Georgina Wroe is a freelance journalist who moved to Moscow in her twenties. She covered stories ranging from wars in the former USSR to serial killers, for magazines including *GQ*, *Esquire*, and *Marie Claire*. She now lives in Suffolk and returns to Russia on assignment.

georgina wroe

slaphead

HEADLINE

First published in 1999
by HEADLINE BOOK PUBLISHING

10 9 8 7 6 5 4 3 2 1

ISBN 0 7472 6203 9

Typeset by
Letterpart Limited, Reigate, Surrey

Printed and bound in Great Britain by
Clays Ltd, St Ives plc

HEADLINE BOOK PUBLISHING
A division of Hodder Headline PLC
338 Euston Road
London NW1 3BH

To Brian Wroe

CHAPTER ONE

I

Should he travel in his only pair of Calvin Klein's, or save them till he got there? Terry took a swig of coffee. He contemplated the grey trunks – apart from the exorbitant price, not so different from the Y-fronts of his youth. And those had stretched to a decade of co-habitation.

If, as he hoped, he was going to be caught with his pants down, he'd better make sure they were his best pair. But if he *didn't* wear the Calvins to travel in, it ruled out scoring with one of those immaculate air hostesses. Women with limbs so perfect they looked prosthetic. Or even a tan-legged Australian who'd smile suggestively as he put her rucksack in the overhead locker.

What the hell. He'd wear them to travel – after all, he could always wash them. They *did* have soap, didn't they? He paused and noted it on his 'Must Ask' list. In any case, Russians had probably never heard of Calvin Klein. They probably thought Prada was somewhere you invaded.

The Calvins had been bought in a heady rush of sexual confidence after his girlfriend left. Terry had thought her

1

departure would be the rocket launcher to uncharted dimensions of sexual experience. It was only in the dark evenings, of Lean Cuisine and abdominising in front of the TV, that he admitted the past year had more in common with the Mir space shuttle than the Challenger probe.

The gym kit would have to go in. Terry stuffed a pair of socks into each Adidas trainer before setting them sole down in the case. Did they have abdominisers in Russia? He doubted it. In his mind's eye he saw a black and white parade of firm-bodied Soviet youths marching through Red Square, smiling at an old bloke on a podium. He frowned. Actually a bit *too* firm-bodied; some might call them *chunky*. But that had been before the brochure arrived. Nothing like seventy years of tyrannical leadership to make women drop a few pounds.

Ah, the brochure! Terry felt a surge of excitement just thinking about it. Pages of them. Rows and rows. So good they actually looked like women off the telly. Some were even wearing swimsuits, like that programme he taped on Saturday afternoons. And yet, at the same time – and this was the thing – at the same time, they looked like they were *gagging* for it (unlike those Thai brochures, where the women looked as if they were just about to take an order for fried rice).

And not just *it* but *him*. Terry Small. 'Hi. My name is Natasha, come live with me,' said one in a mini skirt and see-through top. 'I am Tanya, I want to know all about you. My interests are home-making and aerobics.'

It had seemed too good to be true. Why didn't all men have one? Then Terry thought, maybe like his latest

2

abdominiser, or Tantric sex, not everyone *knew* about them.

He paused for another gulp of black coffee. His only real requirement was skinny. Definitely none of those wobble-thighed British women whose thighs and stomachs *leaked* – there was no other word for it – out of their clothes.

He thought of Grace, his erstwhile partner. Her skin, on the rare times it had been revealed to him, had been like greaseproof paper. And there'd been so much of it. Her stomach had reminded him of the uncooked pastry you got at the bottom of a chicken pie. Or it would remind him if he ever ate pie. Puff pastry (saturated fat 22g per 100g), he smiled, was almost as distant a thought as Grace.

The bed looked like a Boy Scout jumble sale. Odd, the clothes you amass over a lifetime. Terry paused in front of his leather-look suitcase, a Christmas present from Grace. All that time spent in shops, looking, coveting, and what did it amount to? Half a dozen shirts – admittedly, in Terry's case, designer – and some jeans – ditto. The contents of your wardrobe were like a snapshot of your life. Today, Terry's would be shot on a Nikon F4. This time a year ago it would've been snapped on an instant Polaroid.

What to take? He surveyed the room. He'd stripped it of Grace's lacy adornments and pots of dried flowers after a men's magazine had advised him that *minimalist* was the *mot de jour* for bachelor pads. Only when some of his conquests complained it didn't look *lived in* (Mona, from the Gender Awareness Forum, had called it *stark*) had he rescued the odd ornament from under the sink.

Terry was dressed in clothes from his previous life – a Pringle V-neck and polyester trousers, suitable only for wearing around the house, and only then if no one was coming round. Unlike his midnight-blue silk monogrammed dressing gown, a definite on his 'Must Take' list. True, it would take up a lot of room, but it was essential for cutting the perfect post-coital dash. The top gaped over his muscular chest, toned to perfection. That was a point, though – how many condoms? He added it to the 'Must Ask' list. (Russia, he knew from his incomprehensive scan of foreign pages, en route to the classifieds, was currently gripped by a wave of sexually transmitted diseases.)

The dressing gown had been a gift from Grace, who'd presented it in the Taste of India on the high street where they'd been celebrating five years of living together. In a giddy moment they'd ordered wine although she never drank. She'd splattered the dressing gown with rogan ghosh. Dry cleaning had got rid of most of it, though there was still a mark on the back if you looked closely enough. They'd called it a celebration meal, though what they'd had to celebrate in those dark days before his reinvention was hard to imagine. Bleak days of car boot sales, DIY centres and takeaways. Terry frowned just thinking of the saturated fat content in one of those tin-foiled time bombs waiting to explode on his fortieth birthday. He unconsciously passed a hand over his newly abdominised stomach. He shuddered to think of what might have been.

He stared out of the window – a sea of model homes interspersed by strips of lawn, barely recovered from another summer of drought. He'd once read that churches were a community's focal point, now it was the hypermarket. Not that he was complaining. Before the Savacentre, he'd had to go to the sports shop in town for his isotonic drinks. He should add Nutri-Grain bars to the 'Must Take' list.

What would his neighbours think of his wife-to-be? He'd be the envy of the gym. He could just see them, Bob on the pec deck, Steve on the treadex, ogling her arse as it daintily bounced off the stair-climber. He could picture his Natasha. She was petite, even fragile, blonde, green-eyed, and with that *moulded* sort of cleavage. She'd laugh at his jokes and stare open-mouthed at his body. 'I can hardly believe you are thirty-four,' she'd gasp. A heart-stopping five years younger than reality.

Her voice was more difficult to imagine. One of those sexy sounding eastern European Bond girls. Maybe. Though Bond girls had always seemed a bit Amazonian to him. Hippy was the only way to describe Ursula Andress, and he didn't mean flower power. Maybe his Natasha couldn't speak! Lost her voice box in a tragic tractor accident, wearing nothing more than a peasant-style bodice. Perfect.

Terry's lapse into the pages of the top shelf was disturbed by the Edwardian-style phone (rescued from under the sink). It was the man from the agency, telling him he'd be met when he landed in Moscow tomorrow. He mentioned the name of the airport, which Terry instantly forgot.

He replaced the receiver reflectively. *Odd* was the only way to describe Clive, the director of Reds In Your Bed, the agency whose advert Terry had first spotted in the classifieds of *Loot*. He'd been after a second-hand cross-country ski machine.

'Have you tried them yourself then?' Terry had asked him, wanting the type of testimonial the man in Reigate had given him for the ski machine.

'Never mix business and pleasure,' had been the reply. Ominous, thought Terry. O-min-nous. Like owning a gym and not having free turns on the sunbed. Damn, he'd meant to have another couple of tanning sessions before he left. His summer tan, two weeks surfing in Torquay, had all but left him. Now he'd have to make do with fake.

At least Clive had reassured him that he would be going on his own. 'All part of our personal touch policy,' Clive had told him. 'All our gentlemen get a personal service.' It reminded Terry of a smutty film involving prostitutes and luncheon vouchers. Personal was good. Abdominised or not, what if his Natasha fell for someone else?

Not that Terry couldn't pull like a man half his age. It's just that there weren't the *resources* in Britain. After Jean in accounts, who rarely asked for his expenses in person these days, he noted, and Mona, who hadn't signed up for Advanced Gender Awareness, he'd even resorted to putting an advert in an upmarket Sunday paper which he never read.

'Basingstoke-based knight in shining armour, very sporty, dark and handsome [at five foot seven not even Terry dared write tall] seeks Lady Godiva. Must be slim and under 35.' After two weeks, librarians had been the only ones who'd replied. Dried-up women with big arses. What, he had felt like spitting through clenched teeth at

6

the local Harvester, was their definition of *slim*? Vanessa Feltz? He had tried to get his money back from the paper, though the woman on the classifieds had just laughed at him.

His Natasha wouldn't laugh. She would smile sweetly and look at him adoringly.

Shit, he thought. He'd meant to ask Clive about washing powder and condoms and if a pair of Levi's were better currency than a box of Marlboros.

II

Katya knew before she answered the phone who it would be. Sometimes she thought she had a second sense. She'd known the day before the judge passed sentence that her live-in elderly sister-in-law was going to receive a lengthy jail spell. Mind you, with good reason. It had been Katya who had planted the computer in her room. Had the arresting officers, whom Katya had summoned, been less interested in getting into her knickers, they might have stopped to wonder why an elderly book keeper had stolen her office desktop. But that had been her plan. The trial by a troika of three judges with a post-Soviet conviction rate of 98 per cent was guaranteed to go her way. It had been worth the effort and the cost of bribing the office manager. And it had, after all, freed up the spare room for the next ten years.

Katya picked up the phone. She was right. It was the militia. Sasha had been arrested. Again. Could she come down and get him out. Damn, Katya swore under her breath. Not only did she have an order on, but she knew it would take a $30 bribe to get her son out of jail. Money was especially tight this month.

This time she would definitely kill him. Aside from everything else, she had next door's apartment to prepare for tomorrow's client. The woman she was paying $20 a week to move out was still there, and the place was a pigsty. It looked like the old bag had collected every back issue of *Pravda* since the revolution. She glanced outside. Only September and it had started to snow. Even the weather in Moscow was getting worse.

She hurriedly packed a change of clothes for Sasha, dragged on last year's autumn coat and boots, and locked the steel-padded double door to her nineteenth storey apartment. She wondered, not for the first time, why in communism's crime-free society Russian flats had been built with bank vault-style security. Her sister-in-law had said it was to stop you hearing the screams when the KGB took people away. Today people blamed it on the Mafia, though these days everyone in Russia blamed everything on the Mafia.

Someone had pissed in the lift. An empty vodka bottle was discarded in the corner. For the tenth time in as many minutes Katya cursed Sasha.

At first she had been touched by her son's attempts to take over as head of the family after his father, her husband Maxim, had left. But even for a young Russian his entrepreneurial grasp was a little too keen. Today he had been caught with a dog (where in the name of God had he got that?) begging for money for his mother's operation. Though Katya felt fine, according to her son's misspelt cardboard placard she had six weeks to live without a heart bypass. Worse than that, Sasha had been dressed as a Gypsy girl. Worst of all, he was not yet seven. Apparently an elderly American woman had complained not of harassment but shock when she saw Sasha pissing against St Basil's Cathedral from underneath his petticoats.

A thin layer of snow had settled on the crap that surrounded her twenty-four storey home like a moat. The block was identical to buildings from Moscow to Samara. In the great days of central planning the only choice Russians were allowed was to get pissed on Moldovan cognac or Russian vodka. Consequently, Katya could feel at home in every two-roomed apartment across eleven time zones – same cooker, same fridge, even the same flimsy plastic toilet seat, which had witnessed every dump in Soviet history.

She raised a gloved hand to hail a car to take her to the Metro – waiting for a trolley bus would make her even later. A dirt-encrusted Samara Lada swung across three lanes of traffic to pick her up. Katya knew it was a bad sign – the driver was more interested in her than the 10 roubles she had planned to give as a fare. Not that on every occasion she would have objected. If she had the time and the driver was OK-looking, she was not averse to paying in kind. In fact this driver, who just shrugged when Katya waved him on, wasn't bad-looking – unlike the elderly driver of the Volga who pulled up next, who could have been one of Beria's henchmen.

Katya got in. Thank God the only thing coming from his mouth was a Chernobyl-sized blast of toxic waste every time he exhaled smoke from his Russian cigarette. A reproduction icon of the Virgin Mary rubbed shoulders with a picture of a bare-breasted woman who Katya thought had the dumb-eyed plastic look of an American.

Worship them or fuck them, Katya reflected, once you realised the power women had over men, it was a piece of cake. She had grasped this shortly before her expulsion from Young Pioneer camp at the age of fourteen. There was only one male important to her and that was her son. There was nothing she wouldn't do to provide for him.

A bitter draught was blowing in through an ill-fitting window. The car had so little suspension it was like riding in a Roman chariot. Almost to order, the Volga lurched into a pothole. Ash dropped from Beria's pungent *belam-orkanal* cigarette onto the stretched polyester seat cover between his legs.

He didn't wipe it away. Katya sighed inwardly and checked her make-up in the passenger seat mirror. She didn't usually wear lipstick, but when it came to encounters with the militia, it was best to make an effort. At thirty-four she was holding out well, though the skin over her cheeks had started to sag and when she smiled the bags under her eyes were like potato sacks. Her figure, once as hard as an athlete's, had started to soften. But men still wanted her, as much now as in those half-clad afternoons in the one-roomed flat in the small Byelo-russian town where she had been born.

'Can't you drop me off on the other side?' asked Katya, irritated, as they pulled up opposite Fili Metro.

The driver merely nodded to the duo of GAI, traffic police, waiting like vultures further along the road. Every second car was waved down by one of their striped truncheons, and a spurious driving offence was answered with a bribe. Katya had once had an affair with a Gainik who cleared $200 a day, four times most Muscovites' weekly income. She had dumped him when he suggested leaving his wife and moving in with her. At that time she had only recently got rid of her own layabout husband.

The Metro was packed. Moscow did not have a rush hour because people no longer worked nine to five. Now they spent all day criss-crossing the capital, selling, buying, meeting, shagging. Or, in the case of her own young offspring, begging. She changed lines at Kievski station and got off at Ploshad Revolutsii, beneath posters advertising Swiss yoghurts and German aspirin. Not one damn thing made in Russia, thought Katya – but then who wanted the rubbish produced in Russia for the last seventy years?

Katya recognised the desk sergeant from her last trip, when Sasha had been caught selling pirated videos. Sergeant Arkady Korzhakov looked like a walrus. His grey uniform strained to cover his stomach. Dark rings of sweat leaked from his armpits. Quite a feat, thought Katya, shivering. His breath had the unmistakable sour-sweet smell of stale vodka, though there wasn't a bottle in sight. Damn, thought Katya. She could have got away with a five-dollar bottle rather than a hard currency bribe. The combination of the sickly smell of vodka and the low-level dread in the pit of her stomach reeled her back twenty-five years to her childhood.

She dragged a ringless hand through her blonde hair and smiled, she hoped alluringly.

'Ah, Mrs Popova,' said Korzhakov, pushing his chair

back on the concrete floor. 'Nice to see such a lovely lady again so soon.' He leered. 'Tell me, are you trying to see your son put in a children's home?'

'No, no, of course not,' said Katya, though for one head-swaying second there was nothing she would have liked more.

'You are aware that this is the second time we have seen little Sasha in the past fortnight? Perhaps,' he said, smiling, 'like his mother he lacks the firm hand of a man.' His eyes moved down to Katya's chest.

'No, I think he's just going through a difficult patch. Perhaps this will help you understand.' Katya pressed three ten-dollar notes in the sergeant's paw-like fist. His sickly breath was an inch from her ear.

'I'm not sure that will quite cover it.' His other hand moved to start undoing her coat, fumbling for her breast.

'I'm afraid it'll have to,' said Katya, edging away. 'Or do I have to ask the colonel about this?'

'I'm not sure you fully understand the seriousness of your son's offence,' he murmured. His eyes, now fixed on the outline of her breast under her jumper, had a drugged look. 'I'm sure the colonel would agree with me. Breaking article three two four of the Russian constitution is a very serious offence.' He tried to move his hand under her jumper.

'And I'm afraid you don't seem to realise how seriously offensive *you* are,' replied Katya, her knee jerking upwards towards his groin. Before height had ruled her out of serious competition, she had been trained as a gymnast and she still retained the strength of her youth.

The sergeant fell back on his chair. The wooden legs

looked as if they might snap like toothpicks. His shirt gaped to reveal a trail of dark hair, like ants, crawling down his flaccid stomach.

'Bitch,' he hissed at her. Then, before she had time to think of her next move, he started to laugh. The phlegm from a forty-a-day habit bubbled beneath the surface like chemicals heated on a Bunsen burner. He reached under the table for the last third of his vodka bottle and poured it into a dirty tumbler. 'Fancy a drink?' he asked.

Katya shook her head. That was the thing with Russians, she thought. So frigging unstable. Randy one minute, mad the next, and then friendly. No wonder the country was in such chaos. 'No thanks,' she said. 'Just my son.'

'Sure. Cell number four, down the corridor on the left. It's not locked. And for Christ's sake take that fucking dog with you,' Korzhakov added, and drained a clear four fingers of vodka in one. Then he picked up a piece of brown bread, sniffed it, and took a bite.

The cell stank of mildew but it looked clean enough. Sasha's fine mousy hair was spread out on sacking where he slept in the corner. His thin bare arm stretched over his head, grazing the cold bare bricked wall. Katya's heart lurched. In his skirt, he looked like a peasant girl from a 1930s Mosfilm on grain production. She stooped to shake him awake and hug him – his clothes (where had they come from?) smelt of smoke, and were slightly damp.

'Sasha, what am I going to do with you?'

Only as her son was rubbing his eyes on a brightly coloured headscarf did Katya become aware of a low growl and a pair of eyes watching her from the shadows.

'Hello,' said Sasha, ignoring the low canine reverberations. 'Oh, don't worry about him, it's only Leonid. I bought him off a Gypsy. Good investment. Tourists give much more money when you've got a dog. Specially the Yanks.'

'Leonid?' asked Katya.

'After President Brezhnev. Don't you know anything?' he retorted.

Sasha's obsession with the former Soviet leader was as mysterious to Katya as the computer games he pirated. But, like cross-dressing and extortion rackets, she just hoped he would grow out of it.

'Mum, the bastards took all my takings,' he screeched as he searched through the underskirts Katya was trying to strip him of. Leonid was still growling.

'Don't call policemen bastards, darling.' Katya tried to coax him into trousers and a jacket. Leonid had started to bark furiously. 'And for God's sake shut that bloody mutt up.'

'Don't swear, Mum. He's only hungry.' Sasha patted the mongrel's head. Its filthy tail now beat against Katya's leg like a brush.

'Well, he can stay hungry. He's not coming home with us. You'll have to take him back to whoever you bought him from.'

'But Mum,' wailed Sasha, close to tears as his arm went through a blue knitted jumper, 'he's good for business and he's mine. He needs me.'

'Sasha, we live on the nineteenth floor. Now for God's sake, come on.'

Sasha started to whimper as he picked up Leonid's rope leash. The dog followed suit and the trio ascended into the courtyard, heading towards the main road.

'Mum, we're hungry. There's a two for the price of one on Big Macs. I can have one and Leonid can have the other,' trilled Sasha's sing-song voice. Leonid barked his assent. 'Please, I'll pay. I've still got fifty bucks hidden in my trainers.'

Katya was wrestling with the dual concerns of the source of her son's hard currency and where she could leave a stray dog when she saw her. Across Petrovka Street, getting out of a yellow cab. The woman of her dreams. The woman she had gone to bed thinking about and woken up thinking about. The woman who might just deliver her and Sasha from this world of mongrels, pre-teen transvestitism and over-sexed militia. Stunning. One metre seventy. A natural blonde. Blue eyes and a perfect bow mouth.

'Sasha, shut up,' Katya shouted as she dragged her son and the mongrel across the road.

III

If one more mobile phone went off, thought Bob Bridges, he would stuff a hand weight in the face of its owner. It was a gym, for God's sake. Just how indispensable were these people? Five years ago in Russia carrier pigeon had been the most reliable way of communicating. Now suddenly it was like a frigging AT&T convention. He'd read that Finland had the most mobiles per capita. To beat

Russia, he thought, every motherfucker from Santa Claus downwards must own one. Including the reindeers.

For Muscovites mobile phones were the ultimate accessory. The only way, along with a Mercedes 600 and a couple of bodyguards, to the heart of every slim-hipped bottle-blonde here. Well, if not exactly the heart, at least an organ somewhere lower. Bridges glanced at one of the women whose body could have come from a swimsuit commercial. What did they see in these bull-necked, empty-eyed chumps, sweating out their liquid lunches?

No need to think too hard on that score. Dollars. Though they weren't that fussy. German marks would do, even sterling at a push. There had been a time when a whiff of an American passport had been enough to spark a line of women as long as a 1980's queue for imported tights. Not now. These babes were after a bulging wallet, and no one on earth, save for a few Brunei prices, had the money of this generation of Russians.

The pulsating red dots of the random hill-walking programme in front of him blinked to a halt. With a satisfying beep the machine told him it had finished his half-hour session, 242 levels achieved, 340 calories used. That should keep the alcohol he intended to consume tonight off his growing paunch.

He picked up his towel and headed out. As he did so, a woman clutching two pink dumbbells looked at him more out of curiosity than ardour. Bridges found it impossible to tell in Russia if, in encroaching middle age, he still appealed to the opposite sex. Here he was taken at face value, literally. Unable to impress with his diffident charm (his wife's phrase) or a high-profile job, now he had to rely on his dark hair, flecked with grey, blue eyes, more rheumy each year; and once-hollow cheekbones. He was Sting at best, Al Gore at worst. He had a feeling he was worst more often than best.

He glanced at his watch; just after six. If he hurried he'd have time for a sauna and shower before he met Sergei at seven. He draped his towel round his neck feather-boa style, hiding a chest which definitely required work. He even risked a smile at two perfectly made-up women on their way to an aerobics class. His eyes lingered, as he turned into the locker room, on their wonderfully toned backsides as they swayed past.

He stripped out of his Adidas sweats – a present from the KGB nearly a decade ago as they tried to steer him away from his nightly drinking bouts – and grabbed his toilet bag. As he headed towards the sauna, the *thud thud* of his plastic slippers echoed down the hall.

Bridges smiled to himself as he showered. He passed the block of unscented soap over his crewcut hair, unchanged from his days in the CIA. Thank God it was quiet. On occasions the sauna resembled the *Playboy* frieze of a Roman mosaic. For a small consideration the staff turned a blind eye as the men-only sauna turned co-ed. Tonight only a couple of young American investment bankers, stripped of loafers and suits, were perspiring inside the slatted wooden cell.

Bridges knew, even naked, how to pass as a Russian. More than a decade in Russia with only rudimentary language skills meant a lot of body watching. The shoulders bunched, the chest out, buttocks clenched – a posture that showed a pride in physique which only men who live in truly male-dominated cultures can ever attain. From his memories of the States, the Spaniards and Cubans had it, the Mexicans didn't. American men were more loose limbed, less confrontational. British men, he noticed from his time in Russia, lolled as if unaware of their sex. If the Americans took him to be Russian he wouldn't have to talk to them.

Bridges guessed the bankers had been in Russia about six months. Their faked jadedness ('Christ, we paid four grand to customs in bribes last week') had been the give-away. In reality Bridges knew that, like him – like every American brought up in the godfearing middle classes – they were *impressed* by the Russians' fuck-you attitude. They sensed a bravado they could only emulate, an attitude which *really* meant they didn't care if they lived or died.

After ten minutes, the ginger-haired one with a rash of acne turned raw by the heat stood up, a white towel clenched round his waist, to spoon more water onto the coals. The rush of steam bit into them.

Bridges stretched a foot into a scorching plastic shoe. There were probably more fungal diseases in a Russian sauna than a Turkish brothel, he thought as he got up to leave. He pushed the door of the hermetically sealed oven away from him. A blast of cold caused a chorus of disapproval from the bankers. Bridges stumbled as his shoe caught on the step.

'Hey, Boris, pal, hurry up and shut the frigging door,' drawled one of the bankers in English.

'Go fuck yourself,' Bridges replied with a New Jersey accent. If the new Russians were hard to stomach, then

Americans were ten times worse. They actually believed they owned the world.

The bar on Tverskaya, formerly Gorky Street, was opposite TGI Fridays, hidden in the basement of a renovated theatre which had staged the opening nights of some of history's finest playwrights. The nearest tonight's clientele got to literature was the menu.

The decor was American diner-style, checked tablecloths and chrome. Behind a fairy light bar Sergei was doing his best Tom Cruise impression, jiggling a cocktail shaker like a man undergoing ECT. He finished pouring a drink the colour of which Bridges hadn't seen since his last bout of food poisoning. With a flourish Sergei added an umbrella and a sparkler.

'Kiwi Collapser.' He smiled at Bridges as he handed it to a man in a green blazer. Did men actually *drink* those? 'Can I interest you in one?' It was no job for a one-time KGB colonel.

Sergei's English, like his Laos, was perfect. The curious language combo had been demanded by the prestigious military translation school he had graduated from. That was before the Red Army had collapsed into a derisible fighting force, which sent sixteen-year-old conscripts to be killed in an ill-judged war in Chechenya. English and Laos had won in a toss-up with French and Afghan. Now Sergei's language skills were devoted to translating Orange Curacao into English and correcting Bridges' grammar.

'Call me old-fashioned, but I'll stick with a Jack Daniels,' replied Bridges good-humouredly. 'Need I add large with no ice?'

'Coming right up, boss,' Sergei mimicked a plantation slave with a grin. Irony might be dead in the States but it was not lost on Russia's emerging underclass.

Bridges looked round the bar at the usual sort of low-level *nouveaux riches*. Men in cheap Turkish leather jackets. Women in micro-skirts. In America there'd be a couple of beer bottles on the table, here it was vodka. Like everything in Russia, if it was foreign it was more prestigious. Finnish Absolut was the tipple of choice.

Sergei – as if the job itself wasn't humiliation enough – was dressed in a uniform of baby pink blouson and trousers. His blond hair was swept back under a pink peaked cap. He set a half-full tumbler of liquid amber in front of Bridges. At the same time a shaven-headed Russian in a purple jacket waving a $50 bill called him back to his shaker.

Bridges savoured the glass, suggesting to an onlooker that his desperation for it was controllable. Then in one fluid movement he raised it and gulped down three-quarters. A familiar sense of warm wellbeing moved up from the pit of his stomach. After a work-out and sauna, 40 per cent whisky maybe wasn't the best liquid to take on board. Still, he could always order up a beer next.

At a table in the corner four thugs, sitting with two improbably good-looking women, were starting to get noisy. Russians, like any race whose culture is steeped in over-proof spirits, didn't make nice drunks. Sergei eyed them warily from behind a cocktail umbrella and, like the good intelligence operative he had been, noted a potential problem.

Bridges ordered another drink. 'Quiet tonight,' he said.

'Yeah. When it first starts to snow, Russians tend to stay in for a while and screw their wives,' said Sergei. 'Then it's a race to see if it's them or the snowplough that hits the streets first.'

'How come I know you're not kidding?' replied Bridges. 'So what's new?'

'Not much. Visited our old pals at the firm last week. Barely got a pot to piss in these days. Looked like we bailed out at the right time.'

'Some of us had no choice. The collapse of this once great empire had nothing to do with me. I was working for you lot, remember?'

'For all the good it did. You didn't tell us anything we couldn't have got from a "CIA for beginners" manual. I wish I could've squealed for so little and be living in Virginia on a US pension.'

Sergei was right. Bridges' legendary status among defectors had had more to do with the KGB's desire not to lose face than the information he gave them. They had proclaimed him the biggest Soviet Agent since the Cambridge Five. Only when the leaks continued from Arlington after he'd fled eastwards did the CIA realise they had to pin the blame on someone else.

'That reminds me. Don't forget, term starts next week.' Sergei grinned.

Great, thought Bridges as he sank another drink. He hardly needed a twenty-four-hour tail of greasy-skinned secret service recruits practising their tradecraft to tell him how meaningless his life was.

Sergei knocked off in half an hour, replaced by a one-time government chemist who drove taxis by day.

Bridges moved over to a table and sat down, noticing as he did how tight his jeans were. Either he'd have to speak to his cleaner about the shrinking effect of Russian washing powder or he'd have to start holding back on the beer.

Better start now. He ordered up another Jack Daniels by nodding at Sergei, who sent over a waitress wearing the name tag which said Natasha in English.

'*Spasiba*,' said Bridges. 'Thank you' was one phrase from a vocabulary which would have been severely stretched to translate a Janet and John book. He'd always maintained he'd been too old to learn the language – though he was aware that many of his ilk, most of them older than he was, had done so.

He reached into his suit jacket for a packet of Russian manufactured Marlboro Lights, which while proclaiming a tar content of 11g ripped into the back of your throat like the steam of a 120 degree sauna, only the sauna lacked that light-headed, muscle-relaxing buzz as the nicotine hit home. Bridges drew in deeply.

'I thought you'd given up,' said Sergei, sitting down with a bottle, now thankfully changed out of his Baby-gro into a pair of green Levi's and a tight ribbed polo neck. Even in the dimly lit bar he displayed a finely sculpted chest. Sergei at thirty had the physique of a Soviet realist statue, thought Bridges with envy. At just over six foot he looked as if he should be cast in bronze on a street corner, waving a red flag.

'I'll give up when I return to a country where cigarettes cost more than eighty cents a pack,' said Bridges, knocking back another drink with a wince. 'And besides, with the current state of your country's intelligence service, who knows how long my pension is going to last? I'm aiming to exit this mortal coil before I hit fifty.' He flicked his cigarette into an ashtray which already looked as if it had hosted a Philip Morris convention.

'You'll be all right. You should think yourself lucky. I'm reliably informed you get a much better deal coming eastwards than going westwards.'

'You'd have to. I mean, who would volunteer to come here?' Bridges attempted to swoop his head round 180 degrees.

Sergei nodded in the direction of two blondes who had just come in. 'Well, for a start the women are better looking.'

'Not on a barman's wages they're not.' Bridges slumped back as Sergei refilled their glasses.

It was only when he was half cut that Russia started to make any sense to Bridges. It wasn't just the rudiments of Russian grammar that eluded him. He was closer to grasping nuclear physics than he was to understanding Russians. He glanced up at his friend, who'd already zeroed in on the two women now sitting at the bar.

'Guess what? I think I've scored.' Sergei returned to the table, cigarette in mouth, brandishing two drinks so large, Bridges noted, the chemist barman must surely have thought he was back in the labs. *Scored?* Exactly where did Sergei get his vocabulary from? thought Bridges hazily. Surely not the Voice of America.

'Well, unless you've met the never-yet-encountered whore with a heart of gold who takes pity on an impoverished spy, count me out,' slurred Bridges. The room was starting to spin slightly and the level of the techno beat filling the bar had become oppressive. 'Besides, haven't you only just recovered from your last sexual misadventure? What about Olga?' With the deftness of a magician Sergei was transporting his wedding band from right hand to left.

Unlike Sergei, Bridges had more or less given up on sex. He raised another glass to his lips. If it hadn't been a couple of paid-for encounters and a liaison with an American TV journalist, who in retrospect had been after his story, he would have been celibate for the last few years. A long way from those days when he first arrived in Moscow, feted by the KGB; when Sergei would drive into town and pick up whores who were threatened with a spell in the Lubyanka if they refused.

Sergei had always been Bridges' favourite guard. In the early days of his debriefing and shock, after being ripped from a wife and two daughters in less than seventy-two hours, Sergei had been the only thing that kept him sane. Sergei and whisky. It had pretty much been the same ever since.

'Bridges, I'd like you to meet Lisa and Anya.' Sergei pulled out a chair for Lisa, a small, rounded blonde wearing a pair of brown velvet hot pants that put Bridges in mind of *lederhosen*.

Pastoral thoughts were clearly not on Sergei's mind. He knew his friend's type, and this was it. Lisa was young, around twenty-two, Bridges guessed, pudgy-cheeked and busty. He thought of Sergei's wife, Olga, in her towelling robe, her childish bare feet shivering on the cold parquet floor. She was delicate featured with almost translucent skin and a halo of blonde hair cut in a bob. He thought of her bathing her baby daughter, splashing and laughing. Suddenly he felt terrifyingly sober. He wanted to be a million miles from the smoky bar.

'Not bad, eh? Bags I the short one. And fear not.' Sergei winked. 'They don't speak a word of English.' Sergei maintained that an ability to speak English was the entry visa into most Russian girl's knickers. And, unlike Russian border controls, it meant you didn't have to pay. The girls were drinking cocktails whose size made Bridges think the barman really had returned to a career in chemistry.

The smell of cheap perfume and cigarette smoke, as well as alcohol in a dehydrated body, made Bridges start to swoon. Sometimes when he was drunk, for a horrifying minute or two, the reality of his life hit him like a sledgehammer. Disorientated, he staggered to his feet and made his way to the door. Outside, a blast of cold air froze his perspiration to his cheek and back. He slumped on an upturned rubbish bin and retched, covering the fresh snow. Despite the wind, he started to sweat again. He collapsed further down the bin.

It was only after he'd retched again that he became aware he wasn't alone in the courtyard. From the shadows of a gateway a small bearded man, like a character from a fairy tale, approached him. 'Good evening,' he said in perfect, barely accented English. 'May I be of any assistance?' He removed his hat and smiled. His silver-white hair reflected the snow. 'Allow me to introduce myself. My name is Professor Modin.' He bowed slightly and clicked his heels like a Prussian prince.

Bridges glanced up at him before throwing up a stream

of bile, as green against the snow as one of Sergei's Kiwi Collapsers.

IV

Had he or had he not asked for a low-sodium, low-fat meal? He'd specifically told Clive at Reds In Your Bed that he had to have a healthy heart meal. And what had he got? Beef in a red wine sauce and trifle. Did those Finnish stewardesses (Clive said the cheapest flights went via Helsinki) have any idea how much saturated fat there was in a wine sauce?

Not by the look of them. He'd been surprised the one pushing the duty-free trolley hadn't got lodged in the aisle. A couple of them made Grace look young. Hadn't he read of some EC regulation that demanded women retire before they lost their looks? If there wasn't, there should be. When he'd tried to liberate a couple of Nutri-Grain bars from his hand luggage, he'd dislodged his abdominiser, almost concussing the woman opposite.

And now he was here. Moscow. Heart of the evil empire. Standing in line for passport control. He hadn't seen a queue like it since his and Grace's last trip to Ikea, when all she'd come away with was a vegetable steamer which turned out to be (she'd misread the Swedish label) a metal lampshade. Terry checked his bald patch in the angled mirror overhead. No need for those Hugo Boss shorts, it had been snowing when they'd got off the plane. Radioactive snow which would burn off his few remaining follicles.

The cranberry-coloured visa meant nothing to Terry.

Not a bad picture, though. He'd worried that the light in the Insta-flash cubicle outside the Co-op might have bounced unflatteringly off his bald patch, but he seemed to have got away with it. Decidedly debonair and not a day over thirty-four.

Strange, he thought, how the nationality of your fellow passengers seemed to change in mid-air. When they'd left Heathrow there hadn't seemed to be a Russian among them. Now it looked like a vodka-tasting jamboree. He took a good look round. None of the women seemed recognisable from the brochure. Most of them were middle-aged and either yelling or humping huge parcels, the size of which he'd only ever seen in a *National Geographic* spotlight on Africa he'd read at the dentist's. At least those women had had the decency to be topless. It didn't bode well, he reflected as he edged slowly towards the strip-lit immigration booth.

The man in a green uniform gave him a scrunched-eyed look of suspicion which he'd last seen from Marg, the office manager, when he'd tried to put through aloe vera juice as an entertainment expense. The rugby scrum only got worse at the baggage retrieval. Men and women launched themselves from a rabble three deep as shabby suitcases were spat onto the carousel like bingo balls.

Terry's mood only lightened when he clocked the neon sign. Elsewhere in Europe it said *willkommen, bien venue, welcome*. Here it was a busty babe in a miniskirt with the caption 'Do It Tonight' and the name and address of a nightclub in English. Terry made a note of it on a customs declaration form which another uniformed man had thrust into his hand. For currency declared Terry wrote one thousand US dollars. No need to tell them of the four grand for the operation, which he'd stashed in a hollowed-out carton of fat burners.

'Terry Smells' read one side of Katya's cardboard placard (she'd re-cycled Sasha's begging board). She held it chest high, her elbows deflecting taxi drivers from the trickle of passengers disembarking from flight AY 206 from Helsinki.

'That's Small, actually.'

'Small, what's small?' replied Katya irritably. She'd already been propositioned by two drunken Finns and a Russian cabby. The flight was an hour late and Sasha's babysitter had to leave by eleven.

'Me. My name is Terry *Small*. Small by name. Large by nature, if you know what I mean.' Terry smiled, he hoped, suggestively. She wasn't bad, he thought, looking Katya up and down, though she'd obviously been around the block more times than a marathon runner. But not too tall, and definitely on the feminine side of muscular.

'Ah, hello. Sorry, yes, pleased to meet you. Please let's go. There's a car waiting for us outside. All these taxi drivers are owned by the Mafia. The Mafia even stopped the bus route into the centre. Did you have a good journey?'

'Er, yes, thank you.' What did she mean, *Mafia*? What were the Italians doing here? He suddenly felt very tired. Katya was pulling him towards the airport exit.

'You are American or British? The agency didn't say.'

'English. Indeed, yes. One hundred per cent.'

'Good, my girls prefer British. They think they are more cultured.'

'Oh yes, definitely,' replied Terry, perking up.

'Yes. Though, of course, meaner. Do you smoke or drink?' Terry suddenly felt a sense of inadequacy not experienced since he first joined the gym. What a cheek. Wasn't he supposed to be doing the choosing?

'No, actually. Neither.'

'Good, very good. That may make up for the other defects.'

'Def . . .?' Outside, it smelt of low-grade benzene. It was freezing. Katya pushed him into the back of a Lada, throwing his case into an oily boot. 'What do you mean, *defects*?' Perhaps her language skills were poor. A man in a leather jacket started the car and pulled away.

'Height, Mr Smell, height. My girls like a tall man.' Katya nodded briskly, checking her hair in the mirror. 'And usually with hair. But don't worry, we'll find you something.' She smiled.

Terry automatically touched his scalp. He felt like the last boy being picked for the school football team.

They drove into Moscow in silence, Katya occasionally barking orders in Russian to the driver and then laughing. Huge advertising billboards flanked the road on either side. Terry slumped in silence on the back seat, amid a plastic sack full of tools and an empty McDonald's carton, and watched the cigarette hoardings flash past.

It was after eleven by the time Katya had installed Terry next door and liberated the babysitter from a game of cards, where it appeared her son was already 80 roubles up. She poured herself a drink and sat down, thinking, as she looked around the apartment, how lucky she was to live on her own, with Sasha.

She had married Sasha's father Max in order to qualify for residency in Moscow. Max, whom she'd met on holiday by the Black Sea, was from Odessa, but was then lodging, rent-free, with his elder, Moscow-born sister. Residency in the capital was the prize among Katya's friends in her home village, the only chance of a better life than the one primitive Byelorus could offer. They'd married within six months, on her twentieth birthday, and she'd moved to Moscow, to the same flat where she still lived. For years she'd been saddled with an alcoholic husband who worked fleetingly as an oil rigger, and his religious maniac sister. It had taken most of Katya's ingenuity to shift them.

She poured another drink. The Englishman hadn't been too much of a disappointment. He'd looked upset when she'd pointed out his drawbacks. But in Katya's experience it was better to be blunt from the start. This wasn't the good old days of a decade ago when Russian women would have sold their own babushka for the chance to marry a westerner. These days it was a Mafia sponsor they were fighting for, men who wouldn't bat an eyelid at spending $1,000 on a meal. Last month a surgeon from Cleveland had baulked at paying a $200 restaurant bill. How could he complain, when he'd got a first-rate screw out of it? Americans were getting almost as mean as the English, she thought as she went in to check on Sasha.

In the kitchen, Leonid yelped good night.

Terry woke just after seven. For the first time since she had left him, he missed Grace. He looked out of the window at something akin to a *Mad Max* film set: tower blocks as far as the eye could see. Some twenty storeys down, packs of stray dogs roamed between piles of rubbish which were burning despite the faint drizzle of snow.

He'd slept badly on a sofa which Katya had converted into a bed. He swore when he realised he'd forgotten his purpose-made satin pillowcases, guaranteed to be easy on your scalp. The flat had only one room, with adjacent bathroom and kitchen. It reminded him of the interior from one of the Swedish channels he tuned into after midnight. Uninhabitable sort of places, with a bed, dark interior, and little else.

The walls were hung with rugs and a couple of pictures from a western women's magazine. One poster was of a bowl of fruit. The only ray of hope had been the brochure Katya had left by his bed which made better reading than the underwear section of Grace's Kay's catalogue. Only with a supreme effort could Terry blot out the background and lose himself in dreams of his Natasha. He'd thought of going for a run this morning, but unless he left a trail of Nutri-Grain bars he felt sure he'd never find the flat again. To think he was paying Clive at Reds In Your Bed two grand for ten days in this luxury *custom-built* apartment. He had just started his 'Must Complain About' list when the unfamiliar screech of the doorbell shook him like an electric shock.

Katya in daylight looked older than the early thirties Terry had first pegged her. He suddenly panicked. What if the brochure was as illusory as his *custom-built* apartment? Then who could he complain to? Hardly *Holiday Watchdog*. Terry thought of a scam he'd once read about when blokes in American Bible belt towns who had paid $200 for a porn mag subscription were too embarrassed to cancel their cheques when it turned out to be a con.

'How did you sleep, Mr Small?' she asked perkily. 'I've brought bread and sausage for breakfast. Or would you prefer some Russian eggs?'

'Er, um, no thanks, I've already eaten.' His supply of Nutri-Grains would never last.

Terry looked anxious. 'I was hoping to start meeting the girls as soon as possible. I mean what happens? Do they come here or do I go to them?'

'Mr Small,' said Katya tiredly, 'my girls are not call girls. They are sensitive young ladies. You are here to get to know them, are you not? Are there any women you have been writing to who you would like to meet first? If not, you must make your selection from the catalogue, and we'll take it from there.'

Clive had suggested Terry write to a couple, but it smacked too much of pen pals. Besides, he couldn't get the hang of those squiggly letters on the address. But, hold on, *what* had she just said? '*Make your selection from the catalogue . . .*'

In a second Terry had abandoned his 'Must Complain About' list in favour of a 'Must Try To Fuck' list. He was in heaven. It was a cross between his Swedish channel and Argos. He hardly heard Katya leave as he picked up the brochure and started to write.

V

Bob Bridges shuddered awake in a room as familiar to him as the moles on his back. Though the surroundings weren't familiar, the feeling was. A leaden, dry-mouthed head, from which he could actually feel his hair growing in painful spurts. The concept of waking up, as opposed to coming round, was these days as foreign to him as going to sleep, rather than passing out. Like the handstands of his youth or playing the piano, he just wasn't sure he could do it any more.

Other than a radio spewing out Russian voices, Bridges could hear no one. He groped for his watch. Ten twenty. His heart lurched in that Pavlovian way when you know it's a work day and you're still in bed. Then he remembered he hadn't worked for more than ten years.

He raised his head from a cushion and looked round. Then he wished he hadn't. It wasn't just the pounding. At first he took them to be pickling jars, which fill most Russians' homes in the autumn. Then he saw the reddy interiors were pickled *things*. A couple had the translucent look of a foetus. Others were livers, hearts, *organs*.

'Tea?' Bridges hadn't heard the door.

'Where the fuck am I?' he squealed, throwing back his sheet to find himself shrouded in an operating gown.

'Don't be alarmed, young man. I do sometimes forget how disconcerting my collection can be.' It was an old guy. Had they met? Bridges tried to access his memory.

'No, no. Please. You needn't explain to me. Whatever you do here is fine. Really. But I'm afraid I must be going.' Bridges searched desperately around the room for his clothes. Stories of Russian Jeffrey Dahmers were as common in the Russian press as reports of Boris Yeltsin's indisposition. Bridges panicked. Hadn't one nutter in Rostov eaten fifty-three people?

33

'No, you mustn't go yet.' His English was perfect. 'I haven't explained. I've been looking for a foreigner for some time.'

The man was tiny and certainly over seventy. Surely even with a hangover the size of the Empire State Building, thought Bridges, he could overpower him. He edged his way round the divan, heading for one of the smaller jars – what was in it? A hand? – to use as a projectile.

'Oh, darling, good. He's up. Good morning, Mr Bridges.' A neat, precise-looking woman of the same age joined the man in the doorway. 'I hope you didn't mind, we got your name from your documents last night. How are you feeling?'

For serial killers, they were the oddest looking duo since Fred and Rosemary. But then wasn't everything odd in Russia? Why else would this man lure home a foreigner doing an impression of an E-coli victim, with complications of botulism? (Bridge's internal VCR had started to play last night's tape.)

'Who are you?' he stammered. 'And what am I doing here?' He cast round the room. As well as looking like the prop room for *Quincey*, there were photographs showing the guy in front of him shaking hands with every Communist Party leader since Chairman Mao.

'My name is Professor Modin and this is my wife Marina. We met last night, though I'm not sure you were at your best. Among other things I am a doctor of medicine and as such recommend you drink this.' He held out a phial of liquid which was frothing like a rabid dog.

'What is it?'

'A combination of sodium and glucose, with a dose of

34

pure alcohol, the absence of which your organism is now craving. Isn't that right, nurse?' He turned to his wife who silently nodded her assent.

No matter what sort of crazed doctors and nurses game these two were playing, Bridges could feel a raging thirst so bad it was drawing liquid from his eyeballs. What the hell? he thought. The pure alcohol had been the clincher.

'Your health.' He downed it in one bitter draught and drew his hand across his mouth.

'Now I suggest you hydrate with tea.' The old man smiled. 'Shall we go to the kitchen?'

The pure alcohol kicked in, Bridges guessed, like a heroin fix. Sometime soon, he promised himself, he really would stop drinking. Only now wasn't the time. Whoever this little Rumpelstiltskin with his wicked witch sidekick was, he certainly knew his medicine. He almost felt human.

Bridges drew up a stool and accepted a glass of black tea from the woman. The professor sat opposite him. He drew a gnarled, freckled hand over his beard.

'Like all Russians, Mr Bridges,' he started slowly, 'I am a great believer in fate. It is part of the Russian condition.' He smiled.

Bridges tried to focus on the idea of existence outside this flat.

'It is only the powerless who believe in fate. If you have no control over your life, you hand it over to a mystical force. That is why only women – and Russians – believe in horoscopes.'

The effects of the hangover cure were wearing as thin as this mid-morning lecture on the great Russian soul.

'Fascinating,' said Bridges. 'Much as I would love to stay and chat, I have an appointment at midday,' he lied.

'Fate brought you here, Mr Bridges.'

'No, a hastily drunk bottle of whisky after a work-out and sauna and no food. And *you* brought me here, Professor . . .'

The little man ignored this outburst. 'Has it ever occurred to you to wonder what the Soviet Union was built on?'

'Communism?' Bridges was lagging fast.

'Not ideology, not oil, not precious metals. At the heart of one of the most powerful countries in the history of a world is a *corpse*. A dead body. Lenin's body is at the epicentre of this country. Doesn't that strike you as odd?'

'Not as odd as being abducted by the Tweedledum and Tweedledee of mass murder and drinking tea in a home which doubles as a morgue. No, not that odd.' Bridges got up to leave. He noted he was still wearing the green surgical gown.

The old man started to laugh. 'Good heavens, we're not going to harm you. We have a proposition to put to you. Please sit down. Tell me, have you ever considered *embalment*?'

CHAPTER TWO

I

'I'm listening.' The woman's voice growled more ferociously than Leonid before he'd been fed. Why was it, thought Katya, that Russians' idea of a service ethic would make Japanese prison camp guards seem over-courteous. Much as she despised the cultural takeover of Americans, they, at least, had some manners.

'Is that bookshop number one four two?'

'What if it is?' rasped the woman.

Katya consciously held her breath. Even in Byelorus these days they managed hello. 'I'd like to speak to Sonya, please.'

With no acknowledgement that her request was to be granted, Katya heard a thud as the receiver was tossed onto a hard surface.

'Sonya, it's that woman on the phone for you again,' a voice echoed from somewhere in the shop. A muted conversation continued which Katya could only hear one side of. 'You'll have to speak to her, I've got better things to do than lie on your behalf.'

Such as? thought Katya indignantly. Like most Russian

state workers, she probably averaged two hours a day. And one of those would be overtime. Katya grasped from the stilted exchange that Sonya didn't welcome her call in quite the way she had hoped. She was just about to hang up when she heard someone fumbling for the receiver.

'Hello. This is Sonya.' The voice was quiet and precise. Katya's heart lunged with a longing close to lust when she pictured the slender blonde woman on the other end of the line. The woman she had first seen crossing Petrovka Street just after she'd sprung Sasha from jail.

'Hello, Sonya.' Katya tried to control her growing excitement. 'This is Katya Popova. Do you remember, we met the other day?'

Silence.

'I was the one with the young boy and dog,' Katya persisted.

'You wanted to know how big my feet were,' Sonya answered in even, measured syllables.

'Exactly.' In retrospect, asking the girl if her feet were smaller than a size 36 before she had even offered her name hadn't necessarily been the best approach. But her client's instructions had been specific.

'Then you asked if I was interested in meeting foreign men,' continued Sonya.

'Not just meeting. *Marrying*.'

'And I told you no.'

'You said, if I recall correctly, that you would think about it.' That had been shortly before Leonid had started to piss on her leg. It hadn't been the easiest of recruitments.

She continued doggedly, 'I was phoning to see what you had decided.' In the background she could hear the

Japanese camp guard screaming at a customer, slam the till shut, and call Sonya back to work.

'Look, I've really got to go. I've never met any foreigners before. I don't think this is the sort of—'

'Perhaps we could meet to discuss it.' Why, sighed Katya, couldn't this perfect woman – of the natural hair, small feet and green eyes – have been a model or a stripper? Or at the very least a croupier. None of those professions had ever baulked at her suggestions. Why did she have to work in a bookshop and have a xenophobia not seen since Khrushchev? 'Could I come down to the shop?'

'Er, no. I don't think that would be a good idea.'

'Perhaps we could meet for a drink?'

'No.'

'A *coffee*?' This was tough.

'No. I suppose you could come to our apartment, though.' She sounded hesitant.

'Great. Where is it?'

She gave Katya instructions which employed most of Moscow's municipal transport system and ended with a twenty-minute walk. 'I'm usually finished here at six, so I get home by eight. Come then.' She hung up.

A tingle of excitement surged through Katya as she replaced the receiver. She always knew when she'd seen a perfect girl. It must be the same rush that a talent spotter saw in the fluidity of a young ice hockey player, or when a music teacher first heard the haunting melodies of a star pupil. It might even have been the same thrill that her own gymnastics coach had got when he had first seen her spiral across the matting floor at her village school. But look where that had got her. Thrown out of the team when the same coach noticed a post-pubescent growth spurt. He'd told her the only cure, in the absence of steroids, was a twice weekly dose of testosterone to be administered, by him, in the form of screwing her on the cold damp floor of the shower room.

True, her discovery might not have the same *nobility* as a sporting endeavour – she was, after all, trying to pair Sonya up with a man three times her age with an uncontrollable, almost illegal, taste in young girls. But it was more profitable. Where was the money in Russian sport? She'd been right to give up on gymnastics. Any sportsman, or woman, who won any prize money these days was forced to give it to the Mafia almost before the strains of the national anthem had finished. At the time of the Atlanta Olympics, black Cherokee jeeps had hung around Moscow's sports halls like vultures.

Katya hurried to prepare something for Sasha's tea. She picked up some American mayonnaise, a tin of Dutch peas and Israeli sweet corn. Sometimes she wondered how anyone shopped in Russia without the knowledge of five modern European languages.

Her sister-in-law had tried to ban foreign food. She claimed it was all poisoned and part of a worldwide anti-Russian conspiracy. She refused to have anything with a black striped bar code in the house, claiming it was the mark of the devil. Sasha, on the other hand, refused to eat anything identifiable by a Russian label. It had made shopping very difficult.

It would be tinned vegetables for months now that winter had started. Unlike the other mothers at Sasha's school, Katya didn't have time to spend days up to her elbows preserving fruit and vegetables. Leonid watched her as she peeled potatoes and mixed a salad. She'd reached a compromise with Sasha over the dog: he could keep the animal as long as he walked him and contributed to the cost of his food. She didn't always like to encourage her son to break the law, but why should she pay for dog food when Sasha kept an estimated $300, 200 German marks and £50 under his bed?

She should also go and check the Englishman next door. It was not a prospect she relished. The last time she had let herself in unannounced he'd been stretched out half naked on the floor, writhing about with a piece of curved metal. Honestly, the men that brainless Clive sent her got worse.

The Englishman had at least found time to complete his list. The choices were predictable. Attractive, young and sexy, but with a girl-next-door look. They tended to steer clear of the real bombshells. Some of the women he had selected were no longer on her books. A couple were married to Mafia sponsors, two more to foreigners and two, both of them ex-Bolshoi dancers, had gone to dance at the Crazy Horse.

It meant another recruitment drive (not that she'd waste Sonya on the likes of Mr Small) and another evening class advising new girls how to behave with clients. Quiet and shy. With an absurd interest in housework. Sporty was good. Independent was bad. Likewise drinking and smoking. And though it might be *de rigueur* to ask a Russian suitor in the first five minutes how much he cleared (*earned* was never quite the word for Russian incomes), foreigners took it as the sign of a gold-digger. And never seemed too interested in sex. 'Acting like a hooker' had been the Cleveland surgeon's reason for breaking off his engagement with Irina.

Sasha stormed the flat at just after four. He threw his Simpsons school bag on the ground and tugged at his anorak sleeves as Leonid greeted him in a frenzy of barking.

'Hi, Mum. Have you fed Leonid?'

'The deal was you fed the dog. And you'll have to hurry if you're going to walk him. I'm going out, so Mrs Voronsheva will have to sit with you for a couple of hours this evening.'

'No,' groaned Sasha. 'Please, anyone but her. She smells of vinegar and the only card game she knows is patience. What about Mrs Rubelova?'

'Sasha, this may come as a shock to you, but I don't select babysitters on their ability, or lack of it, to beat you at three card brag. Now eat your tea and then take that bloody dog out for a walk. He's already peed in your toy box.'

'Ugh, Mum, you're disgusting. He wouldn't. Would you, Leonuchka?' Sasha flung his arms round the animal and buried his head in its neck.

'You'll have to clean it out this evening,' said Katya, 'after you've finished your homework.' She placed a plate of boiled potatoes, Russian salad and sausage on the table.

'Yuk. I can't eat this. I want pizza.'

'Sasha, I'm starting to lose my temper. Eat this or you'll get nothing. And shut that dog up.'

'I mean,' sighed Sasha, stabbing at the plate with a disgruntled expression, 'this sausage isn't even German.'

Katya missed the last comment. She'd gone into the

sitting room which doubled as her bedroom to sort through her catalogue of men. It was essential to select only the very best to show Sonya. No overweight pig farmers from Utah, no cab drivers from Scunthorpe.

Her eyes fell on a 42-year-old movie producer from Miami. It probably translated into a 50-year-old Blockbuster counter clerk, but Sonya wasn't to know. The photograph showed a paunchy man with good teeth.

If Sonya worked in a bookshop, reasoned Katya, she must be literary. She peeled back the plastic cover to get at an advertising copy writer from Virginia with specs as thick as vodka glasses. Alongside, a sheet of A4 said he owned a six-bedroomed house and station wagon.

She'd better take a pretty boy as well, just in case. Charlie Palmers, 26, from Bristol, UK, always went down well with her girls, even though he lacked the formulaic chiselled chin, capped teeth and blue eyes of an American. Still, she reflected, high time to get Clive to update her records. These photos were starting to get the sepia tinge of a 'Wanted' poster.

At six thirty the babysitter arrived. Mrs Voronsheva had the solid curves of a wooden *matryoshka* doll. And according to Sasha was just as hard. Katya slipped out of the apartment to the squawking protests of her son as he was forced to listen to and recite huge tracts of Chekhov. 'Uncle who? I want to play nineteeeen dooo . . .' was the last wail she heard.

Katya could hardly believe she had travelled such a distance and not required a passport. She wouldn't have been surprised if Sonya's instructions had included a short flight in an Ilyushin 76. Could this still be Moscow? Katya scanned the desolate suburbs. For sheer inhospitality *microrayon* rivalled the surface of Mars.

She pulled on a pair of gloves. It even seemed colder than Moscow, with a gale blowing through the high-rise flats which must have doubled in intensity since leaving Siberia. It was already dark as she groped her way towards Korpus 2, flat 244. The concrete lobby was strewn with rubbish and spray-painted and misspelt English band names. 'Fuk You' said another wall. Metal doors on the rows of green mailboxes were blackened and swung open.

Katya, with her keen sense of self-preservation, had never believed in communism. Years before Gorbachev had unwittingly set Russia on its collision course to what was now referred to as freedom, she had resisted any idea that her destiny was not her own. Only at times like this, when she saw the depths to which her country had sunk, did she feel a pang of regret. Third World was the best way to describe Russia these days.

Sonya's flat was on the fifteenth floor. When the lift doors juddered open, the smell of onions frying cut through the odour from an overflowing rubbish chute. Katya rang the bell to a communal door which allowed access to a further five flats. She heard a door inside open and the noise of slippers as they skimmed along a linoleum floor. A lock clanked undone, then another, before Sonya's face greeted Katya with an uncertain smile.

'Hello,' she breathed. 'Did you find us OK?' She was dressed in a flowery cotton housecoat under which hip bones were clearly definable. She seemed as innocent as Sasha, in a parallel universe, might have been.

'Yes, fine,' lied Katya, following Sonya down the corridor. She looked even more radiant than when Katya had first spotted her. At home she looked younger. Katya stole a glance down at her slippered feet. They were as stunted as a Chinese concubine's. Perfect.

'It's quite a long way from the centre but the area's good and they say the air is quite clean,' Sonya continued automatically.

They entered the apartment. Sonya passed Katya a pair of slippers, and went on, 'They say there aren't many factories around here. It's much better for Nikita.'

Nikita? Don't say she was married. Katya's eardrums started to pound with disappointment.

'Who is Nikita?' she rushed out a little too quickly.

'My brother, he's inside. You should meet him.' She spoke as if she was guessing at social conventions.

The apartment was two-roomed and lined corner to corner with books. But Katya was so caught up with the luminous beauty of the boy sitting on a chair with a huge book of drawings on his lap that it was a few seconds before she realised that he had no legs.

'Nikita, this is Katya,' said Sonya nervously.

'Hello.' His cherubic face had a dazed expression.

'Pleased to meet you,' replied Katya.

'Likewise.' Eyes as blue as his sister's narrowed to a confused smile. He looked about fourteen.

Sonya crossed the room to drape a reassuring hand across his shoulders. A child playing at being a mother. Katya smiled sympathetically. Not that Nikita seemed to notice; his eyes were back on the book in front of him.

There wasn't much to say. He was too young for

Afghanistan, so it had to be Chechenya. Moscow was full of young limbless men begging for loose change along the Arbat, or using their knuckles to propel homemade carts, some little more than teatrays with wheels, on and off Metro carriages, begging for scraps.

'Come on, let's leave him. We should go next door,' said Sonya, and led the way into the kitchen.

'Before the war, Nikita wanted to be a mathematician. He was the one with all the brains. He was due to graduate from MGU when he was called up for military service,' she explained when they were both sitting at the kitchen table. 'Two from his class died and two more lost their legs. Then they said university students didn't have to go to war any more.' Sonya looked at Katya with huge almond-shaped eyes. Her thin arms, as she reached to pour tea, were covered in soft blonde down. She spoke like a child whose knowledge of life was so slight it could hardly be verbalised. She reminded Katya of Sasha when he asked her about pirating laws. On occasion, events took the wind out of Katya's bulldozer-like attempts to earn money for herself and Sasha. This was one of them.

'They said it was a Russian grenade that did that to him. Our parents died when we were children and Grandma died of shock when she saw what had happened to Nikita.' Sonya stared down at the silver spoon she had just used to stir her tea.

Katya thought she ought to try to move the conversation on, before nineteen of the twenty million Russians killed in World War Two turned out to be close family relatives. In Russia it didn't pay to dwell on the past.

Nikita was a stark reminder that if she didn't keep working and saving, then in ten years it could be Sasha, crippled in a war no one knew anything about. Katya took a deep breath and smoothed her hair, breaking Sonya's childlike reverie with a nervous laugh.

'So. I guess you thought my proposal the other day was a bit odd?' She wished she was drinking something stronger than tea.

Sonya blew her nose on a tissue. 'No, not so strange. I've had people come up to me before and ask if I wanted to model. Or dance. Though I'm not sure why. My posture is terrible and I'm not at all rhythmical.'

Her naivety made Katya want to weep. The nearest a Moscow dancer got to a Giselle was a G-string.

'No, it's nothing like that,' she said. 'No, my concern is more *humanitarian*.' It was a long shot but she'd never tried to a recruit a bookshop assistant before. Innocence was not a state of mind she often encountered. 'You may have read about the sad decline in moral standards in the west?'

'No.'

'Well, it's reached such a point that honest, trustworthy men simply cannot find wives who do anything other than work and stay out till all hours drinking. There is hardly a woman left in the west who will agree to bear a child. The society is close to collapse.' She was starting to sound like the Communist Manifesto, but it seemed to be having the desired effect.

'Really?' said Sonya, eyes huge as a cartoon character's.

'Yes. Today, due to the decline, western men have to travel here, to Russia, to find the perfect woman. A woman who could be all the things a western woman is

47

not: loyal, trustworthy and honest. My job is merely to bring the two worlds together, sit back and watch true love unfold.' No need to mention the $20,000 fee her client had promised for a betrothal to a woman who exactly met Sonya's description.

'Er, I don't know. I've never met a foreigner before. Aren't they very different from Russians?'

Katya smiled with maternal reassurance. 'Goodness me, no. If they do differ slightly it's just that the men are more hard-working, family-orientated and drink less.'

'I wouldn't have to,' Sonya paused, her long eyelashes downcast, '*screw* them, would I?' She used the word in a hushed yet straightforward way, which almost suggested she didn't know what it meant. Like when Sasha had learnt of his grandma's death, he had tried to be serious without knowing why. Then she added hurriedly, 'It's just that I haven't done . . . before."

'No, no,' Katya dismissed the idea. 'You won't have to do anything you don't want to.'

'But in any case,' Sonya continued, 'it really doesn't matter to me. I couldn't ever leave Nikita. Without my bookshop earnings he would be destitute. And I couldn't bear that.'

'No, Sonya, of course, I quite understand,' said Katya. 'But one thing I must say about my gentlemen is that they are usually very well off. If you did fall in love, it would mean a new life for you and Nikita.'

'What, in Russia, or abroad? I don't think I would be able to live abroad.'

'That would depend on what you and your husband decided. Together. But just think of the medical services they have in the west. For Nikita's sake.' Sonya's charming childishness, at first so touching, had started to grate on Katya, who viewed an inability to meet one's material potential as a failing. As far as she was concerned, they could live in a yurt on the Mongolian plains, as long as she got her finder's fee out of it.

'I would get the choice to turn him down if I didn't like him, wouldn't I?'

'Yes, of course, though my gentlemen can be quite persuasive. Take a look.' Katya delved into a plastic carrier bag and dragged out the profiles of the three men intended to impress Sonya.

She gave them a cursory glance, like a princess in a fairy tale. 'Ugh, he looks like an old man. He's as blind as a bat and he looks short.'

'This is only a sample selection. I have dozens more at home. What do you say? Would you be interested in joining the agency? There's usually a fifty rouble registration fee, but in your case I'm prepared to waive it.'

'And I really wouldn't have to do anything I didn't want to? I told you I've never met a foreigner before.' She pursed her lips in a girlish way.

'Please, Sonya, this is a respectable marriage agency, not the white slave trade. Now tell me, do you speak English?'

'A bit from high school. But not much.'

Katya started to write on the back of one of the Americans' photos. 'Height?'

'One metre seventy.'

'Weight?'

'Thirty-nine kilos.'

'Hair?'

'Yes.'

'No, what colour?'

'Blonde.'

'Natural?'

'Yes.'

'Measurements?'

'Thirty-four, twenty-two, thirty-four.'

'You're absolutely sure about the hips?'

'Yes!'

'Feet?'

'Two.'

'No, what size?'

'Thirty-five.'

'Good. Age?'

'Nineteen.'

'Ever been married?'

'No.'

'Any kids?'

'No!'

'Smoke or drink?'

'No and no.'

'Religion?'

'None.'

'They usually expect something there.'

'Really? What should I say?'

'I usually recommend Russian Orthodox.'

'OK.'

'Education?'

'Graduated high school. Technical qualification in libraries.'

'Any history of cancer in your family?'

'Sorry?'

'How did your parents die?'

'Car crash.'

'Good. Any history of strokes?'

'No.'

'Any tendency towards bisexuality?'

'I'm sorry?'

'I'll just put no for that. Finally, what are you looking for in a man?'

Sonya hesitated.

Katya looked at her watch. Nearly ten. 'Don't worry. I'll put hard-working, loyal non-drinker.' She put down her pen. 'Most of all we need a photo. If you haven't got any we can get one done at a studio.'

'Well, actually, I went to Yalta on holiday this summer. I think I've some from there. They're only of me in my swimsuit though.'

Katya felt her pulse start to race. Even if she missed the finder's fee she could probably raffle them off and make enough money to pay for Sasha's education.

'They should be fine,' she replied.

While Sonya went to look for them, Katya took a look round the immaculate kitchen. Its shelves were even barer than her own. Wasn't she doing Sonya a favour by trying to save her from a lifetime of *this*? And as she told all her girls, they could easily get divorced after a couple of years.

Sonya returned with a selection of colour pictures that made Katya's palms sweat just to look at them. The $20,000 was so close she could almost smell it. She hardly noticed the trek home.

51

II

When Bridges returned to his cosy dacha 25 miles west of Moscow, his answer phone was flashing like the summit of a random hill walking programme.

'Hi, Bob. This is Susan. Could you give me a call? Don't worry, it's not urgent. It's nothing to do with the girls. It's just that we should talk.'

Bridges heard his wife's voice so rarely now, it took his breath away. That and hearing her New England accent being broadcast around his KGB safehouse. What could warrant a phone call that wasn't to do with one of their daughters? She probably wanted to get started on the divorce. Marry Jean Luc, the French tennis coach whose astronomically priced lessons, along with the huge mortgage, had been one of the reasons he had first started photocopying the odd document in his airless Langley office. It seemed like a lifetime ago.

He thought with a bitterness which bordered on rancour how well things had turned out for Susan. Days after he'd caught her and the tennis coach in a love-all clinch (paid for indirectly by the hard-working citizens of the USSR) he'd been forced to defect to Moscow. Admittedly, Susan had had to stay away from the Wives of America league for a couple of months till the fuss died down. (In the early days he'd seen her on CNN proclaiming her innocence and wailing that she had known nothing of her husband's deviant behaviour.) Then she got to keep the house, the car, and their daughters. And the lover. It was like the perfect virtual murder.

Outside in the garden the hired hands, a couple of married

ex-KGB old-timers, were clearing the garden after the first drift of snow had melted. Bridges waved to them. The old man, Alexander, waved back. There was a time when his every movement, including last night's absence, would have been forwarded to the intelligence service. Now the FSB, or whatever it was known as now, hardly cared.

He glanced at his watch. Gone 4 p.m. Moscow time. Just after 8 a.m. Virginia time. Better to try and catch Susan now before she left for a tennis lesson. Though, if his suspicion was correct, her Yannick Noah would be nearer to her than a closely called ace.

He poured himself a tumbler of Jack Daniels before he dialled. It must be an acceptable drinking hour somewhere in the world, and it seemed a long time since the professor's restorative draught.

The phone rang four times before Susan picked it up, slightly breathless.

'Sorry to disturb you,' he said caustically. There was nothing that rubbed in a lack of a sex life like knowing your one-time partner was at it like a Girl Scout at a Rasputin love-in. 'It's Bob here. You called.'

'Hi, yeah. Hi, gosh. Long time no speak. What're you doing?' He'd definitely caught her doing something other than boiling eggs.

'At the moment counting my phone bill.' Why did she always bring out the worst in him? 'How's Lee?'

'She's great. Really great. Her grades are up and, uh, she's joined the softball team.'

'Fantastic.'

'And Monica?'

'She's fine. Got a new boyfriend. He's OK.'

'Tell them both I've just sent them a letter,' he lied. Postal fuck-ups were one of the few boons of living in the former Soviet Union.

'Great, that's really great.' Her guilt had sent her into eulogy mode.

'Susan, can we get to the point? Why'd you call me?' The mental picture of his wife in bed with another man hurt. It wasn't so much the sex he missed, that had tailed off after the first years of married life in their twenties. It was the lack of domesticity he regretted. And the jarring thought that it might be years before he saw his daughters.

She started slowly. 'Look, there's an election for a new governor here. The Republican candidate is trying to get elected on a far right ticket. It seems he's not been making much headway. Then he decided you were a vote puller.'

'*Sorry?*'

'The guy figures that if he can get you extradited – is that the right word? – it will pull him a lot of votes. You know: so and so reins in red traitor.'

Bridges' heart started to pump like a cardiac machine. 'And exactly who is so and so?'

'Hang on.' A hand over the receiver could barely disguise the pillow talk. It stung more than the prospect of a grand jury indictment. 'His name is . . . wait, yeah, I've got it . . . Somebody Foreman. "Foreman Is Your Man." Yeah, that's it. I thought I'd better warn you. Listen, why don't I fax you this leaflet?'

He ignored that. 'How's all this going to affect the girls?'

'No worries on that front. It seems that Russia is cool

these days among American teenagers. You're a hero among their friends.'

'Well, I guess that's one thing.' He'd promised himself he would not drink while his wife was on the phone but the news had come with a knee-buckling, bowel-loosening shock. She could probably hear as he drained another glass of whisky.

'Are you all right? You sound strange.'

'Me? Strange? Why should I sound strange after learning that I'm likely to be serving life in a state penitentiary in less time than it takes Boris Yeltsin to finish a bottle of vodka?'

'But surely the Russians can protect you? What about the KGB?'

'Susan,' he spoke calmly, 'the KGB couldn't protect the skin on a bowl of custard.'

'Look, Bob, I've got to go.' She giggled in a way he used to think was kittenish. 'Something's just come up.'

'Yeah, I don't doubt it,' he sneered. 'Give my love to Jacques Cousteau.' He threw the phone down. Typical. Just as things here start to look up, albeit with the most unlikely business venture since Burke and Hare, reality hit him in the face.

The wooziness of the third glass of whisky had started to numb the outer neural transmitters when he heard the tinny engine of a Samara Lada limp up his drive. A tune beeped out on to the horn meant only one thing. Sergei. Then he remembered that in a moment of uncharacteristic hospitality he'd invited him and Olga over for shashlik.

In a split second he decided not to tell Sergei his latest piece of news. It might get back to the KGB. He wanted to keep it under wraps until he'd had time to weigh up the consequences. Then, as the alcohol seeped into his brain, he started to view it more rationally. How interested could the great American public be by all that Cold War nonsense? After glasnost and perestroika, weren't we all one world governed by the multinationals and Bill Gates? Then he remembered it wasn't the spying, it was the *betrayal* for which the public felt entitled to their pound of flesh. Bridges was dully imagining his trial when Sergei walked in.

'Greetings, my dear boy. How are we this afternoon?' Sergei was so intent on re-casting himself as a character from a P.G. Wodehouse novel, it was just a question of time before he started wearing plus fours under his leather jacket.

'Knock it off, Serge. My head already feels like it's got the Siberian Express running through it.'

'What, pray, did you get up to last night?'

'I might very well ask you the same question,' said Bridges, silenced as Sergei's wife Olga pushed herself and baby Lena through the door. Though she spoke little English, it was inconceivable to discuss Sergei's philandering in front of her.

Sergei rushed to her aid as she greeted Bridges with a heavily accented, 'Hello, Bob. You are well?'

'Yes, thanks, Olga, I'm good. What about you?'

'Oh. You know, so so.' She shrugged.

In the past six years that had been the extent of their conversation. Through childbirth, poverty, good times, deaths, she had been, 'You know, so so.' But existing with an utterly superficial level of communication, Bridges had to admit to himself, was one of the attractions of living in

Russia. Not understanding meant no involvement – though it hadn't stopped him forming a throbbing crush on Olga. In the many evenings when, too drunk to make it home, he had stayed with them, Olga had risen silently and made up a bed for him on the divan next door. He had ached for her to join him in the soapy starched sheets. While Sergei snored next to her, he tossed and turned in a silent sign for her to join him.

'So, what's on the menu, my good man?' Sergei patted his shoulders in a Stalin-like embrace.

'At the moment, Jack Daniels. Want one?'

'Prefer a beer if you can run to it.'

'Sure, in the fridge. What about Olga?'

'She'll have tea,' he replied, without asking his wife who was walking Lena round the garden. The two-year-old was sheathed in so many clothes, bound like swaddling, that she could hardly walk.

'So what *did* happen to you the other night? We left at two and you still hadn't come back.' Sergei popped the cap of a bottle of Budweiser.

Bridges hesitated to ask who the *we* referred to. 'If I told you, you'd hardly believe me.'

'Listen, my friend, Russians have been accepting the unbelievable for centuries. Try me.' He sat back and took a swig of his drink.

III

After two whole days with his abdominiser as the only form of exercise, Terry felt like a caged beast. Women had started to seem as distant a concept as a rowing machine. More than forty-eight hours and the only woman he'd seen had been the one from next door. And even then she'd forgotten the bog roll. He'd had to use newspaper. It was ghastly. He was thirsty and his bottled water had run out at lunchtime. He didn't trust the sulphurous liquid that spurted out of these taps. The bath, after his shower, had had the yellowish glaze of a jaundice patient. Then he remembered it might have been his fake tan washing off.

He half-heartedly switched on the archaic black and white TV set. Yesterday evening he'd caught part of a Brazilian soap opera which had included some tasty scenes. Why should he have to settle for celluloid when he was paying for real flesh? He'd called next door only to be met by a tiny tot delinquent whose only word of English had been *pleeze* and who had come to the door holding a cardboard placard saying something about an operation. It really was too much.

He switched off the TV, so old it had a dial to find the stations. Grey men in suits speaking in double dutch. He picked up the currency declaration form on which he'd jotted down the address of the nightclub which guaranteed you would do it that night. Screw Drivers. T-ver-ska-ya, U-lit-sa. Num-ber twen-ty fo-ur. Surely he would be able to convey that to even the most backward Russian cabby. He only had US dollars but that shouldn't matter. If Katya didn't show up in the next hour he was going out on his own.

What to wear? He picked up his discarded pair of Calvins and took a sniff. They weren't clean but in the circumstances he thought he could risk getting away with them. Ralph Lauren shirt and chinos cut the right sort of *colonial* dash. Had Russia been part of the British Empire? Probably. Parts of it definitely, how else did they get chicken Kiev? The thought of food made him swoon. He'd only had twenty-three Nutri-Grain bars since leaving Heathrow.

Good for the old weight loss, though, he thought, pulling his belt a notch tighter over his trousers. The shirt could have done with an iron. He draped his dressing gown over the pillow and stashed three condoms under the bed. He should have a shave before he left, but he was starting to like this two-day stubble. Maybe Russia, three thousand miles away from his semi-detached home and nine-to-five job, could be the next rung on his ladder to complete reinvention.

Who could he be? International banker in town for a conference? Humanitarian aid worker distributing food to the starving? War photographer on a *Time* assignment? The last one he liked. Ever since his action shots on his and Grace's holiday in Lanzarote, he'd fancied himself as a Lord Snowdon. This could be his chance.

He grabbed his Fuji sure shot and hung it round his neck. He looked in the mirror over the chipped enamel sink. Just the job. He combed his hair very carefully, picked up his jacket and went to the door. He looked at his watch; it was just after ten. He thought of what he would be doing at home at this time. It was just after seven in the UK; he'd be starting his thirty-minute treadmill programme. He began to jog on the spot as if in sympathy, or maybe it was nerves. Maybe he was psyching

59

himself to go out into this unwelcoming landscape.

'Go on, Terry,' he said out loud like a mantra from his Gender Awareness Forum. 'You can do it.' He jogged harder. 'Go on, Terry, my son.' He was breaking into a sweat. He shook his head from side to side like a horse, the Fuji sure shot beating on his chest like a medallion. 'Go on, you can do it,' and like a small explosion he launched himself from the flat.

He glanced back at the door as he left. Number 133, he must remember that. How? He was *one* person and his age was *thirty-three*. I'm one and my age is thirty-three. He mumbled it as a headscarved woman, hunched nearly double, shambled past him. I am one and my age is thirty-three. Her gaze moved from the scuffed linoleum up to meet Terry's sunglass-shrouded eyes.

'Hello,' he said, smiling his older woman's smile, more reassuring than suggestive. Her furrowed forehead creased into a frown.

'Nice day for it.' He sometimes thought foreigners' inability to understand English was nothing more than stubbornness.

The old woman shook her head, spat onto the floor inches from his feet and walked away.

'Charming,' he said with a tut. He was shaken. 'Absolutely charming.'

The encounter had so unsettled Terry – it had been even less welcoming than the reception he and Grace had got from the guesthouse owner in Lanzarote – that by the time he got to the ground floor he was starting to doubt the flat number. I am one, but how old am I? Thirty-four. I am one and my age is thirty-four.

It was hardly easier when he got outside. A gang of youths was waiting menacingly in front of the building. There was a road, but which way was the centre? The road was unlit and it was practically pitch black. Terry pushed his Gucci sunglasses onto the top of his head. Lada after Lada sped past.

Damn that Clive from Reds In Your Bed. It really was too much. He would definitely be claiming a rebate. What that old crow had done to him inside verged on assault. Personal service his foot, it had all the personal touch of a vicar at a drive-in wedding chapel.

Terry noticed that a yellow car with the word TAKSI in English had pulled up beside him. A middle-aged man in a leather flat cap was winding down the mud-encrusted window. He said something unfathomable.

'Evening,' muttered Terry. He delved for the piece of paper on which he had scribbled the name of the nightclub. 'Screw Drivers. Ter-ver-sky-ya Street,' he said slowly.

The driver nodded curtly. 'Khow much?' he asked in a guttural accent.

The speed of the negotiations threw Terry, who had been congratulating himself on his linguistic ability. This war photographer guise was going to be easier than he'd thought. 'Er. I don't know. What do you think?'

'Fifty US,' was the swift reply.

'How much?' squealed Terry. 'That's nearly thirty quid.' A month's gym membership. The cost of the train fare to Heathrow, which he'd dodged by getting Bob to give him a lift. A tenth of the cost of his operation . . .

The driver's leather-clad arm moved to put the car in first and pull away.

'No, stop. Stop. OK. Fifty is OK.' The thought of

stopping another car was too daunting. And perhaps the club really was a long way away. This area really didn't have much of a *centre ville* feeling to it.

Terry ducked to get in the car, his Fuji sure shot banging on the front seat, while his Gucci sunglasses scraped on the roof. He felt the corner of the packet of Marlboros which he'd brought out with him as intended payment.

As they careered off, Terry looked out of the muddy back window, trying to fix the block of flats in his mind. The number 20/1 was painted in white at the bottom. There was a strange garden shed immediately in front of it, selling vodka. In front of that was the slouched body of an unconscious man, and a pile of rubbish was ablaze to the left – though the last two, he noted, might not be permanent.

When they pulled up outside Screwdrivers it was gone eleven. Terry had never been a drinking man, but as he used his shoulder like a battering ram to open the jammed back seat door, he thought this might be the time to start. A condom had flown over the front seat as he had tried to peel off a $50 bill from his roll. The driver had merely passed the silver packet back to Terry without a flutter of emotion. Strange how he'd almost seemed to *know* where to drop him.

The sign flashed in red and green, alternating with a fifteen-foot neon girl whose miniskirted body and pouting lips at the airport had first caught Terry's eye. The cars parked outside were much flasher than you ever saw outside his gym, Fit To Burst – BMWs, Mercedes, even one Rolls-Royce. Maybe there was some sort of car auction going on. Terry found it impossible to reconcile the Russia of his imagination, honest peasant labourers or bearded revolutionaries (and that was just the women, he smiled to himself), with the reality in front of him.

An Armani store flickered opposite the club and he'd passed a Hugo Boss and a Dior on his way here. He looked down at his Marks and Spencer chinos. Still, at least the shirt was Ralph Lauren. He was, after all, only going for a Martin Bell look, or a paparazzi photographer on the Princess Di Angolan landmines tour.

There were four suited bouncers on the door. One ripped Terry's Fuji sure shot from round his neck while the other pushed him through one of those security checks you got at airports. It was done with the speed and assuredness of a death row jailer taking a condemned man to the electric chair.

From behind a curtained booth a young woman demanded 250 roubles or $50. What was it with this place? thought Terry. Was fifty the only number they knew? But he was so relieved to have a payment option other than the monopoly sized sum of roubles that he paid meekly and continued to the room where a techno beat was pounding like jungle drums.

He hadn't seen so much female flesh since he'd got the wrong day for the sauna at Fit To Burst and walked in on a women-only afternoon. Gyrating, thrusting, lunging. It was only when he noticed that the room had wall-to-wall mirrors that he realised there were only six women on the dance floor. They danced with each other or danced with themselves opposite a mirror. It achieved the desired erotic effect on Terry.

'Vodka and tonic,' he told the barman, handing over a

$10 note from which he got no change.

He moved over to set up base camp leaning against a mirrored column in a spot where his bald patch would not be apparent from the mezzanine above, where women were circulating like Greek goddesses. Men sat at a table around an open bottle scrutinising the women as they walked past.

'Pleeze buy me a drink. Gin tonic.' Terry hadn't seen her approach. His initial irritation at the loss of another eight quid was tempered with a boastful swagger that a member of this swirling harem had selected him.

Quite forward these Russian girls, he thought as he waited for the drink. He couldn't see Grace being so bold even before her waistline disappeared into her chest.

Silently he handed her the drink, which turned opaque under the disco lights.

'My name is Angela. What is yours?' She reminded him of a doll his sister had had which said, 'Hello I want a toffee apple', when you pulled a string on her back. Terry had discovered it when he'd been trying to look up her gingham dress.

'Terry Small.' She wasn't one of the real lookers, but for a first attempt she was more than acceptable. He brushed a hand over his shoulders to check for dandruff and in the same movement looked away, pretending to cough but really cupping a hand over his mouth to see if his breath smelt.

'What do you do, Angela?' said Terry, returning his face to within two inches of her ear. In her platform boots she was the same height as him.

'Er, hostess. Me leetle English.' She laughed and shook her head, then encased the straw in her drink with two perfectly made-up lips. That was handy, thought Terry. If she was an Aeroflot hostess, he could maybe change his flight home and avoid those Finnish witches. 'We go. No?'

'Where?' A line of perspiration formed on Terry's upper lip. He wiped it away with the back of his hand. The hastily gulped vodka had made him feel light-headed.

'My place. Your place. Easier your place.' She had taken a compact from her bag and was reapplying her lipstick. The tip of her straw looked like an oil gauge.

She looked at her watch. Eleven forty-five. 'Pleeze, we go now. Club close at five.' She set off towards the cloakroom.

If the club closed at five, why were they hurrying? Terry felt slightly cheated. He'd spent $50 to get into this paradise (if only he'd been allowed to take some pictures) and now he was leaving, albeit with this charming young lady, after only half an hour.

Angela came back, drowned in a full-length fur coat, her platform-booted feet poking out from under it like hooves. In the gloaming of the entrance she looked about twenty-nine, with short almost spiky dark hair and skin which was slightly pitted.

'You live far?' she asked as she pulled him onto the pavement. The air was a relief after the smoky interior.

'Fili, I think.'

The woman said something under her breath and looked up with the same expression of hatred that the woman who had spat at him had had. 'Sheeet. What about car?'

'No, I don't have a car. I'm on holiday. Well.' Terry gave his suave yet mysterious look. He fondled the Fuji sure shot, which had been returned to him. 'Actually, I'm on an assign—'

'No, do it in a car.'

Terry gasped.

'In car two hundred dollars, your place, three hundred dollars, both places only one time.' She looked irritated. Two bouncers within earshot looked at them impassively.

'How much?' he squealed. It was a knee-jerk reaction of shock to the price rather than the realisation that his young companion was a prostitute. Pay for it when he had a brochure full of free ones in Katya's flat?

'Look, I'm sorry, but I think there's been some sort of terrible mistake,' he said, showing the inside of his palms in a way that he'd read in *Men's Health* showed you were being non-confrontational.

'Meestake? What is it meestake? You not pay?' Her lips snarled over her teeth, leaving splodges of red lipstick.

'No, I no pay.' Terry turned to go back into the club, slightly miffed that he'd been dragged away. Terry Small pay for sex? Not likely.

He felt the crash on the side of his head a millisecond after the scream pierced the hum of traffic and the music from inside. Even the bouncers looked over. The impact felt as hard as a discus. Even though she'd only used a little sequinned bag, it must have had a brick in it.

Terry hit the pavement immediately.

IV

'Sometimes, Bridges, old mate, I think the KGB man who gave you the truth serum must have got a dodgy batch,' said Sergei as he opened another beer and picked at the bones of a chicken leg on his plate.

'This has got nothing to do with thiopentone sodium,' replied Bridges. 'It's a sound business proposition and, what's more, one that could make us a lot of money.'

It was after 3 a.m. Olga and Lena had gone to bed in the spare room. Bridges and Sergei were sitting round a fire, its chimney not up to disseminating the fug of their cigarette smoke.

'Why,' persisted Bridges, 'did our last business venture fail?'

'Because you and I are to business what Solzhenitsyn was to the Russian prison service?'

'No. Because we went at it from the wrong angle.' Bridges thought back to their first and last foray into the quagmire of 1990s Russian commerce. It was only in costly retrospect that they decided that starting a life assurance business in a city where the average life expectancy of a businessman was thirty-three was not a viable idea.

'And let me get this straight. The right angle is?' asked Sergei scornfully.

'Funerals.'

'Funerals. OK. Once more from the top. The other night, when you stumbled off into the darkness, leaving me with two of the most—'

'When I stumbled into the darkness,' Bridges interrupted before Sergei could launch into an account of his debauchery that would probably wake his wife and child, 'I met Professor Nikolai Modin.' No need to dwell on the throwing up part, thought Bridges. 'Had you ever been a student of Soviet history, that name might mean something to you.'

Sergei countered with a blank look, before walking over to the fridge and pulling out two more beers.

'Professor Modin was the man charged with the preservation of the body of your country's founding father. When Vladimir Ilyich Lenin departed this world for that great Central Committee Party meeting in the sky in nineteen twenty-three, Modin embalmed him.'

Bridges thought of the day shortly after he'd arrived when he'd been taken to see Lenin's body in its Red Square mausoleum. Escorted by the head of the KGB's counter-intelligence department, they'd skipped the queue which had snaked as far as Manedzh Square. The body looked like a waxwork model, the pale glassy skin in stark contrast to the shockingly ginger hair. What sort of a country would follow a leader with orange hair? had been his overriding thought. He had, though, bowed his respects alongside a KGB general who still thought it had been ideology, rather than his wife's tennis lessons, that had made him betray his country.

'Yeah, all us Young Pioneers had to visit his body,' Sergei said. 'Spent all morning in the queue. All the girls were crying.'

'Well, what you and your classmates may not have been aware of is that his body has to be re-embalmed every three months. Professor Modin, as head of the Institute of Cosmetology, still does it.'

'You mean he has to be re-pickled?'

'Right. Else the body would start to go mouldy. No method for embalming bodies without a periodic top-up has ever been invented.'

'Fascinating though this undoubtedly is, I've yet to see

how it's going to earn us enough for us to see out our days on the French Riviera.'

'The French Riviera? You forget, the furthest east I'm allowed is Prague.'

'Sorry. See out our days by the Black Sea.'

Bridges nodded and took a swig of beer. Was it the alcohol, or was this starting to make sense? 'Sergei, have you heard the one about the Russian mobster who admires his friend's new jacket?'

'Probably, but carry on.'

'He meets up with his friend and says, "Boris, nice jacket. How much did you pay for it?" Boris smiles and says, "Thanks, it cost two thousand dollars." His friend screeches, "What! Are you mad? I bought one the other day and it cost four thousand." '

'Very good. But can you, as they say, cut to the chase? I'm tired.'

'Sergei. The conspicuous consumption of wealth. You lot lead the world in it. It used to be space travel, nuclear warheads, invading small countries. Now Russians are Olympian money spenders.'

'True. But I don't—'

'When was the last time you went to a cemetery?' Bridges stood up.

'What?'

'When was the last time you visited a graveyard?'

'Grandma. One year ago.'

'Don't tell me. Small grave, plastic flowers, tiny inscription?'

'Roughly, though there was a purpose-built bench to have a vodka shot and toast the bereaved.'

'Look.' Bridges excitedly took a swig of beer. 'Crappy funerals, shitloads of money, and a professor who is to embalming what I am to whisky sales. Put them all together, what have you got?'

'A former CIA spy gone off the rails?'

'No, my friend. You have Bodies Beautiful, Russia's first privately-owned funeral parlour and embalming service. All parties catered for.' He picked up the packet of cigarettes Sergei had thrown on the table and inhaled with a flourish.

'Well,' said Sergei gravely, 'they said Burgess turned to alcohol, Philby went mad. In the spying community, there's only little George Blake who seems to have kept his marbles.'

'Oh, shut up. It's brilliant. Mafia funerals. Basic package twenty-five thousand dollars, includes embalming, coffin and after-funeral party. For fifty thousand you get the mausoleum service. Funerals are Russia's future.'

'You really are serious about this, aren't you?'

'Never more so. Professor Modin's got the know-how but no business sense. He wants a foreigner on board to give it a touch of authentic US panache, essential for the Al Capone special at thirty-five grand. You're the Russian partner.'

'And you, my friend, are mad,' said Sergei. Then he smiled. 'You know, this is so fucked up I think it just might work.'

'Cheers,' said Bridges, raising his bottle. 'Welcome to the firm.'

V

Terry wasn't sure if the clatter was coming from inside his

head or outside. He struggled to get one ear off the ground. One side of his body was wet and very cold. From his limited vision he could see nothing but feet. Stiletto heels clicking past him on the concrete slab. A hubbub of voices which he couldn't understand. He tried to move his head. Nothing. The sudden thought that he'd had a stroke made him flick his head a few inches off the pavement.

Thank God, he could move. He looked down at a body which seemed unconnected to him. His chinos and Ralph Lauren shirt were coated in grey slime. He looked more like a paparazzi photographer *after* a landmine explosion. He felt his chest where the sure shot should have been. The camera had gone.

He edged into a sitting position by the kerb. Men and women were streaming out of the club. The electronic beep of car alarms punctuated women's conversation. He was aware of a mobile telephone ringing. What had happened? He glanced over towards a hoard of bouncers who hadn't intervened when his fur-coated friend had swacked him with her lead-lined bag.

He got unsteadily to his feet and used the inside of his sleeve to wipe the mud from his face. Was it worth going to the police? He wasn't really sure if they had police here. He thought of the inside of a South American jail he'd seen in a film and decided not to. Better just get back. Even the thought of Katya, the only face he knew in this godforsaken town, comforted him like the image of a mother.

He raised a muddy arm for a cab. 'Fili Metro,' he said. 'How much?' asked the driver in English.

'Fifty US.'

'Get in.'

Terry reached for his roll of dollars which he was not surprised to find was missing. He must have collapsed on his wallet because it was still in his inside jacket pocket. He got in the back of the car, relieved to sink into the relative comfort of a Volga.

He tried to think of his apartment number. I am one and my age is thirty-four. Or was it thirty-five? Surely not thirty-nine. He glanced at his watch. He quickly his other wrist. It had gone. His Citizen deep sea diver's watch, readable up to 200 feet underwater, which gave you the time in four major capitals, had been stolen.

Outside, the black sky was turning a bruised brown. For the first time since Grace had left, he started to cry. I am one and my age is forty-one. He sobbed.

CHAPTER THREE

I

Katya's heart dropped like an elevator in a lift shaft when she saw the letters. One, in a coarse brown envelope, was addressed with the jagged curves of Cyrillic script, like the printout from a lie detector. The other was in English with childish rounded letters, edged by the red stripes of air mail. She knew immediately who they were both from. She locked the blackened green letterbox which appeared to double as someone's ashtray and turned to take the lift back to her flat.

She was still dressed in her housecoat and slippers. She looked at her watch. Just after nine. With a sinking feeling she remembered it was the start of the autumn break. Sasha was going to need a sitter. She couldn't put off taking out the Englishman any longer. If Clive got to hear about it he might take his business elsewhere. She knew the representatives at the other agencies – From Russia With Love and European Connections – both had a good database of girls in Moscow. She'd tried to explain to Clive that the supply of unspoilt, *virginal* girls had dried up faster than an open bottle in Boris Yeltsin's drinks cabinet. Sex was one of the few growth industries in Russia. After communism, pornography had arrived in Russia before even the first IMF loan. Now the best girls were in the provinces, simple village girls who still thought Max Factor was a communist principle with a typo.

The lift stopped on the nineteenth floor and Katya shuffled out. She nodded at her neighbour who lived opposite, a pensioner who Katya knew had already reported her to the militia at least twice. It was like still living under the NKVD, she thought as she unlocked the door. Russians couldn't stand to see people better themselves. That was probably why communism had done so well.

No sign of life from Mr Small. She'd meant to look in on him when she got back from Sonya's last night. Perhaps cheer him up with Sonya's holiday snaps. Even leave him a couple. Not that she would waste a find like Sonya on the likes of Terry Small. Instinctively she touched the letters in her pocket. She had one particular client in mind for the lovely Sonya. A glimpse of her would do the Englishman no harm, though. But by the time she had got home, she had been exhausted. Sasha had invited his school friend Misha over and the flat resembled Grozny in the summer of 1995.

'Hi, Mum.' Sasha was wearing an I Love NY T-shirt. Misha's sweatshirt said GAP. 'We're taking Leonid out. OK?'

'Fine,' replied Katya, handing him a jacket. 'But remember, come straight home. No begging, card games or petty theft.'

'For goodness sake, Mum. We couldn't beg around here. It's the pits,' said Sasha. Misha giggled. 'Oh! That bald man from next door called last night. 'Bye.'

They slammed the door. Katya inwardly hushed them as they whooped down the corridor. The longer the Englishman slept, the better. She lifted the kettle before lighting the gas ring underneath it. She sat on a kitchen stool and took out the two envelopes. A letter from her husband was never a good sign.

On impulse she ripped into it. She scanned it like a condemned man reading a last minute reprieve. 'Darling . . . miss you . . . long for you . . . little Sasha . . . sweet caress . . . torment . . . lovingly yours, Max.' Katya smiled with relief. Then a sense of profound irritation swept over her. It must be how Stalin had felt when prisoners in gulags appealed to him for their mistaken imprisonment, not realising it had been him who had sent them to their frozen deaths.

It was written on company notepaper. It was Max's third year with the state-run oil company, 1,500 kilometres north-east of Moscow. Katya had forged the letter from the company director, in the days when employees had no say over where they worked, which demanded he take up a five-year posting in Neftyngansk, a frozen outpost four time zones away. She dreaded the day when he discovered his summons to work had been of her invention only. He'd put his lack of wages down to the fact that no state-sector workers had been paid in the last few years. Little did he know it was because he wasn't on the payroll.

A spell at work would toughen him up. He might *do*

something when he got back from Siberia, other than read American detective books and watch Brazilian soap operas. He was no example to Sasha. Five years on an oil station should at least give him some valuable pointers to his future direction, thought Katya as she sipped her tea. 'There is no work for Russian men now,' had been his constant refrain when she had tried to persuade him out of the house. 'I studied for seven years as a physicist. What do you want me to do? Become a waiter?'

Katya couldn't abide his inability to adapt. They all had to. She had studied English in order to become a teacher. Now the instruction she most commonly employed was, 'Please use a condom. We cannot be held responsible for anything caught on your trip.' (Clive was worried about being sued.) Others who had trained at the Bolshoi were now aerobics instructors. Poets were writing advertising copy. The only artistic expression left in Russia was making money.

She heard the door open and whispers in the corridor.

'You two, come and eat,' she said, taking a loaf of bread out of a plastic bag. 'And shouldn't you be telling Misha's mum if he's going to be staying here today? I have to go out so I'll have to get a sitter.'

Sasha and Misha exchanged glances.

'His mum knows where he is. She says it's OK,' said Sasha.

'Is that right, Misha?'

'Yes, she says it's fine. Er, can we play on the Game Boy?'

'After breakfast. Sit.'

Katya fried two eggs while the boys spoke in a language

she barely understood. Japanese computer games, British bands, German football players.

She went into the bathroom, stripped out of her housecoat and climbed into the bath tub which doubled as a shower. She felt her energy level soar as the hot water cascaded down her back. She thought of Max. At least the sex had been good. She remembered the times, before Sasha had been born, when they had found sanctuary in the bathroom, the only escape from Max's sour-faced sister. He would enter her from behind or she would kneel in front of him while the water poured off their bodies. She thought of his taut hairless chest and lazy smile. No, a spell in Siberia would toughen him up. She was tired of being the man. She rinsed the soap off her body. It was just that she hadn't met a man who was better at it than her.

As she climbed out of the bath she caught the reflection of her naked body in segments. Chest, torso, then legs. Compartmentalised like a woman about to be cut into three. It was a shame not to be making better use of it before it lost its firmness. She hadn't had sex in nearly a year. But once you allowed a man into your life, they thought it gave them rights over you. Russian men she could have understood. They had been so emasculated by communism the only things left for them to control were women and animals. But even foreigners seemed the same. Looking for a wife who would put up less resistance than a blow-up doll.

She started to dry herself on a towel which looked as if Sasha had already used it to bath Leonid. She pulled on a T-shirt and a pair of jeans. She'd wear flat boots. It had started to snow again. She moved into the hall and sat down by the phone. If she was going to stop that Small man from complaining to Clive she was going to have to pull something out of the bag very quickly.

She opened her A list. Possibly not the most attractive on her books but they could generally be called on at the last minute. She looked at her watch. Ten to ten. At least two hours too early for her girls. While they might tell her clients they had been up late tending to an elderly relative or sick child, Katya knew they were more likely exotic dancing or seeing a few clients of their own.

She tried four numbers without success. The fifth picked up on the tenth ring. 'Hello.' The voice sounded drugged.

'Natasha? Hi, this is Katya. Listen, I've got an emergency. Could you—' The line went dead. Katya redialled.

'Popova. Is that you again?' Now it was the voice of a heavy smoker trapped in an opium den.

'Of course it's me. Who were you expecting, Raisa Gorbachev?' Katya was starting to get irritated. 'Natasha, please, I'm desperate. You don't have to do anything. Just meet the guy. Have a few glasses of champagne, then go home.'

'No.'

'Why not?'

'Because I got in at four. And I have only been alone in this bed since seven. I'm exhausted.'

'But the meeting wouldn't be until two. *Please*. He asked for you specially.'

'Don't tell me you've still got my picture in that catalogue of yours?'

'Of course.' Katya sounded hurt. 'Why not?'

'Because. Because, Katya. How much do you think I could earn on the check-out at a supermarket in Oregon?'

'He's not from Oregon.'

'Wherever.'

'Basingstoke.'

'How much do you think I could earn in a supermarket in Basingstoke?' It sounded like basin stock.

'Look, that's not the point. I'm not asking you to marry—'

'Not much. Katya, how much did I earn last night?'

'I don't know, Natasha. How much did you earn last night?' It sounded like the penultimate line from some terrible joke.

'One thousand seven hundred and fifty-three dollars and—'

'Natasha.' It was time to fight back. 'When I first found you, you thought a blow job was something a western hairdresser did. You thought a dose of clap was a round of applause at the Bolshoi.' Katya spoke through gritted teeth so Sasha and Misha couldn't hear her. 'You knew nothing. And now all of a sudden you are too good to come on a date, a *date*, with a foreigner. For which opportunity a couple of years ago, I might add, you would've killed.'

'Well, it's not two years ago. It's now. I wouldn't go with a foreigner these days if they paid me.'

'That much I know. Please, come as a favour. If he doesn't get to meet some girls he'll complain to the agency and I'll be out of a job. Where would that leave Sasha and me?'

'You could always come over to the other side. You're still in pretty good shape.' She paused. 'For your age.'

'Thanks. Look, Natasha, what do you say? Two drinks, a flash of cleavage and that's it. I promise. I won't bother you again.'

'Until the next time.' Katya could hear Natasha smile at the other end of the phone. 'OK. Where and when?'

'Two o'clock. Restaurant of the hotel in Oktaybraskaya Ploschad,' said Katya with relief. 'Oh, and try and get that mate of yours with the wig to come.'

'I'll try. So tell me. What's he like, this man from Basingstoke?'

'You'll see.' Katya smiled as she hung up. She looked at her watch; nearly eleven. She really couldn't put off going next door for much longer. She called Mrs Voronsheva, who was only too pleased to convert two young minds to the pleasures of Pushkin. If that didn't make Misha fly home with the speed of a fighter pilot in a MiG she didn't know what would.

'Mr Small. My most sincere apologies for yesterday. I had hoped to return sooner, only my mother was more ill than we thought and we had to call the doctor.' Katya looked at Terry with what she hoped conveyed sorrow. Only halfway through the spiel did she notice that one side of his face was swollen to elephantine proportions. 'My goodness what has happened?' she asked, putting a hand to his face.

'Aaagh.' Terry shrank away from her as if she, too, was going to clout him.

'Please, perhaps you are needing medical care?'

80

'No. No, thank you. I have treated it from my own well-stocked medical bag,' said Terry, nodding towards a green nylon rectangle with a white cross on the front. 'I'm afraid I was mugged.'

'But where? Not here?'

'Yesterday I decided to do some sightseeing on my own. When I couldn't find you. I am no armchair spectator of life, Miss . . .'

'Call me Katya.'

'No, Katya. Life is what you make it. One of the central tenets of the Gender Awareness Forum is seizing the moment, making others aware of your sexual presence.'

'Really.' Katya glanced at her watch. The boys were alone until Mrs Voronsheva turned up.

'Yes, I am a doer. You'll see that in me this week, Katya. A doer.'

'Your head, Mr Smell.' She was getting cross.

'Yes, well, as I was walking across Red Square I was attacked by, it must have been four, six – no, ten. Probably ten men. Er, with sticks. And knives.' Terry hesitated with the information like a schoolboy before the head.

'But Mr Small, you must report it to the police. This marauding gang which sets about tourists like Genghis Khan must be stopped.'

'Well, while I do agree, I'm afraid I can't report.' Terry winked with his unclosed eye. One half of his face was the purple of Imperial Rome. 'If you know what I mean,' he said, touching his nose. 'Under cover, don't you know.' He smiled.

'*Under cover*, Mr Small? I thought you worked for a company which installed conservatories?'

'Well, of course I have to put that for the visa. My real job is extremely sensitive. Let's just leave it at security.'

'You mean you put the locks on the conservatory doors?'

'Good heavens, no. Katya.' He leaned in so close she could smell the antiseptic on his cheek.

'Do the words M.F.I. mean anything to you?'

'Oh, Mr Small, this is getting us nowhere. Do you wish to report your attackers to the Russian police or not?'

'Er, no.'

'Very well.' Katya looked round the room. At least it was tidy. 'Do you require anything for breakfast?'

'What have you got?'

'Russian porridge. Eggs. Sausage. Bread. Jam. What do you want?'

'A Nutri-Grain bar?'

'I'm sorry?'

'Muesli? Pop tarts?'

What was he talking about? *Tarts* at this time of the morning? 'I have arranged a meeting with some of my girls this afternoon at two o'clock. Several of the girls you selected from the catalogue will be there. I will be there to translate, as not all the girls speak English. Any questions?'

She spoke with the authority of a gym teacher, thought Terry, who could feel himself getting excited. He looked at his watch. Just after eleven. 'Katya. Without saying too much, it is in the interests of British security that I keep this body in shape.'

Terry flexed his fingers and did a sort of paso doble in front of her. Katya looked on in disbelief. Even in her flat boots she stood two inches taller than he was.

'I am therefore charged to ask you the following question.' He paused and continued his paso doble. 'Is there a gym near here,' he spoke in measured tones, 'equipped for the type of training this body might require?'

Terry Small was beginning to make the surgeon from Cleveland look like Rudolf Nureyev.

'Well, you know, Mr Small, us Russians fall some way behind a man of your, how can I say, stature.'

'Oh yes. Oh yes.' Terry had now incorporated his arms into his curious dance. Less a paso doble, more a Navaho rain dance.

Katya continued, 'The discipline of physical fitness is somewhat lacking in our culture.'

'I feared as much.' Terry halted. 'No abdominisers.'

'Exactly. Though I do know of one gym which may go some way to keep this fine fighting machine in peak fitness.'

'Peak is the word,' beamed Terry, forgetting the crater on one side of his face.

'When would you want to go?'

Keen as Terry was to get on a stair-climber, Moscow had, in the last twenty-four hours, taken on the fearful dimension of giving a conservatory quote in one of Basingstoke's more terrifying suburbs, places where Terry knew the only garden activity was re-spraying company cars.

'Er, I don't suppose we could go together?' he asked.

Katya was aghast, though at least he'd stopped dancing.

'I mean,' continued Terry, 'it's not as if *you* have spent a great deal of time with me. Clive promised me a *personal touch*.'

Katya winced.

'And I would hate to have to report back that after forty-eight hours here I have yet to see one of his girls.' He smiled his closing-a-sale smile.

'OK, Mr Small, we go now. Be ready in five minutes. I will show you the gym this once and then we will go to the meeting with the girls.'

Katya swept out of the flat and back into her own in one indignant manoeuvre. If it wasn't enough that she had to get these misfits laid, she now had to get them into shape. Next thing she knew she would be giving them guided tours of the Baltic States. At least it sounded as if Mrs Voronsheva had arrived – Pushkin was booming around the apartment.

Katya picked up her bag and waved at Sasha who barely acknowledged her departure. Misha, meanwhile, was cutting words out of one of her catalogues. She thought better of trying to stop him.

II

In a luxury ten-roomed dacha on the outskirts of Moscow, Peter Raevitch, just twenty-four, picked up his pen and started to write.

> My Darling Emily,
>   Never since Boris Pasternak was forced to live away from his Anya has anyone suffered so much. You are my muse. The sun and moon of my existence.

Darling, I long to be with you to hold you in my arms. Every night I dream of you, of the summer we spent together, and dream to be home again with you. Every fibre of my body yearns to leave this place. I arrived here a week ago and I feel like a stranger.

My father seems odder by turns – he refuses to let me leave the house without an armed guard. And as for my new stepmother, she is loathsome. Her superficiality and materialism represent everything I hate in this society. I cannot describe how it feels to be an outcast in my own country. Imagine if you were to return to Snodsbury-Under-Lyme after the summer term and found everything utterly different.

Peter put his pen down and re-read the letter. He couldn't quite imagine the village where Emily had grown up changing at all. The nearest the parish council had come to open revolution had been when the pub had applied to erect a satellite dish.

He thought of the weekend she'd invited him to the vicarage to meet her parents. Tea in the garden, tennis at the club, a pint at the local with Mr Palmer-Smythe. That was what he loved about England, the timeless unchanging tradition. In Moscow you were lucky if the buildings were still there when you went out in the morning. He could have sworn the name of a Metro station actually changed when he was in it the other day. Damn and blast his father for dragging him back. If he could only persuade him that he belonged in England with Em, finishing his course and starting a life together. He'd smoke a pipe and she'd ride a bicycle with a wicker basket on the front. She'd cycle through the village, a jumper over her shoulders, hair blowing in the gentle breeze. Their golden retriever would gallop alongside.

He picked up the letter again. Not too over the top. Definitely literary. No need to dwell too much on some of his father's more disturbing behavioural traits. Like the time he had walked into his father's office to find him whipping his young wife with the flex to his Panasonic fax machine while she was tied half naked by the lead to his laptop. Somehow, Peter reflected, he thought his father really had failed to grasp the essentials of capitalism.

'You fancy shooting some pool this afternoon?' Alyosha, Peter's bodyguard and oldest friend, looked up from his prone position on the white leather sofa. He was glued to a computer magazine.

'I'd really prefer to stay in and work on my novel.'

'Suit yourself. We haven't been out for days. When your dad told me I had to play nursemaid to you I had no idea how dull it was going to be.'

'Alyosha, I'm sorry but I just can't seem to *connect* with Moscow these days. The last time I lived here I was thirteen. A lot has changed since then. I promise we'll go for a beer tonight.'

'Yeah, that's what you said yesterday and you ended up writing to that English girlfriend.' He flicked on the CD with the remote. The Prodigy hissed out. 'The sooner you realise your old man's not going to let you return to cucumber sandwiches on the lawn, the better,' said Alyosha irritably over the music.

Sometimes Peter had trouble keeping up with Alyosha, so much had changed since his days at School 83 where he and Alyosha had first hung out. But as usual Alyosha was right. His father had not paid for a private education at one of the better minor public schools in England for Peter's benefit. Since the overnight riches forged out of his car and gas empire a decade ago, he'd been priming his eldest son to succeed him. The fact that Peter had no interest in business and no aptitude for commerce was neither here nor there.

'You know you've got your first meeting this week.' Alyosha was taking revenge.

'Don't remind me. I'm thinking of staging my own death to get out of it.'

'Well, that shouldn't be too difficult. The minute you start on that Round Table your life expectancy will be as long as an unarmed Russian private's at Stalingrad.'

He had a point. It was with some trepidation that Peter was taking his father's place on the Round Table, a forum for Russia's most important business interests. The number of men who sat round the table at the monthly meetings was decreasing like the vicarage guests of an Agatha Christie novel.

'Don't rub it in. Exactly how many are left?'

'On the last count, nine. But that was a week ago. I heard there were a couple of deals going down that might have seen off a few more,' said Alyosha.

Nine left out of an original thirteen. Why couldn't there be some laws in Russia? Peter thought back to his degree in business studies which he hadn't been allowed to finish at De Montfort University. He thought of the theory and the endless practicals and how totally *irrelevant* they were to Russia, where the only contract ever drawn up referred to a hired gun.

Peter was not too sure how his father Gleb had amassed his fortune. His nickname, essential for anyone who was anyone in the Russian business world, was Hard Currency, or Hard for short. Even when dealing in foreign currency had been illegal in Soviet Russia, Gleb had insisted all his deals were made in hard currency, money that would later pay for Peter's private education and send Peter's mother into divorced exile in Cyprus.

'I wish I was out with the lads instead of cooped up in here,' persisted Alyosha. 'Why did Hard have to pick me to wet-nurse you? You never used to be this dull. What did they do to you in that posh school?'

'Just give me a few weeks. I'll get used to it. It takes time to learn how to be Russian again.'

'Crap,' sulked Alyosha. 'You're just stuck up these days. The sooner you piss off back to Britain and that girlfriend the better.' He paused. 'I bet she's nothing compared to our girls.'

Peter thought of his stepmother. At her peak she could average an hourly spending rate of $10,000. If she took the driver and started in Moschino and Dolce and Gabanna on Okhotni Ryad, she could probably get it up to $15,000. Especially now that there was a new underground shopping centre next to Red Square. A couple of weekends away would probably be enough for her single-handedly to re-boot most of eastern Europe.

He remembered shopping with his mum when he was little. How her grocery catchment area had been fifteen square kilometres. How she'd cross Moscow for a piece of cheese or sausage.

Within one generation the entire world had become a shopping mall. His stepmother traversed the globe (Paris, London, New York, Milan) like a Dior-clad twentieth-century explorer.

Had it been inevitable, wondered Peter, that seventy years of communism would spawn one of the most materialistic societies on earth? Had equality been nothing more than the subjugation of greed, which was as basic a human instinct as eating? He picked up his pen and made a note to include the question in his modern Dostoyevskian classic.

'I said,' repeated Alyosha tiredly, his head straining off the white leather sofa like a Borzoi, 'was she as good a fuck as a Russian girl?'

'I don't know,' sighed Peter. 'I've never made love to a Russian woman.' He thought back to the afternoon in the vicarage when Em's parents had gone to a garden party. If only he could explain the purity of his love for Em to his oldest friend. The essence of their feeling for each other.

'You what?' Alyosha screeched with incredulity. 'You mean to say you have never in your life screwed a Russian girl?'

'Correct.' Peter picked up his pen again.

'Let me get this straight. You, a Russian man in the prime of your life, a Russian man whose veins pulsate with the century-old blood of Cossacks, have never experienced the joy of a Russian girl?'

'Oh, for God's sake, Alyosha,' said Peter, irked.

'I'm sorry. But it is my job – no, my *duty* to rectify this. It's . . . it's *unnatural*.'

'Why? How many English girls have you screwed? I mean made love to,' he added hurriedly.

'That is not the point. I am no believer in the cross-cultural relationship. Look what happened to Lenin.'

'What do you mean? What happened to Lenin?'

'He started on a French mistress and died a couple of years later with the pox.'

'Oh, for goodness sake.'

'Anyway, that's far from the point. It's your failing libido that is under discussion here.' Alyosha stirred from the sofa and moved to a marble fireplace. 'Take me, for example.' Alyosha was launching forth like Khrushchev at Yalta. Any second now, thought Peter, he'll take off his Nike Airs and start banging them on the table.

'I considered it my duty as a Young Pioneer to spread my seed as far around the former Soviet Union as possible. It was,' he added gravely, 'one of the duties of the Empire. I lack only a female from the former Russian republic of Kirghizia to make up the full set.'

Peter looked up from his letter. 'You make them sound like a set of spanners.'

'If that Tumpy, Thumpy or Grumpy, whatever her name was, had only lowered her knickers in Bishkek, I'd have had the whole set. Every nationality in the USSR.'

'Fascinating. And exactly what sort of Order of Lenin would that entitle you to?'

'You may mock, but if every Russian had tried as hard to integrate this country as I have we might still be one of the world's foremost powers.'

'Really.'

'No doubt. In any case I haven't given up. This country may have crumbled but my resolve is still strong. Call me nostalgic, but having a Kirghizian girlfriend remains one of my life's ambitions.' Alyosha reached for a copy of *Iz ruk V Ruku*, the Russian *Exchange & Mart*.

Peter returned to his letter. '*Oh, Em. Do you remember that afternoon in the vicarage? When we made a bed on the sitting-room floor . . .*'

'These days I have to look through the classifieds. Here we go,' said Alyosha.

'*You were wearing your blue dress which I lifted over your . . .*'

'Look, mate. Why don't I fix you up with one while I'm at it? High time you lost that cherry for real.'

'*. . . head. You unbuttoned my shirt while I caressed your . . .*'

'Galine, aged eighteen, statistics thirty-six, twenty-four, thirty-seven, looking for a Russian boyfriend. Why can't she say where she's from?' He sighed. 'She might do for you, though. Shall I call her?'

'*. . . breasts. I can still smell the scent of your hair. Feel the hardness of your nipples under my palms . . .*'

'Now this one might be Kirghiz. Altonai – that's not a Russian name, is it? Twenty-seven years . . .'

'*My hand slipped into your cotton briefs . . .*'

'I said, is Altonai a Kirghiz name?' repeated Alyosha. 'The trouble with these Central Asian names is that they all sound the same.'

'*Between your thighs I felt . . .*'

'For Christ's sake, are you listening to me?' he bellowed. 'What's the point in me trying to do you a good turn if you're not even listening?'

Peter put down his pen. Perhaps he was getting a bit carried away. Truth be told, he had spent longer grappling with the fastenings of her Marks and Spencer bra than feeling her nipples.

'I really couldn't tell you,' he said. 'She may be Hindustani, for all I know. Now please, I beg you, shut up.' Peter returned to his letter. But, like his erection on that summer afternoon, the inspiration had gone.

He stood up, smoothed down his green cords and stretched for his Burberry. 'Come on. This is like being locked up with a sex offender. Let's go. You never know, a Kirghiz women's football team might be playing Spartak.'

'You don't really think so?' Alyosha grabbed his Tommy Hilfiger jacket and followed his friend.

Gleb 'Hard Currency' Raevitch heard some laughter and then the door closing. At least Alyosha still found some common ground with his son. These days Alyosha was more of a son to him than Peter would ever be. He'd always suspected it was a mistake to send the boy away to school. America he could have understood at a pinch. But England? It had been his mother's idea. What, since the beginning of the century, had they ever contributed to the world? The Psion and Margaret Thatcher. Even Thatcher had plummeted in his estimation when she'd embraced that fool Gorbachev.

No, Russia was the only place to learn about Russia. Peter had come home with his head stuffed full of fancy ideas. Romantic poetry. Plans to be a novelist or poet. Nonsense. 'Daddy,' he'd said, 'I'd like you one day to meet my girlfriend Emily.' English girlfriend? What was wrong with a woman like Tanya? Only a Russian woman could understand the soul of a Russian man. He remembered the first time he'd beaten Tanya with his hand-held phone. She was like a wild animal. Even her hair had that mottled two-toned look of a Siberian tiger. She understood passion. Understood what drove him. Two things seemed to move Peter. The World Service and letters stamped with a picture of the British monarch.

The phone rang on his dark wooden desk, a legacy from his days at Gazprom. He picked up the receiver. 'Hard here.'

'They want one hundred thousand dollars.'

'For the whole thing?'

'For the whole thing.'

'Then go for it. I lose that much money running for a bus.'

'As if you ever travelled by bus.'

'Go on.'

'There's a problem. The Fridge is offering double.' The man on the end of the phone paused.

'Shit. I thought we'd seen him off last time.'

'Must have got someone to bail him out.'

'It's not the money, it's the lack of respect. In the old days everyone knew their place. This is mob rule.' Hard paused. 'Maybe we should just have him liquidated.' He spoke with the casualness of someone ordering from a takeaway menu.

'Might be the best option. If he left that gang, they'd most likely kill each other.'

'Exactly. Leave it with me.' Hard replaced the phone.

Business in Moscow was so much more difficult these days. Newspapers all over the world were full of this phenomenon of the Russian Mafia, comparing his country to America's Wild West a hundred years ago. What they failed to see was that Soviet Russia had been one of the most successful organised crime syndicates in the world. Communism had practically invented it. The whole country was kept running by the deals done behind the scenes. In this finely tuned shadow economy oil quotas were fiddled and sold on the private market, as were semi-precious stones and uranium. The idea that it was only after 1991 that illicit nuclear arsenals began to be sold off made him want to laugh. They'd been doing it for years. Selling to western companies, to the east, to whoever would pay. Communist apparatchiks like him had had it sewn up. Only with the advent of these sneaky little mobsters – Armenians, Georgians, Chechens – had things started to get more difficult, with the old structure breaking down. And now Moscow was awash with shell-suited hoodlums doing things they would never have taken part in – extortion, prostitution, drug-running. No, there was no doubt about it, the country was going to the dogs.

He would be glad to get out of it, hand it all over to Peter and see the balls-up he made of it. He'd made a fortune and he intended to enjoy it. Clear out, buy a villa in France or Greece and watch Russia sink further into chaos. Then all he'd have to worry about was keeping

Tanya in the style she was used to.

The door to his office clicked. Hard looked up. She was naked apart from a pair of stilettos. She had bound her wrists with DHL tape and had a Fedex envelope on her head from which she had cut two eye holes.

'I've been a naughty girl. Someone needs to punish me,' she breathed.

For the second time in ten minutes Hard earned his nickname.

III

Bloody hell. If the lads back home could see me now, thought Terry as he beamed his seriously-working-out smile to the woman on the pec deck. This gym made Fit To Burst look like a kindergarten playground. Treadexes as far as the eye could see, but the women! Certainly kicked the Thursday evening step aerobics class into touch. He suddenly felt back on track. Admittedly it had cost a staggering $40 admission, but – *blimey*! That woman on the inner thigh machine looked like something from his Swedish channel. Instinctively he adjusted his shorts.

Up until an hour ago he'd started to think that the operation might be the only thing he'd get out of the whole trip (that reminded him, he must ask Katya about the institute). But now he felt on top of the world. He thought of the unsightly bruising on the side of his face. The swelling had gone down a little and he could almost forget about the throbbing, but he'd noticed a couple of double-takes when he'd come in. Optimistically he'd put them down to his stylish Polo Sport shorts.

So far so good. He'd only made one serious error. That had been on the treadmill, when he'd programmed in his kilo weight for speed required and found himself running at 80 miles an hour. Apart from that, the disasters of the past forty-eight hours were almost forgotten. In retrospect, anyone could have fallen for that woman at the club. How was he to know she was a working girl? He'd found his way home eventually – after he'd tried every door from 34 to 46 (the known parameters of his given age).

Wasn't prostitution against the law in Russia? He was surprised that recreational sex of any kind was allowed. He tried to refocus on his Natasha. Where was she now? Finishing after a morning teaching at primary school, the tops of her tights – no, make that stockings – rustling as she crossed her legs. She pushed a pair of glasses to the top of her head where her long blonde hair was tied up in a bun. The buttons on her too tight shirt strained over her chest.

She speaks: *'Ooh Terry, you've come for me at last. Take me, take me from this terrible, terrible place,' she sighs.* (Note to self: Calvin Klein jeans, Paul Smith shirt, loafers.) *Terry gives his mysterious stranger smile. Pushes Gucci sunglasses on head. Natasha's hand moves to her throat. She starts to unbutton her blouse.*

Terry replies, 'Can I—'

'Aaaaaaaaagh,' Terry screamed in a way last heard when Bob beat him to the 1994 salesperson of the year award.

He'd missed his foot on the treadex and been catapulted into the free weights section. Two Russians, who in any other country would have had a ring through their noses, were lifting iron bars.

'Oh my goodness, I really am most terribly sorry.' He stumbled as he tried to extricate himself from the chest of one of them. He had a faint sour odour, Terry noted. Most unlike his own aftershave. 'Here, allow me.' He stooped to pass a hand weight to one of the men but, like a cartoon character, his whole body buckled as he tried to pick it up.

'Recovery, Terry. Recovery and poise,' he breathed to himself and did a few side stretches to account for his position. The Russians looked at him in silence. Terry scanned the gym. He gave an all-part-of-the-routine smile to any onlookers as he flexed his hands, stuck out his chest and headed back towards the machines.

Best not to return to the treadex, make them think it was a complex ending manoeuvre like a double somersault off the box, he thought as he sat astride the rowing machine.

He strapped his feet in and sat back in the chair. It was the first time he'd been able to study Russian men, apart from the back of the taxi driver's head. They weren't necessarily the work-shy drunkards the blurb from Reds In Your Bed had assured him they were. He started to pull on the handles of the rowing machine reflectively. In fact, several of them would not be out of place on an Olympic podium. All in all they made the members of Fit To Burst look like a Saga holiday brochure. He glanced at the weight-lifting duo who, after his untimely introduction, had gone back to puffing like a steam train.

Terry adjusted his towelling headband nervously. Thank God he had invested in a new gym kit before he left. If only he could get the woman on the inner thigh machine in the red Lycra shorts which, he had noticed earlier, went right up her bum, to look at his Adidas trainers (MRP £129), he might be in with a chance.

There was only one thing for it. He would have to chant. As they were taught at the Gender Awareness Forum, even if you just say a mantra in your head while you concentrate on the object of your affections, it will happen. He closed his eyes, swayed his head from side to side like Stevie Wonder and started the GAF mantra.

'*Mm Nyo Korengy Kan*,' he said to himself. 'Red shorts, look at my trainers. *Mm Nyo Korengy Kan*, I said look at my trainers, you red-arsed bitch. *Mm Nyo Korengy Kan*, look at my shoes, red bum. *Mm Nyo Korengy Kan*, look at my trainers, you—'

'Excuse me, have you finished with this?' asked an American voice. Even the steam train had stopped. A couple of stair-climbers ground to a halt. Terry's chant had coincided with the end of the techno tape and his murmuring was the only sound to punctuate the rhythmic beat of the runner on the treadex. That was the thing with chanting, it was easy to get carried away.

'Yes. Oh yes. Absolutely. Be my guest. Take it away.' Terry leapt from the rowing seat. He made two peace signs with the fingers of both hands and raised them to his towelling headband. 'Wow, man. Endorphins. Triffic,' he said to anyone still watching him. He winced as one of his fingers jabbed his black eye. He gave a parting wave as he backed out towards the changing rooms.

Katya remembered the gym from when she had first come to Moscow. She had used it in the days when she still had some pretensions to becoming a gymnast. Then the admission fee had been 2 roubles a year. Now Swedish-owned, it was $5,000 and there was a waiting list. She was waiting for Terry in the marble walled reception half listening to a conversation between two uniformed instructors.

'Tennis courts have been closed for a week. There was a fire,' said one matter-of-factly.

'Did it start in the sauna?' asked the other.

'No, it was a bomb. They must have forgotten to pay the *krisha.*'

This exchange was lost on the half-dozen foreigners waiting to pay a $10 deposit for a freshly laundered towel. *Krisha* meant roof in Russian. The two instructors were talking about the gang you paid protection money to, to stop your business being razed or your workers beaten up. Every enterprise in the country, foreign or not, had to pay. Even Sasha complained he had to pay for his begging pitch on Red Square.

She looked at her watch. One thirty. He'd been in there an hour. She looked at a couple of articles in the English language *Moscow Times*, instinctively turning to the personal columns of the classifieds.

Busty Anna gives good massage. Blonde nymphet is longing for your call. Katya thought about ringing them but doubted if it was worth it. She'd already tried to recruit a couple of the younger women at the gym and been told where to go. Women with the money to come here already had a Mafia sponsor and were unlikely to want a foreigner. Especially one who had to travel three thousand miles to get laid. No, she really would have to go on a recruiting tour in the provinces one of these days, perhaps when Sasha was at summer camp next year. Or at least put a few ads in some of the regional papers. Samara, she recalled, had yielded a couple recently. The provinces were definitely where the talent was to be found now.

She thought of Terry. She would be lucky to make her $1,500 commission on him. At least he didn't want them young. Some of her clients were after girls so young, they stood a better chance of becoming their legal guardians than of marrying them. She smiled. Then frowned. She suddenly remembered she still hadn't opened the air mail letter from this morning. She took it out of her brown shoulder bag and sucked in her cheeks. As she opened the envelope she thought of the thick, slobbering tongue that had licked it.

Dear Katya,

I hope you and little Sasha are well. How is our search going? I trust you received my requirements. Feet no more than 7 inches. I am less concerned about bust. Age range up to 18, for legal reasons. Though younger appreciated. I enjoyed my last visit very much and, if everything goes according to plan, I hope to come back soon. I will let you know when.

Yours sincerely . . .

'Fantastic work-out.' Terry walked through the reception after dropping off his towel. 'I can really feel the adrenaline start to kick in. You know, when your body is a fighting machine, you suffer if you can't get a good work-out.'

'Really,' said Katya as she stuffed the letter back into her bag. She looked up at Terry. What little hair remained was plastered to his ruddy scalp in dark stripes. 'We should hurry, the girls are meeting us at two. Luckily the hotel is not far. We can walk. Come. Do you have a hat? No hair and no hat in Russia is not a good combination.'

Outside, the cold air set Terry's teeth on edge. He looked around at the grey concrete buildings. Men and women, heads down, scurried from doorway to doorway. It all looked so drab. He suddenly yearned for the hustle and bustle of Saturday morning at the Savacentre, following Grace's polyester-draped backside as it pushed the trolley up and down the aisles while he tried to catch the attention of women in bright pink uniforms asking you to taste a cube of cheese on a cocktail stick.

Maybe it was the work-out but Terry had started to feel light-headed. His mind seemed to bounce in and out of Moscow like a ping-pong ball. He got a buttock-clenching rush of excitement. In a few moments he would meet his Natasha. She'd grin nervously. He'd give his man-in-charge smile.

A Cherokee jeep swerved to avoid him.

'Please, Mr Small, watch the traffic. You are aware that here we drive on the right.' Katya grabbed his arm as they stepped to cross Oktaybraskaya Ploschad. He looked up from his reverie to see a huge bronze statute of a bloke with a beard. His legs were parted, denoting movement, and he was waving a flag.

He looked like Robin Cook. Why would Russians have erected a statue of Robin Cook? He pondered. Apart from the fact that he was a rabid lefty, of course.

He was just about to ask Katya when she bundled him through two pairs of double doors and into the dark interior of a building. The sign above the door said 'Pectopah'. Katya propelled him towards a curtained booth where a man was taking coats. She manhandled him out of his jacket like a mother with a toddler.

'Oi,' protested Terry petulantly, 'don't you know that jacket is a Cecil Gee original?'

Katya sighed and turned to comb her hair in a full-length mirror. Terry did the same. He pulled out his YSL shirt slightly over the belt of his Calvin Klein jeans. In silence he marched after her into the interior.

It was so dark inside the restaurant it was a couple of minutes before Terry's pupils had adjusted. Until they did it was the unfamiliar squawk of women that his sensory locators followed to the table in the corner.

'Terry, this is Masha and Dasha,' said Katya with a smile. Christ, thought Terry as his eyes roamed around the room as if through night vision goggles, they sounded like reindeers. In the gloaming he was aware only of flashes of hair and thighs. And the noise. What was this *pectopah* place Katya had brought him to?

'And this,' continued Katya, 'is Natasha.' He swung round to see her enter. The light from the cloakroom highlighted her in silhouette. Like an angel, thought Terry. Slightly too tall, slightly too broad and with slightly too much hair. Terry couldn't see her face, but his heart leapt. His stomach fluttered. There was no doubt. This was *his* Natasha.

IV

The operating room on the fourteenth floor of Moscow's Institute of Cosmetology was thick with the smell of formaldehyde.

'The time, gentlemen, is precisely two o'clock. Let us begin.' Professor Modin was speaking in English, though Bridges was the only English-speaker there. Sergei, in green operating smock and mask, was opposite the body. A couple of others, who looked like a pair of Epsilon Minuses from Brave New World, hovered.

'I'm going to puke,' said Sergei, staring at the corpse.

'Come off it. An ex-KGB man like you must have seen worse than this.' Bridges was trying to be brave. It was the smell that was the worst. Formaldehyde and dead flesh.

'No, really, I'm going to chuck. We might have had some questionable interrogation techniques, but we never frigging cut them up.'

'Gentlemen, please. This is a solemn moment.' The professor raised a scalpel and made an incision in the chest. 'The moment of embalming is sacred. From Egyptian times, only the very highest cultures have preserved their dead,' he said, not looking up from his work.

The dead man had a bluish tinge. The skin was glassy. How people could look at a dead body and think they looked as though they were sleeping, thought Bridges, was beyond him. This was like a waxwork, though worse. He was no older than his mid-thirties. The hair was dark and cropped. His flesh on the slab was flabby. The nipples were dark buttons on hairy podgy mounds.

'Observe, gentlemen, the bullet wounds. These are most demanding to the embalmer. To build up the cavity I have to take bone and tissue from another part of the body.'

'Jesus Christ.' Sergei started to sway.

'If it will revive your spirits at all, gentlemen, might I remind you that in the past twelve months in Moscow alone there have been one thousand one hundred and forty-five murders. I estimate that if only one-third of those avail themselves of the services of Bodies Beautiful, and if they ask for the cheapest package in the St Valentine's Day Massacre range, at fifteen thousand dollars, we will clear nearly half a million dollars a year.'

'Well, as long as I don't have to participate in any of the embalming,' said Sergei.

'We all have our roles in the firm and each is vital. You, Sergei, are responsible as the Russian partner, in charge of security. My expertise is not in that area. Especially not in this city.'

Bridges smiled encouragingly.

'You, Mr Bridges, as well as adding that essential touch of American authenticity – Russians always believe westerners know what they are doing – are in charge of marketing.' He looked up from the body. Over his mask, Sergei and Bridges saw his eyes crinkle in a smile.

They looked at each other over the body.

'No, gentlemen. Death is the future of Russia.' The

knife cut down the chest like a zip.

When Sergei came round he was lying on a cold concrete floor. The sweat was clammy on his forehead. Above him, Bridges, still in his operating gown, hovered like a green giant, a glass of water in his hand.

Sergei spoke. 'If you ask me, that professor has done one embalming too many. The formaldehyde has affected his brain.'

'Here, drink this.' Bridges passed him the glass of water.

Sergei struggled onto his elbows. 'Look, Bridges.' He paused. 'I just don't know if I'm up to this.'

'Come off it. I'm sure everyone gets like that at their first embalming. It's just a case—'

'No, really. It's not only that.' Sergei hauled himself onto a chair behind a huge wooden desk. 'It's not something I want to get *involved* with. I've got Olga and Lena to think about. Any sort of business in Russia these days is dangerous. Say we do start to make thousands, how long before someone comes along with a couple of AK 47s or whatever they use these days and tries to take it off us?'

'Then we'll get someone in to do the security.'

'It would have to be more than just a couple of bouncers on the door. And in any case, what happens if we fucked up? What happens if our resident Frankenstein in there botches a job? Or the client doesn't like the frosting on the Al Capone coffin? It's a risk.'

'Hey, what isn't these days?' Bridges drew a hand over his mouth and stopped when he remembered he hadn't washed since the operating room.

'It's easier for you. You haven't got any family. It's not you they come after, it's your wife, your kids. No, I've still got my KGB pension and my job at the bar will pay enough until something better comes along. Something a bit more legit.'

'This is legit. The mad professor's right. The money to be made here *is* in funerals.'

Sergei stood up, his head still bent lower than his shoulders. He ripped the gown over his head. 'No, mate. No offence, but if you want to go ahead with this one, you're on your own.' He walked towards the door. 'Drop into the bar when you've got a free evening. We've got a Rocky Horror night next week.'

'Yeah, great,' said Bridges, slumping into the chair Sergei had just left. Rocky frigging Horror was about right.

CHAPTER FOUR

I

Katya sat back warily. The restaurant's interior was dark red and she was aware of soft velvety textures. The rich density of colour reminded her of an internal organ.

'Ask them if they could ever love a man who might be follically challenged,' urged Terry, a snail's trail of perspiration on his top lip. 'Then casually introduce the fact that I'm one of the most respected conservatory salespeople in the south-west,' he blurted, almost uncontrollably.

Katya turned to the women sitting round the table and stifled an inward sigh. 'Sorry, girls, I really do appreciate you turning up but I'm not even sure this one is mentally stable.' With one movement five women turned to survey Terry who was caressing the back of his head and flexing his pectorals. Katya couldn't be sure, but wasn't he *mouthing* something as well?

'Try to ignore the facial abrasions,' she counselled as the women continued to stare dumbfounded. 'They are, of course, temporary.'

'Unfortunately that's more than can be said for the rest

of him.' Natasha inhaled deeply on a cigarette. A finely manicured red thumbnail flicked ash into a silver foil ashtray. Her expression showed utter disdain. With the other hand she smoothed the creases from a lilac linen two-piece.

Terry grabbed Katya's elbow with the intensity of a chiropractor. 'What did she say? What did she say?' he breathed. The line of perspiration was seeping via a wrinkle into his chin, where a scab had started to form. Katya suddenly thought of a geography lesson at school in Byelorus. *The natural course of a river is to meander.* Sweat was meandering in streams all over Terry's face.

'She says she likes France and admires the Impressionists,' Katya said, trying to convey a sense of wonderment as if it really was the meeting of two minds.

Terry beamed. 'Tell her I like the French Impressionists, especially Van Gogh.' His gaze fastened on Natasha round about chest height. 'But don't dwell on the painters. Don't forget the bit about salesperson of the year award. Two years running.' Terry adjusted his belt in a self-congratulatory way.

Katya pretended to translate. As she did so Terry interrupted her with something about a camera and a well-known British hobby called readers' wives. She ignored him and turned to Natasha, who appeared to be smoking two cigarettes simultaneously.

'Look, in essence they're all pretty bad,' she said. 'Get the visa, then you can divorce him. Come on, girls, don't any of you fancy it?' As she looked at them imploringly.

Terry pushed his face close up to hers. 'What are they saying?' he pleaded. He smelt of coconut oil. This close his skin, still flushed from his work-out, had the texture of a red sponge. A gobbet of saliva ejaculated onto Katya's lip. He continued his instructions with military precision. 'Don't worry about the others. You must stick to the blonde. I repeat. Focus on the blonde with the chest.'

'Mr Small.' Katya took a tissue from her bag and dragged it across her face. The restaurant was starting to fill up with lunchtime diners. A sickly smell of frying meat came from beyond a double swing door. 'Please try to contain yourself. This is a romantic encounter. I am asking all the girls about their favourite French artists. I know, for example, that Masha is very keen on Monet.'

Katya turned to a woman with red hair and a short A-line skirt which reminded her of her gymnast days. It had no sartorial place on a female over the age of eleven. Katya raised her eyes heavenward. 'Go on, Masha, what about it? I know he's a freak. But as I always say, western divorce laws are very favourable to women. You've got a kid. Wouldn't you prefer your Lisa not to grow up in the murder capital of the world?'

Masha had taken out a Chanel compact and was removing clogs of mascara from her lashes. She was wearing knee-length black PVC boots. Terry was squirming as if a testosterone-fuelled funicular railway was running up and down his spine.

Masha sighed wearily. 'We're all doing very well here now. What would the deal be if I married a westerner? No Russian would dream of letting a woman work. I've heard that in the west all women do.' She winked at a man sitting opposite and continued preening herself with nails so long Katya wondered how she managed to remove a tampon without performing female circumcision.

'I know.' She glanced at Terry, who was adjusting his flies. 'Don't worry, I'll tell him. But do me a favour, Mash. You couldn't just say Toulouse-Lautrec, could you?'

'Why?' She snapped the compact shut and watched a waiter deliver an unopened bottle of Smirnov to the table of businessmen, two of whom were raising a glass to her. She smiled coyly in return.

'It's complicated.'

'Toulouse-Lautrec.'

Katya turned to Terry with a smile. 'You see, Mr Small, my girls are cultured as well as beautiful. Now you really wouldn't get that in Thailand, would you?'

'Er, no.' He looked askance as if art really wasn't his main concern. 'Would the girls like to ask me anything about myself?' He tried to look self-deprecating. 'My lifestyle, interests?' He sat back. Then sat bolt upright and smiled. 'Perhaps the girls would like a drink?'

Katya nodded.

Terry did a quick ready reckoner around the restaurant. 'What, then? Five glasses of what? Orange? Coke? Surely not *lager*?'

'I usually advise champagne. Two bottles would suffice and of course some snacks.' Katya watched the blood drain from his cheeks. 'Fifty dollars should cover it.' She turned to flag down the waiter. The champagne came from the Crimea and cost a fraction of the real stuff. She could pocket the difference. Usually her cons had a little more guile to them than straight deception, but she was tiring of this idiot Englishman and she owed Mrs Voronsheva a week's pay. Terry would never know the difference. He

110

didn't strike her as a wine connoisseur. In fact the only thing he was a true connoisseur of was himself.

A middle-aged waiter with blond hair specked with grey handed Katya two green bottles with a conspiratorial wink. In recent years Russians had become more adept than airport cab drivers at ripping off foreigners. From Yeltsin's rendition of the trustworthy old fool to extract doomed billion-dollar loans from the west to Sasha dressed as a Gypsy girl outside the Metropole, pretending to be what foreigners thought Russians should be, had become the country's greatest new skill.

Katya set the bottles on the glass-topped table. 'There you go, girls. Let me know when you want something else. I've ordered some *zakuski*. Might as well get our money's worth.' She turned to Terry. 'Please open the bottles. In Russia it is inconceivable for women to open a bottle.'

He looked anxious as he picked up the bottle with one hand on the neck and another underneath. Then he began shaking it with the ferocity most people reserved for spray deodorants.

'What the fuck is he doing?' asked Natasha incredulously. Terry looked to Katya for translation.

'She says you obviously know how to handle a bottle,' said Katya, smiling.

'Tell her I have been voted salesperso—'

Before he could finish, the bottle exploded like a firework, spraying the women with alcohol. Natasha's dress mopped up most of the overflow while the cork ricocheted over the bar like a bullet. A cheer went up from the Smirnov diners.

'For Christ's sake, the man's a complete buffoon,' yelled Natasha, now on her feet. 'What the hell does he think he's doing?'

'Goodness me. Yes, what a pop. Quite a kick to it,' Terry beamed. 'Glasses, ladies, if you please.' He pointed to the flutes on the table which had champagne cascading down the outside. None of the women moved. He grabbed the nearest flute and upturned the bottle but it contained only enough to fill one glass. He picked it up and downed it in one. 'Cheers.' He wiped a freckled hand mottled with dense, dark hair over his mouth.

Katya looked imploringly at the waiter, who smiled and walked casually to the bar. It was a slim-hipped swagger, suggesting a confidence in his own sexuality that she rarely saw in foreign men.

Terry belched. 'My my, got quite a kick to it, that stuff,' he said. More perspiration had appeared on his forehead, along with a crop circle of dampness on his shirt where he'd rested his champagne glass.

The waiter returned with another bottle and a trayful of glasses. Katya admired how well his tailored trousers fitted the curve of his backside. Grooming was all that Russian men required. Get them in uniform and they were made. Hence her doomed romance with a traffic cop and a six-month affair with a baritone in the Bolshoi, with whom she could only become aroused when he arrived at her apartment still in costume from the evening's performance. She blamed a Russian version of *Les Misérables*, staged to attract the American audience, for the relationship's demise.

'Who's your friend?' the waiter asked her.

'It's a long story,' she replied with an apologetic smile.

'Perhaps you'd like to tell me about it later.' He nodded at the bottle. 'Over a glass of champagne.'

'Never mind that,' Natasha blurted. 'What about my suit? It's ruined. You can tell your pal it's a Dior and he owes me two grand.'

Katya watched the waiter return to the bar. She asked irritably, 'Does he look like the sort of man who can afford two grand?'

'Precisely my point,' said Natasha triumphantly, 'and precisely why I should never been dragged out of bed at this ungodly hour and subjected to him. I'm not surprised he has to come three thousand miles for a shag. Look at him.' Natasha picked up a glass and drained it in one seamless gulp. She reached out for another.

Terry was adjusting his belt buckle while gently pulsating his groin upwards like a flasher. He was cradling another empty glass of champagne in his hand.

An afternoon hadn't gone this badly, reflected Katya, since the time a lay preacher and part-time children's entertainer had asked one of her girls what tricks she could do. It was only halfway through telling him how she could play the entire Soviet national anthem on a mouth organ – without using her mouth – that Katya had stepped in. The lay preacher had never quite recovered.

Natasha picked up the bottle and poured another glass. Women's laughter punctuated the trill of mobile phones from a red booth where a party was in full swing. The puffs of smoke emanating from the booth made Katya think of cardinals electing a new Pope.

Terry seemed to come to with a start. 'Tell 'em that I have a personalised number plate and once recorded a Country and Western record.' He hiccuped and took another drink. 'With Kenny Rogers.'

Katya forced a smile. 'OK, girls, anyone want to go on another date with him? Natasha?'

'I would rather—'

Natasha clenched her teeth.

'Whatch she say? Whatch she hafta say?' slurred Terry, the second bottle now empty beside him.

'She said Country and Western never really caught on in Russia.' Katya turned to Masha and Dasha who were swapping numbers from two identical leather address books. 'You two, what about it? Any chance?'

They both shook their heads. Masha got up to go.

'Come on, what about as a personal favour?'

Masha delved for her bag under the table.

'Fifty dollars?'

Masha looked up. 'Per date?'

'For two.'

'Sex?'

'At your discretion.'

'No physical contact.'

'Whatever you say.'

Masha looked at Terry with such revulsion it almost evoked a sense of maternal pity in Katya.

'Whatya talking about? 'S it me?' Terry was hitting his stomach with the back of his hand. Considering what he'd had to drink, Katya didn't take it as a good sign. 'Look at it. 'S a six-pack. Thas the abdomis. Thas the abdimon—' he stopped.

Katya thought better of inquiring what he meant. 'Terry, listen. Young Masha here was hoping she might be able to see you again.'

'What about my Natasha?'

'Unfortunately I've just learned from Natasha that her mother is dangerously ill in Saint Petersburg and she must visit her immediately.' Katya looked at Natasha. Now on her fourth glass of champagne, she hardly portrayed the devastated daughter.

She sniffed loudly and turned to Katya. 'You can tell Don Juan there that I'm off. I've got an appointment at three thirty and I haven't shaved my bikini line,' she said, belching quietly.

Katya grimaced. Terry had narrowed his eyes and was trying to focus on Masha. His bruised face was now the colour of week-old bananas. He looked like Chairman Mao after a bar-room brawl.

In the corner of the room the pontiff's table was close to riot. Three empty bottles were on the floor and a couple of full ones on the table. A woman wearing a skirt the size of a belt was thrusting her hips in the direction of a man in a purple blazer. Closer to Katya, Terry was swaying from side to side.

'It's gone to my head,' he said. 'Issa bubbles. Ya know affletes have very low tolerance for alcohol.' He hiccuped again and put his hand to his mouth, swallowing hard. Just as Katya was considering the logistics of getting him into a cab, he swivelled his body to face her and clenched her knee. 'Katya. Where's sa Insatute of Cosmatology?'

Katya removed his hand as she watched Masha and Dasha disappear out of the gold-studded exit. 'I'm sorry?'

'I said, where's the Insatute of Cosermatology. Where's—' Abruptly he flopped back into the velvet booth, his eyes closed. The base of his skull rested on the wall while his chin collapsed onto his chest. In less than ten seconds a bubble of saliva had formed at the side of his mouth which seemed to inflate in rhythm with his chest. As he exhaled he gave out a snore which seemed to be generated from behind his loose-skinned Adam's apple.

Behind the bar the waiter raised a glass to Katya and smiled. She tried to smile back though she felt like crying.

II

On the ninth floor of a fourteen-storey block, identified on the outside by a greening brass plaque that read 'Building 324 for the Advancement of Cereal Production', Peter steadied himself on an ornate wrought-iron banister moulded in the shape of a sheaf. A man who looked as if he'd grown up with his head in a vice told him and Alyosha to wait until the meeting was ready for them.

'Fancy a shot before we go in?' Alyosha wiped the neck of a pewter hip flask before passing it to him.

'Do you think it would help?'

'Well, let's face it, what harm can it do? Look at it as a last request.'

Peter's face fell. 'You don't think anything could actually happen to me when I'm in there, do you?' The low level of dread he usually experienced on the streets of Moscow had become outright nausea.

'To my knowledge, no. But there's always a first.'

'Thanks.'

'Relax. You've got me.' Alyosha smiled and pulled a cigarette from a packet using his teeth.

'I seem to remember you telling me that when we were at junior school about to storm the barricades of the Young Pioneer canteen.'

'There is one essential difference, my friend. In those days,' Alyosha patted the hard bulge in the left-hand pocket of his Pierre Cardin blazer, 'I didn't have this.' He lit his cigarette and inhaled. 'As our great former leader Vladimir Ilych told us then, we must always be prepared.'

'Oh God.' Peter sank a few inches down the banister. Small firearms had never featured as recommended office equipment on his business management course. He nervously stroked the handle of his leather briefcase which contained his business plan. He thought of Emily. What was she doing now? Not that the letter he'd received this morning had filled him with much confidence. 'Spending two weeks of the autumn vac with Bodge,' she'd breezily informed him.

Who the hell was Bodge? If the sight of his stepmother at breakfast wearing nothing but a G-string and a top fashioned from what looked suspiciously like fax paper hadn't been enough to put him off his food, the letter had. More important than *who* Bodge was, what sex was it? The trouble was, Em's friends all had such implausible names. And why did she insist on calling it a vac? It had been two terms before he'd twigged she wasn't referring to the new Dyson. Why was it only Em and her friends who referred to their parents as mater and pater? If was, after all, only the one-time polytechnic, De Montfort

University, not the dreaming spires of Oxford.

'You don't think the suit is too much?' Peter turned to Alyosha, who was drawing a moustache on a photograph of a woman pinned to the green baize of a noticeboard.

He capped the pen and fished in his pocket for his gun. 'Not at all. It may be the first time the Russian Round Table has seen clothes made of . . .' He paused. 'What did you call that stuff?'

'Corduroy. It comes from the French—'

'Cord roy. But the suit will pale into insignificance when you hit them with your *business plan*.' He said it in English to underline his disdain.

'Alyosha, business, as I'm about to explain to our esteemed colleagues, is governed by *rules*.'

'Not here it's not.' Alyosha ground out his cigarette with the heel of his shoe, took another swig from his flask, wiped the neck and tilted it towards his friend.

Peter ignored it. 'Not yet it's not, but it will be. Business, like nature, abhors a vacuum. This country is in a period of transition. It's like the Wild West used to be, sheer chaos until the business classes decided for their own preservation if nothing else that law and order was the future.' His words owed more to a *Guardian* leader than empirical evidence.

'And you think one unfinished course at some poxy British institute qualifies you to secure the future when all others have failed.'

'It took Leon Trotsky a couple of weeks in a library to learn how to mobilise the entire Red Army.'

'Yeah, and look what happened to him.'

'No one has ever really tried it here. It hasn't been in anyone's interests. That's where this comes in.' Peter's eyes gestured down to his briefcase. 'And besides, I can't help having this nagging suspicion that killing people is wrong,' he added sarcastically.

'Christ. This is worse than I thought. You do know this gun fires only one round?' said Alyosha with what Peter assumed was feigned horror.

'And another thing, my father dragged me halfway round the world to sit at this damned table. At the same time, for right or wrong, he sent me to England to get an education.'

'That was never Hard Currency's idea, that was down to your mum. He's sending your half-brother to school right here in Moscow.'

'True, but I still feel I owe him something.' Peter adjusted the white handkerchief in his top pocket and flicked the dandruff from his shoulders. 'And in a strange sort of way I would like to make a go of it. For years my father has regarded me as, I don't know, *useless*. Now I intend to show him what I'm made of.'

Alyosha looked grave. 'This really is much worse than I thought.' He was checking the barrel of the small Beretta when the door opened and a man with a flattened face ushered them in through a pair of double doors. For a second they were unable to locate the table for the fug of cigarette smoke. As the haze cleared, it wasn't the *men* sitting round the table that struck Peter. It was the gaps. Gaping holes, like the teeth of an Armenian taxi driver. Five missing from a possible thirteen. The table looked like a dinner party recently deserted by its female diners.

Boy, gap, boy, gap, boy, gap. Or rather boyar, gap, boyar, gap. Despite looking like a scene from the St Valentine's Day Massacre before the cake came in, Peter reminded himself that these were some of the most important men in Russia.

He recognised all of them, despite the fact that at least two of them had never appeared in the media. Three of them were like his father – apparatchiks whose illegal manipulation of resources had pre-and post-dated per-estroika. Despite their wealth they dressed in a style hardly changed since Brezhnev: dour grey double-breasted suits and eastern European slip-on shoes. Men trained to keep their wealth hidden.

Not so the other men talking among themselves and pouring tumblers of Sprite from a plastic bottle each had in front of him. They were dressed in the finest Europe could offer, Italian suits, French ties, British shoes. In front of each of them were a mobile phone and a packet of cigarettes. A couple had brought their bodyguards who were sitting in an outer circle like mothers watching their offspring in a paddling pool. As Peter sized up the inner circle, Alyosha gave the bodyguards the once over.

'Gentlemen, please join us.' One of the older men stood up and beckoned them in expansively. He was Gennady Bortshov, a middle-aged former Central Party member from Yekaterinburg who, according to legend, had paid cash for two Silver Shadows when Rolls-Royce first opened in Moscow. He flew the vehicles the one thousand miles back to his home in the Urals in his private jet. In Yekaterinburg which, as every hoodlum worth their weight in platinum knew, boasted the most ruthless Mafia in the former Soviet Union, he was known simply as the Godfather.

'Do you know everybody here?' he growled.

Peter felt the floor move under him. He tried to smile. Alyosha, meanwhile, was beaming like the homecoming prodigal.

'Morning all,' he said, assuming the role of Peter's spokesman. 'Yes, we do indeed. If you will allow me to introduce us, this is Hard Currency's son and now appointed representative on the Round Table, Mr Peter Glebovitch Raevitch. Mr Raevitch has recently returned from business in Europe.' Alyosha nodded suggestively at the 'business in Europe' bit.

If only, thought Peter, they knew that the nearest he'd got to crime in the UK had been watching *The Bill*.

'Gentlemen.' Peter nodded nervously and set his brief-case on the table. Maybe the green corduroy hadn't been such a great idea. He focused on a display of silk flowers in the centre of the table.

The Godfather rose. His dark hair was speckled with grey above jowls modelled on Marlon Brando. His shirt was pulled taut over a paunch.

'Before we start,' he said, 'I would like to call for a minute's silence for the death of one of our number, known to you all as The Fridge, who died two days ago in a tragic road accident.' Two men silenced a cough. The Godfather bowed his head. 'A hit and run accident.'

Peter felt a dozen eyes focus on him. He turned ninety degrees to look at Alyosha who winked back and tapped his breast pocket twice.

'Actually, as we've got quite a busy meeting,' the

Godfather continued, 'we'll use the same minute to remember our dearly departed colleague Raspberry who was blown up' – Alyosha started to snigger – 'in a freak incident of spontaneous combustion.' He paused. 'Or a car bomb – depending on whose version you believe.' He smiled ghoulishly. 'Gentlemen, a minute.'

Peter tried to calm himself by listening to the hum of the traffic roaring round the Garden Ring. Twelve lanes of traffic had been built for tanks to quell civil disobedience. He thought of his beloved Shaftesbury Road designed for nothing more than hansom cabs.

After nearly thirty-two seconds the noise of a loud bang disturbed the men's reflection.

'Car backfiring,' said one of the older participants as he checked a Cartier watch. Mikhail Metzel was a car and gas magnate whose personal worth was estimated at seven billion dollars. He spoke with smug assurance, as if he knew it was anything but a faulty exhaust.

'At least *we're* all still here,' said Alyosha, grinning. The click of his Zippo as he lit up a Marlboro sparked off another couple of smokers. 'It's amazing just how dangerous backfiring cars can be.'

Peter glared at him. The Godfather smiled paternally.

'Don't I know you from somewhere?' Bortshov asked. 'You're one of Hard Currency's boys, aren't you?'

'Cemetery shoot-out of ninety-four,' replied Alyosha, bursting with a pride others of his age would have kept for swimming certificates. The gunning down of fourteen Afghan war veterans in Krapotkinskaya cemetery had made Moscow's gang rivalry plummet to even lower depths than before. No sense of shame disturbed Alyosha.

'Those two Armenians taken out by the gates. That was me.'

Peter shook his head. He had a vague idea of the rationale behind the killings. After perestroika, war veterans and sporting institutions had been given huge breaks on import duty for spirits and cigarettes. The concessions had been one of the most closely fought over agreements since the Ribbentrop-Molotov Pact, though the latter had probably been responsible for less bloodshed.

'Terrible business, that,' said the Godfather, shaking his head in mock sympathy. Alyosha joined him. 'Terrible.'

'Yes. Just two months later the government cancelled the tax breaks.' Others around the table joined the general commiseration.

'Ah well, gentlemen, we must look to the future. Now to the business in hand. We are all aware that the auction of Rosneft is just weeks away. I need hardly remind you of the profound significance that will have for all of us.' The Godfather looked around the room which was echoing with murmurs of assent. 'Whatever the government might say, it is crucial that foreign investors be discouraged. This, I'm sure you will agree, is vital to us all.'

There was general assent.

'Now, as far as we know there are, or should I say *were*, two among us who are seeking to buy into Rosneft – at what I need not add will be an extremely favourable rate. The first is, or rather *was*, our former colleague The Fridge, the second is our esteemed colleague Mr Hard Currency whose plans will now be outlined by his son.'

Peter stood. The moistness usually found in his mouth was seeping out of his palms like stigmata. He cleared his throat and opened his briefcase to take out a list of figures showing Rosneft's production rates over the decade.

The men exchanged confused glances around the table. The nearest they'd got to examining figures in the last five years had been comparing mistresses.

'Gentlemen, I would like to thank you for my hospitable welcome and pass on to you my father's regards. As a few of you may know, in recent months Gleb Alexanderavitch has been scaling down his Moscow affairs.' Peter thought involuntarily of his stepmother astride a laptop; a couple of men murmured, 'Pity, pity.' He continued, 'And it is with great pride that I have answered his call on me to take charge of things.'

Alyosha beamed. No one spoke.

'My first undertaking concerns the auction of Rosneft for which I have drawn up the following business plan.' Peter started passing photocopied sheets round the table. A dozen eyes looked imploringly at the Godfather to make him stop. The older ones hadn't looked at a production profile since the demise of the five-year plan. The lines of the graph went up and down like a child's drawing of a mountain range.

'As you can see, production levels throughout Siberia have been consistently falling since nineteen ninety-one. I am convinced that to make the buy into Rosneft profitable would require a considerable investment on our part.' He dared not look up. 'If we add to this the world slump in oil prices, my recommendation is that we withdraw from the auction.'

Mikhail Metzel, who for most of Peter's speech had been whispering into a mobile phone, spluttered into his plastic beaker of Sprite. Even Alyosha gasped. The God-father spat out his cheroot.

'However, I have been researching the investment potential of,' hesitantly he looked up, 'original English spring water.' He couldn't have floored them more effectively if he'd let off a tear gas canister. 'Very close to my alma mater in Leicester, De Montfort University, can be found some extremely palatable mineral water.' Boris Belyakov, the vodka magnate, was actually fighting for air. 'In my own experience the water in Moscow is of a very variable quality,' Peter persisted as Alyosha clamped him round the shoulders and forced him to sit down.

Alyosha smiled round the table and spoke as if he was a ventriloquist and Peter the dummy. 'What the hell are you trying to do, get us killed?' he spat.

Peter's face was close to his. 'I am merely trying to apply a little long-term business logic to the situation. The water in Mos—'

'You just don't get it do you?' Alyosha hissed as the hubbub continued around them. 'Can't you understand why these men are some of the richest in Europe, if not the world? The selling off of the former Soviet Union was never to the highest bidder. Here you use your connections to buy it cheap and sell it dear. And you don't rock the boat. Didn't they at least teach you that at your so-called business school? *Mineral water*, for God's sake. You'll be lucky to see your bed tonight, never mind your next birthday.'

Peter looked hurt. Metzel was speaking to the God-father in an animated way which suggested mutiny.

Alyosha straightened and extended his arms by way of

apology. 'Gentlemen, I'm sorry about the distress this must have caused some of you. It's just that Mr Raevitch has been under a great deal of stress recently and—'

He was interrupted by the arrival of a man in a black leather three-quarter length coat. He scraped his leather flat cap from a balding scalp. The meeting, now close to riot, was hushed immediately.

He addressed the Godfather. He was sorry to interrupt but there'd been an accident. Details were sketchy, but it appeared to involve Hard Currency, his mistress and a Jiffy bag.

III

Katya very rarely smoked but this morning she felt a disconnectedness with her surroundings which a burst of nicotine often helped. She dug out a packet of Turkish cigarettes from Max's drawer in the kitchen. A few personal documents, his passport, his Crimea key fob and a penknife were all that remained of her husband.

Sasha and Misha had gone out in a flurry of secrecy. She thought with a pang of the times when she'd known everything about her son. She'd soon be usurped by another woman. In fact, knowing Sasha's precocity, she probably only had about five years left. She sucked on the pungent cigarette and nearly retched.

As the tobacco turned to ash she started to feel better. In a few years she and Sasha would have enough money to start a life elsewhere in a country where you didn't have to worry if there was going to be a government, never mind an economy, when you woke up.

They'd both miss the place. Katya thought of the dozens of girls she'd sent to a new life in the west. A dream as embedded in them as Marx and Engels. But, like communism, it was better in theory. They had traded their families and friends to become model wives in a country where they couldn't speak the language and whose customs they couldn't understand.

She knew that Sasha would miss his friends, especially his constant companion young Misha. Misha was one of the new brand of Russian children, indulged by *nouveaux riches* parents whose own childhoods had been characterised by longing. Now they were spoilt, literally. Last week a mother at Sasha's school had been shovelling chocolate into her offspring like milk. When she had questioned the woman, she'd tartly replied that the child had to experience as much chocolate as possible in case it disappeared. A few years ago you never heard a baby or toddler whine; now 'I want' wailed around every shopping mall in the city. Sasha had grasped early what whatever he wanted he paid for. An unnerving self-reliance, especially in a six-year-old. Sasha seemed to have abandoned his childhood almost as soon as he started on solids.

Katya stared out of the window – snowing again. In Byelorus the snow had stayed crisp and white all winter long. In Moscow the fluctuating temperatures, one day minus twenty, the next plus one, meant a filthy sludge which froze to black ice. Then in the spring the ice would disappear and the detritus of winter would come to light. It was always her least favourite season, a murky greyness which stretched from September to May.

She sometimes wondered why any marauding gang galloping across the steppes had ever dismounted in Russia. If they'd only carried on till Paris, or even Germany, she and Sasha would be eating pain au chocolat. She half-heartedly cut a slice of salami from a roll of dubious origin. And yet with a perversity she recognised as uniquely Russian she knew that she would miss the place like the convict misses prison. Freedom offered so many choices. Oppression was so much simpler. Of course it was more difficult for the elderly, the men and women who demonstrated in Red Square beneath the communist banners and pictures of Stalin. But she had a good fifteen years' work left in her to save for her retirement and provide for Sasha's education.

If that was the case, she'd better start now. She heaved herself up by her elbows.

As she did so, the phone rang. The quickened trill of an international call. She looked at her watch with the assurance of an international trader. It was too early for Europe, the UK, or East Coast America. It meant two things: mid-America and her client had been up all night committing the sort of atrocities he usually paid her to procure on his visits to Moscow. She contemplated leaving the machine on but resisted, knowing it would only mean another phone bill, barely large enough to accommodate the noughts.

'Katya, hi. This is Baz. How ya doin'?'

'Very well, thank you. How are you?'

'You know. Hangin'.'

What did he mean, *hanging*. Surely not literally? 'Glad

to hear it.' She waited, picturing him inhale on a dog turd sized cigar.

'You know it's kinda late here.'

'Really?' *Had he really called her to acquaint her with international time differences?* She looked at her watch again. What had happened to Sasha? She thought of speaking in order to hang up (it was always less suspicious to hang up when *you* were speaking) but she knew he'd only call back.

'Guess what I'm doin' right now? *Right* now?'

She forced herself to smile to convey a happy interest. 'I simply can't imagine,' she said through gritted teeth.

'Playing strip twister with three young ladies.' Katya heard giggles and the sound of flesh being slapped. 'I am, of course, on my mobile,' he added superfluously. 'It's the sort of fun that puts me in mind of my trips to Moscow. You know what I mean?'

Katya thought of a belly like a bag of flour hanging over a Star of Texas belt. She thought of Sonya's spiky thinness, her hip bones jutting out from her housecoat. In a terrifying moment she imagined a coupling. She calmed herself by thinking of Sasha.

'Yes, I think I do,' she said.

'So what have we got lined up? Remember, Katya, this time I'm after one for keeps.'

Katya winced. What did he think they were, *pets*? 'Yes, I know that and I'm doing everything I can. In fact I think I might just have found the perfect girl.' She grimaced as she thought of Sonya.

'Really?' Whatever he'd been doing, the information halted him in his tracks. Katya tried hard not to imagine him jettisoning a teenage girl from his lap. 'What size?'

'Very, very slender, a natural blonde, and practically no feet to speak of,' replied Katya, flicking through a Rolodex of possibles for Terry.

'Any family history of stroke?'

'None that I know of.'

'Is she now or has she ever in the past been a prostitute?' He sounded like the Vice Squad version of Senator McCarthy.

'No, absolutely not. In fact by profession she sells books.'

'Any *whore* mentality?'

'Absolutely not.'

'OK then.' He paused. 'Have you put in an offer on her?'

'I thought it was better to leave the negotiations until you got here.'

He seemed to weigh up the information. 'How old?'

'Nineteen.'

'But looks?'

'Fifteen.'

'Perfect. Truly inspired.' Katya heard the click of ice in glasses in the background and a snort closer to the phone. 'Wow, Katya, I gotta tell you. I gotta say I'm really *psyched* about this whole thing. Seems to me I just gotta get my butt out there before any other horny men snap her up.'

'Quite,' said Katya, contemplating her chances with another of Max's cigarettes.

'And it just so happens work is gonna take me back out your way real soon. Real soon. This is outstanding.

130

Outstanding. So whaddya say you slap a *reserved* notice on that pretty little ass of hers a.s.a.p.?'

'Consider it slapped.' Another echo of flesh on flesh, followed by a whoop, echoed twelve thousand miles across the world.

'Just to recap, Katya. Exactly how small are her feet?'

'Metric or inches?'

'Inches.' She could almost hear the saliva drip.

'Thirty-six.'

'Wow. Katya, look, I'm gonna have to hang up now. I . . . I'm gonna have to . . .'

'Goodnight, Baz.' Katya put down the receiver.

She tapped the side of the phone with a profound sense of unease. If she was going to get her 20K finder's fee by hooking him up with Sonya, she would have to make Baz seem as normal as possible. And there was only one way to do that: introduce Sonya to more freaks than a nineteenth-century freak circus. There was no doubt. She would have to introduce Sonya to the Englishman.

IV

It was one of those days, as rare in Moscow as twenty-four hours when the rouble holds its own, when the sky shone an icy blue. On the few occasions when it surprised you, it was best to make the most of the weather. On a whim Bridges decided to exit at Park Kulturi and walk to the office. He corrected himself. Walk to the morgue. A brisk walk would also provide some muscle-tightening exercise to stave off the paunch, in case a run of bodies (he winced) meant he didn't make it to the gym today. He looked around the carriage – a few acned youths with limp, greasy hair and skin the colour, he thought with new-found authority, of a corpse, two miniskirted women clutching vanity cases, who looked as if they hadn't made it home last night, and a pug-faced elderly couple, sporting a chestful of medals.

As the train clattered into Park Kulturi, he leapt up and flung himself onto the platform just as a Russian recording reminded him to take all his belongings. Since Chechenya the authorities had become very urban terrorist conscious. Waiting until the doors were about to close before he left the carriage was a hangover from his CIA days. It gave anyone who might be tailing you little time to do the same. Which was why when two doors down a man in dark blue followed suit, Bridges made an uneasy mental note of it.

He joined the lumpen proletariat as it was funnelled towards the escalator. They streamed past a uniformed guard who was paid to sit at the bottom of the shaft. Bridges thought for the zillionth time just how low tech the greatest threat to the west since Hitler had been. He remembered marvelling, when he first arrived, at an elderly road cleaner sweeping the street with a broomstick made of twigs. He had to concede that Russia's status as an aggressive superpower had been more the invention of his friends at the CIA, intent on keeping their budgets, than it ever was in reality. Had the west ever wanted to take over Russia, they could have done it with a few crates of vodka and an armful of *Playboys*.

He stared up at the people sinking into the improbably

deep Metro. It was just after ten o'clock. A 37-year-old one-time Soviet spy going to work in an embalming parlour. He smiled, feeling ridiculously at ease. For the first time in as long as he could remember he'd woken up without a hangover.

Previously he'd used the nausea as a focus to the day, its relief about the only thing he had to look forward to, the relief usually coming in the shape of a bottle of Jack Daniels. Bizarre as it might be, now at least he had some purpose. He considered the day ahead. The company's first advert was expected in today's *Moskovsky Komsomolets*, chosen because it was the most widely-read Russian rag, though only a few steps up from the *National Enquirer*. Freedom of the press hadn't lasted long in Russia. No sooner had journalists been freed by communism than the papers they worked for were bought out by huge business interests for which they became the hired mouthpieces.

Bridges felt so good he treated himself to a round of his favourite elevator game. Who would you screw on the opposite staircase? It put a whole new spin on the phrase going down. The only rule was that you must choose someone, otherwise you had to take the last person, regardless of looks. Once you'd made up your mind there was no going back. He usually stuffed up. In a parallel universe, he'd had sex with more Russian hags than Gregory Rasputin. He'd been a bit like that in his non-staircase relationships, always holding out for something better to come along. Even with Susan he'd never been totally convinced that the perfect woman hadn't been about to board the escalator just behind her.

He stared across the impressive teak balustrade, dotted

with brass candlesticks. Had he been right to pass up both the blonde in the mink *and* the brunette whose red made-up lips had puckered to a smile – in favour of what?

As the elevator ejected him onto the wide concourse he saw that, as usual, he'd been left with a bulky middle-aged woman who was loudly berating a wiry husband. Shit. He turned back down the stairs to see if he couldn't extract another smile from the brunette he'd spurned. But the pressure of people bundling him onwards was too much. He did, however, spot the man in the blue coat. He was the same striking dark-haired man who, on reflection, Bridges was sure he'd noticed yesterday waiting on the platform at Kievski station where they'd accidentally made eye contact. He'd noted him not for his blue Chinese down coat, habitual in Moscow, but his piercing blue Siberian eyes which were as cold as the region's winter.

Now the hairs on the back of Bridges' neck leapt to attention. A cold sweat momentarily doused his body. It was the same feeling he'd had when the FBI had him under twenty-four-hour surveillance before he'd managed to skip town. He turned to be jostled through the ticket barrier with the rest of the worker drones. First rule of espionage, never confront a tail. He kept walking, crossing the bridge over the Moskva, past Gorky Park, up to Oktaybraskaya Ploschad and then on to the institute.

The best way to check a tail was to double back on yourself. When he got to Gorky Park, Bridges joined the early morning queue for entry tickets. Despite his preoccupation he registered the hordes of children, denoting a school holiday. He paid 5 roubles to a woman in a black headscarf whose face was covered in warts sprouting grey hair like fountains.

As he turned to continue walking away from the road, he saw Blue Eyes had crossed the street. When Bridges continued, Blue Eyes looked up from a tampon display in a newly opened western pharmacy and followed him. Bridges began to sweat again. Surely the colouring was wrong for the CIA and he was dressed too smartly for the Russian secret services. He must be a hit man. But even for one of Moscow's extortion rackets this was a bit quick off the Russian mark. Bodies Beautiful had been running less than a week. Besides, subtlety was not the hallmark of the Russian Mafia, whose motto was shoot now, ask questions later. He reached in his jacket pocket for a cigarette. Even by his standards 10 a.m. was a bit early. But this was an emergency. He was being hunted and he had no idea why.

V

Taking the passport from Katya's kitchen drawer would clearly have been wrong. But he was only borrowing it and it was essential for the operation he had in mind. It could even have been fate that had put it in such easy reach – he'd been searching rather desperately for a loo roll while Katya's back was turned. In any case, he wouldn't have had to borrow the passport if that bag-wielding troll hadn't stolen all his money. Disappointing was definitely the word he'd use to describe the women he'd met so far. Not looks-wise or even size-wise, but confidence-wise. It was difficult to be a knight in shining armour to a princess who was on forty a day with a drink problem. Take the other afternoon, the champagne disaster. Terry now confidently attributed his passing out to drinking on an empty stomach – he could no longer remember eating anything. Ever. He hadn't even wanted champagne.

Wasn't Russia supposed to be a peasant economy? How many peasants drank champagne at lunchtime? Even on *The Archers* they only managed a pint of Shires. At least on his dates at the Harvester the women had paid their way. At the most he'd fancied two of the girls, excluding Katya, for whom after all it was a job of work, and he'd had to stump up for drinks for six.

It was worse than a single person room supplement. It was one of those hidden holiday extras that Anne Robinson had based an entire career on. Clive hadn't warned him he would be subsidising a round of drinks for half of Moscow. He could still see their look of blithe expectation, staring at him with the confident knowledge of children waiting to be bought sweets by their parents. A wave of loathing swept over him. He'd certainly shown them, though, when he opened it. He hadn't been voted salesman – salesperson, he corrected himself – of the year, gazebo division, twice in a row, without knowing how to open a bottle of bubbly. It had been like a cross between the Grand Prix and a wet T-shirt competition.

As the meeting had progressed he had become more and more disillusioned with Natasha. His Natasha had *surely* never been a smoker or a drinker. Not for the first time he considered the advantages of living in an Islamic society. Whatever they did to female genitalia certainly seemed to do the trick. Calmed them down. Leave a woman with a clitoris and they became so *confident*. Also, you wouldn't get the snide type of comment he'd increasingly received from Grace towards the end. You wouldn't *have* to satisfy a woman. It would be her job to satisfy you. All in all it hadn't even been worth drying off his Calvin Klein underpants in the oven, a laundering method which had only left a deeply suspicious scorch mark on the back.

Terry looked up from the sofa in his flat in mournful silence. The evening date had, if anything, been even worse. Four hours with a woman whose only knowledge of English had been 'Yes please' and 'Princess Di'. And he'd had to pay for the privilege. A hundred and seventy dollars for a meal and when it had come to getting his just desserts in the taxi, *her hair had come off in his hand*. Not only not a redhead, but not even her own hair. Even in Terry's darkest moments he'd never stooped to a wig.

No, it was time to take control. He picked up a child's drawing pad which he'd found in a kitchen cupboard and the green pen which he'd brought with him. With a flourish he started his 'Why Clive Must Pay' list, ignoring a wave of light-headedness which had wafted over him. He stood up and felt dizzy. The assumed fat content of last night's meal, at a hamburger joint, had ruled out his eating anything more than a green salad with no dressing. Last night he'd dreamt of a man-size Nutri-Grain bar. But when he'd tried to unwrap it, it was full of maggots. He shook his head from side to side, exhaling heavily.

He picked up his abdominiser ponderously and rotated

it round his head, loosening his shoulders. 'No, Terry. Time to regroup and reassess,' he said out loud as he twirled.

As the thought occurred to him, he let go of the abdominiser which hurtled towards the wall, denting the crossbar. Terry ignored it. He flew to the notepad and scratched out the 'Why Clive Must Pay' list and wrote 'Objectives'.

1. *Find wife*. He paused, then scored out the first objective.

1. *Get laid*. He paused again, then scratched this one out too.

1. *Get photographs of the women*.

2. *Get hair*. Then for no obvious reason he started to laugh like a maniac.

VI

'Are you sure this is going to work?'

'Have I ever let you down yet?'

'No,' replied Misha meekly. They were hiding out in their favourite bolt hole, a janitor's cupboard accessed through a rabbit warren of corridors in the basement.

'Then just pass the scissors,' said Sasha with a smile.

CHAPTER FIVE

I

The noise was superhuman. A piercing wail usually reserved for Muslim burials, it screeched, above the familiar two-time beat of a Russian love song, like a peacock.

'Christ, what's that?' asked Alyosha incredulously as the series 600 Mercedes swept into the parking space outside a dacha more imposing than a Bavarian castle. The driver, Alexander, smelt of stale cigarettes. His fingernails were black and the index finger of his right hand, as it gripped the steering wheel, had the nicotine-induced dull glow of a jaundice patient.

'I have a horrible feeling it's my stepmother,' said Peter, his gritted teeth pulling nervously at a loosened nail. He looked at the man in the front passenger seat wearing the leather coat, a Ukrainian called Pavel, whose prowess with a machete had appealed to Hard Currency. Hard believed an over-reliance on firearms was no good thing.

'Are you sure you haven't got a better idea of what happened? I would have thought that the wounding effects of a Jiffy bag were somewhat limited,' said Peter.

'Depends what you do with it,' replied Pavel, addressing him through the rear-view mirror.

Peter and Alyosha's eyes met and looked away. No matter how close a friend, Peter preferred not to share his father's more bizarre office antics with the wider world. But by the lack of shock registered on his face, it seemed Alyosha had a pretty keen grasp of the fact that the Jiffy bag wasn't being used to send something fragile through the post.

The doors slammed in tandem and Peter and Alyosha strode to the front entrance while Alexander and Pavel hung back like uninvited guests. An ambulance emblazoned with the name of a European medical service with a green cross on the door was parked in the driveway.

Inside, the wailing had reached a terrifying pitch.

'Alyosha, you couldn't try and calm Tanya down while I go and see what's going on? You've always got on with her much better than I have.'

'I'll try,' he replied, straightening his jacket.

A dapper doctor in half-moon glasses, dressed so smartly that Peter knew he couldn't work for the Russian emergency services, came up to him and extended an exquisitely manicured hand.

'Good morning, my name is Dr Hans Brecht, like the playwright,' he said in hesitant Russian. 'May I—'

'Do you speak English?' asked Peter.

'Yes, of course.'

'Please continue,' Peter smiled. Despite the gravity of the situation, a part of him was thrilling to the responsibility of it all.

The doctor continued, 'I regret to tell you it was asphyxiation that did it.'

'Did what?' asked Peter incredulously.

'Was responsible for your father's death,' he said gravely, taking off his glasses as he delivered the news.

'*Death*? What are you talking about? How the hell can you die from a Jiffy bag?'

A wail two octaves lower joined Peter's stepmother's. Alyosha had joined the mourners. He was theatrically staggering down the stairs, bouncing from banister to wall like a wounded cowboy in a saloon.

'He was like a father to me,' he sobbed, wringing his Dolce and Gabbana T-shirt in grief.

'What do you mean he was *like* a father to you?' said Peter, sinking into a Louis XIV armchair in the hall. 'He *was* a frigging father to me.' He looked at the doctor who was cleaning his glasses on the sleeve of his immaculate white coat. 'Are you absolutely sure he can't be brought round?'

The German shook his head.

'What exactly were they . . .?' Peter let the question hang, hoping the doctor would fill in the blank spaces. Then he considered. Given the circumstances, it might be better to keep the exact details of the death on a strictly need-to-know basis.

'I am obliged to ask if you want to see the body,' said Dr Brecht.

'Do you think I should?' asked Peter.

'Some family members say it helps with the grieving process.' He smiled. 'Though I must say,' he added, replacing the tortoiseshell frames, 'it's not a pretty sight.'

141

Peter let out a subdued yelp.

'You see,' the German glanced around furtively, 'it appears your father and your . . . your mother—'

'Stepmother,' corrected Peter.

'Stepmother were in congress at the time it happened.'

A wave of Valium-like relief went through Peter. They weren't *at it* at all. Simply *in congress*. Like a business meeting. They had been addressing envelopes and his father had accidentally choked on one. It probably happened all the time, an unreported office hazard like radiation from mobile phones. A tragic, though domestic, accident. The home was where ninety per cent of all accidents took place, he remembered from a British safety council advert.

Then the doctor continued with uncalled-for Teutonic honesty, 'Your father was attempting to achieve heightened orgasm by restricting the flow of oxygen, using a Jiffy bag. Unfortunately, covered by the envelope, your stepmother was unable to see that he had in fact passed out.'

Peter started to reel. How the hell was he going to explain this to the waiting world, never mind his halfbrother? *Never mind Emily.*

'In any case, it is unlikely she would have been able to prevent it. Being, as she was, trussed to a fax machine at the time. I am advised that they usually took the precaution of using a small metal device to keep the trachea open in case he passed out, though there is no sign of it on this occasion. Truly a terrible business.'

'Oh shit,' said Peter. 'Could I have a glass of water, please?'

'Certainly.' The doctor spun on his Cuban heels and made his way to the kitchen.

Peter became dimly aware that the dacha was full of Hard Currency's entourage, a batch of bodyguards and a collective of chauffeurs. For the second time that day he was going to have to take up the Raevitch mantle. First, though, he'd have to comfort his stepmother, whose breathless whelps continued to fill the house. In another room a Russian pop song boomed out. A fitting parody, thought Peter, of the solemn music played by the radio round the clock when a Soviet leader died.

The doctor returned with a cut-glass tumbler of water.

'Where is the body?' managed Peter between sips.

'Congress was taking place in the study.' Dr Brecht made it sound like the signing of a peace treaty.

'Is that where he is now?'

'It is. In these circumstances we usually remove the body to our morgue, where we await instructions for the funeral. I have signed the death certificate,' he said, passing Peter a brown envelope. 'And if you would be good enough to sign this, we'll put it on the bill, which now stands at,' he glanced down the list, 'one case of whiplash and release from handcuffs. Twice.'

Peter groaned as the doctor proffered him a form in triplicate and undid the top of a Mont Blanc pen.

II

It was unusual for her to lie in. If it wasn't her ninety-minute commute to the bookshop that got Sonya up at seven, it was knowing Nikita would need seeing to. It was already ten thirty and there hadn't been a murmur from the kitchen where they made up a bed for him.

She ought to check on him and she *would*, only after another five minutes. The apartment was freezing. She knew from her friends at the bookshop that the city municipality had switched the heating on throughout most of the city, but their *rayon* in the back of beyond tended to get overlooked. It was even worse for Nikita with his lack of mobility. She bundled him up with blankets but he still complained.

'Sonya?' The call from the kitchen was apologetic. She knew Nikita liked to give her as long a lie-in on her days off as his bladder would allow.

'Coming.' She threw back the cover and rubbed her eyes, unused to the extra sleep, as her feet felt on the wooden floor for her slippers. 'Is it just a pee?' she asked. Any pretensions to modesty had left the brother and sister weeks after Nikita had been flown home on a stretcher.

'Yes.'

'Hang on a tic.' She fetched a plastic bucket from the bathroom. 'Did you sleep OK?'

'The dream's come back.'

The dream needed no explanation to Sonya. It was a horrific tableau from the war, replayed in various guises.

'Was it the worst one?' she asked, struggling to pull his wheelchair into the kitchen. The worst was being stalked house by house by the Chechen separatists.

'Not the worst. The burning plane one.'

'Poor darling,' Sonya kissed him on the forehead as she took the bucket from him.

She emptied it in the lavatory and returned to the kitchen to brush her long hair in a mirror above the sink. Then she passed the brush to Nikita.

'You know it won't always be this bad, don't you?'

'The dreams?'

'Well, the dreams and . . .' She looked around the kitchen. 'Well, everything.' She smiled.

'I know.'

'Tatyana told me a joke in the bookshop yesterday. Do you want to hear it?' She was cutting bread.

'Go on, then.'

'A New Russian goes to a travel agent and tells him he really needs a holiday. "OK, sir," replies the travel agent. "What about Paris?" "No," says the New Russian. "Not a city. I really need to relax." "OK then," says the travel agent. "What about Egypt?" "Ugh," replies the New Russian. "Too hot. I told you I really need somewhere I can *relax*." "Well, sir. There is one holiday. But it's very expensive." Of course this excites the New Russian. "Go on," he said. "Well, sir, it's called a safari. What you do, sir, is drive around in a jeep shooting anything that moves." "*Are you deaf?*" thunders the New Russian. "I said I needed a *holiday*."'

Nikita threw back his head and laughed. Moscow was full of jokes about the detested New Russians. The anecdotes were as popular as stories a generation ago about Chuckchas, a tribe of northern Siberian Eskimos then the butt of all Soviet humour.

Since the accident Sonya had become an adept joke-teller. She was Nikita's only live medium with the outside world, especially after the visits from his army pals tailed off.

She hauled him up into a sitting position and handed him a glass of black tea poured from yesterday's pot and topped up with boiling water.

'Jam OK on your bread?'

'Fine. You're not going out today, are you?'

She knew how much he hated her spending her precious free time away from him. 'Only shopping.'

'Good.' He took a bite.

Sonya looked at him. 'I don't suppose anybody's called for me this week?' She tried to sound offhand. The phone was kept a couple of feet from Nikita's wheelchair, a sort of base camp surrounded by jigsaws and books, in the sitting room which doubled as her bedroom. In the days when their parents had been alive the whole family had slept in the same room. Now Nikita claimed to prefer the kitchen, though Sonya knew it was only in case his nightmares woke her.

'No one. Most people call the shop, don't they?'

Sonya nodded. She had been half expecting a call from the middle-aged woman who had visited her the other evening.

She wiped the crumbs from the table onto her curled palm and shook them into the bin. As a child, it used to make her feel sick, watching her mum scrape the debris into her hand. Today she couldn't imagine why.

Katya probably wouldn't call. It was only in retrospect that she'd started to think it might make sense. She had grown so used to telling Nikita things were going to get better, she'd lost sight of how. The money from the bookshop was hardly enough to keep them in food. If Nikita needed more money for medicine or an operation they'd be lost. His monthly disability allowance and army pension were hardly enough for a new pair of shoes.

Things will get better. It used to be one of her mum's constant refrains. Or if they didn't get better, at least you'd get used to them, she would say. Sonya didn't want to get used to them. Improvement had never been an option for her parents. Her father, a chemist, had been bounced around the former Soviet Union without a choice for years, until he was sent to Moscow to work on a research project where she and Nikita had been born. The day they had collided with a tractor driven by a drunkard on an icy road on their way to visit her grandmother in Magnetigorsk had been the worst of her life. In retrospect, Nikita's accident had been quite easy to bear.

'Did you hear me?' said Nikita, rejecting a second slice of bread.

'Sorry?'

'Were you expecting a call from anyone?'

'No, not at all. I mean who could call us?' She pushed the wheelchair over to the sofa, using all her strength to lever Nikita onto it.

III

'What the hell was in that tablet?' Peter registered that the sobbing from Tanya's room had abated for a full five hours.

'The doctor called it Tamazapan or something.' Alyosha had his hip flask in his hand. 'I gave her a vodka to wash it down with. She shouldn't wake up for the next twenty-four hours. I don't suppose . . .' His grey eyes viewed Peter with cowed expectation. 'It's just that she's got very olive skin.'

'So?'

'Almond-shaped eyes and the sort of dumpy figure you associate with women from . . .'

'No,' said Peter, 'my stepmother, a woman still in shock after the untimely death of her husband, my stepmother is *not* from Kirghizia.'

'Sorry. Worth a try though, wasn't it?'

'No, Alyosha, it wasn't worth a try. Trying to screw my stepmother before my father's body is cold is not what I would call *worth a try*.'

'Not even before the effects of the sleeping pills wear off?' Alyosha started to laugh, an infectious tear-inducing explosion of mirth. Peter tried to keep a straight face in the interests of dignity but failed.

'Hell of a way to go, wasn't it?' spluttered Alyosha.

'On the job.' Peter held his sides.

'With a Jiffy bag.' Alyosha couldn't continue.

'On his head.' Peter sank to the floor. It lasted for three side-splitting minutes. Then, just as quickly as mirth had overtaken them, they got serious.

'Sleep is probably the best thing for her,' said Peter, decorum restored, choosing his lines from the soap opera bereavement manual.

'How are you feeling?'

'A bit numb. You know. What about you?'

'I can't really believe it.' Alyosha paused. 'What happens next? I mean, what about the funeral?'

'God knows. Any ideas?'

'None. Someone needs to tell your mum what's happened.'

'Yeah, I'd already thought about that. I'll ring her tonight.'

'Do you think she'll fly back?'

'I wouldn't have thought so. Relations between her and Tanya aren't exactly great.'

'Then we've got to decide who's going to tell the boy.'

'I know. It should be Tanya, but she's in no fit state. In any case, I haven't seen him all day. I don't suppose you know where he hangs out these days?'

'No idea. Hard Currency never seemed to have much interest in the under eighteens.' He paused. 'Unless they were female.'

'You don't have to tell me that,' said Peter forlornly.

'What a day.' Alyosha unscrewed the top of his flask and took a swig. He wiped his mouth on the back of his hand. 'Still, look on the bright side. Your dad never got to hear about your inaugural speech at the Round Table. The repercussions of which are yet to hit us.'

'It wasn't *that* bad.'

'*That bad*,' echoed Alyosha. 'I'll tell you how bad it was. You know when Yeltsin gets so pissed he can't get off aeroplanes?'

'Yes,' said Peter petulantly.

'And when he conducts German brass bands in front of the world's press?'

'Yes.'

'And when he's in such a state of confusion he doesn't know what country he's in?'

'Look, I fail to see—'

149

'Well, your performance today would make Boris Yeltsin look like Kofi fucking Annan.'

'That bad?'

'That bad.'

'But nothing will come of it. Will it?'

'Peter, these days in Moscow you can get shot for asking the wrong woman to dance in a nightclub, never mind threatening the livelihoods of some of the city's most powerful hoods.'

'Shit.'

'Shit is the word.'

Above them the chandelier twitched as a thud echoed in the silence. They jumped.

'What was that?' hissed Peter.

'Relax. That was your stepmother falling out of bed,' said Alyosha. 'Allow me to assist her.' He got up and stubbed out his cigarette on a silver plate.

Peter said, 'Don't forget, before you get too carried away, that both her parents come from Saint Petersburg.'

'Duly noted.'

Peter watched Alyosha walk to the door then flicked the CD from Oasis to Rimsky-Korsakov and started to consider the implications of his new circumstances. He outlined a letter to Em.

> Darling,
>
> What a tragedy! Pater has been struck down in congress. A heart attack while negotiating his latest business deal. We are devastated. I will have to stay on here until I can at least put his affairs in order. I—

Alyosha was standing at the door with a letter in his hand. He held it out towards Peter. 'This has just been delivered.' His face was pinched. 'Open it carefully.'

The envelope was addressed in capitals TO WHOM IT MAY CONCERN.

'It's probably from a well-wisher passing on commiserations,' said Peter.

'Something tells me not,' said Alyosha.

Peter gently eased a sheet of white paper out. He looked up at Alyosha. As usual his friend was right. Their faces fell like shooting stars sinking out of the firmament.

III

Katya hadn't had sex in the afternoon for more than a year. A few minutes after they'd finished the coupling, from which by the sounds of it he'd derived more enjoyment than she had, she remembered why. Sasha was due back in less than an hour.

She rolled over. 'What time does your shift start?' She tried to murmur it in a post-coital sigh but was aware it came out with the bluntness of a production manager.

'Seven. Though I must say you are a persuasive case for calling in sick.' He reached round Katya's waist and felt upwards for a nipple.

'Well, much as I would love you to stay,' she said, pushing away his fingers which had the eager frustration of a radio ham trying to tune a station, 'I'm afraid my son will be back any minute now.'

He groaned. 'Please, say it isn't so. You'll be telling me

next your husband is expected in time for dinner.'

'No,' said Katya. 'Short of a heat wave in Siberia, I can confidently predict that there's very little danger of that.'

'I'm sorry?'

'Nothing.' Katya edged further across the bed, torn between the luxury of a lie-down and the risk of more sex. She heard him clear his throat.

'Perhaps we could meet up later. My shift finishes at midnight.'

Katya thought about it. He would still be in uniform and it had been, after all, the fit of his clothes that had made her give him her number in the first place. That and the dry cleaning bill after the Englishman's champagne accident. He'd called, as she'd expected he would, the same day. He'd arrived twenty-four hours later with a bottle of cherry liqueur and five red roses.

Not that the sex hadn't been good. Even more than that, it had pulled a temporary security grille down over a clutch of problems which were in danger of swamping her. In this regard sex was better than alcohol, especially now that the older she got, the worse the hangover. This way you were up, showered and back at work before the scent of the lover had worn off. There was much to be said for it. Over the years she'd tucked away more condoms, left behind by her clients, than the average Moscow pharmacist got through in a month. They were more reliable than those supplied by the Moscow Rubber Company and thinner than a pair of gumboots. You could probably populate an entire Central Asian republic with the unwanted offspring resulting from faulty Russian condoms. Not *unwanted*, she corrected herself, *unexpected*.

Even Sasha had been the result of a burst prophylactic.

She was aware that the hand was back and had returned to her breast while the other hand was caressing a buttock. Both actions were accompanied by a nibbling of her earlobe. She couldn't help thinking it was a level of ambidexterity which must come in useful as a waiter. She felt herself starting to yield when she remembered Sasha.

'No, darling, we mustn't,' she sighed, trying to convey lusty confusion.

'Baby, please. Once more. Come on, baby.'

That killed it more effectively than a bucket of water. Katya couldn't stand being called baby. She shook him off. 'No, I mean it. My son will be here any minute.' She pushed him away with a powerful right arm and swung her legs off the sofa bed. 'Maybe another time. Just not now,' she relented, seeing a look of what she guessed was genuine hurt in his eyes.

She pulled a dressing gown over her shoulders and headed for the shower, praying he wouldn't follow her. In less than five minutes she was dressed, hair and teeth brushed. She returned to the sitting room where he was still crumpled under the pair of sheets kept for afternoon trysts.

She silently cursed. A typical Russian man, only happy when horizontal. And, like cockroaches, impossible to get rid of once you'd got them.

'Hey, wakey wakey.' She shook him gently, hoping he wasn't going to turn nasty. He rolled over, still asleep. Katya looked at her watch. Sasha had only gone to a friend's house locally, he could be back at any minute.

She suddenly stood stock still in a moment of rare clarity. Perhaps it was westerners' complicated attitude to sex which made their relationships so difficult. From what she understood of western women (albeit from magazines and dubbed Hollywood films) women held back on sex till it *meant something*. No wonder they got so screwed. In Russia it was a recreational sport, like volleyball. She'd even slept with men who had flashed their telephone numbers out of passing cars. In the rest of the world, sex was steeped in some sort of Christian morality. One of the good things about communism was the lack of guilt associated with it. Western women came to Russia preaching feminism, but where was the equality in waiting by the phone for a man to ring? No, there could only be real equality when women had devalued sex as much as men had. And she was certainly doing her bit.

'I said *wake up*.' She punched him again and felt him stir. 'Time to go home.' She began to throw his clothes at him. There was a grunt of recognition as his trousers landed close to his head. She was pulling the sheet from under him when the phone went.

'Hello, Katya?' The voice sounded hesitant.

'Speaking.' She sank into a chair and found a stray pair of boxer shorts which she launched like a kite over to the bed.

'This is Sonya. Do you remember me? We met—'

'Sonya, yes, of course. How are you?' She dropped the receiver, estimating she had four seconds to launch another kick before the reply came back. She dashed to the bed and then back to the phone.

'Sorry, I missed that.' She was slightly too late to hear

the tail end of Sonya's reply. At least, though, he was out of bed.

'I said I wondered if anything had come of my application to join the agency.'

'Of course, Sonya. Could you excuse me for just one minute?' She hurled herself over to the bed, thrusting two grey socks in his face. '*Hurry up*,' she snarled. Then back to the phone. 'Well, I've checked our database and I'm pleased to tell you that your application has been successful. Congratulations, Sonya.' She flung down the receiver and tugged the sheet off the bed. As she picked the receiver up again, she heard, '. . . step was.'

'Sorry, Sonya, this is a terrible line.'

'I was wondering what the next step was.'

Really, thought Katya, this was going much better than she had dared hope. 'The next step, Sonya,' she put a hand over the phone, '*Your shirt is behind the chair.* – is to find your ideal partner. And it so happens that I have one very cultured gentleman from England currently staying in Moscow.' England always went down well with Russian girls. It had connotations of Shakespeare, afternoon tea and Romantic poets. Though a pot of yoghurt had more culture than her present client.

'English?'

'One hundred per cent. *Your shoes are in the kitchen.*'

'Sorry?'

'Help in the kitchen. All of them, it's a well-known fact. I know that this gentleman has a very busy schedule, Sonya, but I'll try and arrange a meeting that would suit both of you.'

'Oh yes, please.'

'I'm not promising anything, understand?'

'Of course.'

'Well, expect to hear from me.'

'Katya, thank you so much.'

'Not at all. Remember, if it doesn't work out with the first client it might be that you are more suited to a different type.' She paused. 'American, for example.'

'Whatever you say, Katya.'

'Goodbye, Sonya.'

'Goodbye, Katya.'

Katya might have felt a pang of guilt if she'd been able to stop smiling.

The smile was misconstrued. Now dressed, her lover had joined her in the hall. 'Mmm. That's more like it,' he said.

Katya struggled to fight off two engulfing arms.

'I know you must have enjoyed this afternoon as much as I did,' he breathed.

'Well, as they say, all good things must come to an end.' She pushed him away. 'I'll call you. But now you really must go.'

'Promise to call?'

'Promise.'

By the time he turned to go, Katya had gone back to her Rolodex. She looked up as she heard the door open. 'Oh, sorry, I forgot,' she said distractedly. A hopeful glow returned to his eyes. 'What did you say your name was?'

'Sergei.'

She wrote it down. 'I sometimes need a driver. I'll be in touch. 'Bye.' After the door closed, a smile spread across her cheeks, still ruddy from lovemaking. A phone call from Sonya! It was all starting to fall into place.

IV

'Do. You. Sell.' He paused to let her take it all in. 'Nutri. Grain. Bars?'

The woman in what he took to be a bloodstained white overall and pantomime make-up looked blank. The shop was divided into sections, one devoted to bread, one to meat and the other to vegetables. Because of the pyramid display of 'slimma shakes' piled next to one of the cash registers, Terry had thought they might sell health food.

'A nutritious combination of all your daily vitamin requirements,' he continued jauntily, mimicking the advert and ignoring the fact that she appeared to have picked up a meat cleaver and her nostrils were flared like a bull ready to charge. 'Low in fat.'

The hairs on her moles started to quiver.

'I said *low*.' Terry lowered his voice and simultaneously bobbed down. 'In,' he elongated the word. 'Fat.' Seeing nothing that might provide a visual aid, he picked up a ruler lying on the counter, extended it towards her and jabbed it into her. Just above the waist.

A couple of younger assistants with heavy blue eye shadow dived for cover.

Terry looked exasperated. 'Low in fat. What's the matter with you? *Low in fat*. It's hardly surprising you don't know what I'm talking about. Look at you,' he prodded her again. 'More spare tyres than Quickfit.' He started to laugh out loud. One arm, bent at the elbow, rested on his hip, his other hand balanced on the counter.

He grinned down the queue which stretched nearly to the door, half registering the fact that he may have pushed in, and laughed out loud again. 'I said more spare tyres than—'

The meat cleaver missed his little finger by millimetres. The blade sliced an abacus in two.

Terry yanked his hand away as if it had been burnt. 'Well, really. I—'

The woman extracted the cleaver from the abacus and placed one pudgy knee on the counter, heaving her bulk closer to Terry. He felt a rugby tackle round his knees and they landed under the meat counter. Still stiff from the nightclub incident, he had forgotten how tender the left-hand side of his body was. Despite the stab of pain, he felt a palpable sexual thrill when he discovered a woman on top of him.

The meat cleaver sailed past Terry's right ear and shattered a row of pickled cabbage.

'What the *fuck* do you think you are doing?' Katya's voice breathed in his ear.

In a moment of confusion, Terry mistook the vinegar dripping into his ear as a kiss. 'Katya? I didn't know . . .'

'Stand up. Walk to the door, leave the shop and do not, I repeat *do not* turn round.'

'Roger wilco.'

She sounded like a member of the Russian resistance. If she had been in uniform this would definitely have qualified as a four-star sexual fantasy. He got up and made a Nazi salute, turned and goose-stepped out of the shop.

Christ Almighty, sighed Katya as she dusted herself off and made her way over to face the music. God knows what would have happened if she hadn't been stocking up on fish fingers for Sasha. There was no question, the man had to go.

V

The opened letter lay before them.

'Do you think it has anything to do with the Round Table meeting?'

'It's difficult to say. If it is they've been bloody quick off the mark. Even in Moscow a kidnapping takes a couple of days to organise.' Alyosha picked up the letter.

'Careful how you handle it, the police might need it for forensics.'

'For God's sake, Russian police would be lucky if they knew what forensics was, never mind what to do with it. The police here wouldn't issue a parking ticket unless there was something in it for them.' Alyosha sniffed the paper. 'And besides, you don't go to the police with a thing like this.' He slumped back in his seat. 'What a bloody day this has turned out to be.'

'You can say that again,' said Peter, massaging his temples. 'How much do they want again?'

Alyosha looked at the words made up of letters cut from newspapers and magazines. 'Five thousand roubles.'

Peter frowned. 'How much is that in sterling?'

'Christ, what's the matter with you? This isn't a bloody shopping trip to Harrods. May I remind you, you are Russian and your native currency is the rouble.'

'I know, it's just that I still think of everything in pounds. If they knocked a few noughts off, it might make it easier. It just seems so monopoly like.'

'It just seems so *monopoly* like,' Alyosha mimicked. 'While you struggle with your exchange rate, your half-brother is in captivity. These people don't mess about, you know.'

'Yes, quite. Absolutely. Well pointed out.' Peter hesitated. 'So exactly how much is five thousand roubles in sterling?'

Alyosha sighed. 'Sterling. God knows. It's about a quarter of a million dollars.'

'Christ.'

'Exactly.'

'What do we do?'

'Exactly as the ransom note says. We await further instructions.'

'Are we going to pay?'

'That, my stuck-up little friend, depends. In the meantime we tell no one, and that includes sleeping beauty upstairs.'

'She is his mother,' protested Peter.

'And currently about as much use as Boris Yeltsin at an AA meeting. If she does come to and realises he's missing, then we tell her we thought it best while the funeral was being arranged for him to stay with his grandparents in the country.'

'She might check.'

'I doubt it. At the moment she's got more drugs coursing through her blood than a dissident in a psychiatric hospital.'

'My God.'

'What?'

'What about the funeral?'

'Well, on that score, at least, it seems help is at hand.' He flicked over a copy of *Moskovsky Komsomolets*. 'Page twenty-three, after sexual aids, before cut-price terrapins, bulk orders not required.'

Peter screwed up his eyes and started to read like a child. Then he stopped. 'Could you read it for me? You know I've never really got to grips with reading Cyrillic.'

'Oh, for God's sake.' Alyosha caught the paper as it floated back to him. "For the special corpse in your life. Be the envy of your friends. Full funeral service including embalming. For details, including the Al Capone funeral package, call blah blah." What do you think?'

'Sounds disgusting.'

'Exactly. Pass the phone.'

VI

The face had the flat look of an ancient Roman coin. The hooded eyes and protruding chin definitely put it on the BC scale.

The young woman who was tweaking and blow-drying the hair was pulling so hard, Bridges was afraid it would come out in handfuls. Not that the client was likely to complain. His days of telling the hairdresser the water was too cold were definitely over. Amazing, thought Bridges, how *intact* a body stayed on death. Even the hair and nails continued to grow. Or was that an old wives' tale? He noted it as a question for the professor.

He could see the attraction of preserving someone

you loved when they died. The days his own father had spent in a coma before he passed away had been some of the pleasantest they'd shared. Funerary rituals fascinated Bridges. As rites of passage went, his own funeral had always interested him the most. His wedding, a $50 a head buffet, in Susan's parents' New England home, had been noteworthy only for the bottle of vodka he'd consumed in record time (twenty-seven minutes with his best man, Susan's brother, an accountant from Delaware) and the subsequent row. The wedding was full of friends of Susan's mother, the three-Martini lunch brigade, who saw Susan's marriage to a junior government officer as a scandal. Guessing who would attend his funeral was much more difficult. People as yet unmet. It was like knowing that girls were born with all their ova inside them and waiting to see what life would spring from them. Funerals, like the unborn, existed in the imagination only. Maybe there'd be a Jackie O second wife, her heart-rending grief kept in check by a black veil and strength of will and a trio of beautiful daughters leaning on each other for support.

The hairdresser worked in silent concentration. Was she an embalmer, or just seconded from the local *parachmacheskaya*, the interminably long Russian name for barbers? Bridges tried to make himself look useful by rearranging steel tools on the side. They smelt faintly of lighter fuel which left a tinny taste in the mouth, like drinking out of a can.

It was part of his programme to familiarise himself with all aspects of the firm.

Outside, it was nearly dark. He viewed the onset of a

Russian winter with the trepidation of a long-distance swimmer, not knowing if he would make it to the other side.

The institute was in one of Moscow's more attractive districts, not among the endless anonymous high-rises that Russians craved on account of their functioning plumbing systems. He liked the older *rayons*, the buildings of the revolution which were painted in the incongruous pastels of a Greek fishing village.

'*Vot krasivi.*' The woman stood back to admire her afternoon's work. She rummaged in a vanity case and pulled out a handful of half-used women's foundation creams. Automatically he looked at the beautician's own colouring. Mousy with pale freckles. Did she share her make-up with dead people?

She frowned and flicked her head from side to side as she picked one after the other, swinging round to test their colour against the corpse's hair and skin. She settled on a more putty-coloured one and snapped the case shut. Above the smell of formaldehyde Bridges caught a waft of cosmetics which reminded him of his mother's handbag when he was a child.

'My friend, I'm heartened to see you take such a healthy interest in your work.'

Bridges jabbed himself on what looked like a potato peeler as he spiralled to see the professor, who had soundlessly appeared.

'Familiarising myself with the product,' said Bridges, squeezing his spiked finger to see if the potato peeler had drawn blood. God alone knew what sort of diseases you could pick up from a Russian embalming parlour. He'd been horrified to see the professor carry out all his embalming without gloves. Modin was absently twisting the dead man's hair as he spoke to the make-up girl in Russian. He pointed to the bridge of the nose and one of the eye sockets.

'I was just saying, Mr Bridges, that this was a filthy job. The deceased was thirty-nine, though I think you'll agree Alyosha has done a super job on making him look a good ten years younger. He had been shot and garrotted.'

'I thought that cravat looked slightly out of place.'

'We are seeing so much more mutilation these days than ever before. A cruel race, the Russians, Mr Bridges. The Slavic blood makes us very unforgiving.'

Fear bubbled up through Bridges' oesophagus as the thought of mutilation combined with the icy-blue Siberian stare of the man following him. Bridges put it down to coincidence. At the same time he found himself trying to gauge the alcoholic potential of embalming fluid. If a common tipple in Russia was a draught of eau de cologne, how dangerous could it be?

'What did he do?'

'Wrong, or by profession?'

'I was thinking by profession, but either will do.'

'Mr Alexei Ivachenko had recently opened a nightclub on the Garden Ring. White Nights. Maybe you know it.'

Bridges shook his head. There had been a time in Moscow, not so long ago, when a kiosk selling Cinzano had been the nearest the city had got to a nightclub. Now they seemed to blister up like boils.

'Well, Mr Ivachenko, whether he knew it or not, was stepping on the feet of other interests in that part of town. And, it appears, was determined to stand his ground.'

'And now he will shortly be in the ground,' finished Bridges with a bitter smile.

'Precisely. But as you say in English, every cloud has a silver lining.'

'More importantly, every coffin has a silver lining.'

'Or red or royal blue or purple. Yes, you are absolutely right.'

'What service is he going for?'

'The Godfather Two.'

'Which includes?'

'Embalming to last two weeks, oak coffin, service, funeral cortège and wake.'

'I thought that was the Godfather Three?'

'The Godfather Three includes a police cordon.'

'I thought that was Al Capone.'

'The Al Capone is with full orchestra. Really, Mr Bridges, I think a little revision is in order before we go into full operation.'

'Well, our first advert has appeared in the papers and I intend to start a flier campaign in the banks which is where I expect to hit our target audience.'

'Hit our target audience? Very good, Mr Bridges.' Modin started to laugh in terrifying gulps.

Bridges wasn't aware he'd made a joke.

'Oh yes,' guffawed the professor. 'I knew it wasn't a mistake to have a foreigner on board.'

Bridges looked down and saw a drop of blood on his starchy Kazakhstan cotton shirt. He put his bleeding finger in his mouth and then pulled it out when he remembered where it had been. He waited until the laughter had died down.

'Professor, I was wondering if you ever considered that going into business yourself might attract the same sort of problems that seem to have befallen our friend.' He nodded towards the corpse, whose limp hand the professor was massaging with the tenderness of a lover.

'I would say there is no question. Why do you think I have taken on a staff? How do you say it in English? You don't have a dog and bark.' He gulped like a drowning goldfish.

Bridges felt as if he was falling.

CHAPTER SIX

I

'Are you sure we shouldn't be trying to find these kidnappers? Hard would be going ballistic if he . . . if he were still here.' The words hung in the air more heavily than the smoke from Alexander's cigarette.

Peter caught the eye of a headscarved old woman as the trolley bus clattered past them. Alyosha swore on the driver's behalf. The bus driver, a woman so old she looked as if she pre-dated the invention of the combustion engine, stuck her middle finger in the air. Even Alyosha appeared shocked.

The four-wheel-drive Niva weaved in and out of traffic with the deftness of a shuttlecock, random but precise if you knew what you were doing. Alyosha pulled his black woollen hat, which when fully extended doubled as a balaclava, further down his head. He turned to Peter, whose reddened eyes seemed to have retreated into his skull. They reminded Alyosha of miniature dartboards at his pool club. He felt an immediate wave of sympathy.

'Look, believe me, I understand kidnapping.' He

cocked his head to one side as if assessing evidence. 'In fact I used to do a bit of moonlighting for a couple of firms who specialised in it. Nothing's going to happen to him. He'll be treated like the goose who laid the golden egg. Which, in a manner of speaking, is what he is. Keep your head and await further instructions. Trust me.' The speech exhausted him and he sank back into his seat and tore aimlessly at the stuffing. 'Alexander, pull over at this kiosk. I'm dying of thirst here.'

The car veered to the side of the road in front of a hut selling an array of coloured drinks, twinkling like fairy lights.

'Get me a Sprite while you're there.' Peter leant out of the window, succumbing to a hangover from a bottle of Stolychnaya drunk over the course of last night. He watched Alyosha half-heartedly chat up a dark-haired woman struggling to push a pram over wasteland. The body language of the exchange – she smiling, he arms outstretched, suggested to Peter that his friend was on target.

Alyosha returned with two cans.

'How did you get on?'

'Bastard tried to overcharge me.'

'I meant with the girl.'

'Thought it was going to be a LENIN, turned out to be an ENGELS.' Alyosha abbreviated his pulling for ease of reference. A LENIN stood for a leg over expected, no involvement necessary, whereas an ENGELS meant expectation not good for an easy lay.

Peter nodded. 'Bad luck.'

Alyosha frowned, still thinking of his change. 'Still, I

suppose they've got to make money somehow.' He snapped back the ring pull and drank half before wiping the sleeve of his jacket over his mouth. Peter winced and straightened his cuffs.

'I mean to say, each of these guys gives us . . .' Alyosha looked up. 'When I say *us*, I am of course referring to all our underworld brethren. They each give us on average two grand a week. That means they've got to make . . .' He pulled out a calculator from the cavernous pouch of a bum bag bearing the legend 'Lucky Stripe'. 'They would have to make at least that again to stay afloat.' He jabbed a few numbers into the machine as the car dived back into the flow of traffic. 'That would be two hundred dollars a day. Open let's say eighteen hours . . .'

Peter was remembering fondly his seminars in profit and loss and the economies of scale. Extortion did not feature on the syllabus at De Montfort University.

'That's twenty dollars an hour.' Alyosha glanced over his shoulder at the kiosk and it disappeared from sight. 'Say we were his only customer—'

'Alyosha, is there a point to all this?' A globule of Sprite settled unabsorbed on Peter's trouser leg as the car swerved to avoid a jeep.

'Just trying to interest you in what looks like being your future profession.'

'*Extortion?*'

'We prefer to refer to it as security.'

'When, and if, I take over the reins of this . . . empire, I would hope to run it along the lines of fair play.'

'Fair play? This isn't the bloody playing fields of Eton, you know.' He sunk into moody silence and crushed his empty can in his fist. He lobbed it out of the window into the line of oncoming traffic.

Peter put a hand to his hair.

Alyosha said, 'In any case, why couldn't we sort all this out on the phone?'

'He said it would be better if we went to see them. It's part of their mourners' charter. "Our promises we keep, while you wail and weep" is what the brochure said.'

'You're kidding.'

'Sadly not.'

'Bollocks. More like, "You grieve, we thieve". Respect, that's what this is all about. How much did you say it's going to cost us?' Alyosha was digging dirt out from under his nails with the corner of a packet of French cigarettes.

'It depends on the service. What did Tanya say when you told her about the funeral arrangements?'

'Not a lot. Mind you, she's been funnelling those sleeping tablets down her like there's no tomorrow.' Alyosha looked moodily at him. 'She should show a little more respect.'

Peter thought how high respect loomed high on everyone's list of funerary expectations. Not grief or mourning but *respect*.

'What do you mean?'

'He put her up there, didn't he, and now she could as easily fall.' In the uncharted territory of death, you stuck with what you knew – the platitudes of commiseration cards and cheap fiction. 'Besides, she was knocking on a bit.'

The car swerved to avoid a pothole. They braced

themselves against the jolt. Up until a few years ago the twenty-minute journey into town along the Roubleovsky Shosse from the Central Committee dachas to the Kremlin had been one of the smoothest in the country. Now it resembled the surface of the moon.

'Why is he driving this bloody Lada?' asked Alyosha petulantly. The menacing black ZiL of the Party chiefs had long since been replaced bumper to bumper with the blackened windows of four-wheel-drive jeeps. By comparison the rust-stained Lada looked as if it would have struggled to get off the production line in Samara. It stood out like a pair of Bulgarian shoes at a Russian casino.

There was no response from Alexander the driver. Neither of his passengers had expected one. To say Alexander was a man of few words was an understatement. In the ten years Peter had known him, Alexander had been known to speak twice. Alyosha's ambition, along with achieving his full set of Soviet women, was to elicit a complete sentence from Alexander's beard-framed mouth. Once, in a shimmering afternoon four years ago on the banks of Lake Issy Kul, accompanied by a bottle of Moldovan cognac, Alexander was reputed to have sung 'Candle in the Wind' in its entirety. Since then he'd remained as mute as the oracle at Delphi. Conversations with Alyosha, on the other hand, were a bit like lunchtime drinking – irresistible and senseless.

'Alyosha, Tanya is twenty-four.' Peter watched the Lada's windscreen wipers struggle to push away the spray of sludge which a weak midday sun had temporarily released from permafrost.

'But these women have a shorter shelf life than a bottle

of milk. Aside from that, she's got stigma.'

'What do you mean *stigma*? She's not a venereal disease.'

Alyosha's expression, already driven by recent circumstances to profundity, took on the studied gaze of a lecturer. 'It is, in a way, as you say, like the clap. Only worse. Your dad was one of the best-known bosses in Moscow. No-one would go near Tanya. She's sort of *shop soiled*. It's the equivalent of Indian widows throwing themselves on the funeral pyre.'

'Oh, really, professor. Well, we'll just have to see if that's a service on offer at Bodies Beautiful, won't we?'

Alyosha's face was a mixture of horror and delight. 'You don't actually think they—'

'No, you prat, I don't actually think they provide a burning bonfire for grieving widows.'

Peter leant forward to tap Alexander on his brown leather shoulder. 'I think it's next left, just past Oktaybraskaya Ploschad.'

The driver nodded in mute acknowledgement as he punched the dashboard cigarette lighter with a clenched fist. The knuckles showed blue tattoos, the sign of an ex-con. Peter wondered if Alexander's Trappist silence stemmed from his time spent in Russian prisons, in which he was rumoured to have had more stretches than a boxful of elastic bands.

'Poor Alexander,' hissed Alyosha in a theatrical stage aside. 'I think he's taking this worse than any of us. They went back years, ever since Hard Currency's emerald days in Yekaterinburg.'

'Really?' Peter was staring moodily out of the window,

contemplating how little he still had in common with the city of his birth. 'What do you mean *emerald* days?' Was it like Picasso's blue period? Shelley's Italian summer? Chekhov's ennui?

Alyosha looked up. 'Emeralds, you know. Their wholesale theft of precious stones direct from the factory. He netted millions.'

Peter sighed. 'Hang on, Alexander.' He stared out of the window. 'I think this is it. Yes, the Institute of, does that say Cosmetology?'

'Yes,' Alyosha replied tiredly. Reading was yet another of the duties he had had to take on for Peter. 'Pull in anywhere.'

They slammed the doors shut in a purposeful echo. Alexander was sucking on a cigarette, staring into the middle distance. Peter clutched his purple and blue scarf, the colours of De Montfort University, which he wore over a Burberry. His cords, described on the label as jumbo, were the colour of sour milk. His hair was styled into what he liked to think of as a Byronic fop. Another of his De Montfort affectations, encouraged by Em and her friends, was running his fingers through it while loosely shaking his head.

Alyosha looked him up and down. 'Christ, is that an Aston Villa scarf you're wearing?' Ever since Russian TV had taken to showing the premiership, Alyosha had become an expert on English football. He was wearing his Tommy Hilfiger jacket over shiny tracksuit bottoms over his Nike Airs. 'With that haircut you could be bloody—' A blast of 'Yankee Doodle Dandy' came from Alyosha's jacket pocket.

'What the hell is that?' Peter asked as Alyosha pulled up the antenna and gave a beep.

'Hello. Brazil Nut here.'

Peter shuddered. With the demise of his mentor, Alyosha had decided he was old enough and experienced enough to have a nickname of his own. It was as important a rite of passage for the would-be gangster as a young Masai warrior's need to kill a lion with his bare hands. After a long discussion with anyone with the patience to listen – in this case the Tadzhik cook who was rumoured not to understand Russian – he'd come up with Brazil Nut – because they were hard and Brazil was his favourite football team. It also had the potential to be shortened to Brazzer which he liked for its associations with female underwear.

'Calm down, calm down,' Alyosha said. He looked imploringly at Peter.

'Who is it?' hissed Peter.

Alyosha frowned and shook his head and turned his back, staying close to the car. Even the most adept mobile users liked to hover near a fixed object. A gust of wind caught his tracksuit bottoms, making them balloon like a spinnaker.

'What did it say?' Alyosha sounded worried.

Peter watched a bird the size of an eagle crap on the bronze head of a statue in the middle of the courtyard. He tried to test his Cyrillic by reading who it was and whether Bodies Beautiful commemorated the dead in a bas-relief.

'What do you reckon?' Alyosha had snapped the phone back into its fleecy home.

'About what?'

'About all *that*.'

'About all *what*?' Peter raised his voice in irritation and above the wind.

'The hair. His frigging hair. Tanya reckons she got a letter today with a lock of hair in it.'

'Oh shit,' said Peter sinking on to the base of the statue. 'We'll never get her sober now.'

'Shit indeed,' agreed Alyosha. 'And it's on your trousers.' He pointed at Peter's left leg.

II

Even Terry had to admit he hadn't been feeling himself. Maybe he was still recovering from the lead-lined blow to the side of his face (note to self: could he sue Clive?) from that demented troll at the nightclub. Maybe it was the culture shock – the strangeness of the alphabet, the lack of a coherent customer care ethic, the peculiarly militarised world in which he found himself, the number of soldiers on the street. Perhaps it was the women themselves, their customs – drinking champagne at lunchtime (weren't they supposed to be communists? Not even Tony Blair's lot did that). Maybe, though, it was just the lack of food.

The taxi had dropped him off ten minutes ago. Even though he said it himself, he couldn't help thinking he was getting the hang of this Russian language. He'd managed to scale down one of the world's most complex languages; the key was, quite simply, t add *ski* to the end of every word. The square nearest to the institute was October *ski* something and there were several Leninskis.

The money was posing more of a problem. Previously he'd overcome the counting part by handing out a wad of brightly coloured notes and allowing the taxi driver/shop keeper/Metro ticket vendor to pick at it like a bird of prey. But he did seem to be getting through it remarkably quickly. Hadn't Katya exchanged $500 worth for him just the other day? Where had it gone? He'd calculated a hamburger and green salad with Masha, she of the wig fame, had set him back nearly two hundred. But then she had said the word 'Manhattan' to the cocktail waitress more times than a New York A-Z.

There was the loss of money and the lack of sleep. He'd returned to his monkish truckle bed at midnight only to wake up in the early hours covered in unopened condoms which he'd optimistically placed under the pillow. He'd taken their scaly exterior to be cockroaches and leapt out of the bed in horror, simultaneously concussing himself on a dangerously overhanging book-case. By the time he'd added it to the 'Why Clive Must Pay' list it had been nearly five. Sleep was almost as distant a memory as food.

No, food was definitely the order of the day. Especially bearing in mind the task ahead of him. He looked around the concrete slabbed square, where the taxi had expelled him in a bubble of benzene and cigarette smoke. He fingered the passport in his jacket pocket. True, Katya's husband didn't look much like him, but how choosy would a hospital be? The plan was so cunning. So *daring*. So brave. He was starting to feel like Andy McNab behind enemy lines.

Why was he suddenly so caught up with military

images? He felt under siege, fighting for freedom over oppression, truth over lies, choice over dictatorship. He was on his feet. 'Freedom from oppression. Free gym membership for all,' he boomed out.

A woman dressed from head to toe in black (surely they didn't have women vicars here as well) looked up from minding a toddler and gave him a benign smile. A couple jigsawed in an embrace came apart and laughed.

Terry, feeling conspicuous, sat down abruptly. It was very much time to raise the old blood sugar levels, he thought. He looked round for a McDonald's, the international purveyor of more saturated fat than a Japanese whaling ship, and saw none. He thought he might even risk one of those *pectopah* places which Katya had assured him meant restaurant in Russian. Then he remembered the globules of grease that seemed to float on everything on the menu.

It was this morning's glance at a thermometer, tacked to the kitchen window, reading minus five, that clinched it. He strode across the square back towards the Metro where a youth with a lunar complexion was selling confectionery and pornographic magazines which looked as if they'd been photocopied.

'Snickers*ski* bar*ski*. Please*ski*.'

The boy didn't flinch.

Terry tried again. 'Mar*ski* Bar*ski*. Now*ski*.'

Not only nothing, but crater face served a woman behind him.

Terry was just about to give up on the chocolate to sate himself on some pornograph*ski* when it dawned on him. The vendor couldn't equate him (body of finely chiselled

177

athlete) with this bizarre dietary request. He would have to level with him.

He gave his best master-to-pupil smile. 'Yes, my friend, usually I steer well clear of the old Snickerskis, but I am,' he winked, 'leader of an Arctic exploration and we have to keep the old calorificski levelski definitely upski.' He smiled. 'If you get my meaningski.'

The youth's look seemed to go straight through him. He picked up the chocolate and passed it in silence to Terry. Even his volcanic skin seemed to be bubbling in anger. He snatched at the 10 rouble note held in Terry's upturned palm and went back to studying the paper.

Like a caveman Terry hauled the confectionery back to a bench in the most secluded corner of the silver birch-lined square, and set about devouring it in undisturbed silence. The first wave of sugar hit his brain like a vodka shot, a soaring euphoria he never thought it would have been possible to achieve from food.

He rammed the rest of the bar into his mouth with the ferocity of a bulimic. Toffee and chocolate coated his teeth. A stream of discoloured saliva cascaded over his chin. He had to have more. The craving to saturate himself with this sticky nectar was overwhelming, an aching yearning he'd last felt when the Swedish channel refused his credit card. The guilt was the same.

He lumbered back to the teenager now sitting on an upturned orange crate. 'Moreski. I must have moreski,' he groaned, lurching at the cardboard container and thrusting a confetti of notes onto the stand before retreating to his lair.

After the fourth he started to slow down. Strange. He

was calming down now, feeling nothing but the urge to sleep, like a bear that has feasted on salmon's eyes and needs to lie down until the spring. He looked at his watch: 11.10. He really should be getting on. If nothing else, he wanted to make the appointment today. Start the final, most essential stage of his reinvention.

When he woke it was just after two. A fine layer of snow had settled on the ridges of his clothes, tatty clothes brought deliberately for his operation. He had to look the part. His clothes were so unfashionable he'd had to dig them out of his BR drawer reserved for manmade fabrics and anything brown. BR: before reinvention. Before Grace had left. Even the thought of her brought a funny taste to his mouth.

His tongue glazed his plaque-encrusted teeth and he cupped his hands in front of his mouth and puffed out to see if his breath smelt. He caught the bitter smell of air belching from a pedal bin. He had a post-binge headache. A nagging worry from the pit of his stomach that only exercise ever quietened. The stale breath made him think of Grace. He thought of her with a venom no worse than the day she'd walked out. The letter had even been written on a notelet from her *second drawer*. Cheap paper with two hedgehogs in the corner, which he happened to know were not her best. Paper from a 99p pad to end a decade of cohabitation.

Terry chewed the skin on the inside of his mouth. How he hated her obsession with furry animals! Save the Spanish donkeys, stop people eating dogs; she'd even had one of those chequebooks that had 'payee only' tattooed to the nose of some bloody beaver. As if a love of small

179

animals somehow absolved you from paying £1.99 for a Fray Bentos pie.

His head thumped. She was *unfulfilled*. She had to *find herself*, she'd written. How did she think he *found himself* after nearly fifteen years selling conservatories. He'd tell her. He *found himself* pretty pissed off.

Eight months of boarding the 147 bus for a WI for a class in Ikebana, which in reality was eight months of Women's Assertiveness Training, had done it. He should have smelt a rat when the only foliage introduced over the course of two terms was a sheaf of plastic ivy to hide the pipes in the downstairs toilet. He'd give her *reaching out to the inner me, finding the hidden child*.

Christ, he was cold. One thing about manmade fibres, they didn't keep you warm. With the suddenness of a Siberian blast, he knew he couldn't go through with it. Not yet. He fingered the passport in his pocket and looked at the absurd cheapness of his clothes. He would do it, but not today. A manoeuvre like this took precision timing. Guts. This was a recce only. He was a foot soldier in the war against . . . Against what? Against mediocrity and polyester. And like a military campaign, the strategy had to be in place.

He put his Man At C&A-clad arm out to hail a cab, thinking as he did so what a difficult word *Taxiski* was to say.

III

Again came the insistent ring of an international call.

Katya shut the kitchen drawer. Even the phone company seemed to have rigged it so foreign calls sounded more important than Russian. Please let it not be Baz again – no, he'd still be sleeping off the excesses of the night before. And please not a stray lonely European drop-out. Katya had become a number in black books from Reykjavik to Rome. *Try Katya in Moscow, she'll set you up. Social misfits and physical freaks her speciality.* She picked up the receiver.

'Katya? It's Clive.'

'Clive, hello.' Katya stood to attention.

'Not much time. Calls are bloody expensive. We should be e-mailing. Embrace technology, Katya. That's the future.' He paused as if waiting for the telegram-taker to catch up. 'How's he getting on?'

'Who?'

'Little, Large, Big, Small. Small, man with no hair.' On the rare occasions Katya thought of Clive she imagined a general astride a campaign table sending plastic armies of single men to open up the eastern front.

'Very well. He seems to be enjoying himself.'

'Copped off yet?'

'I'm sorry?'

'Rumpty tumpty. How's your father. Has he had any yet?'

'No, not yet. Early days, though. He seems quite fussy.' She thought of Masha.

'On what he's paying he should be happy with a one-legged leper.'

'Quite.'

'How many have you got on your books?'

181

'Oh, about three hundred,' she lied.

'Top notch or old has-beens? We really need to update the files this end. Also, I think it's time to get on the Net.'

'Quite.'

'Technology is the way ahead. The World Wide Web will reap dividends, Katya. All these nerds are on the Net.'

'Quite.' Katya rarely knew what Clive was talking about. 'Quite' usually seemed to keep him happy.

'South America, Katya. Cuba. They worry me, I don't mind admitting it.' In the background Katya heard a whistle.

'Really?'

'Economy in Brazil. Rock bottom. Women, highly skilled in the bedroom department, anxious to leave. Not just that. Good in the kitchen. Then there's China. They're coming at us from every angle. The whole Far Eastern economy gone to rat shit. But as I always say, we've got one thing on our side. And what is it, Katya?'

'Country about to sink into civil war?'

'No, Katya. Whiteness. Our women are Cau-bloody-casian. Men don't want to let it be known that their lifelong partner comes from a catalogue, like a set of garden chairs. Our men want to be able to walk to the supermarket with pride.' He thought about that. 'Or send them to the supermarket with pride.'

'Quite. Do you want me to do anything in particular?'

'Get that little man laid and start another recruiting drive. ASAP.'

'OK. I forget, what's the commission on Mr Small?'

'I'm feeling generous, Katya. Best form of defence is attack. We need testimonials. Five hundred dollars for a screw, the grand for a fiancée. Oh, and Katya?'

'Yes?'

'Any progress on the love boat down the Volga? Got the slogan. *More than a girl in every port. Use your cock in every dock.* Aggressive marketing, that's what's required. Any thoughts?'

'No, it's all going very well. Very well,' she lied.

'That's my girl. I'll be seeing you.'

Katya longed for the day when she would be able to tell Clive where he could stick his love cruises up the Volga. But until then he remained her biggest money spinner. She made a mental note of Clive's requests and turned into the kitchen with a heart heavier than a Russian blini.

She paused by the cooker and thought of Sasha's latest dietary fad. 'Only orange food this week, Mum.' She knew she should have stuck to her guns, but with Sasha, the path of least resistance was always best. Not so long ago he'd become convinced that over-use of aluminium pots led to senile dementia; he had cited – with some justification, Katya had to concede – the strange kleptomania of his aunt as a case history in point. He'd taken to this orange food obsession with relish; it included sweet corn, naturally, which just scraped in at the far end of the colour spectrum. In fact, Katya thought as she threw another half packet of fish fingers into the Tefal frying pan, Sasha was eating a lot, even by his standards.

'Sasha?'

'Yes, Mum?' He looked up from a copy of *Forbes* magazine. Unable to read the words, he liked to study the lifestyle.

'Have you been feeding Leonid with your food?'

'No, Mum,' he answered a little too quickly.

'Then can you explain why our current grocery bill approaches the Russian debt to the World Bank?'

'The under-tens require an average calorific intake of three thousand kj daily,' he replied, stressing the daily.

Katya tried to equate the contents of the frying pan with the platter held by a bearded trawler man on the packet. Sasha returned to his magazine.

'Sasha?'

'Yes, Mum,' he said exasperatedly.

'You're not *selling* it to that man next door, are you?'

'No!' he tried to sound shocked but Katya could tell he was kicking himself for a missed opportunity. 'Why? Can't he get his own food?' he asked cautiously.

'He *can* get his own food. He just can't get the food he likes.' Katya was opening a tin of spaghetti hoops, aware that with characteristic ease Sasha had changed the subject.

He tutted. 'Oh, Mum, can't I have baked beans?'

'You'll eat what you're given.' It was a small but, she felt, important point.

IV

Bridges jumped when he heard the doorbell. He dropped the Russian manual of embalming that Professor Modin had lent to him onto the desk, where a Russian/English dictionary was jammed open at the page containing the word 'corpse'.

'Customer,' he heard the professor call out from the

laboratory. Bridges stood up and tried to tidy the desk of an unemptied ashtray and four dirty coffee cups.

Modin had told him to expect a lull before the winter set in, when bodies tended to go straight into the Moskva before it froze over. But the advert had reaped dividends. As Bridges walked to the door he felt like a cartoon character whose eyes showed dollar signs. He urged himself to relax as he opened it. If the professor was up to his elbows in embalming, he helped with the customers. After four days of learning his spiel by heart he could just about cope with the Russian language.

At the door were two men, both in their twenties. The taller one looked as if he should be having tea at the Ritz, the shorter one resembled an international soccer hooligan.

Bridges was two sentences into his speech when the taller one, with the hair, stopped him.

'Do you speak English?' The accent was flawless.

'Actually, yes. I'm from the States.'

'What a curious profession for an American,' he said with a wry smile which Bridges took exception to. He sounded like a stuck-up Brit.

'Well, it's a long story.' The shorter one was looking round the office, making the sort of motion with a cigarette that one of the Marx Brothers did with a cigar.

'He wants an ashtray,' said the taller one, as if speaking for a recalcitrant toddler.

'Oh, right.' Bridges passed him a heavy black dish which still showed the grey traces of his earlier mental travail.

'Sorry, I should introduce myself. My name is Peter Raevitch, and this is my,' he paused, 'assistant, Alyosha.'

185

They both looked at Alyosha, who was finishing his cigarette with the frenzied intensity of a condemned man. He smiled and nodded.

'Yes, we spoke earlier. Your father recently . . .' Bridges stopped. This was precisely why he had devised his Questionnaire For the Bereaved, so he wouldn't have to enter the mourners' world which he had last visited eighteen years ago when his father had died of a heart attack.

'Passed away,' supplied the English speaker.

Luckily these two seemed to have come to terms with their grief, thought Bridges.

There was a brief silence. Alyosha, unconscious of the solemnity of the moment, started whistling the Soviet national anthem.

Bridges coughed. 'Usually at this time I ask our mourners to answer a few questions.' Peter Raevitch looked up. 'On paper,' continued Bridges. 'In another room.'

In case the misery of the recently bereaved was infectious, he liked to keep them at arm's length. Besides, dealing with the public in any size, shape or form had never been one of his fortes. That was why the faceless bureaucracy of Arlington had suited him so well. It also avoided stretching his nascent embalming lexicon.

'Would you like to follow me to our mourners' antechamber?' Bridges led them down a corridor covered in black and white pictures of, according to Modin, some of embalming's most celebrated sons and daughters.

The pair shuffled behind him, speaking in Russian. After they had walked some fifty yards they came to a small boxroom which, in the glory days of the 1960s when the bodies of communist world leaders were queuing up to be preserved, was used for admin. Bridges sighed as he closed the door. That was another one in the bag, literally.

'It reeks in here,' Alyosha said, pretending to hold his breath. After a few seconds he noisily exhaled. 'What was that bloke? American?'

He ignored him. 'You can always tell an American by their obsession with tasselled loafers. And did you see that jacket? It was so green, it could have been made out of pool-table felt.'

'Lursha!'

Peter nodded and started massaging his temples.

'Strange job for a—'

'Lursha, can we get on?'

The room was windowless and gave the impression of being cramped although it only contained two chairs and a table on which had been placed a vase of plastic pink flowers. A Russian icon stared down at them. Inexplicably a video of *Godfather II*, dubbed in Russian, was also on the table.

'Fine. Shoot.' Alyosha sank into a plastic moulded seat which bore more cigarette scars than an inmate of a Nicaraguan jail.

Peter picked up the photocopied paper onto which a silver foil cross had been pasted. 'Actually, could you do the honours?' He sounded sheepish. 'You know my reading isn't very good.'

Alyosha nodded with the weariness of the needed. 'Name. That's easy.' He accepted the Biro Peter extended to him, wrote and paused. His tongue circled from one side of his mouth to the other. 'Height. What do they want to know that for?'

Peter shrugged. 'I suppose it affects the amount of stuff they need.'

'What stuff?'

'Fluid. Embalming stuff.'

'How tall was he?'

'Big. One-eighty?'

'Weight. How much did he weigh?' Violin music suddenly filled the room. They both jumped as if it was poisoned gas.

'Not a clue. Would Tanya know?'

Alyosha tapped the Biro on the melamine table in thought. 'I'd doubt it. Anyway, she's not been conscious for the last seventy-two hours.'

'Put one-eighty and ninety-six kilos.'

'Any serious disease?'

Peter looked aghast. 'Yes, he's *dead*. How much more serious do they need?'

'No, I imagine they mean did he suffer from any diseases when he was alive?'

'No idea. Why do they want to know?'

'I'll put no. Cause of death. If violent please state if death was by bullet wounds, stabbing, poisoning. If other please state. Would you get a discount for a Jiffy bag?' Alyosha was smirking and intently tattooing the back of his left wrist with the Biro.

'Put suffocation.'

'How long do you want the embalming to last – one week, one month, one year? If other, please state.'

'What do you think?'

'He's your dad. How long do you want the old geezer hanging around?'

Peter shuddered as the details of this embalming started to sink in. Maybe a conventional by-the-board funeral would be better. 'Do you think it's too late to call the whole thing off? I mean it's all so *sordid*.'

'It's respect,' said Alyosha gravely.

'Let's go for a week then. What happens with it? I mean him. Does he go back to the dacha?'

'We'll ask. Do you wish to preserve the internal organs separately?'

'Jesus Christ. What for, a fry-up?'

'Look, I'm just reading the questions. We'll put no then. That's the personal details. Now the service. Casket required. Lead-lined? Gold leaf? Copper? Crystal? Oak?'

'Put crystal.'

'The service. Orthodox, Catholic, Christian, other?'

'Orthodox.'

Alyosha paused and read: 'Now go to Box Four. Will you be requiring the services of a priest?'

'S'pose so.'

'He did have quite a lot to do with the Church.'

'Really?' Peter looked up.

'Yeah, we used to nick the gold leaf from the tops of them. Do you think I can smoke in here?'

'Don't see why not. Alyosha, let's tick Box Four for priest.'

'Music? Tick. Police to cordon off road? Tick. Armed guard?'

'You'll look after that, will you, Lursha?'

'No problem. Cemeteries are my speciality.' He smiled ghoulishly. 'Cars required? If yes, see Box F. Right, Box F. Mercedes Series 600, BMW, Rolls-Royce.'

'What about a ZiL? Let's keep it traditional.'

'A ZiL would be good. Traditional. If it was good enough for Stalin, it should be good enough for Hard. Last question. Do we want to deliver it or will they pick it up?'

'What do you think?' asked Peter.

'Make them pick him up. It's the least they can do. Yeah, we'll put delivery required. Shows a bit more respect.' Right, final thing before signature of the prime mourner. Will you be requiring the will-reading service?'

Their blank expressions met somewhere above the *Godfather II* video and the Russian icon.

'Shit, that's a point,' said Peter. 'I'd forgotten. What about his will?'

V

She was wearing her signing blouse, on which the third button undid if she arched her back and pushed out her chest. The knock had gone unanswered. She rang the bell. Surely he hadn't gone out? He barely had the initiative to make a cup of—

'Katya. Good afternoon. Come in. I was just working out.'

'Working out what?'

'No, you misunderstand me. I was *doing* a workout.' He was dressed in a pair of shiny blue shorts and a singlet.

An oval of sweat had formed on his chest. Hairs sprang from around the V neck. He gestured her in.

'I've just had Clive on the phone from the UK. Reds In the Bed? Remember?'

'Yes, yes, of course.' Terry was towelling himself and flexing his chest muscles simultaneously. He was hardly listening to Katya, who couldn't help noticing that her catalogue had been left open at page 145, showing Yelena Busterova, twenty-one years, wearing a see-through negligee.

Katya smiled lazily and walked slowly towards Terry, who backed away. Katya used a voice she thought might be described as girlish and pulled her blouse tightly down over her breasts. She craned her neck. 'He's concerned that you aren't getting . . .' She had him with his back against the wall. She arched her back and the button popped open. 'Enough, how can I put it? *Satisfaction* from the service.' She flashed her eyes. 'Can I ask you, Terry, if you are *satisfied*,' she fiddled with the undone button under which her black bra was visible, 'with what you've been getting?'

A vein in Terry's forehead was throbbing like a police light and he'd started to perspire again. He adjusted his shorts. 'Well, actually, I would like to . . .'

Katya ran her tongue over her top lip and pulled her blouse still tighter. She looked down at her breasts, where Terry's gaze met hers.

Terry swallowed. 'No, actually I think you can tell Clive that I'm very happy. Really. That I have no complaints on that score. At all.'

Katya relaxed and whipped a piece of paper from behind

her back. 'Good. I wonder if you'd be good enough to put that in writing. It's just in case Clive should question the quality of the service.' She paused. 'You do understand, don't you, Terry?' She smiled. 'What huge muscles you have.'

'Really? Do you think so? My upper body workout has—'

'Please sign here.' She thrust a pen into his hand.

'Te-rry. Sm-all,' he said and signed with a flourish.

'Good, that sorts out any misunderstandings.' When Katya suspected that a sexual encounter was doubtful, she liked to get it in writing that it in no way reflected on the quality of the hospitality the client had received. 'Now, what about Masha? Are you seeing her again?'

'No, we decided it wasn't a meeting of minds.' Terry looked down. 'In fact, I may be absent over the next few days.'

'Really?'

'Yes, I'm afraid the Official Secrets Act restricts me from saying too much at this stage. Affairs of state. Lives at risk. Protection of the innocent.'

'What a pity. It's just that I have a special woman who is dying to meet you.'

'Really?' He sounded cautious.

'Yes. Her name is Sonya.' She produced Sonya's holiday snaps from her bag.

'Oh my goodness me.' Terry looked at the blonde woman in the bikini with the evening sun sinking behind her. A cross between Uma Thurman and Barbara Windsor. He decided on the spot. He would make inquiries, but the operation could wait.

VI

'Where would he have kept it?' It was the first time they'd been in Hard's office since the accident. Peter avoided the place on the floor where the body had been found. He imagined the outline if the police had drawn a chalk line round it, like they did in American films. A barrel-shaped body with a rectangular head where the Jiffy bag had been. He tried hard not to look at the fax machine, on which he was sure he could still make out the buttock prints of his stepmother.

The light from the Anglepoise lamp on the desk bounced off the windows, showing their reflections. Apart from the unheralded intrusion a week ago, it was one of the few occasions Peter had ever been in his father's study.

'I know he's got a safe in here somewhere,' he said. 'And I'm sure he mentioned a safety deposit box.'

Alyosha yanked open the bottom drawer of a filing cabinet. 'One Uzi, four grenades and a pistol of,' he fingered the weapon, 'unknown origin.'

'Any sign of a will?'

'No. Are you sure he had one?'

'I spoke to Mum this afternoon—'

'How is she?'

'Very well, actually. She says there was a will drawn up when they divorced. I imagine she didn't want Tanya getting everything.'

'Fair enough.'

'If he died intestate—'

'In what?'

'Without a will, she'll get everything. And while that

might benefit Messrs Armani, Dior and Lacroix, it would leave Mum pretty penniless.' Peter was rifling through the second drawer of Hard's oak desk. 'Can you read this? I can never read joined-up Russian writing.' He passed Alyosha a sheaf of papers.

'Contracts, mainly.'

'You'd better hang on to them, then.'

'Why?'

'Christ, I don't know. Someone's going to have to take over this lot. And I've a horrible suspicion it's going to be me.'

'Well, in that case, I'd bin them as soon as possible.'

'Why? I'll need all types of contracts for, I don't know,' Peter shrugged and went back to the filing cabinet, 'tax.'

Alyosha shook his head in pity. Peter noticed the gold hoop earring he usually sported in his left ear had been replaced by a cross. He put it down to respect.

'Point number one. First rule of Russian business is that no one, I repeat, no one who is anyone pays any tax.'

'Really?' Peter murmured distractedly. He'd just discovered a box file devoted to photocopies of his father's and, he imagined, Tanya's genitals. He snapped the lid shut.

'Why do you imagine the Russian Cabinet has more reshuffles than a dodgy casino?'

'Something to do with politics?' The reply was vague. Peter was trying to shed the grainy impression of his father's foreskin.

'Wrong. Because every time the latest finance minister decides it's time to pay the miners in Donetz – who last received a wage sometime before nineteen seventeen – the business interests, such as your father, make sure he's sacked.'

'Oh.'

'Why do you think the tax authorities here are armed with semi-automatics?'

Peter didn't reply.

'And besides, George Soros, these aren't those sort of contracts.'

'What do you mean?'

Alyosha held one towards the light and read, 'I.V. Potanin to be paid ten thousand dollars in the event of the death of one Ivan "Big Cheese" Basurin.' Alyosha let out a whistle. 'S.D. Horavitch to be paid seven thousand pounds in the event of – blimey, I always wondered who'd done that one.'

'I see,' said Peter meekly.

'There's more.'

'No, thank you, Lursha, that'll be enough for the time being.' Peter picked up a steel peg from the box he was going through. 'What sort of a weapon is this?' He passed it for Alyosha's scrutiny.

Alyosha turned it over in his palm. 'That, unless I'm very much mistaken, is a nipple clamp.'

Peter slumped down on to the edge of a purple velvet chaise longue. 'Maybe you should do this. I'm not sure I've got the stomach for it.'

'Hang on. This one's marked personal.' Alyosha was burrowing through a hanging file in the top drawer of a cabinet. 'Arms bought, arms sold. Banks bought, banks sold, bank fraud. Bribes. Charity – *charity* – oh, charitable donations to. Quite organised, your dad, wasn't he?'

'Alyosha, is it there?'

'Hang on. Underground, underworld. Vice, refer to category.' He halted. 'Bloody hell.'

'What?'

'Will.' He pulled out a sepia-coloured sheet with a gold-embossed cherub in each corner. 'The last will and testament of Gleb Alexanderavitch Raevitch aka Hard Currency.' His eyes scanned the page. His expression became solemn. Then there was the beginnings of a smile. 'The old sod.'

'What is it?'

'You're not going to like it. You're *really* not going to like it.'

VII

'It's Katya. Sorry to call you so late. I'm not disturbing you, am I?'

It was ten past eleven and she'd been in bed since nine thirty. She forced herself to sound awake. 'No, no, not at all.'

'How's Nikita?'

'Fine, thank you, we're both well.'

'Good. Listen, I've spoken to the English gentleman who is staying with me at the moment. Remember?'

'Yes, of course.'

'It seems your luck's in. I've checked his diary and it appears he may have some free time between meetings and in fact might be able to see you tomorrow evening. What do you think?'

Sonya hesitated.

'Hello?'

'Hello, yes, I was just thinking. He really asked to see me?'

'Amazing, isn't it? What do you think?'

'Gosh. Yes, tomorrow evening would be fine.' She lowered her voice in case the call had woken Nikita. She was anxious to keep Katya a secret. 'Where should we meet?'

'Sonya, this line is terrible.'

'Where should we meet? You will be there too, won't you?'

'Yes, I'll come too. This Englishman,' she stressed every syllable, 'is very keen on keep fit. That's very good, don't you think?'

'Er, I suppose so.'

Well, let's meet outside his gym. Klebny Pereulok, close to the square. It's called Premier Fitness.' She paused for Sonya to write it down. 'Let's say seven.'

'OK. Great. Well, I'll see you there then.'

''Bye.'

'Oh, Katya? What should I wear?'

'I usually recommend something short in the leg and low at the front.'

'Oh.'

'It's just that that's what western women wear and the gentlemen are more used to it. They're quite traditional, you see.'

'OK, then. I'll try. See you at seven.'

'I'm looking forward to it.'

Sonya put the phone down and stared at the paper in front of her.

'Who was that?' Nikita called from the kitchen.

'Nothing for you to worry about, darling.' She tucked the instructions in the pocket of her nightdress and smiled as she went back to bed.

CHAPTER SEVEN

I

He had jolted awake with a feeling of deep unease in the pit of his stomach. It was more than just a fear of piecing together the events of last night.

Then Father Georgi Bulgakov remembered. It was Friday. God, how he hated Fridays. The runt end of the religious week. Just when the rest of the world was preparing for sloth and excess, he was embarking on the weary road to Calvary, culminating in a Sunday.

What it meant – and your average parishioner totally failed to appreciate this – was simply no decent food. If there was one thing that had lured him into the priesthood, it had been the food. That and a religious mother who was attempting to atone for her husband's affairs by offering up her only son as sacrifice. Two things had made him acquiesce: the opportunity to miss his National Service. Not even communists, he'd thought – wrongly, as it transpired – could send the clergy to the front. And the food. Never, in any culture on earth, did you ever see an un-fed priesthood. From rotund medieval monks to plump pontiffs, they never looked short of a meal. The money in recent years had been a bonus. But Fridays meant famine. Very few people served a decent buffet on a Friday. Meat was at a minimum and rarely was there alcohol, if at all.

Father Georgi raised his finely sculpted head a couple of inches from his pillow and exhaled in a memory of stale Campari and peppered steak. He looked round. Through the double-glazed Italian-style windows with shutters he could see that it had started to snow. Worse and worse. Unless he wanted to freeze his bollocks off he'd have to dig out his salopettes, which usually kept the worst of the Moscow winter at bay under his cassock. Bollocks, that was a point. He levered his head up another couple of inches and scanned the room like a periscope.

What it meant – what the debauchery of last night translated into – was that he'd have to iron his cassock before he went out. At moments like these, even Father Georgi had to admit there was always a payback for self-indulgence.

Ironing his cassock was an hour-long operation, even after he'd cleared his desk, which doubled as an ironing board, of his Toshiba laptop and the smattering of red, gold and green icons full of moody-faced elongated men who looked like he felt. He tried to focus on the garment, discarded at the end of his bed like a reproachful black labrador waiting to be taken out. And just as smelly. The unmistakable odour of religion – dampness and incense.

Georgi Bulgakov, a religious man of twelve years' standing, extended a well-toned though hesitant leg backwards. Had he, or had he not, brought that woman from the restaurant back last night? His ankle met with no resistance. Relief. He'd made it home on his own. He tried to remember how. Taxi, car, horse-drawn carriage, hovercraft? Nothing. In fact since the indecent proposal in the kitchen, his memory appeared to have ceased to function. What had been the girl's name? He'd have laid a bet that her legs would have parted as easily as the Red Sea. What was it about women and priests? They were so eager to defrock him. That in itself, even without food, would have been reason enough for the five years in the seminary.

He struggled to find his watch, knocking over as he did so a bottle of holy water which he made a mental note he must stop drinking to stave off a hangover. Father Georgi thought back to his performance last night. It had been a restaurant opening, always one of his favourite blessings because it guaranteed a knees-up after the service. Well, he called it a service, but as his freelance career had progressed, he'd refined the speaking part to a succinct fifteen minutes. The singing had been scrapped four years ago. In general he found his latter-day parishioners preferred it short.

Of all the different types of people Father Georgi came into contact with, there were two he could identify at twenty paces: old-style believers and virgins. Both for different reasons made the hair on the back of his neck stand up. With both he knew he had to push the boat out a bit, lay it on thicker. Luckily the Authentic New Orleans Bar and Grill had been as lacking in spirituality as it had been in Creole. Counting the dressing-up part, he had got it down to less than half an hour.

He drew up a mental profit and loss account for the week. Three Cherokee jeeps, $100 each, two *nouveaux riches* apartments, $200 each, one new vodka distillery and a shop, $75 each. Not bad.

Today he had a dacha and a one-time parachute factory which now specialised in tampons and a funeral which he needed to bone up on. Funerals, he thought with distaste, seemed so passé. He rarely had to do them, and then it was usually as a favour. To cap it all, it was Friday, which meant a very limited wake afterwards. He spent all of Lent on an incognito early holiday in the Crimea.

It was as he was imagining the topless sunbathers oiled and laid out along the Black Sea like sun-dried tomatoes (he would pack the cassock in case of emergencies) that he heard the key in the lock.

'Good morning, Father. It's only me.'

In shock he smeared cigarette ash on the sheet – shock mingled with relief. Mrs Pegova could at least iron his cassock.

'I see you're still in bed, Father,' she said, crossing herself as she walked in from the corridor.

'Indeed, I'm afraid I was up half the night praying.' In a moment of confusion he returned the sign of the cross. Was that three fingers or two that she'd used?

'It's a terrible burden you have as a father, Father. Were you praying for anything in particular?'

'You know, save us from famine, fire, drought. That sort of thing. More of a pestilence roundup really.'

'Thank you, Father.' Mrs Pegova usually cleaned – he hesitated to use the verb – the six-roomed downtown apartment, well on its way to becoming luxury, twice a week, usually with her husband. The doubling of manpower rarely affected the cleanliness of his home. Father Georgi not only suspected, he knew that when he was absent they rarely engaged in any activity more strenuous than drinking tea and watching his wide-screen Sony wall-to-wall sound TV. He knew this because on the Tuesdays and Fridays the couple came, he counted the tea bags and hid the remote. Unfailingly the tea bag count was down between four and six and the TV was tuned to All Russia Television, the Brazilian soap opera station.

Mrs Pegova's latest celluloid obsession was Sao Paolo's *The Rich Also Cry*, the sentiments of which had almost universal appeal in Russia, namely that misery follows success as surely as a hangover follows vodka chasers.

Not that he was in any position to complain; his business was based on that very principle. Why else would the *nouveaux riches* pay him to bless everything from cars to microwaves? Like the peasants they were, they feared that their success, avarice – call it what you will – might disturb the dormant god of greed which had lain undisturbed for the last seventy years.

'Would you like a cup of tea, Father?' Mrs Pegova had shed her outer layer and was wearing a pair of tracksuit bottoms which made her backside look the size of a Russian oil spill. She was without her diminutive husband. What was it about a couple (he less than 100 pounds, she more than 200) that meeting them made images of them fornicating come to you faster than an outstretched hand? The Lilliputian trying to scale Gulliver. Captain Ahab and Moby—

'I'll just put the kettle on then.' Her silhouette filled the doorframe. A black and red apron came down to her knees.

'Yes, thank you, Mrs Pegova. I'm just reciting matins and will be with you shortly.' He had been contemplating an early morning wank before the intrusion of Mrs Pegova; now he'd have to put it off until he was in the bathroom. 'Mrs Pegova, I'd be much obliged if you could iron my cassock this morning. In my fervour last night it seems to have fallen on the floor.'

'Of course, Father.' She handed him a cup of tea. 'As soon as *Santa Barbara* is over, I'll get straight to it.' She returned to the sitting room and positioned her bulk opposite the screen. Sometimes he really did wonder what he paid her for.

'It's just that I have a baptism.' The synthesised blare of the opening shots drowned his words. For God's sake, even his half-hearted midweek erection had left him. He inhaled. 'Mrs Pegova, when I said I had a baptism to attend—'

'Sshhh. I can hardly make out this dubbing as it is.' He heard the creak of the leather of his highly prized swivel chair (was she spinning round on it?) and the slurp of tea. Less a workplace, more a day centre. He readjusted his hair, which he kept fashionably long, and straightened his boxer shorts.

He picked up the black robe with distaste and walked to the kitchen. 'Ohs' and 'ahs' were emanating from the sitting room like a matinee performance of the Moscow State Circus. He lit and sucked on a Camel Light hoping the smell of tobacco would be strong enough to rouse Mrs Pegova (*the cleaner*, he added in parenthesis) from her current five-year-plan to consume as many New World soap operas as was humanly possible and come into the kitchen, if only to tell him that smoking was forbidden anywhere but on the balcony. At which point she would see the iron, tangential to the crumpled mass, and be *shamed* into working.

A bowel movement followed the first cigarette. On the third, which coincided with the adverts, a verbal chastise-ment came from next door. On the fifth, he conceded defeat and spat on the iron in disgust.

The iron hissed its revenge. He hauled the unwieldy bulk of the cassock onto his desk like a mainsail. Its mustiness and crusty hem took him back twenty years to the seminary in Murmansk to which his mother, a wiry Orthodox woman whose asexuality clung to her like the odour of incense, had sent him after his father had run off with the red-faced wife of a railway engineer from Norilsk.

The iron was made in the Ukraine. No wonder it didn't work. He had hard-ons hotter than the cotton dial. He turned it up optimistically to the three dots recommended for heavy garments. Even the three dots suggested a wait with no conclusion. A belch of steam caught him on the forehead.

'Jesus Christ,' he breathed as the credits of *Santa Barbara* came to an end. He could make out the bored voice of the dubber, a Russian economy which meant one man read all parts. After translating the main players, the dubber was close to giving up. 'Directed by Chip Hogmonkey, produced by O fuck-it.' The audience prob-ably took him for an Irish American. 'Assisted by I Quit,' probably from the Pacific Rim.

'Mrs Pegova, *will you get your fat arse in here.*' The second part he said in the whispered tones of the confessional. At that point he spotted a bunting of yellow post-it notes stuck around his red phone like flags on an African day of independence. He tried to decipher Mrs Pegova's threadlike scrawl (why couldn't the nosy bag just leave the answer phone on?) 'Masha called please phone back. Natasha said meet her at five. Olga will try later.'

'Mrs Pegova.' She'd entered swinging her huge hips and empty cup with the nonchalant air of a Brazilian call girl. 'Have you any idea how many Mashas, Natashas and Olgas I know? If you insist on taking my calls while you're here, at least find out who these bloody women are.'

That was one of the problems with having approximately ten Christian names in circulation. You could have an hour-long conversation with a woman only to discover, after reminiscing on a theme unfamiliar to them, that you'd got the wrong one. Now, after he'd twice almost propositioned a wrong number, he took precautions with an extensive filing system, cross referenced by patronymic names and grid reference (address).

'Father, may the good Lord forgive me.' She crossed herself, he noted, with two fingers. 'I took them to be parishioners, sick people, in need of spiritual guidance.'

'Quite. In these days of Sodom and Gomorrah, have you any idea just how many of my flock *are* sick? It is vital I know which ones they are. Now what, for example, did Masha sound like?'

'Very young, Father, very young. And yet her voice was husky.'

Georgi took out a pen. That would be Masha Alexevna,

a nightclub singer from Lithuania who could do remark-able things with her throat.

By the time they had fleshed out all the women and factored them onto a spreadsheet, smoke was coming from the kitchen.

'My *cassock*! I've left the sodding iron on.'

The scorch mark was the shape of a small boat, viewed from above, and the colour of rust. When he pulled the garment over his head, it stuck out like a medieval codpiece made of burnished gold.

'Heaven preserve us, Father,' said Mrs Pegova. 'It is burnt straight through to your unmentionables.'

'What's the time?'

'Half past eleven, Father.'

'Yes or no. Can you sew it?'

Mrs Pegova fingered the smouldering material like a first-time whore. 'It's burnt straight through. Have you a piece of black cloth?'

It was twenty minutes before they had discounted the Levi 501s (on price) cushion cover (wrong black) and sock (too small). Only when Mrs Pegova's head was retreating from his groin, rather too post fellatio-like for comfort, did it come to him.

'Give me your apron.'

'But it has a picture on it and says Love Is Never Having to Say You're Sorry.'

'As fine a Christine sentiment as ever there was, Mrs Pegova.' The first job promised $300, this was no time to worry about detail. He would just have to invent a religious faction en route. He struggled to get his arms round her indefinable waist before jerking the apron clear.

He dashed for the door, pausing only to stuff a packet of Camels under his belt. He had just over twenty minutes to get to the home of the recently departed Gleb Raevitch.

II

Peter had slept so fitfully after the effects of Alyosha's nightcap had worn off around four that waking had come as a relief. His dreams had been ghoulish. His father lying naked in an open coffin. His stepmother, also naked, throwing herself into the grave. Pornographic pictures received through the fax. And in the background his young half-brother, locked in Hard's office, clutching a lollipop which by turns changed to a pulsating dildo painted blue.

He welcomed the grey morning, even if it did herald the beginning of what might turn out to be the worst day of his life.

The rain clouds fought with Athenian smog for space in the sky. All that could be said for it was that the day would be short. By the time the sun had limped into the sky, it would be time for it to collapse. Even the silver birches surrounding the dacha looked ashen. Peter held the fob watch in his hand. Was it too much of an affectation? It had been an heirloom from his maternal grandfather who had descended from the nineteenth-century British merchants in St Petersburg. That might have been where he got his Anglophilia from. That, or he was a changeling, swapped somehow at the maternity hospital with Alyosha, the real heir to the Raevitch dynasty. It was after all,

Alyosha on whom his father had rained down gifts, mostly small arms, like a doting parent. Even this last request from beyond the grave was aimed more at his humiliation than maintaining the family's dignity.

At least, though, he could find some decorum in a black blazer bearing the royal arms of De Montfort University and a black tie. Alyosha would, no doubt, be in trainers and an Arsenal strip.

Peter was alone in the dining room. It was uncharacteristically quiet. The incessant calls inquiring about the death had tailed off after Alyosha had let it be known that silence was a mark of respect. Peter had so far managed to ignore his friend's ominous warnings that unless they consolidated their position they would lose their territory. Alyosha made it sound like a football match. Already a couple of gangs were moving in. 'We have to make a stand or we're sunk,' he'd said, shaking his head. 'We must act.'

Peter couldn't manage a walk-on part in a pantomime, never mind act.

He heard a thud from upstairs. His stepmother was either up or searching for more tranquillisers.

He thought back to yesterday's conversation with his real mother in Cyprus.

'He who lives by the sword shall die by the sword,' she had intoned on hearing that her ex-husband had died rather suddenly. Peter wasn't sure but she seemed to have swayed towards religion since her move. A curious religious blend which sanctioned her taking young Cypriot lovers who doubled as domestic staff. A male who sounded no older than a teenager had answered the phone. 'Who was that?' he asked her.

'Um, that would be Dmitri. The gardener.' There was a pause. 'How exactly did he die?'

'An accident.' He'd thought it best to keep the details vague.

'What sort of accident?'

'A tragic accident.'

'With what?' She sounded more intrigued than concerned.

'At home. In the office. Electrical.' It came out in an avalanche of implausibility. 'The fax blew up. There were bits everywhere. The phone receiver hit him on the head. Death was instantaneous. The fax was ruined.' He nervously waited for a response. 'As I said, tragic.'

'Sue.' Did she mean Tanya?

'Who's Sue?'

'No, you idiot, sue the manufacturers. There could be millions in it for us.' She'd been reading John Grisham books again.

'We'll see,' he said heavily. He hadn't expected much from the call but he had hoped that her concern for his father might have extended further into grief than the possibility of a successful legal action. Hurtful as it might be, he had to admit that his sepia images of them holidaying happily on endless hot summers were as selective as the half-erased photographs of the Central Committee under Stalin.

The doorbell disturbed him. Out of respect Alyosha had changed the usual Waltzing Matilda chimes to a funeral march.

The man at the door was a good six foot tall. He was lean and in his early thirties. His hair was dark, nearly black, long at the front and trimmed over the ears. His eyes were dark brown and hooded. Peter thought they were what women's magazines referred to as come-to-bed eyes. He had a diffident look, almost embarrassed. But then again, he had good reason to be. From the waist up he was dressed as an Orthodox priest. But tied round his waist was an apron bearing some sort of cartoon. It reminded Peter of a game called Misfits he'd played at prep school, in which cardboard cut-outs of a dozen different professions (nurse, farmer, policeman etc.), were divided into three. When you mixed up the sections and then laid them together again you got all sorts of interesting combinations, like an athlete's legs attached to a dancer's middle with an undertaker's head. It has been one of his favourite games.

'Father Georgi Bulgakov. Pleased to meet you.' The man held out a slim-fingered hand.

'Please to meet you. You are?'

'Bodies Beautiful?' He said it more as a question than a statement. 'Clause Twenty-three. Where there's a will there's a way?' His dark eyebrows were raised in a perfect arch.

'Of course, yes, please come in. I'd almost forgotten, the will-reading service. I'm Peter, Gleb Raevitch's son. You must be their dignitary. We, I, was expecting something more,' he paused, 'legal.' A priest was the last thing Peter had been expecting or wanted to see.

Georgi stepped onto the marble flagstones. In the middle of the Tudor-style hall was a huge log fire.

'Nice place he had. I mean, you've got.' He handed Peter an Italian cashmere coat.

'Thanks. We moved here about five years ago. Before that we were in Moscow, near Taganka, perhaps you know the church—'

'Tell me how many you're expecting,' Georgi interrupted, pulling down the cuffs of his cassock.

Peter tried to read the slogan on the apron. *Love means . . .* 'Why, will it affect the acoustics of your service? I take it there is going to *be* a service?' For decency's sake he wanted to keep numbers to a minimum. Apart from himself, Tanya, Alyosha, Alexander and the Tadzhik cook, that would be it.

'Yes, but I was wondering about the meal. Buffet, or sit down?'

Peter had tried to communicate with the Tadzhik cook that a small buffet might be appropriate. Communicate was the word, as opposed to tell. He had entered Hard Currency's payroll in 1993 when Chinese food had become *de rigueur* among the Moscow glitterati. Authentic Chinese chefs were as sought after as the latest Mercedes.

'I'm sure our cook will come up with something.' Peter tried to sound more convinced than he was.

The priest nodded.

Peter asked, 'What sort of service is it likely to be, exactly?'

'Exactly.' Georgi weighed up the word in his mouth. 'Exactly, I'm not sure. Was he religious, your dad?'

'Not really,' answered Peter.

'No churchies expected, then?' The grandfather clock in the corner struck midday.

'I'm sorry?'

'Churchies. Religious nuts, those sort of people.'

Peter thought of those expected to attend. The nearest they got to formal religion was Alyosha's Black Sabbath T-shirt. 'Not as far as I know, no.'

Georgi exhaled and offered up silent thanks. 'In that case, if we leave out the singing part, I could do you a nice little service which would last about ten minutes.'

'Fine. Look, I'm sorry, I have to ask, what is that apron?'

Georgi looked shocked. 'This is the very latest in religion. In fact, as far as religiosity gets, this is the main thing.' He seemed to be groping for something under his belt. 'Do you mind if I smoke?'

'No.' Peter wondered if he was in some way related to Alyosha. 'It's just that I've never heard of the "Love is" series having any place in religious belief—'

'Christ, what was that?' Both men looked up at the ceiling above them, where a crystal chandelier was quivering after an Armenian earthquake-style jolt.

'I think that was my stepmother. She's been in bed since it happened. She's very upset, you know.'

Georgi flicked his cigarette ash towards the open fire. It left a grey trail which he rubbed into the floor with his foot. Outside, the snow continued to fall.

'What was your father's profession?' Georgi asked. 'It helps for the eulogy.'

'You do a eulogy *now*? I thought that would be at the funeral.'

Georgi inhaled and rotated his cigarette packet in thought. 'Look, to be honest, this is all a bit new to me,' he said. 'I only met the guy from Bodies Beautiful after a few too many in a bar in Krapotkinskaya. He said something about will reading combining the spiritual and temporal. Seemed okay to me.' He looked apologetically at Peter. 'You tell me what you want. You know, incense, prayers, that sort of thing.'

Alyosha and Alexander burst in through the door.

'This is Father Georgi,' said Peter. 'He's here to oversee the reading of the will.'

Alyosha let out a small yelp which was half laughter, half pain.

Peter continued, 'Which I suggest we get on with as soon as possible.' He looked at Alyosha. 'Do you know if Tanya will be joining us?'

'I doubt it,' he replied. 'Since the Tamazapan ran out, she's basing herself out of the drinks cabinet.' He grinned, then lowered his head and bowed slightly towards the priest. 'Sorry, your worship,' he said reverentially.

Georgi vaguely made the sign of the cross, a cigarette between his fingers. Then he flicked the butt into the fire and gave a beatific nod. 'If we could get started,' he said.

'Of course.' Peter swung round on his Italian shoes and led the mourners to the sitting room. He waited while Alyosha jostled for a front row position.

'We are here to listen to the last will and testament of Gleb Alexanderavitch Raevitch, whose loss is felt by us all.' He looked up. Alyosha had the rapt expression of a toddler. The priest was lighting another cigarette and looking in dismay at the Tadzhik buffet. Alexander, as usual, was expressionless.

'Here goes.' Peter unravelled the will. It had been Alyosha's idea to wrap it up like a Roman scroll. 'I, Gleb Alexanderavitch Raevitch, being of sound mind . . .' Alyosha let out a giggle. Peter hadn't seen him this excited since Spartak won the Russian league. '. . . hereby lay out my last will and testament.' Peter picked up a cut-glass tumbler of water. He saw Alyosha pull out his hip flask from his Lakers baseball jacket and pass it round. Only Alexander refused. Alyosha looked shocked by the diminished weight of the flask when the priest handed it back to him. Peter inhaled deeply.

'But before I read my father's will, I would ask Father Georgi to say a few words to the assembled, um, congregation.'

Alyosha tutted disapprovingly and clicked his fingers in disgust. 'Oh man,' he said. Since the advent of Tommy Hilfiger, Alyosha had modelled himself on a black American.

Georgi looked up from his cigarette. 'Oh, right. Absolutely. Do you want to do a religious type thing, or just a few words?'

Peter thought rather wildly that if this went on much longer God might show his displeasure with an act – a tornado, earth tremor, nuclear bomb. Still, anything would come as a bit of light relief to the task in hand.

'Just a few words would do it,' he said.

Georgi tripped on the hem of his cassock as he stumbled to the front of the marble fireplace. He stood head on to the audience, who had a full frontal view of the 'Love is' apron. Before he could begin, Alyosha rose to his feet unzipping his bomber jacket to signal action.

'For God's sake, give it here.' He pulled the will from Peter's hands. 'OK then.' He scanned the preamble. 'Sound mind blah blah, do divide my worldly goods.

Tanya, lump sum, five hundred thousand dollars. First wife, Lisa, lump sum, the same. Second son, Mikhail Glebavitch, one million, kept in trust until he comes of age. To my first son Peter Glebavitch I leave the not inconsiderable contents of my personal safe and my safety deposit box.'

Everyone in the room looked at Peter who was holding his head in his hands.

Alyosha continued, 'The key to the deposit box is kept about my person. The combination of my personal safe which,' Alyosha looked up to check that he had the full attention of his audience, 'I have taken the precaution of tattooing . . .' he sucked on his Lakers sleeve to stop the guffaws, 'which I have taken the precaution of tattooing on my,' Alyosha spluttered, 'penis.'

Peter groaned. Even Alexander let out a 'Shit'. Georgi choked on his cigarette. Alyosha was doubled over.

'Which can only be read,' he stuttered between sobs, 'when fully erect.'

After a minute's silence, apart from Alyosha's hysterics, Georgi spoke. 'Anyone fancy something to eat?'

III

Potentially it was the biggest day of his life to date. He wiggled his toes and curled and uncurled his tongue in excitement. So much to gain, but how much to lose?

'No, Terry, old son, we've been through all this before,' he told himself. 'You've got to do it. The completeness of your reinvention demands it.' Quite right.

Terry thought about the day when it first happened. The worst day of his life. He could still remember the date. The ninth of October 1987. A Saturday not long after they began living together. Grace was downstairs engaged in her Saturday morning ritual of polishing the ornaments. ('Don't disturb me, I'm polishing the ornaments. I can't, I'm polishing the ornaments.') He'd been upstairs getting ready for their pilgrimage to the Savacentre when it happened. He combed his hair and it came away in handfuls. Not just a clump that you found in a plughole or the usual residue of a brush, but bushes of it. Like small furry animals. Finger puppets. Hand puppets. Cuddly toys. Entire toy departments.

'Don't worry, sweetheart. It'll grow back,' Grace had said. She had laughed. 'Anyway, you've got plenty more, haven't you?'

That was it. There was hair all over his body – front, back, legs, arms, hands, toes, matting you could make a carpet out of. But somehow it had given up the will to grow on his head.

Since then he'd examined the residue of every comb with the care of a nit nurse. He *smoothed* shampoo into his hair as opposed to lathering it, slept on satin pillowcases, and combed – he snorted out loud at the word – the back pages of the *Daily Telegraph*, amid the gardening trousers, for the latest in hair restoratives.

Part of his gym programme, though he never admitted it, was aimed at boosting his testosterone so that it might somehow cling on to his follicles harder. He even tried to justify his sticky half-hour encounters with the Swedish porn channel as a way to halt his hair loss. The doctor had recommended a scalp cream which he'd stopped using in case the circular movements necessary to apply it eased the hairs out.

His father, a one-time trading standards officer whose speciality was noise abatement, at the age of sixty-nine still maintained an averagely full scalp in his retirement bungalow on the south coast, as did his mother. Why him?

Close to accepting defeat, he'd spent hours chanting at the hairs on his chest and back to migrate upwards to his scalp. 'Move, you follicles, walk, you bastards,' had been his mantra for an entire summer after an especially savage trim had left him balder than a newborn.

'No, Terry, you've definitely been putting the cart before the horse with this one,' he said. 'First you get the hair then you bag the woman.'

The taxi driver turned to stare at Terry. He appeared to be conducting a conversation with an imaginary friend.

'The wig woman, pah!' There would be no women with hairpieces in Terry Small's new world. Sleek women in tight black cocktail dresses, that would be the future for Terence Le Petit.

'Terence Le Petit, full head of hair, pleased to meet you,' he recited, as if reading from a business card. He smiled.

The taxi driver, a wiry blond man with a cardboard box full of knitting patterns on his front seat, turned the dial of his radio up. Queen blared out as the Moscow suburbs gave way to the centre of the city.

'I want to break free. I'm going to break free of my baldness, my horrible baldness,' Terry sang along. He thought of the day when he'd first seen the article in a men's magazine which somebody had left at the gym next to the water dispenser.

There it was, in the index after 'Two weeks to a six-pack' and before 'Pecs to die for'; *Miracle cure for baldness*. Terry had almost dropped his plastic cup on which he'd inscribed the initials T.S. in blue felt tip. 'Russian doctors have pioneered a revolutionary new cure for baldness. Scientists once famed for the manufacture of nuclear weapons are turning their attention to the vital question of hair loss', sneers our full-headed Moscow correspondent, thought Terry. 'The technique pioneered at the Institute of Cosmetology guarantees a complete head of hair.'

He'd read the last part again: *guarantees a full head of hair*. He'd ripped the page out and dashed home.

In the Moscow taxi, he still had the dog-eared original. True, it was going to be painful; the technique, as he understood it, involved inserting a plastic sack under a part of the scalp where hair growth existed. Then the sack was slowly inflated with a saline solution until it stretched to twice its size, so that double the area of scalp was able to grow hair, and then the top of your head was sort of *turfed* with it. Steady though, Terry, he said to himself, this was only a recce. What did Andy McNab say? In the SAS, as elsewhere, preparation and planning were the keys to a successful mission.

The baldness operation had been designed for burns victims from the Afghan war but now appeared to have a commercial application attracting, the article said, foreigners.

'I'm going to have hair. I'm going to have ha ha hairy hair,' he boomed out to the Queen chorus.

'Foreigners, however,' continued the long-haired Moscow correspondent, 'have to pay in dollars whereas Russians receive the treatment for roubles, approximately $43 compared to the $3,000 a foreigner could expect to pay.'

'I'm not going to pay,' Terry sang on to the Queen song. 'I have a plan a nice little plan oh yeah, nice little plan. I'm not going to pay.'

The driver launched a knitting pattern into the back seat and abruptly switched off the radio.

Terry stopped singing. 'Charmingski,' he said. 'Pull in here, my good man. We have arrivedski.'

IV

Sonya looked at her watch. Nikita's telephone call had thrown her. She had another hour before she'd arranged to meet Katya. She didn't know whether to change at work or later. She'd brought her only smart dress, a neat black one, which she'd bought for her parents' funeral.

She'd spent most of the day looking at the English author section. Maybe he'd be interested in literature. Dickens, Conan Doyle, Poe. Her favourite was Oscar Wilde. He was bound to be sophisticated. Cultured, well-dressed, thoughtful and attentive. A bit like that man who had been married to Princess Diana, though better looking of course.

Nikita had sounded frantic.

'Sonya?'

'What is it?'

'Nothing, I was just worried about you. I thought something might have happened.'

'No, darling, I'm fine. What sort of thing?'

'Nothing, I just felt worried for you. What time will you be home?'

'I'll be a bit late. One of the girls from work wants me to go shopping with her for shoes.' She crossed her fingers behind her overall. She hated lying to him. She quickly changed the subject. 'How are you today?'

'OK. Though I can really feel them today. They're even itchy.'

'Poor darling.' Nikita had constantly felt sensation in his amputated legs just after the accident. Now he only felt them when he was tired or worried about something. He said they were like an early warning system. 'Listen. I'll bring some cake home after I've been shopping. I'll make that apple tea you like.'

'Chocolate cake?'

'If you like. Why don't you try and sleep now?'

'OK. But be careful today, won't you?'

'Aren't I always?' She said goodbye and hung up.

She was half-heartedly pricing a new batch of translated American detective novels all about the KGB which had just come in. The shelves were full of trashy American novels these days. Russians seemed to think foreigners knew more about their own intelligence service than they did. Maybe they did. All she knew was that they used to sell Lermontov and now they sold Tom Clancy.

221

'Comrade Arakadia. There's another call for you,' yelled the shop supervisor, a matronly woman nicknamed dinosaur because of her stubborn fondness for communism. 'I have told you, have I not, that receiving personal calls during office hours is not allowed?'

'Sorry, Supervisor Comrade. I've got some problems at home today.' Sonya squeezed past her into the book-filled back room.

'Sonya, it's Katya. How are you? All set?'

'Yes, I think so.' The supervisor had left to reprimand someone else.

'No second thoughts?'

'No.'

'Good. OK then, see you at seven.'

'Outside the gym or inside?'

'It's cold, let's make it inside.'

IV

'I say we take the priest. It'll make it look authentic.' Alyosha was trying to pick the flesh off an unguessable cut of meat. 'Do you think this is chicken?' he asked, contemplating the bone like a palaeontologist.

All things considered, thought Peter, the morning hadn't been as disastrous as he'd expected. The priest, now on his third bowl of rice and fourth glass of wine, had barely batted an eyelid.

'We really need to get a decent look at the body and I think a priest would be a good cover,' Alyosha went on. 'You know, the rites and everything.'

'Isn't it a bit late for that?'

'Well, not last rites then, some sort of funerary blessing.'

'Aren't you forgetting one thing?'

'You're right, ketchup would help disguise the taste of this.'

Peter ignored this. 'Even when we,' he stopped, 'even when we discover the combination for the safe we'll still need the key to the safety deposit box.' He lowered his voice and the priest smiled across the dining table in his direction. 'Do you know if he kept his money in the safe or in his safety deposit box?'

'Haven't got a clue.'

'Do you know where he kept the key to the safety deposit box?'

'No.'

'So we're stuffed. Did you see it in the office?'

'No.'

'Was it among his belongings? The will said he kept it *about his person*.'

'No. There was only a pair of handcuffs and a packet of ribbed condoms.'

'Maybe Tanya knows. Maybe she had it.'

'I doubt it, but I'll try her.'

'Look, about this tattoo thing. Maybe we could just ask for the body to be returned to us before the funeral. Couldn't we do it then?'

'Ordinarily, I would say yes. But this came this morning.' Alyosha pulled an envelope out of his inside jacket pocket. 'It was addressed to Tanya but I recognised the handwriting.'

'Oh shit.' Peter's stomach clenched and churned, though that could just have been the fermented mare's milk.

'Yes. They want the money by the end of the week.' Alyosha looked grave. 'So I suggest we get cracking.' He looked at Peter firmly. 'And I suggest we recruit the priest.'

Peter felt as if a lead weight was balanced on the crown of his head. He ran his fingers through his hair and nodded. 'Whatever you think best.'

V

'Sasha, can I ask you something?'

'What?'

'Exactly how much of the *Financial Times* do you understand?' Katya was hand-washing clothes at the kitchen sink. Sometimes she thought it was wrong to take the Mickey out of her six-year-old son, but sometimes she couldn't resist it.

'It's what reading it says about you, Mum, not how much you understand.'

'Oh right, sorry.' She stifled a giggle. 'Sasha?'

'What now?'

Katya was aware that it was usually children who badgered their parents for attention rather than the other way round. 'Why am I washing Misha's I Love NY shirt?'

Sasha quickly looked up from the shares list. 'We swapped them after football. He's got my Gap one. You don't mind, do you?'

'No, not at all. But there does seem to be a huge amount of dirty clothes. I'm sure I haven't even seen you in this Power Rangers shirt this week.'

'Mum, do you mind? I'm trying to concentrate.'

'Sorry.' She waited a few seconds. 'Where's Leonid?'

'Out.'

She wrung out a T-shirt and put it on the draining board. A washing machine was first on her list when she claimed her $20,000 fee. *If* she collected it, she corrected herself. She looked at the kitchen clock; three hours to go.

'With whom?'

'Mum, can we continue this conversation later? You might not have been aware of the recent floating of Rosneft, but some of us have to keep up.'

'Oh, righto,' said Katya, pretending to be chastised but smiling. Not even Sasha could disturb her equilibrium. She had a date for the Englishman tonight. She'd found a possible for one of her most difficult though lucrative clients and she'd had sex in the past twenty-four hours. Her mood bordered on relaxed.

'Sasha, I'm out tonight, so you've got Mrs Voronsheva.'

'Fine.'

It was an unheard of response from Sasha who usually viewed the babysitter in the same mould as dentists or his head teacher. Even by his standards Sasha had been behaving oddly recently. But with her son, Katya reasoned, it was usually due to something quite oblique like the Tokyo crash or the kiosk running out of Kinder eggs. One thing continued to puzzle her, though: why did all her magazines have words cut out of them?

CHAPTER EIGHT

I

Terry fingered the burgundy Russian passport in the back pocket of his beige stretch-with-you polyester trousers which had already curved to fit the shape of his right buttock, and looked up. It was a huge grey edifice, built round three sides of a quadrangle. It must have been twenty storeys high. Perhaps it signified an epidemic of baldness in the Soviet Union, thousands of workers queuing to have their pates adjusted. Perhaps it had been part of the Communist Manifesto. 'Workers of the world unite, you have nothing to lose but your bald patches.' He sniggered. If only British politicians could be that inventive. In Britain these days you had to be a black disabled lesbian before you got anything.

What a dump it was. How few opportunities he'd seen for Pagodas R Us, the south-west's premier conservatory outlet. He'd barely seen a garden in the entire week. Put up a shed here and you'd get a family of ten living in it before you got the door on. Or they'd turn it into a revolutionary meeting place. It was difficult to keep cheerful, he thought. He must stay focused on the important things. He sat down on a bench hemmed by a valance of beer cans.

He didn't really look like the man in the passport picture, but that could be explicable by sudden hair loss. They were both dark, and how often did anyone look that closely at a passport?

He was pretty sure, when it came to making the appointment, that his lack of hair would be explanation enough. In any case, he wasn't banking on the operation on this visit. The purpose of this trip, he reminded himself, was to ascertain the possible. At best get booked in. Besides, he had a date tonight with one of Katya's girls. One of, he felt it was no exaggeration to say, the most beautiful women he had ever seen. Not even a woman but a *girl*. Not a girl in the way that Lionel Blair referred to the ageing hags on that charades TV programme, but young, girlish, *pure*. He had christened her Umababs in deference to Uma Thurman and Barbara Windsor. Could Umababs love a man with no hair? More to the point, could she shag a man with no hair? Or would she be like all the rest, the Olympic bag thrower and the woman in the wig? She looked so innocent, so untouched by human hands.

He should really get into character now if he was going to pull this off. What irony, to be playing the role of a mute just when he'd mastered the language. Getting into the taxi he'd felt exhilarated, despite the sleet. How many of his acquaintances would be so brave? Confronting the red menace behind the Iron Curtain James Bond style. Infiltrating the very heart – an undercover mission. He weighed up the potential dangers. How many of them would have thought of it? Posing as a Russian in order to get the operation for free. Stealing a passport. The mute bit had been the icing on the cake. It had come to him when he'd been trying to scrounge the loo roll from Katya.

While she was out of the room, he'd rifled through an open drawer and filched the passport. Later, on the loo – if that was Andrex he was a Dutchman – it had come to him. The passport would verify his nationality but, only by posing as a mute could he get away with his limited, though not inconsiderable, vocabulary. What ingenuity. What bravery. Passing himself off as one of them. The nearest Bob and Gordon at Pagodas R Us had got to disguise was fancy dress at the Christmas party. Even then Bob had gone as Joseph and spent all night asking Mary, the short-skirted temp, if she wanted to take part in the second coming. Bastard.

This would show him. In a flash of anger Terry leapt up and yanked open the double doors to the institute. Immediately he was halted by a dauntingly large entrance foyer. It was the furthest he'd got to being behind enemy lines. It was empty apart from a hefty woman in a green apron selling newspapers and a few toiletries including, he noted with distaste, Old Spice deodorant, from behind a trestle table. Identify the potential danger, thought Terry. That's what Andy McNab would do. Enemy agent at three o'clock, he breathed out loud. If only he had a walkie-talkie. Luckily, the enemy agent appeared to be filling in a crossword.

Terry instinctively took cover behind a Doric column

made from marble. He did some deep diaphragm breathing exercises learnt at the Gender Awareness Forum.

Think cripple, he urged himself. Disabled was the key to success. Method acting, Robert De Niro, *The Professionals*. He started humming the tune. What he needed was something more to add to that overall *disabled* look. He experimented with a walk between two pillars, out of eye range of the enemy agent, dragging his left foot behind him. Not bad, but was it enough?

Out of the corner of his eye he spotted a full-length double mirror outside a twin set of lavatories identifiable more by their smell than the silver representations of pre-revolutionary men and women on the door.

Terry limped over to them and started practising his walk. He was not impressed. Andy McNab on enemy soil would have known every element of his persona weeks before the drop. He was shambolically making it up as he went along. Poor, Terry, very poor, he chided himself. In self-reproach, he stopped humming *The Professionals* theme tune.

Facial contortions were a plus. Here we go. *Limp* two three. *Grimace* two three. *Limp* two three. *Grimace* two three. He was only five lengths into his routine when he noticed that Enemy Agent Number One had put down the crossword and was watching him.

Terry gulped. He had no doubt that to masquerade as a native, never mind a crippled native, was a capital offence in Russia. He acknowledged the disguise of her grey hair and portly figure, the wooden abacus which doubled as a poisoned dart gun. There could be no doubt she was a KGB agent. This was no time for blunders.

He hauled himself across the foyer to her.

'Aaaaaaaaagh,' he said rotating his head wildly. 'Aaaagh aaagh aaaagh ski,' he added in desperation. The woman's face took on a look of abject horror. She cast around the foyer for help. A globule of Terry's saliva landed on a canister of shaving foam in front of her. She instinctively pushed her chair back and crouched semi-foetally on her plastic chair.

Terry decided to change tack. 'Eeeeeeeh eeeeeeegh eeeghski.' He pointed at his bald patch. Surely the old bat could understand that? 'What floorski for baldski operationski?' he groaned and added 'Aaaaaaaaghski' with a theatrical flourish.

The scream that the newspaper vendor emitted, Terry thought, had a wounded animal element to it. Not that he'd ever heard any wounded animals. But there was undoubtedly a raw edge to the noise that you might associate with an injured female protecting her young.

Terry made a mental note. Enemy Agent One alerted, take avoidance action immediately. He lumbered over to the lift and pressed the illuminated red button. He threw himself to the back of the wooden cavity and took several long deep breaths. With all his senses heightened, Terry noticed the lift smelt of cigarettes and formaldehyde.

II

The rust-coloured Lada pulled in just as the taxi was leaving. It was starting to get dark and a fine drizzle of snow was peppering the ground. Gusts of wind blew the priest's cassock above his knees, revealing a red pair of salopettes, Alyosha noticed. What sort of a priest wore a frigging apron in any case?

For reasons of propriety Peter had elected to stay at home. Even Alyosha had to agree that reading a tattoo on the embalmed penis of your recently deceased father did not make for that special afternoon.

Alyosha spat out his cigarette and flicked up the collar of the camel coat Peter had lent him, arguing that a Lakers bomber jacket would give the wrong impression. He hadn't objected.

The spray from the yellow cab as it plummeted into a pothole caught Alyosha on the left leg of his jeans.

'Jesus Christ, watch where you're going!' he yelled at the driver, who middle-fingered at him. 'Sorry, Father,' he added as the priest jack-knifed himself out of the back seat.

'Listen, can we dispense with this Father stuff?' Georgi dug under his belt for a packet of cigarettes. 'Besides, strictly speaking, this isn't a Lord's mission. I'm on your payroll this afternoon. And a very handsome payroll it is.'

Alyosha had been more in favour of doing the whole thing by force. In his experience everyone co-operated better with a pistol aimed at their head. But *no*, Peter had to do it above board and pay the priest for services rendered.

'Are you sure you haven't been here before?' asked Alyosha as they made their way towards the building. 'I thought you worked for Bodies Beautiful.'

'I do, but I've only met one of them – in a bar. In fact, yours was the first job I've done for them. I'm usually more of a freelance. And I wouldn't be here now if you hadn't been so *persuasive*.'

Alyosha grunted by way of acceptance, not sure if the priest was referring to the money or the menacing way it had been offered. He wasn't convinced $1,000 to gain admittance to the morgue wasn't over the odds but, as Peter had pointed out, it wasn't the sort of service that came with a price list.

There was no doubt that in matters like this Peter was about as much use as a pork chop in a synagogue. Take this kidnapping thing. He himself had been kidnapped twice and could say, hand on heart, that he'd thoroughly enjoyed the occasions. Both times he'd been snatched by rival gangs as a gentle reminder to his boss that a couple of outstanding debts hadn't been paid. The kidnappers had apologised for having to tie him up and compensated by letting him choose the video. *Die Hard III*, if he remembered correctly. On the second occasion he was hand-fed pepperoni pizza. A charming touch, he'd thought.

They weren't serious, especially not when it came to a little boy. Kidnappings were the Russian equivalent of a letter from the bank telling you you'd exceeded your overdraft, or a reminder that your library book was overdue. And if Peter really *was* intent – as his disastrous maiden speech to the Round Table had suggested – on threatening every carefully constructed dodgy business empire in the country, he had to take the consequences. After a $250,000 fine, he wouldn't do it again. Non-payment meant trouble. Hence their spot of afternoon grave robbing.

The pair stood in silence in front of the lift. A flustered

woman, who was actually on her knees praying in front of a newspaper and toiletries stand in the foyer, crossed herself wildly when she saw the priest. Father Georgi waved at her, less like making the sign of cross, Alyosha thought, than inquiring the price of a roll-on deodorant.

He sighed. Unless he took over the reins of the Raevitch empire it would crumble before his eyes and with it Peter's livelihood and his as well. But it wasn't just the money. He owed Hard Currency. Without him he would be just a two-bit hood. Hard had treated him as one of his own since before he could hold a Beretta. He'd been the unofficial gang mascot for years ever since he and Peter teamed up in the playground at junior school, when he had stepped in to stop Peter being bullied in return for the fee of his packed lunch. A month of smoked salmon sandwiches later they'd been inseparable – the posh kid and the poor orphaned boy. Two months after that Peter kept his lunch in return for completing Alyosha's home-work. Even after Peter left to go to school in England, the relationship endured.

Alyosha did have parents though they'd been, as far as he could tell, *in absentia* for the last twenty-three years, ever since they had dropped him off at Children's Home Number 102 (a temporary facility for parents in difficulty) before going to a party, or so the sour-faced matron had told him. It must have been a hell of a do because in more than a decade they'd failed to return. After five years he was moved to Children's Home Number 753 (a perma-nent facility for children with no parents).

He'd excelled in metalwork and developed an embry-onic PR company approximately two decades before the concept was ever known in Russia. After six years he had a steady income and an enviable cache of small arms. Grooming was the key to his success. Of the 127 inmates of Children's Home Number 753, 126 dreamed of being adopted. He was the exception. The home was visited twice a month by couples wanting to adopt, the younger the child, the better. Alyosha groomed toddlers to put themselves ahead of the pack in return for six months' six kopek allowance. Of those who joined the programme, only one remained unselected, the mixed-race progeny of a visiting African athlete to the 1980 Olympics. Russians, Alyosha argued, lacked a civilised attitude to race. His coup had been pairing Olga Pulskova, a charming podgy toddler with a nose-picking problem – which Alyosha had been instrumental in overcoming – with an American Embassy couple from Milwaukee. He often wondered what had become of little Olga.

As they marched down the institute's corridors, Alyosha instinctively hated the building, hated its bone-freezing, institutionalised smell.

'Look, if we bump into anyone official here, anyone from Bodies Beautiful,' Alyosha thought he had better spell it out, 'introduce yourself and tell them that, as mourners, we've decided to go for the full service, including the last rites package.'

'Isn't it a bit late for that?' asked Georgi.

Priest or not, the man was starting to get on Alyosha's nerves. 'Look, tell them anything. That we just wanted to have a last look at the body. We couldn't believe it was really true. Had to see the body one last time. Tell them any frigging thing.'

Deep on the maze-like fourteenth floor, they found the door they wanted. It bore the words Bodies Beautiful in large 15 point letters. Underneath, it said 'Friends to the Bereaved. All Mourners Welcome'. Alyosha tried the handle. The door was locked.

'Where are the bodies kept, then?' He turned to Georgi accusingly.

'I've told you, I've never been here in my life.'

Alyosha kicked the door and cursed under his breath. They turned and walked moodily back along the corridor.

III

Friday was always a long day for Staff Nurse Irina Stepanova. It was even worse when, like today, the barometer read depression. On those days the pressure experienced by the patients became unbearable. Many who were halfway through the treatment, with heads swollen to the size of footballs, had been known to break down under the excruciating pain and cry. It was a very unnerving sight. Added to which, Friday was the day outpatients came in to have their salination treatment before they went home for the weekend. The ward patients, who had travelled vast distances for the operation, were always moodier, sensing another two days of swollen-headed imprisonment while others were off work.

Since the Russian health service had collapsed and the institute had been advertising the hair treatment, there had been a run on the miracle cure. The treatment had been pioneered, she was proud to say, by herself and Dr Jakob Panchenko, a Ukrainian surgeon whose contribution to follicle study was known throughout the world. Lesser known was the fact that she had been in love with Dr Panchenko for more than a decade. She could remember exactly the moment, when he was delivering a paper on Baldness and the Regressive Gene to a stunned audience at a conference in Stockholm in October 1989, when her stomach had started to turn somersaults. She pictured him running his hands, fine surgeon's hands, through his bushy grey hair as the applause rippled through the lecture theatre. How magnanimous, they must have thought, that such a well-endowed man, follically speaking, should take such an interest in those less hairy than himself. Since then – the doctor was married with three sons – she'd been content to act as his assistant. Irina was forty-five and unmarried, having devoted her adult life to an ageing mother and the curtailment of baldness. On good days, she prided herself on being his tireless muse.

Today she was more than a little fractious. The doctor had not turned up for his afternoon ward round. It meant that she had worn her plunge bra – which showed an enticing crevice of cleavage when she bent to hold a patient's head – in vain. Her Swedish-made bra, bought two hours after the conference, could only be washed under the most exacting circumstances and with expensive western soap powder. She sank down behind her desk in the reception office and consoled herself with another Dutch-made macaroon (a gift from a Georgian import/ export trader from Tblisi whose hair growth had increased from 15 square centimetres to 42). It was her eighth macaroon of the day.

She was halfway through an interview with Tom Cruise in *TV Park*, before drawing up a viewing schedule for that evening, when two men disturbed her. With a trained medical eye she noted that both were in a state of some agitation, though both boasted a full head of hair. The same trained eye registered that one was dressed as a priest.

Did she know where the embalming parlour kept their bodies, the younger one wanted to know. The clinic took up one floor of the mountainous Institute of Cosmetology. The exact practices of the other twenty-four floors she could only guess at – apart from a Lithuanian plastic surgeon of dubious credentials on the fourth floor who had been responsible for a botched varicose vein operation on her aunt. The taller one was more diplomatic. They were trying to locate the morgue of Bodies Beautiful, Moscow's first privately owned funeral and embalming parlour. Could she help?

Morgue? Were they trying to be funny? She told them where they could stick their embalming process and slammed the door in their faces before returning to the macaroons and ticking the programmes she would watch after she'd put her mother to bed.

No sooner had she sat down when she heard the door click open again. She barely looked up from the interview with Tom Cruise, assuming the duo had returned and determined to ignore them.

She looked again. Most of their gentlemen clients (apart from two burns victims from Chechenya) were quite well-to-do and smartly dressed. For most Russians, even at the reduced rouble rate, a baldness cure was not high on their list of essentials. She had never, she felt safe in saying, ever seen anyone quite like the man standing in front of her.

His head was twisting from side to side and he appeared to be trying to speak. He was short, no taller than herself, and dressed in a bizarre arrangement of ill-fitting clothes. One side of his face was bruised, and when he lumbered into the office she saw he was dragging one foot behind him.

'Aaaagh. Aaaaagh,' he said jabbing a finger towards his mouth and shaking his head. After a few seconds he stroked his palm over his bald head and looked imploringly at her like a dog.

'Can I help you?' Staff Nurse Irina Stepanova had treated veterans from Afghanistan. She had seen madness in many forms. The man in front of her reached into his back pocket. She instinctively flexed. Sometimes men who weren't completely satisfied with their treatment returned to the clinic. Sometimes they were armed. But she'd never set eyes on this man before. Even a treatment which went wrong left them with more hair than he had. He pulled a passport from his back pocket and flung it on the desk. At the same time he put his hand over his mouth and continued to shake his head. Tentatively, Irina picked it up. She read the information at the back. 'Maxim Davidovitch Popov. Born 13.02.60.' She looked at the man opposite her. Time had not been kind to Maxim, she thought. The man in the photograph was handsome and the owner of a full head of luxuriant dark hair. The man pacing up and down the office, revealing a pronounced limp, was neither. Silhouetted against the pictures on the wall, which boasted some of the clinic's proudest before and after shots, his face looked as if he'd gone several rounds with a heavyweight boxer.

'Hairski. Goneski.' It was gibberish. She thought of Dr Jacob Panchenko, at this very minute no doubt in the arms of his young mistress, the hair stylist who came in on a Tuesday afternoon to add the finishing touches to the patients' new coiffure. She thought of the girl's smudge-resistant lipstick and hair-diffusing drier. She thought of the number of times she'd worn her bust-diffusing bra and how long the doctor had resisted. She thought of another evening at home with *TV Park* and her disabled mother.

She shouldn't even be here on her own. Dr Panchenko should be dealing with all this, not indulging in illicit afternoon affairs. She picked up a crowbar she had kept behind the desk ever since a bodybuilder from Bishkek, whom she'd suspected of taking steroids, made an unscheduled return after his scalp failed to return to its normal size. He'd been forced to take up a job in a kitchen in order to cover the bulge with a chef's hat, and was far from happy about it. That had been yet another afternoon the good doctor had spent with his lithe young mistress.

She wrenched the crowbar free and slammed it down on the desk, shattering the remaining trio of macaroons. 'Take your bloody bald head and get out of here,' she yelled as the man started another limping tour of the office. 'I never want to see another bald-headed *man*,' she spat the last word, 'as long as I live. You are vain.' She slammed the crowbar down. 'Egocentric.' It shattered a paperweight of a snow scene of San Francisco. 'And ugly.' On the last word she let go of the crowbar and sent it soaring from the sixteenth-floor window. Then she ransacked the filing cabinet containing Dr Panchenko's notes, which she had religiously maintained for the past twenty-two years, and flung them from the broken window. They rained down onto the forecourt. Then she picked up her remaining macaroons, her copy of *TV Park* and the Russian-made bra she kept in her top drawer for comfort and left the clinic for the last time.

Terry watched her go. Even Andy McNab would have been hard pushed to call it a successful mission. Russians had so much to learn about the service ethic and customer care. It was his second near assault by a public servant in as many days. He looked at the shattered paperweight. The leaking snow and water were covering the desk, slowly being absorbed by the papers which had landed there. A large book was soaking up most of it. He picked it up. On the front it said 'Appointments' in English.

He picked up a saturated pen and dried it on his tattered cuff. Very slowly he copied the Cyrillic name of Katya's husband from the passport into the appointments diary, for Monday at 10 p.m. He smiled. What guile. After that he wrote, in English, 'Payment In Roubles Only', and underlined it several times. He looked at his watch and smiled again. The persona of Maxim Popov, *crippled mute*, was discarded. He was Terry Small, and on the way to the gym for a well-deserved workout and date with the lovely Umababs.

'Look, you must have contact numbers for these people. Give them a ring.' Alyosha thrust a mobile phone into Georgi's hand. Georgi demurred. Alyosha had already tried the number listed in the paper for Bodies Beautiful and hung up two lines into the piped verse set to music: 'Dear mourners, try to stay calm. Our job, as stated, is to embalm. Fear not, bereaved, help is at hand, though at present the office is not manned.'

The number Georgi had for one of the directors of Bodies Beautiful was at home, programmed into his spreadsheet after Anna (Alexeyevna, 115 Domededskaya, gives good head, princess type) and before Clavdia (Vladimerevna, 54 Klebny, busty, no transport).

'Sorry,' he said, 'I haven't got the number on me. All I know is that one of the directors is old and the other is foreign.' He looked at his watch; the tampon factory beckoned at five. 'Look, is there much point in us hanging about? I—'

'They *do* keep bodies here, right?' Alyosha was pacing up and down the corridor. Since his encounter with the world's least helpful nurse on the sixteenth floor, he had started to doubt the existence of Bodies Beautiful.

'I really couldn't tell you. I imagine—'

'So all we have to do is find them, right?' Alyosha sniffed the air, as if trying to detect the odour of rotting flesh, before returning to the door to give it another try. When it failed to open, he slammed a fist into it. 'Christ Almighty,' he breathed and thrust both hands into his pockets. Georgi, meanwhile, had sunk onto a ledge of skirting board.

'Why don't we just come back on Mond—'

It was the whistling which first alerted him to the man leaving the gents at the far end of the corridor. Georgi peered down the corridor. 'That man looks about as Russian as a Romanov pretender.'

Alyosha was battering the door with his shoulder. 'What of it?'

The man disappeared into the lift.

'As I just told you,' Georgi said patiently, 'one of the directors is foreign. You met the bloke. What did he look like?'

'White Americans all look pretty much the same to me,' Alyosha replied, nursing his shoulder. 'Badly dressed with a green jacket and an unfortunate pair of tasselled loafers.'

'Come on.' Georgi pulled Alyosha along the corridor to the lift, which was descending to the ground floor. When it returned two minutes later, the doors opened with a belch of aftershave.

'It smells like a Turkish brothel in here.'

'I wouldn't know, Father,' replied Alyosha as they creaked to the ground floor.

Father Georgi's motives for leaving the institute had, as usual, more to do with his alimentary canal than altruism. It was four hours since the culinary disaster at the Raevitches' dacha and he didn't expect the tampon factory would offer much in the way of gastronomic delight. His next best option was to grab something from a buffet on the ground floor, which he had noticed on passing closed at three.

'Hang on, Alyosha,' he said as the doors opened. 'I think he may have gone this way.' He strode off down a corridor away from the main entrance.

'But isn't that . . .?' Alyosha's expression of bewilderment resembled that of a dog who has been thrown two sticks. By the time he caught up with Georgi, the priest's cassock was covered in pastry crumbs.

'Could've sworn I saw him go this way,' he said, his cheeks full of food.

'Well, *I* think he was leaving the building. Hurry up or we'll lose him,' said Alyosha petulantly.

When they arrived in the courtyard it was starting to get dark. The air smelt of benzene. There was no sign of the foreigner. They went back to the car. Alyosha slammed his fist into the bonnet. 'Shit.' He knocked on the driver's window. 'Alexander, did you see which direction a bloke in a green jacket went, about five minutes ago?'

Alexander nodded and gestured for them both to get in.

'Gymski, please, nowski.' Terry smiled his plantation-owner-to-slave smile, superior yet empathetic.

The driver looked baffled and turned to drive away.

'Stopski. Dollarski.' He sighed. It had all become so routine.

The man was indistinguishable from most other taxi drivers Terry had stopped in the last few days, thick-necked and dressed in a leather coat. One huge plus point, however, was that he rarely saw any women drivers here, apart from, ironically, on the buses. Maybe they had been outlawed, as indeed they should be the world over. He thought of Grace vaguely swerving round a roundabout, no sense of lanes and barely aware of left and right. No, in an ideal society the driving licence for women would be the next to go after the clitoris.

244

'Get in,' the driver said to Terry in English.

'Premier Fitness,' said Terry as he stooped to coil himself into the car.

'American?' growled the driver.

'Englishski.' Changing into his loafers at the institute had been a mistake. Or was it his green jacket? It was a bit flamboyant.

'Charlton Athletic,' spat the driver. 'Bobby Moore,' he added in unwavering angry tones.

Terry had never followed football, though he had felt some sympathy with Bobby Moore's receding hairline over the years. He now felt so removed from the baldness camp that he felt he could comment.

'Ah yes, old baldie. No hairski. Ha ha.'

The driver retreated into moody silence until the car stopped in the forecourt of the gym, past the impassive Kalashnikov-slung guard on the gate. Terry produced a clutch of low-denomination dollars which he showed the driver, inviting him to make his selection. Without hesitation, he pocketed them all. He didn't acknowledge Terry as he hauled himself and his bag out of the car. Terry in turn didn't notice the rust-coloured Lada pull in behind them.

IV

The stair-climber at least allowed him limited capacity for thought. He'd tried to prop an English language paper in front of him but it kept collapsing or became too truncated to read. In any case, most of Bridges' concentration was given over to staying alive. Any remaining red blood cells in his brain had mutinied to fight on the heart front. If this was what cutting down to five cigarettes a day meant, you could forget it.

Friday was always a knock off early day. Even the professor swabbed down early to make way for the week-end. 'The start of the week is always busiest for the embalmed. Most people die over the weekend. Remember that, Bridges,' he'd told him when he'd downed tools and departed for whatever passed as recreation for the embalmer.

Bridges did have other reasons, other than near physical collapse, for the perspiration cascading off his body. The fax for one. Blue Eyes for two. He pressed a few buttons to learn just how long he'd spent climbing mountains. One minute ten seconds. He consoled himself with the thought that there might have been a power cut. Then, with the shock of an electric current attached to his genitals, the fax returned to him like the headlines in a black and white fifties film spinning onto the screen: 1926, Wall Street Crashes; 1919, *Titanic* Sinks; 1999, Soviet Spy Sentenced to Life Imprisonment.

Usually the Polish-made fax at his dacha only juddered into action with a request about an expired pension fund, an inquiry from a journalist, or a letter from his wife's lawyer. Last night it had borne different news.

To: Bob Bridges, Moscow
From: Senator B. Foreman
I am obliged to tell you that in the near future I hope to secure the necessary legal documentation

that will allow for your extradition from the former
Soviet Union so that you can be tried before a
Grand Jury in the United States of America on
espionage charges dating from the early 1980s
until your defection to Russia in 1987. As you may
or may not be aware, the crimes for which you
stand accused carry a life sentence.

The letter went on to outline the fate of other Soviet spies,
cheerily concluding with the execution in the electric chair
of Ethel and Julius Rosenberg on 19 June 1953. The fax
had been followed by a handwritten note which Bridges
had struggled to read.

Dear Spy,
    You may be an enemy of the people but I'm an
honest man and therefore prepared to do a deal.
If I arest [sic] you, thereby securing the votes of
every law-abiding citizen in the county, I will
personally see to it that you serve no more than
five years max (easy terms). If you play hard to
get I will chase your ass around the globe.
    Yours,
    B. Foreman, Senator.

It only confirmed what Susan had told him a week ago,
before she faxed the senator's picture and manifesto, that
his prosecution was forming the campaign platform for
this redneck's re-election. Maybe he should face the
music, but the thought of a state penitentiary froze his
blood, even at 170 heartbeats per minute. He decided to

stop. He jammed his hand over the control panel, hoping his palm would activate the stop button. After another lung-collapsing twenty seconds the mechanical feet halted.

Bridges stopped. As things stood he was sure that the Russian authorities, such as they were, would prevent his extradition. But how long until Boris Yeltsin offered him up as a sacrificial lamb when he had his hand out for another IMF loan? The number of countries he was welcome in was shrinking faster than a declining empire. He used to be able to holiday in Prague and Budapest, but since they'd applied for EC membership he was about as welcome as a Nazi war criminal. It was only a matter of time before he would be spending his vacations with Martin Bormann in a yurt in Mongolia.

He walked unsteadily over to the water dispenser. He wouldn't mind, but the closest he'd got to revealing any state secrets had been retyping a couple of chapters of Norman Mailer and disguising it as a secret CIA text. He now realised the Soviets had bundled him out of America as a fall guy for a truly prolific spy responsible for more leaks than an incontinent alcoholic. A man now serving life imprisonment who, in another world, would have been looking forward to happy retirement in the dacha next to his own.

Should he try the rowing machine or call it a day? He was, as ever on a Friday, due to meet up with Sergei in a couple of hours to swap the latest from the world of embalming for the best part of a bottle of Scotch. This afternoon he was early. A long session in the sauna would kill time. He positioned himself in the rowing machine, trying to fit his trainers into the pedals. It seemed that his oldest friend had been right to keep out of the death business. He might not have been followed by Blue Eyes on and off for the last thirty-six hours if he, too, had thrown in the embalming towel.

Who was that man he'd observed this afternoon from the fourteenth storey lab as he stubbed out cigarette after cigarette onto the forecourt of the institute. Not Blue Eyes this time but a man in an ankle-length leather coat.

Bridges shuddered and instinctively looked around the gym as he drew the pulley to chest height. Apart from a man wearing a towelling headband and an inane grin as he contorted himself on the ski machine, it was pretty quiet. Friday afternoon was a good time for the gym, most of the *nouveaux riches* having already left for the country, leaving him and the halfwit on the ski machine, together with a couple of mistresses temporarily jettisoned for a weekend with the family.

He looked at the clock above the juice bar where a woman in a pink leotard was squeezing oranges. The man in the headband began muttering to himself. God, thought Bridges, he must be a westerner. If the agonising pain of the rowing machine wasn't reason enough to leave, the probability of being forced into conversation with a madman was. He stood up, pulling his shoulders back and walking balls first, Russian style. As he draped his towel over his shoulders, he walked towards the sauna with his eyes locked on the door. He knew it was a mistake to look back, but he couldn't resist it.

The man in the headband was swaying from side to side on the ski machine. To no one in particular he was saying,

'Look. It's ski *ski*. Geddit? It's ski*ski*.' Then he laughed like a maniac.

V

Peter considered whether or not to answer the phone. Alyosha would have known what to do. He picked it up.

It was Alyosha.

'Look, that bloke, the foreigner at Bodies Beautiful, what did he look like? I remember the jacket, not the face.' Typical Alyosha, no preamble.

Peter paused. 'Your height, darkish. You know.'

'Yeah, I thought so.'

'Why?'

'Because I'm gonna pick him up.'

'What do you mean, *pick him up*?' Peter had an inward vision of Alyosha elevating him in a fraternal embrace.

'Well, which word don't you understand? Pick, him, or up?' Alyosha was tired of dealing with idiots. A frigging priest who had a date with a tampon factory, and a namby-pamby ex-public school boy. If any of the other gangs got to hear about it he would be a laughing stock. It was high time for some action. And action in his book meant unwarranted violence.

'Why?'

'*Why?*' Alyosha half breathed, half screeched. 'Because I can't find your father's sodding body. Your friend Georgi is about as much good as a . . .' he searched for the right word, 'as a *priest*. So I thought Frankenstein from the embalming empire might be able to point us in the right direction. That's why.'

'Oh. So no luck yet, then?'

'You could put it that way.'

'Where are you now?'

'Outside his gym.'

'OK then, well, good luck.' Peter hung up.

Alyosha snapped the phone shut with force. He swore and felt a dig in his ribs. He looked up at Alexander who had stopped flicking through a manual on Lada maintenance, his eyes, through the glass double doors, focused on a man in a green jacket in the lobby.

'It certainly looks like him. Come on, let's get him.' He gave Georgi a sharp nudge to get out of the car.

VI

When Katya turned the corner on the way to the gym she was ten minutes early. It was an eventful ten minutes. In the first thirty seconds she watched Terry being bundled into the back of a car two hundred yards away by two men, one of whom looked like a priest. Thrilling though the sight momentarily was, she knew it didn't bode well. There was no doubt that force had been used. She'd seen the flash of dull gun metal at his back as he'd been pushed in. The car had driven off before she could try and stop it, though she thought she'd glimpsed some of the licence plate. Terry had been flanked in the back seat by the two men who had grabbed him. She reached in her bag for what was left of Max's cigarettes, lit one, inhaled deeply twice, then, realising how cold it was, went through the

251

double doors leading to the gym. A blast of chloroform hit her as she sat down. It was eight minutes before Sonya was due to arrive. Hopefully, like all Russian women, she'd be half an hour late.

The shock of witnessing Terry's abduction very soon gave way to reason, and in the spirit of revelation several thoughts came to her mind at once.

Firstly, she didn't care if Terry Small had been kidnapped by Shi'ite gunmen or passing aliens; it was the implications that disturbed her. Any harm to Terry meant harm to her (via Clive, the node that linked them), and harm to her meant harm to Sasha.

'Excuse me, do you speak English?' The man was in his thirties and wore a white shirt and pair of jeans. He sounded agitated.

'Yes,' replied Katya cautiously. The last thing she needed was an American asking for Russian lessons, when the only thing meant by the locative case was finding her underwear.

'A man just left, did you happen to see which way he turned?'

She frowned. 'Well, yes, I did.'

'And?' The man was addressing her as if she was stupid. She didn't like him.

'And,' she paused, 'he was forced at gunpoint into the back of a car which has since left.' That, she thought, would knock the smugness off his face.

She was right. He collapsed.

At first Terry assumed he must have wet himself. It was only when one of the men elbowed him off a crushed carton of Just Juice that he realised that his bladder, at least, was intact.

Terry had known fear. Few in the jungle of garden sheds had not – lured to dangerous locations for a quote, at the very least disarmed of your mobile and measuring tape on the alleged site of an extension. But it was nothing compared to this. One of them, for Christ's sake, had a gun at his head. They were babbling incoherently like Middle Eastern terrorists. He thought of *Bravo Two Zero*.

Then the one on his left spoke.

'We want,' he started in slow, accented English, 'we want Hard Currency.'

Terry's heart stopped.

'We want Hard Currency. Or you die.' He repeated it more matter-of-factly. 'We want Hard Currency or you die.'

The salt from Terry's tears stung his cuts. At first he hadn't recognised his would-be murderers. Then he placed them. It was the couple he'd seen leaving the baldness clinic. They were on to him. He'd booked in for the operation in roubles and they wanted dollars. They were undoubtedly KGB. Poisoned darts, torture, disfigurement. Another tear landed on his gym bag.

CHAPTER NINE

I

He was getting used to coming round in a strange room after a workout. In fact, passing out had become an almost Pavlovian response to the stair-climber. The first time, admittedly after a bit to drink, he'd ended up at Professor Modin's makeshift morgue.

He looked round. Two walls were covered by dark red rugs, and another had a laminated photograph of a bowl of fruit which, Bridges thought, could have counted as pornography in the food shortage days of the eighties. The room was lit by an Art Nouveau lamp. The curtains were green velvet. There was a feeling of fading opulence to the room. He had the sensation of being part of a Chekhovian stage set. Two doors led from the room, where he noticed an incongruous neatly packed holdall with an overturned bottle of Hugo Boss deodorant resting on top.

He had a raging thirst. Luckily, whoever had laid him to rest on the sofa, covering him with a Spice Girls duvet, had thought to leave a glass of water on the table next to him. He eyed it suspiciously before automatically feeling his back pocket for his wallet, which was still there. But if anyone was going to slip him a Mickey Finn, he reasoned, they'd have done it before rather than after he'd passed out. At the back of his mind, deep in his short-term memory banks – like the amnesiac in a Hitchcock film – he knew something had gone horribly wrong.

He looked round for his jacket and couldn't see it. What *was* he doing here? Even more suspiciously, he couldn't even remember alcohol being involved. Then it came to him. Falling asleep in the sauna. The woman. The jacket. The kidnapping.

He got up and walked to the door, tripping over as he did so a misshapen lump of metal. At first he took it for a torture device, but then recognised it from the gym as something to flatten stomachs with. The door was double-locked from the outside. He returned to the holdall and flicked half-heartedly through the contents. A couple of bad taste shirts, all western labels, none of which he recognised. None of it was in keeping with the rest of the flat, which looked as if its greatest gesture towards modernity was an antique television set.

He sank back down on the sofa. His trousers were caked in a dry dirt. He tentatively removed them, aware of a stiffness in his right side, and laid them over a ladder-back chair opposite the sofa. He badly needed a drink. Even a restorative draught of embalming fluid wouldn't go amiss. His watch read eight thirty, though he had no real way of knowing if it was a.m. or p.m.

He lay back down on the sofa and moved his feet under the duvet. He reached over and switched off the lamp, comforting himself with the thought that few international terrorists FBI agents or members of the Russian Mafia listened to the Spice Girls. In case he was wrong, he took the precaution of leaving the stomach flattener by his bed, though short of killing his abductors with two hundred abdominal crunches he wasn't sure how much good it would do him.

It was the scraping noise on the floor between the carpet and the parquet that woke him up. Momentarily, in the tar-black darkness of his disorientation, he took it to be an infestation of mice which was plaguing his dacha. Then he remembered. As he did so, he lowered his right hand to grasp the abdominiser. In one movement he found the lamp switch and lifted the abdominiser over his head, at the same time drawing his feet to his chest. He clicked the light on. While his eyes tried to adjust, more light filled the room. It felt like an explosion.

The door burst open and a woman appeared.

'*Stop!*' she yelled with a fury that made Bridges' aim swerve violently off course. Straight off, he noticed the gun in her hand. Beneath him, he was aware of a small animal crawling under the table.

The woman pointed the gun at his head with the precision of a trained markswoman.

'Drop that now and don't move,' she yelled. Then her pitch and tone increased. She started to scream in Russian. 'Sasha, what the hell do you think you are playing at?'

Bridges heard small scuffles under the table. He looked at the woman. He looked down, trying to cover his unclothed bottom half with the abdominiser.

'Nothing, Mum. It's just that you said he was an

American. I wanted to see his credit cards.'

'You were *stealing* his credit cards?' The gun was still fixed on Bridges.

'Mum, no! Of course not,' he said plaintively. 'I just wanted to see which ones I ought to apply for. You know we—'

'Sasha, unless you really want to see me lose my temper, I suggest you get up, go next door and get on with your homework.'

The small boy, dressed in a Power Rangers T-shirt and jeans, got up and ran out, slaloming round the woman. She looked at Bridges. She was tall and blonde with hair that looked as if it was periodically cut with a pair of nail scissors and dried in the gas oven. She was wearing a pair of jeans and a sweatshirt. Her skin, as much of it as he could see, was tanned. She wasn't young, though she had the sort of face he thought looked better now than it had a decade ago. And even then it would have looked pretty good. Her brown eyes were tired and lively at the same time. Despite the small arms element to her character, which he hoped might be temporary, he wanted to touch her. He adjusted the position of the abdominiser.

'And you,' she said in English, 'are you in the habit of assaulting young children?' The gun dropped a couple of inches to chest height.

'No. Are you in the habit of kidnapping grown men, Mrs . . .?'

'Miss,' she snapped. 'Pah! That is, how do you say, *charming*, considering I am no less than your,' she ran her left hand through her hair, '*saviour*.' The word was more spat than spoken.

Bridges blinked. It was the second time in as many weeks that a kidnapper had claimed to have his interests at heart.

'And exactly how do you work that out, Miss . . .'

She shook her head in irritation. She looked like the sort of woman who, when you were eighteen, you hoped you'd end up married to when you were older. She looked spunky, maternal and sexy. She didn't look as if she'd spend your money on tennis lessons and three-Martini lunches.

'At the gym this afternoon I witnessed two men kidnapping a friend of mine.' She looked him straight in the eye. He tried to smile, though it came out as a gulp. 'On hearing this news, you passed out. I have no idea why my friend, who is new to this country, should have been abducted. In the hope that you might be able to assist after you came round, I thought it best to bring you back to my home.'

Bridges was as far from understanding the fuller implications of this explanation as he was from renouncing drink or setting up home in the Pentagon.

He felt an explanation of his own was in order. 'It was simply the heat of the sauna that knocked me out—'

'I neither know nor care.' There was an attractiveness about Russian women, thought Bridges, that had nothing to do with the sexual insatiability of Catherine the Great. It was their off-handedness combined with suppressed passion.

There was silence. He broke it.

'You live here?' His eyes swept the room.

Katya was insulted. 'Not exactly.' She saw no reason to

expand on that. 'I live next door with my son.'

Bridges slumped back into the sofa. It crackled under him. Unthinkingly his hand felt behind the cushion and retrieved a rainbow of foil Nutri-Grain wrappers.

He found himself speaking. 'I don't suppose you've got anything to drink?'

Katya bit her top lip and frowned slightly. Bridges smiled. One thing he did know. If he'd been playing the escalator game and seen her at the top, he probably wouldn't have looked any further.

II

Not since he'd had to bless a microwave with holy water – sparsely, as it turned out, so as not to fuse it – had he felt so uncomfortable. How did you sanctify a tampon factory? Georgi smiled beatifically towards the director, Alexander Pishkov, the 32-year-old entrepreneur who, as he'd proudly explained, had plugged the hole in feminine hygiene.

'Tell me,' he'd demanded, 'what do you think Soviet women used to use when menstruating?' When Georgi had shaken his head animatedly as if this was a question that kept him up most nights, the reply had been triumphant: 'Rags and cotton wool!' Pishkov's breath, Georgi had noticed, smelt of garlic and something metallic. 'Is that any way to herald in a new democratic country?' Pishkov asked. 'Would Hillary Clinton be caught one week in four with a pair of socks down her knickers?'

'No, absolutely not,' Georgi had replied with as much dignity as he could muster while focusing on a cartoon poster of a truncated woman with her knee raised to demonstrate the correct method of insertion.

'Women are our tomorrow. Tampons are the way ahead. Problem-free periods are our future.'

Half a dozen earnest young women clustered near Pishkov's desk gave him a round of applause. As a slogan it was unlikely to catch on, thought Georgi as he nodded and joined in the applause with a broad smile. An older woman with tightly coiled black hair was showing rather less enthusiasm for the director's vision of the future, he noticed. She looked like one of the spinster victims of the Second World War, the hard-faced result of a generation of women deprived of men.

When the applause had died down, Georgi spoke. 'Now, let us bless this brave endeavour.' Periods made him sick. No wonder they called them the curse. You could spend a week's wages taking a woman out to dinner only to be told, later, that she was on her *holiday*, as Russians euphemistically termed it. Once he'd even tried to factor them into his spreadsheet – it was amazing what you could do with Windows 98 – but despite the software, few of his girlfriends managed to adhere to a lunar cycle.

The director, who was dressed in a white linen suit, said, 'No, please, first I would like to introduce you to our factory's deputy manager, Mrs Kharkova.' He turned to the black-haired spinster who acknowledged the introduction by lowering her eyes and fastening them on Georgi's crotch. He felt his testicles shrivel.

'Tell me, Father,' said the director, following the

woman's gaze, 'what exactly does that represent?' He pointed at the 'Love is' apron still suspended from Georgi's midriff.

Georgi relaxed. Of course, it must be the apron that held Mrs Kharkova's interest. Clearly, nobody here understood English.

'It represents the passing of the ten commandments to Moses,' he said smoothly. 'The one with the biggest heart is God on Mount Sinai.'

The director nodded. 'I see. And now I'd like to introduce you to our designer, Vladimir,' he said, apparently in no hurry to proceed with the blessing.

A man as thin as a broom, with sinister brown glasses, and clothed head to foot in manmade fabrics, stepped forward. His handshake was limp and damp. Georgi smiled.

The director was beaming like a father. He shook his head and sighed self-effacingly, 'From parachutes to tampons.' Georgi glanced at his watch and shot a look towards Alyosha, who was fingering a box of tampons. Georgi wondered how long his explanation that Alyosha was his altar boy could realistically be maintained.

'The porous material used in the canopy is what we actually use in the product,' the director went on as Georgi extricated his blessing kit from his bag and cast around for somewhere to stick the candles. Tampon production must result in a fearful chemical reaction because it was awfully hot in the factory and the smell of glue was overpowering. A stream of sweat was trickling down his back, unabsorbed by the salopettes. This was fast turning into one of the worst days of his life. The Raevitch debacle had been bad enough but the abduction had been even worse. They'd stuck the bald guy in the cellar of a nearby outhouse, accessed through a mud courtyard and shrouded by bushes, for the duration of the service. Neither of them had been sure what to do with him. His dogged refusal to speak had impressed rather than irritated Alyosha. As they were driving, he'd said, 'This is worse than I thought. If he's refusing to speak, there's a reason.' He'd scratched his head. 'Maybe, *maybe* he understands the importance of the number. Maybe one of the other gangs has got to him first. Maybe—'

At this point the man jammed between them on the back seat had released an unnatural-sounding groan and started rotating his head from side to side. Whether because of the baldness or the subhuman noise, Georgi was reminded of a serial killer who had appeared behind bars in a Rostov court, charged with fifty-three murders. It might have reminded Alyosha of the same thing because they both instinctively edged away. That had been shortly before they'd decided to imprison him next to the factory.

'Perhaps he's been hanging around with corpses too long,' Alyosha had murmured as they manhandled him out of the car. That had been twenty minutes ago.

Now the tampon director continued with a smile, 'It means so much that you are here as a representative of the Church to bless our enterprise.' He touched Georgi's black sleeve. God! He hated it when they did that. Not only did it represent an unwanted intrusion into his personal space, it was so often the sign of a more general malaise.

263

'Why exactly?' he asked, a nervous feeling in the pit of his stomach.

'Why what?'

'Why does it mean so much that I bless your enterprise?'

Pishkov looked hurt. 'Because, Father, despite the spiritual privations of communism, I was brought up a true believer. In fact it was sympathy for the plight of the Virgin Mary and her kind that drove me to ease women's burden.' He smiled and lowered his head. 'Remember, Father, only women bleed.'

'Quite.' He looked aghast. At the other side of the office Alyosha had eased himself into the company of the female workers with an expression which suggested he was after a practical demonstration. A trill of indignant laughter punctuated the silence. The sense of expectation was becoming intolerable.

The director said, 'How long do you expect the service to last, Father? I calculated an hour or so.'

'Of course, yes, naturally, if you go for the shortened ceremony,' bluffed Georgi. He was racking his brains to think how to translate his usual mumbo jumbo, issued to people who thought an icon was the first person of a verb to deceive, into a credible religious incantation. He glanced at Alyosha as he strode purposefully across the flagstoned floor, looking for somewhere to insert a candle. When he returned, the director crossed himself and bowed his head. His scalp was red and scaly with lumps of dandruff in it the size of sleet pellets.

Georgi inhaled and raised his hands, calling for silence. Then he started, reading from an American poster on the far wall, speaking in accented though very creditable English, 'Oh Lord. First wash hands thoroughly before removing the wrapper.' He lifted his incense carrier shoulder high and waved it from side to side. He raised his voice to a falsetto. 'Father, to insert the tampon sit with legs apart or raise one foot on the lid and relax.'

It clearly wasn't what the workers of the former Factory 347 for the Production of Parachutes were expecting. Mrs Kharkova had gone pale. Georgi ignored her as she nudged the director and whispered indignantly in his ear. Her boss's scaly pate twisted up from looking at the floor and stared at Georgi in disbelief.

Georgi strode from one side of the office to the other, shaking the incense like a carpet cleaner as he went. He looked up. 'Oh Mother of God, toxic shock syndrome is a rare but serious illness which can occasionally be fatal—'

'What are you trying to do?' said Pishkov in a low voice which seemed to be restraining temper as a muzzle restrains a pit bull. A cotton ball of saliva was lodged in the corner of his mouth. 'Why are you using the words from our tampon brochure as part of a religious ceremony? Are you by any chance seeking to make fun out of this venture?'

Shit. Mrs Kharkova could actually speak English. '*Make fun?* Christ, no. Not at all. It's just that—'

'I don't think there's anything remotely amusing about menstruation. Do you?' Pishkov's finger was index deep in Georgi's cassock.

'Goodness me, no. Some of my best friends menstr— I mean, where would we be without peri—?' Georgi looked to Alyosha for support. He was exchanging numbers with the dark-skinned secretary.

The two guards seemed to appear from nowhere, but Georgi worked out later that they must have emerged from the other side of a fire exit on the far wall, probably summoned by the outrage emanating from the director. They looked like twins cleaved from the same demonic egg which Georgi, given the context, couldn't help wishing had disappeared twenty-odd years ago embedded in a regular tampon. Both wore identical black suits.

Even as one sank his squat fist into the soft part of his cheek, he remembered thinking it odd that a factory devoted to feminine hygiene should require a security service. Maybe it was time for him, too, to move with the times – employ a minder, take on a bodyguard.

Two things saved him from a much more serious beating – the salopettes and Alyosha, who entered the fray with unconcealed joy. The women scrambled for the door amid hysterical screaming. The director, however, stayed to watch.

Georgi had never been much of a fighter, basing his combat skills – or lack of them – on the fact that no one would hit a man of the cloth. As he received another blow to the face and a globule of blood or mucus landed on his assailant's black suit, he thought it was high time to update this view. While Alyosha and his partner twirled and wrestled like demented ballroom dancers, he and his adversary clasped each other in a clumsy embrace. Georgi was aware of the guard's sour breath panting in his ear and half attempted a head butt, then realised his neck was clamped to the bodyguard's chest.

It was the gun that saved the day. As Alyosha sent a knee into his adversary's groin, he yanked his Beretta from an inside pocket.

'OK, gentlemen, I don't intend to use this unless you make me.' Blood was pouring from his nose. 'Now, you put my friend the priest down and turn round.' Georgi could have hugged him. 'All three of you walk towards the fire exit.'

As the trio turned, Pishkov looked at Georgi who had hauled himself off the floor and was visibly shaking. 'What kind of a priest do you call yourself?' he asked contemptuously.

'What kind of a tampon manufacturer do you call *yourself*?' George retorted, aware that it wasn't the most grown-up of rejoinders. He sniffed loudly.

'Come on, Father, let's go.' Alyosha barricaded the fire exit with a bench and strode out of the door. Georgi hobbled after him.

III

Under pressure it was amazing the resources the human body provided you with. He corrected himself. It was amazing the resources the body of a finely-honed athlete provided you with. He looked around the lockup where he'd been dumped. Even by Russian standards, surely, it didn't comply with international guidelines. What about the Geneva Convention? The smell was the worst, like some sort of chemical glue mixed with mildew. As his eyes adjusted to the gloom he made out clouds of fabric against the walls. Like all good commandos he'd made a mental note of where his captors had taken him – fourteen steps down, across some sort of courtyard past a group of outhouses which, apart from the 1950s feel, had reminded him of the industrial park headquarters of Pagodas R Us.

He tested one of the fabric piles with his foot to see if it shrouded anything.

At least he hadn't sobbed outright which, admittedly, he had done when he'd been locked in that gazebo overnight by an unsatisfied customer in Penge. Though in retrospect he'd put that down to the noxious-smelling weedkiller in the corner. No, all in all, he felt he'd acquitted himself quite well. He'd risen to the challenge. He might even get a book out of it when he got home. Serialised in one of the Sunday papers. *Tango* (for Terry) *Two Zero*. All he had to do was bluff it out. Maintain his disguise behind enemy lines.

In theory they could never prove he wasn't the Russian mute he claimed to be. You only got caught out when you were off guard, like when that bloke in *The Great Escape* (who also used to be in *The Professionals*) blew it when he replied to the German guard in English. He just had to keep schtum.

They'd kept going on and on, especially the young one in the Tommy Hilfiger shirt with his laughable accent: *we want hard currency. Hard currency.* Christ, he knew the country was on the ropes, but did they really have to bring in the security services when someone tried to diddle them out of the price of one baldness operation? It was almost worth writing to Anne Robinson about. See how she twitched herself around the *Watchdog* studios explaining that one.

He sank onto a pile of something soft in the corner. As the adrenaline started to seep from his veins, he thought how cold it was. He was also extremely hungry. He still had his bag with his disguise in it with him. He reached in and pulled out a beige acrylic jumper.

He wasn't yet shaken from his course. He was booked into the clinic on Monday at ten o'clock. In theory, all he had to do was escape this makeshift dungeon, evade his captors and get back to the hospital. Nil desperandum, Terry old chap, he said to himself. He hadn't come three thousand miles just to fall at the last. If he could only obtain a few more follicles, who knew what else might fall into place? A date with the lovely Umababs. He might never return to Basingstoke. They might marry. He could open a branch of Pagodas R Us in Moscow. She could model the joys of the outdoor life in her bikini – though not, he conceded, in winter. Suddenly he felt invigorated and leapt to his feet to pull on the acrylic jumper. It was then that he noticed the jacket he was wearing wasn't a Cecil Gee original (MRP £199.99) but a Far Eastern copy.

Damnation, he must have picked up the wrong one at the gym. He tentatively went through the pockets. Nothing but a telegram in the inside pocket and a business card in Russian with the silhouette of what looked like an ancient Egyptian mummy. The telegram was in English: 'Dear Spy, Coming sooner than you think. Prepare to meat your maker. Senator B.'

He screwed it up and tossed it over the hump of a hillock of material. Less than five minutes later, feeling like

Alice Through the Looking Glass – the macho version –
he was asleep.

IV

'I suppose you want a cup of tea as well?' How Katya
hated wasting resources on someone who wasn't, or
shouldn't be, part of her life. The American, who had just
downed a second glass of vodka, shook his head.

Sasha sauntered into the kitchen clutching a pen and
paper. He looked at his mother with earnest inquiry. 'Ask
him what the interest rate is on his American Express and
what income bracket is required for a Gold Card.'

She took a gulp of black tea. 'Ask him yourself.'

'He doesn't speak Russian.'

'How do you know?'

'He's American, they never speak Russian. Language is
the imperial tool of the conquering race.' Under the table
Leonid had started licking his bare feet.

'Who told you that?' Katya was smiling.

'Mrs Voronsheva. She hates all foreigners.'

They both looked at Bridges. Some colour had returned
to his cheeks. Katya picked up the remaining half-bottle
and poured out two more glasses.

'Sasha, fascinating though this is, could you excuse us? I
have to talk to this man in private.'

There was obviously something on his mind. He started
to skulk. 'Where's the bald one gone?'

'He's been called away on business. Now please go.' He
started to hop from foot to foot. It was possible, Katya

thought, he was about to launch into a list of reasons why he should be allowed a mobile phone. She sighed. 'Was there something else?'

'No. Er, yes. Can Misha stay for a couple of days?' He was doodling on the pad.

'Yes, as long as his mum knows.' Before she'd finished, Sasha had disappeared out of the front door. 'Where do you think you're—?'

Leonid leapt up and followed him, barking.

'He's quite a kid,' said Bridges. 'Was it your husband, the guy who got kidnapped?'

Despite her antipathy towards him, Katya found it intolerable that he could imagine anything between herself and Terry. Then she remembered, he'd never met Terry.

'It it's any of your concern, which I doubt, my husband is away on business. We are in any case – how do you Americans say – having a trial separation.'

A draught was coming through the kitchen window. Katya got up to close the curtains, pausing as she always did to watch the stream of headlights in the distance. It was her favourite time of day. The limbo after work and the calm before she had to straitjacket Sasha into bed. By some happy coincidence she'd spotted an old woman selling pumpkin yesterday. Orange vegetables were so hard to find and it was important for Sasha to get enough vitamins at this time of year.

She compartmentalised her tasks. Feed her son. Interrogate the American. She glanced at him as she stopped to pick the pumpkin from the vegetable rack. She caught him staring at her with the same demented expression Leonid wore when he was mounting the furniture.

He cleared his throat. 'He'll never eat that. Kids hate squash.'

'Exactly how much do you know about the eating habits of the post-perestroika Russian child?' She'd been trying for haughty but it had come out as fury.

'Nothing at all. I'm just saying that kids don't like vegetables at the best of times, never mind ones that look like they've been grown in the Chernobyl fallout zone.' He drained his glass again, though he'd finished the drink some time ago.

'When I need your advice on nutrition, I will—' Sasha and Misha walked in. 'Jesus Christ, what have you been up to?' Misha looked as if he'd spent the last few weeks as a foot soldier at Borodino. His hair was matted and his clothes appeared to be forming the compost layer of a vegetable experiment.

'Can he have a bath, Mum?' Sasha asked. 'He's just got back from a trip to see his, er, gran. In the country. They didn't have any running water and then the train ride was four days. Isn't that right, Misha?'

Misha sniffed and nodded. He looked as if he'd been crying.

'Do you both think I was born yesterday? I'm going to phone your mother, Misha.' She stalked towards the phone.

When she returned three minutes later Sasha was cutting the pumpkin into chunks of a flushable size before passing them to Misha, who formed the solitary link in a human chain en route to the lavatory. The American was peeling potatoes onto the inside pages of a Russian newspaper,

Katya noted with annoyance, that she'd been keeping for the classifieds.

The betray was worse than the waste of food. 'Sasha, stop that immediately.' She clipped him lightly on the back of the head. 'Misha, there's no reply from your house. You may start running the bath.' She turned to Bridges. 'What do you think you're doing?'

'I thought they might eat some fries.' He smiled. 'Fries are my speciality.'

Katya picked up the knife Sasha had obediently flung onto the table. 'Look, I think it's time you and I had what you might call a little chat.' She put the knife in the sink and returned to the table to pour two more glasses of vodka.

She sat down opposite Bridges, simultaneously exhaling and running a hand through her hair. She noticed he was looking at her again. She tried to put it down to the alcohol but something told her otherwise.

'Is there something wrong with you?'

'Sorry?'

'You seem to be staring at me. It's unnerving. Please desist.'

'Sorry.' He looked away. The noise of splashing from the bathroom was followed by childish whoops and then a yelp.

Katya stood up wearily. 'They've got Leonid in the bath again. The mess will be terrible.' She left the kitchen. Bridges heard raised Russian voices. Katya returned, self-consciously trying to cover the front of her sweatshirt which was soaking.

She sat down heavily and took a long contemplative

swig of her drink. She'd already called to apologise to Sonya. She'd told her Sasha had 'flu. Other matters were more pressing. The Englishman was due to fly back in less than a week. The implications of his not being on the flight were unthinkable. She imagined a uniformed Clive stooped over his military campaign table arranging to send wave after wave of fighter planes to blanket-bomb her apartment block.

She narrowed her eyes and stared at Bridges, aware now that she had closed the kitchen door, of the tap dripping loudly into the enamel sink. Bridges had gone back to peeling potatoes. In a curious way, she registered, it made an acceptable domestic scene.

'So please tell me, who are you? For whom do you work and why would anyone want to kidnap you?'

V

The tampons had done very little to stem the blood flowing down both their faces. Also, having one up either nostril meant you had to breathe through your mouth and the string got in the way.

'I don't know how women cope with these things every month,' said Alyosha, ramming one further up his right nostril.

'Well, I might not be as well versed on the finer points of human reproduction as some, but I feel fairly confident that they're not designed *strictly* for use up the nose,' replied Georgi.

'S'pose not,' replied Alyosha in a sulky, nasal way as the

Lada turned illegally past McDonald's on Pushkin Square and left into Tverskaya Ulitsa.

'Are you sure we were right to leave him there?' Georgi wound down one of the windows and prepared to launch the tampon past a street corner babushka selling bottles of beer and dried fish.

'Certainly. What harm can he come to? A couple of nights in a warehouse might mean he'll be happier to relinquish Hard Currency on Monday,' said Alyosha.

Much as he might try to resist, Georgi was finding it impossible not to get drawn into this tragi soap opera. He said, 'Look, what's the rush? Surely you're going to get the body back soon for the funeral?' He lobbed another tampon out of the window.

Alyosha tutted loudly and shook his head. 'Don't you know it's bad to litter, man? Have you no civic pride?'

Both men studied the grey slush-splashed tableau outside. On one corner an unemptied dumpster overflowed with rubbish. Cardboard boxes lined a side street. Discarded vodka bottles were left at monotonously regular one-metre intervals. Shoppers sidestepped to avoid comatose drunks, a couple of whom may well have been dead.

'Not a great deal, no,' replied Georgi.

Alyosha nodded, suggesting he thought the priest had made a valid point. He continued, 'The reason we need the body pronto is because we have what you might term a cash flow problem. One of our fraternity has been . . .' It really was family business, but then again there was nothing like a punch-up for a bit of male bonding. In any case, he had a dim memory that all information given to priests was confidential. It had been in *The Godfather*. 'One of our number has been kidnapped, so we need to open the cash box sooner rather than later.'

While Georgi weighed up this information, Alyosha sank into the seat and considered. The benefits of having a priest on the firm's books were beginning to become obvious. Apart from that fracas in the tampon factory, he imagined very few people would harm a man of God. He glanced at his apron-clad friend. Or a man of the 'Love is' cartoon series, or pioneer of the feminine hygiene religious service, or whatever else this man claimed to be. Take the kidnapping. Say Father Georgi turned up with a suitcase full of money which was only *half* full, how many people would produce a semi-automatic weapon to fill him with more holes than Christianity's theory of evolution?

He delved in his jacket pocket and fished out a packet of Marlboro Lights and offered Georgi one. He lit them both and snapped his Zippo shut. Both inhaled deeply.

'So, Father,' Alyosha said, letting the smoke out in a series of perfectly formed rings, revelling in the post-fight bonhomie – which he personally preferred to the post-coital cigarette – 'how about joining the staff full time?'

VI

Deny everything, admit nothing and make counter-allegations had been Bridges' modus operandi for so long he was unsure if, even in these circumstances, he had the ability to change it.

It had been the interrogation technique of the CIA and subsequently his tradecraft had been refined by the KGB. It was an obvious conversational ploy, but none the less successful for that. Most proficient liars mastered it early on. It went something like this.

Husband: 'You are having an affair with your tennis coach.'

Wife: 'I most certainly am not and besides, what about you and that secretary at the Christmas party?' Or

CIA officer: 'You are spying for the Soviets.'

Spy: 'I am not. If I were why would I be driving a beat-up Chevy?'

So when a beautiful woman asked him straight out about the nature of his employment, it was inevitable he would lie. It was inbred. At one point in his post-defection reincarnation he had laboured under fifteen aliases – a situation which often, especially after alcohol, left him flailing for an identity. Generally he took it as fitting that he should so rarely know who he was. He had, after all, a past he couldn't allude to and a future he could hardly guess at. Only recently had he experienced the slightest sense of belonging, of contentment. Sitting in this strange kitchen with this spiky woman and her delinquent son, his friend and their dog as a swirl of snow bellowed past outside, he felt it more keenly. He wanted to belong. But old habits died hard.

'My name is Ivan Ivanovitch. I am thirty-seven years old and was born in Ohio of Russian parents, which is why,' he used the same self-deprecating smile he always did, 'my

Russian is so lousy. I came to Moscow two years ago to work as an investment consultant for a multinational. And no, I have no idea why anyone would want to kidnap me.'

As he was speaking he was aware of Katya's fixed attention; she was scrutinising him as if he was attached to a lie detector. She didn't speak. Neither did he. The need to fill a conversational gap was a sign of weakness. He'd learnt that from his wife rather than the CIA.

In the event it was a full five minutes before she returned from the sink and placed the vegetable peeler, which had sliver of pumpkin peel lodged between its silver jaws, on the melamine table. Pushing a strand of hair under a clip on the top of her head, a move which Bridges was finding increasingly adorable, she said, 'Well, I have to find him. It's a matter of, er, life and death.'

'Why? I mean who is he to you?'

'That, Mr Ivanovitch, is none of your business. What is your business is that I have to recover him before the week is finished.'

Bridges started picking at a mole on the back of his wrist. 'Maybe they were in fact after this friend of yours and not me at all.' He was trying to work it out. Someone had tried to abduct him, but thanks to a million to one mistake they'd got the wrong man. If it was the Mafia, they were likely to shoot and ask questions later. He could do the honourable thing and come clean about the nature of his employment and possibly help to save the life of an innocent man. Or he could walk away.

Like two grand masters hunched over a chessboard, they were both locked in a world of separate thoughts.

Katya was the first to speak, and when she did, it seemed to him that her entire aspect metamorphosed in a way that only women and lizards could manage. Her eyes became larger and her mouth, which until five minutes ago had been tightly shut, was now slightly open. Her upper body seemed to have moved closer to him. She spoke with her head lowered and through eyelashes which seemed to go up and down as fast as her chest. 'It's just that . . .' She shook her head. 'It really would be awful if I didn't retrieve him. Not just for me, but for Sasha. But no, I couldn't ask.'

'Ask what?' Bridges knew he was walking into a trap.

'It's just that I wouldn't know where to start looking for him. I work at the university. He's a visiting English lecturer, did I mention that?'

'Then why can't the people at MGU help find him?' asked Bridges.

'He's not supposed to be here yet. I offered to put him up as we share a love of Pushkin. Why are you asking all these questions?' she added irritably.

'What about the police? If the man was your lover—'

'I said a love of Pushkin,' she interrupted harshly. Then, much softer and while caressing her throat, she continued, 'Oh no, he's certainly not my *lover*.' She looked hard into Bridges' eyes as she said the word. 'Personally, I prefer a much *younger* man. A man who can satisfy me not just intellectually but sexually. We Russian women can be very demanding.'

Bridges swallowed.

Katya's voice lowered confidentially. 'Very demanding indeed.'

In retrospect, he wasn't sure what happened. But in less than five minutes he'd promised to devote every waking moment to tracking down Professor Terry Small. He'd sworn that no stone would go unturned. No lead not acted upon. And for once in his life he meant it.

VII

The boys were topped and tailed in Sasha's bed. Misha's feet were cold and Sasha was worried about verrucas. He didn't think a facial wart would do much to help him ingratiate himself among the movers and shakers in later life.

He thought of the American his mother had put to bed in the flat next door where the bald man had stayed. He could understand stocks and shares, but he never really understood what it was his mother did. When he was little she'd told him that whereas in Russia they had a shortage of bread, in the west they had a shortage of women. It was like a fairy tale. The men were like knights marrying Russian princesses and they all lived happily ever after.

But if that was the case, why did he only hear fighting from the flat next door where the foreigners stayed? Men and women seemed to wrestle with each other all night long in there. The moans, groans and rhythmic bangs sometimes woke him up. He just hoped his mother knew what she was doing until it was his turn to look after her.

'Sasha, are you awake?'

He'd almost forgotten about Misha. 'What's the matter?'

'I want to go home. I miss Mummy.' He seemed to be choking back a sob. This was no time for tears.

'Not much longer now, Mish, I promise. Then everything will be OK.' He hoped he sounded like a true leader of men. 'Forever,' he added more definitely.

CHAPTER TEN

I

'You left him in the tampon factory?' It was not the sort of question Peter expected to be asking before nine o'clock on a Saturday morning. Or in fact at any time.

Alyosha nodded, his hands flitting across the table with the precision of a croupier, trying to scoop up all the jam jars before Father Georgi got a look in. Only an improbable mango and passion fruit eluded him. 'Well, not the tampon factory, *as such*, more a sort of outhouse. We meant to take him with us, it's just that things got a bit out of hand.'

'I can see that.' Peter exhaled ostentatiously as he surveyed his friend's battered face. Two bloody scabs had formed at the base of both nostrils. The priest seemed to have fared better; his only obvious injury was a battered eye, more purple than black. Peter sighed again. He was finding it difficult to play anything other than the admonitory big brother to Alyosha's irresponsible younger sibling but didn't seem able to halt it. It made him think of one of the volumes from Em's extensive self-help library, *You*

Can Make Others Do It. He resolved to track down a copy.

He adjusted his De Montfort tie. 'Is it impossible for you to do anything without violence?'

Alyosha grinned by way of reply and went back to eating breakfast. Or more exactly eating *around* breakfast – the usual Tadzhik special of fermented mare's milk and unleavened bread. 'Where does he find this stuff in Moscow?' he asked. 'I mean, can you imagine *milking* a horse?' He stopped chewing. 'Then again, why milk a horse and a cow and not, say, a dog or a rabbit?'

'Udders would be too small,' said Georgi, rousing himself out of a moody silence at the other end of the table and in a simultaneous pincer movement retrieving two jars of jam from Alyosha's condiment cache.

'What about elephants, then? I would have thought elephants would be the mammary pin-up of the animal kingdom.'

'Elephants aren't domestic animals.' Georgi spoke with the authority of an ordained man.

'Camel?' Alyosha ventured.

'Ditto.'

A silence for physical and mental digestion followed. Sun streamed into the dining room, shafts of it lighting up dust particles above the table. Alyosha, sitting at the head of the table, had rigged up a speaker out of which a Radiohead CD had just finished playing. Peter could half hear the early morning Radio Moscow phone-in from the kitchen. The topic was economic meltdown and Olga, along with the rest of her family, had lost everything. The slick DJ commiserated briefly and then cut her off, saying he had more calls waiting. Too right, thought Peter, approximately 200 million of them.

Elsewhere in the house a telephone rang. Peter chose not to answer it.

'Why can't we have cereal like everyone else these days?' Alyosha was spreading peanut butter on something like a chapati. At the other end of the table Georgi was on his fourth bowl of Russian porridge.

'And another thing.' Peter spoke through gritted teeth. 'Why is he still here?' He jerked his head towards Georgi who, he saw, had defrocked himself down to his salopettes.

'Because,' said Alyosha, 'I think having a bone fida priest on our books would be an asset to the firm.'

'Fine, if he were a bona fide priest, but if that man,' he pointed at him with his eyes, 'is a representative of any recognised religion, I'm the Pope.' The strain of the last few days was starting to take its toll on Peter. The week's grace Hard Currency's business partners – he used the words in their loosest sense – had given him had elapsed. The phone in his study rang constantly. Some wanted details of the funeral arrangements, others simply talked in tongues. What about these share options, that gas company, this factory? That was aside from his missing half-brother and comatose stepmother. He had a recurrent dream that he was drowning, a feeling that stayed with him most days. Or that he was a long-distance swimmer too far from either bank ever to make it back.

He longed for a couple of pints in the student bar at De Montfort, discussing nothing more taxing than the cricket scores, but something told him he was unlikely ever to return to the rarefied atmosphere of the drawing room of the Palmer-Smythes. He was finding it harder and harder to even imagine Em, despite the time he spent staring at a picture of her, scantily dressed and covered in mud – she was captain of the De Montfort ladies' rugby team. What did she sound like, how had she smelt? In a more terrifying panic yesterday he'd found it impossible to recall anything of his father. He needed something to cling to, to stop his entire life being swept out to sea like sand.

'It never did Rasputin any harm,' Alyosha was saying. 'Having a monk on our side might give us the sort of – how can I put it? – credibility this outfit has been lacking for some time. Isn't that right, Father?'

Georgi spoke without looking up. 'Absolutely.'

Peter suddenly felt very tired. He'd read in another of Em's self-help books that mourners shouldn't be afraid to hand over their grief, stop feeling responsible. Like all that American stuff, he'd considered it self-indulgent claptrap. But today he agreed with *It's OK To Feel Bad*. He, undeniably, felt the need to hand over something to someone.

Alyosha's chair scraped the parquet floor as he stood up to speak. 'Let's clarify our position. We need the combination to the safe and the key to the safety deposit box, which we can't find. So we need to see your father's body. I suggest we try the embalming parlour again.' After dabbing the corners of his mouth with a paper towel he made to leave. 'Gentlemen, shall we go?'

Peter followed Alyosha to the car, Georgi trailing after them. Alyosha was halfway through a cigarette by the time he turned to Peter and said, 'Listen, I've put the priest on five hundred US a day. In my opinion it's money well spent.' Alyosha winked.

Peter nodded mutely. He was suddenly back halfway across the English Channel, trying to stay afloat while a passenger ferry steamed straight towards him.

II

'Do you mind if I call you by your Christian name?' The day had started approximately two hours too early for Katya. The American sitting in the passenger seat in front of her had, in the small hours of the morning, pledged to find Terry Small. But she never completely trusted a man driven more by testosterone than logic. Hence at 9 a.m. the next morning she found herself careering towards the city centre in a clapped-out taxi. She'd volunteered to clamber into the back, thus avoiding both paying and having to communicate with the driver. The plastic knob underneath the front seat's polyester cover, which she'd flicked to move the front seat forward, had reminded her of the genitals of a man in a pair of tracksuit bottoms. This had done little to improve her mood. Nor had the thermometer, which this morning had shown minus 5. The fuzziness from two glasses of vodka the night before was making her even more fractious. She had a million things she wanted to do. Traversing the capital in search of a missing Englishman was not one of them.

'Not if I can call you Ivan,' she replied sulkily.

'Why would you want to do that?' The American had her focused in the rear-view mirror.

'What?'

'Call me Ivan?'

'Because it's your *name*?' she replied sarcastically.

'Oh Christ, yes. Of course. My name. Yes, please do call me Ivan.' He paused. 'It's just the way you said it, you know, it sounded nicer.'

On occasions it shattered Katya to consider how much Americans had achieved on a global scale, how the country and their over-sexed leader effectively ran the world. She sat back and watched the cityscape flash past. She saw pensioners, their chests heavy with medals, out begging, men and women who had seen their families decimated by war, famine and Stalin, who had clung to the Party's promise that tomorrow would be different. It was different. Now they had to sell their hair to pay for food to live, eat dog food, beg for scraps at street markets. The heartache she felt for her country was almost physical, like the emotion felt for a lover – along with the same sense of betrayal when you found yourself trying to leave. Emotion irritated her.

'Where are we going?' she demanded. Not being entirely in control further irritated her.

'I have to go to my office to check messages,' he replied, craning his neck to look at her.

'You work at the Institute of Cosmetology?' she asked incredulously. 'I thought you worked for a bank.'

'I do. Why do you ask?'

'Because you told the driver to take us to the institute on Oktaybriski.'

'The office is near the institute. What's the matter, don't you trust me?'

'Whether I trust you or not, Mr Ivanovitch, is neither here nor there. All I care about at the moment is retrieving my client.' She was trying for officious but it came out schoolmarm.

'Your *client*?' He eyed her in the mirror. 'I thought he was a visiting professor.'

'I call all my visiting lecturers clients. Look, we're here.'

The car, which drove as if its driving mechanism was distinct from the chassis, swung into the car park – empty but for two green dormer vans with a red cross painted shakily on the side. She remembered the institute from the 1993 coup when TV cameras showed the overflow of dead and dying being taken there. Bodies covered in a blood-soaked sheet had been lined against one wall.

They both remained in the car, neither anxious to trade the companionable fug for the bone-chilling sleet.

'Where did you say your office was?' she asked him.

'Round the back. Actually, the best way to get there is through the institute.' He reached in his back pocket for his wallet. Katya had lent him one of her husband Max's old jackets. It generally improved the look of him, she thought. It tempered that dental floss sheen that went with all American men. It also squared up his shoulders and added some bulk.

She watched him trying to negotiate the price, apparently unaware that the first rule of Russian cab driving was to agree the fare first. She looked at his eyes as he struggled to iron out the misunderstandings with the pug-faced driver who was intent on trebling the price. They creased into a smile. Humour, she saw, was his way of communicating. With Russians it was always the best way. He didn't have that look of baffled disdain which most foreigners used on them. He liked them, she could tell, admired them. That was good.

He had half opened the door with his elbow before he said, 'You might as well stay in the car.' She could tell by the way he paused, with the door neither open nor shut, that he was expecting an argument. That he was used to dealing with difficult women. She didn't want to disappoint.

'Absolutely not. If you think I'm—'

'Come on, then.' He reached behind to open her door. She beat him to it, got out and slammed it shut. The American looked pensive.

III

Bridges had known all along that it wasn't going to be easy to make Katya understand why, as an international banker, he worked out of an embalming parlour. The imminent explanation had exercised his thoughts for most of the ride. Sometimes, he knew, the truth was easier but, like ordering a soft drink in a bar, it just went against the grain. He wasn't even sure what he would gain by calling in at Bodies Beautiful. Maybe the kidnappers had left a message or a note. Hell, he just didn't know, but there was nowhere else to start. Maybe Professor Modin, who hadn't answered the phone all morning, could throw some light on it.

He looked at the woman beside him. Her hair had

blown across her face. Unlike any other Russian woman he'd ever met over the age of fourteen, she didn't wear make-up. He couldn't remember the last time he'd walked down the street with a woman who was in some way connected to him. Passers-by would take her for his wife. He smiled at her. She looked cold. He wanted to offer her his jacket but was scared of her reaction.

They climbed the short staircase to the entrance and he pulled on the sculpted brass door handle into the foyer. He stood back while she went into the foyer first.

'You'd better wait here for me,' he said as they entered the building. At the weekend it was nearly deserted. Even the cloakrooms were closed.

'Why?'

'Because security is tight and you wouldn't be able to get in.'

'Well, let's worry about that when we get there,' she replied with a common sense that he associated with mothers. He liked the sense of communality, it might even have been intimacy, he got from having spent the last fifteen hours in her company (fifteen hours minus the sleep time). He was close to smiling as he hit the red button to call the lift.

Katya was the first to hear the sound of the brass door handle as three men entered the foyer behind them. Or maybe she felt the blast of cold air, which sent strands of hair across her face.

Bridges instinctively followed her gaze. He immediately recognised the two younger ones as the corpse Raevitch's son and his friend. The other one, who looked like a priest, he didn't know. Unlike Katya who gasped. She looked at Bridges and then back at the men, who appeared to be as shocked to see him as Katya was to see them.

They were sizing each other up like gangs of schoolboys before a fight. It lasted a split second before degenerating into an ear-splitting explosion of Russian argument that Bridges hadn't heard since he'd last seen a televised debate in the Duma. He had the same feeling he'd first encountered waking up in the professor's apartment – that things were never going to be the same again.

Katya seemed to have singled out two of the men for the most abuse. The taller one had turned to his friend, who was staring at Bridges in bemusement. Katya started poking the younger one, who was wearing a Tommy Hilfiger jacket, in the chest.

Bridges had once read, in a relationships magazine, that the best way to defuse an angry confrontation was to laugh. It was a technique he'd used with his wife, though he'd recently learnt she was citing it in the divorce under mental instability. Allegedly the shock stopped protagonists dead. Not inclined to mirth, he thought a blast of English might have the same effect.

'Look, would someone mind telling me what the hell is going on here?'

His interruption had no impact. He coughed loudly before appealing to the Raevitch boy for an explanation. 'Look, please, tell me what's happening.'

Raevitch said, 'Your girlfriend here is accusing my friends of kidnapping one of her clients.'

Bridges noted that *clients* word again.

Peter Raevitch did a double-take on him. 'And *you're* the funeral director.'

The penny had started to drop. These were the men who had kidnapped Katya's client, thinking it was him. He instinctively checked the exits were clear and started to edge away from them.

'What of it?' he asked hesitantly. Admit nothing, deny everything and make counter-allegations, his inner voice shouted at him.

Raevitch nudged his friend, who disengaged Katya's index finger from his chest. Slowly the fracas died down. As the last man fell silent, Katya did something for which Bridges, on the spot, pledged her eternal love. She dipped into the plastic bag she was holding and pulled out the same grey-blue pistol that she'd last applied to his own head.

She adopted a very credible FBI stance and motioned the group into the corner.

IV

When Terry woke up, he didn't think it was much of an exaggeration to say he felt on top of the world. It wasn't just the puffy nature of the parachutes he'd fallen asleep on that reminded him of clouds. It was this amazing feeling of light-headedness.

He remembered one day last autumn, when he'd been driving up the M4 to give a quote on an authentic crofter's summerhouse (thatch optional) in Slough, how he'd listened to an interview on Radio Five Live with the first man to fast for a hundred days successfully. Terry hadn't eaten, he now guessed, for two days, yet he didn't feel that peckish. Only this week he'd read a chapter in the *Rough Guide To Russia* which said that people in St Petersburg had licked glue off wallpaper during the Second World War. How undignified. He thought of the flowery borders throughout his semi. He couldn't imagine sucking them. But then again, he wasn't foreign.

He was, however, thirsty and cold. Escape was very much on his mind. First, though, like every good hostage, he should do his exercises. He considered the muscle wastage possible in the twelve hours since he was last at the gym. Not much, but it was essential he started to go on. Even Steve McQueen kept to his exacting regime, and that was in the Cooler. And it was jolly cool in here. In fact it was bloody freezing. A few push-ups would warm him up. He flung himself onto the ground, which was compacted soil and smelt of damp vegetation. It was also, he noted, no recognised method of erecting a lasting outdoor structure.

He managed seventy-five press-ups before building up a sweat and halting for lack of a water resource. Next on the hostages' list of essentials was a journal. This would be valuable for selling his story to a Sunday paper. (Note to self: try *Times* and *Mail On Sunday* first.) What he didn't want was some grubby hack writing the story for him, though admittedly that way it might incorporate some sex.

Olga the chesty – no, make that busty, chesty sounded as if she was in need of expectorant – *banged on the door. Though his captors were cruel and merciless, they still allowed Terry an occasional morsel.*

Her short skirt was pulled tight over her thighs. Her shirt buttons were bursting.

'See anything you fancy?' Olga asked the bare-chested prisoner.

'Got any Nutri-Grain bars?' our hero, a fitness professional to the end, asked.

'I'll have a look.' She started to unbutton her blouse.

Actually, he might be better trying for a contract with the *Sunday Sport*. He looked around the lockup again. Three walls were concrete, as was the roof, one wall – effectively the door – was made of corrugated iron. He kicked it before trying to haul it up. It didn't budge. Where were his captors? Even Terry Waite had got breakfast. He shifted uncomfortably. But from what he'd heard he'd got more than a couple of Weetabix in the morning.

His mind started to wander. Hadn't he intended to start a journal? He looked in his bag for paper. There was nothing but the passport. Normally he wouldn't dare deface an official document, but reasoned it was Russian and therefore, like their currency, probably not worth the paper it was written on. In any case, this would serve as a vital archive. He looked at the project as a sort of Anne Frank thing, despite the fact the only diary he'd ever read had been written by Adrian Mole.

He opened a pink sheet at page three and from his inside pocket took out a pen bearing a logo PrUS underneath a stylised umbrella. He felt a stab of nostalgia for the old firm as he began to write.

'Terry's Log' – he glossed over the defecatory suggestion, though it did remind him he would have to go soon – 'This is the first day of my incarceration caught after posing as a Russian in order to gain admittance to a top secret institute.' No need to mention the baldness operation. 'I suspect my captors to be the KGB. I have been provided with no sustenance since my arrest'. (Note to self: check Geneva Convention, possibility of suing Clive/entire Russian Federation). 'Like all captured members of the British armed forces behind enemy lines, I have pledged to escape.'

V

'So let me get this straight. Your associates,' Katya nodded towards Alyosha and Georgi, 'kidnapped my friend because you mistook him for a man who runs an embalming parlour?' She had identified the tall one, Peter, as the most likely of the triumvirate to know what was going on. She'd corralled them into a corner, sheltered from the main entrance by the lee of a staircase, but had not eased them from the gaze of her Makharov pistol.

'That's right.' Peter was massaging his temples.

'Look, would anyone mind if I went to the buffet?' Georgi (Peter had politely made all the introductions) was slouching away from the group in an effort – quite reasonably, thought Katya – to distance himself.

She ignored him. The one introduced as Alyosha was seeking solace in a packet of Marlboro Lights, the paraphernalia of smoking – packet, lighter, inhalation, smoke rings – taking up all his attention.

She turned to Bridges. 'So how is it possible that the Marx Brothers here mistook a banker for the director of an embalming parlour?'

'It's a hobby.'

'You mummify people as a hobby? Most people go fishing.' Katya tutted and slumped down against the bronze statue of a man she didn't recognise but who lacked the facial hair of a revolutionary. 'Any other surprises, Mr Ivanovitch?'

'No, er, yes. One. My name is Bob Bridges, not Ivan. Most people call me Bridges.'

She turned back to Peter. 'Why did you want to kidnap him?'

Peter fiddled with his tweed cuffs. 'Look, they didn't mean to kidnap him. They got carried away.'

Her forehead creased. 'Just tell me where the man you kidnapped is now.'

'I have every reason to believe he is being held in a tampon factory.'

'A tampon factory,' she echoed.

Alyosha spoke for the first time: 'Not *in* a tampon factory. *Near* a tampon factory. And I'm sorry, miss, no offence, but we're here for a reason.' He gestured towards Bridges, which was difficult because he was standing next to him. 'This guy has something that belongs to us and we want it back.' He halted. 'Well, not so much back. Just to have a look at.'

'What?' asked Katya.

Alyosha didn't move. 'A body.'

'Why?'

Alyosha pushed his shoulders back and his groin forward, a move guaranteed to annoy Katya. He sucked on his cigarette as if it was a cheroot and he was the Hilfiger Kid. It was a pose she could imagine Sasha undertaking in a few months' time. He exhaled four smoke rings.

'That, lady,' he said, 'is for us to know and you to find out.'

VI

Terry started to dig. He had tried to customise an old chair that had been left in the corner by breaking it into shovel-sized pieces, which had all disintegrated on contact with earth. Next he'd tried a chipped saucer, which looked as if it had been used for paint brushes. This was slightly better, though the ground was still too hard. He used an elongated steel screw to loosen the topsoil. Then there was nothing else for it, he had to use his hands. He tried to cheer himself up by whistling the tune from *The Great Escape*, but increasingly he felt like the demoralised blind bloke who wasn't allowed to go down the tunnel. (Until James Garner saved him.) He started whistling the tune from *The Rockford Files*, which had once been Grace's favourite programme. Then he stopped. He should really maintain some sort of silence in case his captors were close by. Or he should listen for rescue parties, or passing members of the French Resistance.

He had the feeling that his mind was starting to wander in the same way it did just before he fell asleep. He sat back on his haunches to consider the cast of *'Allo 'Allo*. How ridiculous that the old French restaurant owner should have had so many gorgeous young women running after him. Still, women *were* undoubtedly attracted to the older man. He thought of what the catalogue had said: 'Russian women prefer a partner at least twenty years older than they are. Age to them is immaterial.' It hadn't mentioned hair, though, had it? It hadn't said, 'Hair to them is immaterial. Russian women prefer a partner at least twenty times balder than they are.'

All those catalogue women! Yelena, Olga, Natasha, carefully numbered with customer service in mind, like his Argos catalogue. He thought back to the Natasha of his dreams. Not the one with the wig, but the *real* Natasha who had lost her voice in a tragic tractor accident wearing nothing more than a peasant-style bodice.

What high hopes he'd had for the trip. No more evenings on his own in front of the TV, but with Natasha abdominising alongside him instead. The borscht (onions boiled, not fried) as a starter before a his 'n' hers lean cuisine.

He looked round his cell and felt very very sad. Even Paul Newman had been given boiled eggs during his imprisonment.

VII

Katya weighed up the options. She could either demand that this odd trio took her to wherever they'd left Small, or she could bide her time and wait until they'd completed whatever macabre charade they were engaged upon.

The institution's foyer had been deserted. Then from nowhere a couple sauntered arm in arm across its marbled floor. They didn't spot the odd group hunched in the corner but in case they turned, Katya lowered the gun. The couple walked out of synch, the sway of her hips clashing with the bump of his. They could only just have started dating or they'd either have co-ordinated the walk or moved to holding hands. She was wearing skin-tight jeans which emphasised her fragile bow legs. It was an odd venue for a Saturday morning first date, thought Katya.

She sighed and returned to the matter in hand. After the frenetic opening scene, the four men lined up in front of her were waiting with the passivity of an identity parade. Like children. And if having a child had taught her anything – other than the finer points of the Russian privatisation programme – it was to prioritise your tasks. She was, as far as she knew, the only member of the band in possession of a small firearm, and could therefore, in theory, do as she chose. But in her experience, when dealing with a pre-teen or the mentally unstable, patience paid dividends.

Her mind unconsciously shifted screens to last night's telephone conversation – an hour after she'd put the American to bed to await the hangover from half a bottle of vodka. She'd been rinsing the glasses when the phone rang.

'Katya? Clive here. Reds In The Bed. Can I have a word with that Small chap? There's a men's magazine who want to do a piece on us. Publicity, frankly, would be a shot in the arm. I was after some sort of testimonial. Has he got his leg over yet?'

She'd hardly missed a conversational semi-colon. 'I'm afraid Terry is out on a date with a young lady, otherwise I'm sure he would want—'

'Look,' Clive cut in – women to him were nothing more than a necessary evil, pornography with a voice –

'international calls are bloody expensive. Make sure he calls when he gets back. Oh, and don't forget to remind him of our motto.'

'The hammer and sickle can be your slap and tickle?'

'No. The clever nightclubber always uses a rubber. Company policy is to wear a prophylactic at all times.'

'*All* times?'

'No room for flippancy in this game, young lady. Good night.'

Her last thought before she fell asleep was to contact the old bat from next door and arrange to rent out her apartment for longer. Despite the inclement weather, she'd gone to stay with her son at his dacha which, like most Russian dachas, was less country home, more garden shed. She was impossible to reach by phone. Then there was Sonya, Sasha's new oddness, the American client . . .

Considering everything, she'd slept remarkably well. She had hauled herself out of bed to the sound of Sasha, Misha and the Cartoon Network at eight. When Bridges had emerged from next door she'd been in the shower. Sasha had let him in, and she'd greeted him wearing a towel. He'd been sheepish, embarrassed to look her in the eye. She'd put it down more to last night's advances than to the puddle he'd stepped in which Leonid had left in the hall.

In the foyer, she glanced over at him. He was leaning against a marble pillar. She caught him looking at her expectantly. He was expecting *her* to do something. That was the westerners' way. Had the men really been so emasculated that *women* had to chase *them*? No wonder so many of them had to travel three thousand miles so they could feel free to select women from a catalogue.

She remembered one evening when she was in her twenties having to repel a man – in any other country it would have been attempted rape – using the wooden butt of a hotel key. The next morning he'd been charm itself. She responded. Within two days they were lovers.

She forced herself back to the miscellaneous gaggle of post-Soviet manhood in front of her. Tommy Hilfiger next to a man in a priest's cassock and a 'Love is' apron, alongside one who looked as if he'd just emerged from the pages of a Conan Doyle book.

The foyer had gone quiet. She needed more time to think. The priest seemed to have nodded off and Alyosha was playing a Game Boy. Peter was pacing.

She'd hardly thought to inquire why they needed to recover a body. Not asking was as much a Russian trait as alcoholism. The Russian psyche had a lot in common with that of a battered wife. It had been beaten for so long that it only responded to displays of strength but, like any victim, lacked the confidence to make the break. One day Russians might seek a dynamic leader prized for his intellect. Until then they were stuck with army generals or Boris Yeltsin. Boris might change his governments more times than his underwear but he was respected because he was a *muzhik*, a real man. Sometimes Katya despaired but she realised she was as much to blame as the rest of them. She *would* change, stop being attracted to men who attacked her in hotel rooms – only not just yet.

She stood up. Her clothes still felt damp from outside. Even indoors there was a cold schoolroom chill to the air. She looked around at the abandoned opulence of the foyer – styled, like every other Russian building these days, on the looted Winter Palace – and said, 'OK, then, let's look at this body.'

Bridges thought it was one of those inescapable things that you always focused on the backside of the person walking in front of you. He could have had the hanging baskets of Babylon to his right and the Serengeti to his left and he would still have been following Katya's rotating buttocks like a beacon. It must be an evolutionary strategy, in movement, that groin and backside were naturally where your eyes fell. Or naturally where his fell. He was never surprised by office romances. The jaw-aching boredom of the nine to five, from what he remembered, had only been broken by watching the lumbar regions of his female co-workers. Every time his wife Susan had aimed a serve, it had been at the balls, literally, of her tennis coach. It had only been a short cross-court lob to launch herself in the same direction.

Enjoyable though his vantage point was, traipsing around the institute with a hangover was not his idea of fun. The fuzzy details of what he'd said to Katya last night had hit him harder between the eyes, when he awoke, than the hangover.

The lure of alcohol. It made everything that, in the sober light of day, was untenable, plausible, or worse still, achievable. He regarded bouts of drunkenness as a holiday from himself. He was a dice man who had substituted the dice for the number of chinks of ice in a glass.

He flicked his tongue around his mouth; a scaly dryness. He'd used his finger to brush his teeth this morning.

Then he scratched his head and wondered how any man, even one as under-qualified in attracting the opposite sex as himself, could have transformed last night's opportunity into viewing a corpse. He'd asked Peter Raevitch why they wanted to see it.

'Last rites, that's why we've brought the priest.'

'Aren't last rites usually performed on the living?' he'd asked.

'It's an Orthodox thing,' came the reply.

Not that Bridges minded. The whole idea that the kidnapping had been masterminded by these three had sent a Mexican wave of relief through his body. He wasn't being tailed by a Mafia hit man or disgruntled CIA officer but an over-affectionate son and his friend.

He looked at Katya's back. One hand was intermittently flicking her hair as she walked. She'd taken the news that far from being an international financier he was a New Wave embalmer very well. She'd even asked how much they charged.

Bridges had always considered the first lie, and its subsequent confession and forgiveness, more important than the first kiss. Any two people could touch lips, but how many could share duplicity? He smiled. Like most people, some of his finest relationships had been based on fiction.

As the lift door closed on them and five pairs of eyes strained to read the maximum weight allowance, he smiled at her. It might have been more of a grimace, because it seemed the priest's cassock was rubbing on her cheek, but he was sure her lips parted.

Peter thought there was really no need for a gun. The woman was clearly potty. What interest could it be to her whether they viewed his father's body or not? Admittedly, if Alyosha and the idiot Rasputin hadn't gone in feet first with that damned kidnapping, they wouldn't be in this mess. But now that that had been ironed out, was there really any need to frog-march them off to the morgue? It was so unnecessary. So military. So *Russian*. Hovering like vultures over the last undignified act, in a lifetime of many, performed on his father. He felt in his pocket for his notebook. He should write all this down.

He tried again to think of his father on better days, but the mental black-and-white photo album most children had to flick through at these times just wasn't there. It was like trying to retrieve a lost file, a chapter on his laptop, and being told it didn't exist. He tried again to imagine how his father had sounded, closeted in his office or holding court in a vodka-steeped sauna, which he had been made to attend when he was little. He could remember the nostril-burning heat, the red velvet booths and the condensation on the bottles which he and Alyosha had poured from, like tiny Roman handmaidens. Actually he should get that down on paper too.

The woman with the gun flickered when he groped in his pocket for a pen. She ignored him when he started to write.

The sauna. The hairy bodies, stomachs swaddled in white towels, yet he could not remember what his father looked like. He hoped that when asked to recall by his (his and Em's) sons and daughters, this wouldn't be the image which sprang to mind – a funeral procession of strangers in an institute smelling of vegetables.

Nobody had spoken since the woman had gestured them into the lift. They'd split into pairs to enter it, himself and the American behind her, Alyosha and the priest at the back. They sprang from the lift like socks from an over-full suitcase.

The corridor had a Soviet sterility to it, which reminded him of a time when the workforce had been saturated by cleaners, when cleaning was as virtuous a task as doctoring or physics. Children queued to join the ranks of the *subotniks*, people who worked on a Saturday to clean up the neighbourhood. In those days civic pride was inbred. Now it was every man for himself, or herself, he thought, looking at Katya's blonde hair falling over the shoulders of a dark red ski jacket.

Bridges told her in which direction to walk and she led them to the door of Bodies Beautiful – a company Peter now wished he'd never heard of. But, he thought as he scanned his companions, it was impossible to turn back the clock.

What would happen if his old father could see him now? Georgi thought maliciously. Not the man who'd left his mother and himself to run off with a railway clerk but his seminary father, Father Mikhail. It must have been the institutional smell, disinfectant and cooking, that had made him think of him. Father Mikhail had been a mountain of a man, coated in layers of rough black cloth like an overdone boeuf en croute. His head and neck had been obliterated by bushy, mousy facial hair of pubic density. In the middle he'd worn a pair of brown-rimmed glasses which distorted his eyes from pig to dead fish.

He'd spoken of hell and damnation as if they were a God-given right. The tail end of Georgi's time at the seminary had coincided with the start of perestroika. A crusade against pornography and foreigners had become the mainstay of Father Mikhail's teaching. Naked women and George Soros were the backbone of his lessons. Say what you liked, there was no way the Orthodox Church hadn't moved with the times.

Now Georgi was charging $500 a day to lend an air of respectability to a couple of hoods. He smiled, happy that his education hadn't been entirely in vain.

The place looked even worse the second time round, thought Alyosha. If midweek in an institution was bad, then the weekend was worse. And he should know. It was like being locked in your bedroom when you could hear the funfair in the distance. In any case it wasn't just the smell which was putting him on edge, it was being told what to do by a middle-aged woman with a gun so old it could have been handcrafted by Alfred Kalashnikov. What was this country coming to when armed elderly women were allowed to roam the streets? He could have stopped the rot himself by pulling out his Beretta, but it was hardly polite to threaten a woman. Especially one that age.

Every time his Nike Airs landed on the shiny linoleum they made a noise like a handbrake turn. Everyone else's footwear was noiseless. That was good, he liked to make his presence felt. It also broke up the silence which had started to get on his nerves. Peter had gone into one of his superior moods and even the priest was withdrawn. Maybe he was praying, though more likely he was hungry. In the two days he'd known Georgi, he'd learnt that his moods were governed by blood sugar levels. And it was well past lunchtime. As for himself, his moods were governed by sporting fixtures, designer sportswear and Central Asian women. Corpses barely featured, unless of course it was a combat situation. This was not his idea of a fun morning.

The huddle drew up alongside a door he recognised, though the words were in English. They had reached the Central Office (incl. admin) of Bodies Beautiful.

VII

Ridiculous as it might seem, and he knew it was ridiculous, Bridges couldn't help but feel a sense of pride when he let them into the laboratory. As usual it was the chemical smell that hit you, just before the chilling realisation of what went on there.

For the first time in as long as he could remember, he was calling the shots. He mentally rephrased that when he caught the reflected glint of Katya's gun in an aluminium tray. Well, if not *exactly* calling the shots, he was the only one who knew where the body was. He adjusted his belt, pushed back his shoulders fractionally and, if it was possible to swagger in a morgue, swaggered. He turned to Peter.

'So what exactly are you after?'

'Don't you mean who?' said Katya, who had taken up a position in the far corner by a fire extinguisher. She was framed by four glass-fronted cabinets, two above her and one on either side. Some were stacked with books, others with a miniature scrap yard of metal instruments. The light which streamed through half a wall of windows hit her hair like a figure in a Renaissance painting. Her eyes had become luminous and her hair shone like a halo. By comparison the other three had taken on a deathly pallor. Some people shrank in the presence of death; others, like Professor Modin, seemed to come alive. Katya actually appeared turned on by it. Bridges figured it was the people for whom death didn't seem the worst option that felt the most at home.

'All we want is a moment alone with my father,' said Peter in his hoity-toity English. 'A moment of quiet reflection.'

'Pah!' said Katya. 'And for this you were ready to kidnap someone?' Her words, heavy with sarcasm, sounded strongly accented in comparison to the boy's flawless speech. She really was magnificent, thought Bridges, like something from a Wagnerian opera. Without the hips.

'Look, can we get on?' Peter pushed back his hair and looked at his watch. 'This is a difficult time for us. And to be honest, with the prices you charge, one might have thought seeing my father would not have been too much to ask.'

Boy, did that phoney British voice really start to grate. It was bad enough that a two-bit island race should have such an exaggerated sense of its own importance, without exporting it. A kind of superiority by proxy. Bridges winced. Not only that, but something about the way the tall one fiddled with his tweed jacket cuffs reminded him of the big-eared one in line for the British throne.

But his own innate service ethic, bred into Americans more than Marx into a Russian, forced a smile. The son, of course, was right. The amount of money charged by Bodies Beautiful should, in theory, qualify the next of kin to cannibalise the body if they really wanted to.

'Yes, of course,' he said. 'We keep the bodies – I mean, if you would just like to . . .' He gestured with a tail flick of the hand that they should follow him. Elsewhere in the building a distant and prolonged bell suggested a fire alarm had been set off. They looked at each other and then turned to Bridges for advice.

'Don't worry, it happens all the time,' he assured them.

The corpses were kept in a refrigerated room off the main lab. The door was heavy and metal, and on a spring which meant everyone passing through it had to give it a shove. Styx was the name the professor gave the tiny antechamber they entered.

Bridges gave Katya a look, half smile, half shrug. A morgue was not only no place for a woman, it was no place for any sane individual. To his disappointment Katya grimaced and joined the queue. Despite the surroundings she still hadn't let the barrels of the gun drop below chest height, though on whose chest they were trained wavered from minute to minute.

The room was cold and lit by a fluorescent strip light that gave out a bluish hue. A table in the corner had an aged black telephone and a few newspapers on it which gave the room a ghoulish air of recreation, but otherwise it was uncluttered. The air smelt of metal and school experiments.

Bridges stood back when the door finally snapped shut, while Alyosha let out a stream of what, in any language, could only be expletives. The air was so cold he could blow condensation rings. Within thirty seconds he'd issued four perfect Olympic rings.

'It's a very difficult time for him,' Peter explained. 'Alyosha and my father were very close.'

Bridges nodded. Out of reverence for the dead he usually loitered for a few minutes instead of heading straight for the corpse's drawer like a shopper at a Macy's summer sale. The tone of Alyosha's next comment made him wonder if his sensitivity was appreciated in this instance.

Peter translated. 'My friend,' he nodded towards Alyosha, whose entire face was shrouded by the zipped-up hood of his jacket, 'says he's feeling very upset, so can we get on?'

Katya giggled. If she was having this much fun on a trip to an undertakers', Bridges observed, any other date stood a reasonable chance of success.

'What he actually said,' Katya volunteered, 'was that he's freezing his bollocks off and the Dynamo match kicks off at four.'

'Oh, right then. OK, if we could all just . . .' Bridges moved towards the drawers where the bodies were kept. He turned to Katya. 'Are you sure you should be here?'

'I'm not letting these jerks out of my sight until we've got the professor back.' He liked the 'we' part.

Like any participant in post-war American culture, even before he signed up with Bodies Beautiful he'd been no stranger to the morgue. 1970's TV's obsession with the

311

postmortem meant he already knew how bodies were kept – laid horizontal, in outsize grey filing cabinets. A vernacular twist – not one from the set of *Quincey* – stemmed from Bridge's inability to read Russian and the lab technicians' inability to read English. Professor Modin had pioneered an ID method which involved drawing a picture of the deceased, plus any distinguishing features, and their cause of death, and taping it to the outside of the drawer. They'd refined the system by adding initials, in Russian, because most of the pictures ended up wearing a fedora (indicating Mafia) with a semi-automatic beside them.

Luckily the Raevitch body had presented no such graphical problems. It was with some embarrassment that Bridges guided the group, like bewildered tourists, to a childish drawing of a man with a Jiffy bag on his head. In an unnecessarily cruel moment, the professor had added a striking erection. The result was a cross between primitive cave art and Cluedo. All but Alyosha pretended not to notice. As Bridges' hand grasped the silver drawer handle they instinctively looked at Georgi as if for guidance. Georgi, quietly burning holes in the top of a cigarette carton with a lit cigarette, didn't look up.

'This then is the temporary resting place of . . .' Bridges coughed. 'I mean this is how . . .'

From behind him Katya reached over and yanked the silver handle. 'For God's sake. Can't you even—' As she tried to pull the drawer, her cuff got caught on the edge of it. Bridges intervened to help, tugging at the material. Katya tutted. For a second the group was mesmerised by the impromptu wrestling. Then Katya broke free and, expecting the resistance of a heavy weight, pulled hard.

Her arm shot out. The group watched as the rollers kept spinning. There was an audible gasp. Circles of condensed air formed like speech bubbles in front of them. The drawer was empty.

'Shit,' said Alyosha.

'Well,' said Katya briskly as the silence engulfed them, 'bad luck, gentlemen. That was your body, now it's time to find mine.' She turned to Peter and, as if to emphasise the point, let the safety catch off her gun. 'After all, as westerners say, fair's fair.'

Alyosha turned to her. 'Listen, lady, no offence but,' as he spoke he delved into his breast pocket. Luckily for Katya he was hampered by the number of zippers in his sports jacket. By the time his gun emerged, Katya had trained her pistol on him as if his head was a magnet. Suddenly the room broke into a cacophony of noise. It sounded, thought Bridges, like the audition for a Japanese game show.

Peter called for silence. 'Look, I don't know about the rest of you, but I find all this aggression quite unnerving. I'm sure we can come to some sort of arrangement without all this *nastiness*. We're all responsible adults, aren't we?' He looked at Georgi. It was five seconds before the flag went down again and the screaming started.

Bridges felt his headache was about to be rebooted. Though one thing had to be said: with her arms raised to chest height, squeezing her elbows in line with the gun, he had an unparalleled view of Katya's cleavage. He thought that as the dominant male – well, certainly the eldest – he should really take charge. Not only that, but he was American and the *de facto* natural leader. Also, women liked a man who took charge.

He put his arms in the air and flapped his hands up and down like wings. 'OK. OK. Let's have some quiet. Guys, listen, I think this is what they call a Mexican stand-off. Now let's sort this out. OK, first of all, does anyone have anything to drink?'

CHAPTER ELEVEN

I

As the Boeing 747 tipped to start its descent, the senator marvelled at how the country ever got the name superpower. Above him the 'fasten seat belt' sign pinged on. His sausage fingers felt down the cleavage of his thighs to find his buckle, which had disappeared into his stomach midway over the Atlantic. The middle-aged American woman with the loud voice, sitting behind him, who twitched worse than en epileptic, thudded into the back of his seat. The chair rocked like a barn door in a gale.

He swore. Economy class, God how he hated it. He felt a black ball of sheer anger bubble up and lodge itself at the back of his brain. If only those limp-brained women who staffed his so-called fundraising drives had gotten their act together, he'd be in first. No question.

'Yo, miss, could I get another drink here?' He tilted his glass in the direction of the Lufthansa air hostess.

'I'm afraid the fasten-your-seat-belt sign has gone on. We are about to land.'

'I don't give a shit, excuse my language, ma'am, if the

plane is about to go into free fall. I *want* another goddamned *drink*.' He watched her forehead furrow, weighing up the danger to passengers against the scene he'd hinted he'd create. It pissed him royally. In first class, they were still pouring drinks practically as you entered passport control. In cattle, you were lucky to score more than a pre-meal aperitif. Shit.

'I'll be right back.' The blonde hostess jammed a bagful of headsets under her armpit as she hurried towards the drinks trolley.

The senator sat back and smiled. Asserting his consumer sovereignty was as dear to him as obliterating all people of colour. Any colour, other than white – especially ones who wore a towel on their heads.

He adjusted his Star of Texas belt and checked his watch with its cute yellow rose face and a second hand in the shape of a bee. It read 10.20 a.m. The flight was early. He looked down at the grids of grey high-rise suburbs surrounded by dirt-poor smallholdings that looked like something from the Midwest in the last century. A superpower made up of outhouses. How did *that* work?

Alongside him a dark-haired man was counting worry beads. He was one of them. The senator was surprised airline companies still allowed them to fly at all, after Lockerbie and the rest. Ordering halal meat and moving his lips while he read some goddamn book backwards. No wonder these chicken Shiites and their brethren found it so easy to take on the civilised world. He wouldn't trust a Russian to run a faucet, never mind a decent security service.

The air hostess returned with a measure of vodka, not

enough ice, and a can of tomato mixer. He decided to let it pass. She was followed by another humourless Eva Braun passing out face towels with a pair of industrial-sized tweezers. He didn't like to see Krauts get ahead of themselves. What was the point of crushing the Germans if they ended up fifty years on with their goddamned Teutonic precision intact and stronger than ever.

He gulped the drink, aware that a decompression headache was likely unless he kept the alcohol levels fully fuelled. A slump could mean the trough of despair. Another drink would have him scaling the mound of happiness.

Further down the fuselage babies had started screaming, their heads appearing above the parapets. He felt his toes curl in irritation. He remembered a game he'd played at high school, when they'd driven an open-topped car down a suburban street, smashing the mailboxes with a baseball bat. He wondered if it would work with toddlers.

'Could I take your glass, sir?' an air hostess asked with a basket of boiled sweets in her hand. 'Would you care for something to suck on as we come in to land?'

'No, thank you, ma'am.' He winked at her and smoothed down his hair, feeling the vodka start to kick in. 'I'm saving myself for later.'

II

Sonya wasn't cross, more disappointed Nikita had been right. Something was on the point of going wrong. She had been about to make a fool of herself. How could she have thought that a foreigner would be interested in her? She looked down at a cigarette butt stamped out on the marble floor of the Metro. She'd just missed a train when she arrived, feeling the vacuous rush of air as it disappeared into the tunnel under an LCD counting the seconds before the next one.

The only good thing about working on a Saturday was that the Metro was less crowded. Though even as the clock read forty seconds and the rail tracks started to crackle to indicate that another train was coming, the platform had filled.

Station Prazhskaya, last stop on the grey line. At least it guaranteed you got a seat, especially on a Saturday. The brown leather was torn and the carriage smelt of something horrible but it was warm. A young man with a cardboard placard and one leg hopped in as the doors were about to close. He was Russian, and his leg had been blown off in Chechenya. He had a wife and two children to support. Sonya thought he looked even younger than Nikita. She gave him five roubles and a smile as he passed by with an upturned hat. At least Nikita didn't have to beg. She would always look after him.

How could she have even *considered* turning their lives upside down for a foreigner? Especially one who didn't even bother to turn up when he was supposed to. She'd waited for nearly an hour at the gym. No foreigner and no Katya. She'd been told by the older women in the bookshop how rude foreigners were; well, now she knew it for a fact.

She tried to shut out the snippets of conversation around her. All worry. All money. Money lost, money not earned, prices spiralling out of control.

Old woman: 'Have you seen the price of potatoes? I swear we can't even afford bread these days.'

Daughter: 'They want two hundred dollars for a pair of shoes. It's ridiculous.'

An army captain in uniform: 'No one's been paid for six months.'

Sonya opened her book. She hardly needed to read Dostoyevsky these days. She felt as if she was living a scene of it. She looked up, only realising they'd pulled into Chekovskaya station by the number of people leaving the carriage. The sweet sickly smell of the station hit her in the back of the throat as she ran out behind the ashen-faced commuters.

The bookstore, was another stop on a different line. She weighed up whether to continue on the Metro or walk. It was cold and she was only in her autumn coat, but a walk would do her good, clear her head before the shift.

As usual, when she arrived twenty minutes later, there wasn't much to do in the shop. The staff had long since stopped pricing the books because by the end of the day they'd gone up. A couple of customers bought the latest American blockbuster, a few more the latest Russian detective novel, but most loitered, just glad to be out of the cold. She watched the hands on the clock haul themselves to midday with terminable boredom. She only worked till lunchtime on a Saturday. She planned to go to the Tretyakov Gallery in the afternoon to see the exhibition of Russian icons and wanted to get there before the queue got too long.

Outside, the coldness made her eyes water and her nose

run. She was reaching in her bag for a tissue when the sound of horns made her look up. An ambulance was swerving across the lanes of traffic. It was packed with people, making her do a double-take until she reassured herself it was merely a driver supplementing his state wage by working as a cabbie. Then it shuddered to a halt beside her. Sonya recognised the woman driving. The back door slid open and a man pulled her inside.

'What the hell do you—?'

'Sonya, it's me. Don't worry. Get in,' said Katya as she jammed the ambulance into gear and screeched off, drenching a woman shopper standing on the pavement.

III

Stealing the ambulance had been Katya's idea. She reckoned there was no way five of them would fit in one car, and neither party was anxious to let the other out of its sights. Also, although she'd known how to steal a car from an early age, she had been struck by the challenge of hot-wiring an ambulance which had been left unlocked outside the institute.

'My God, I think there's actually *blood* on this seat,' Peter had complained as he got in.

'Wicked,' said Alyosha as the rusty engine started to tick over.

'Will you all just get in?' Katya had dispensed with the gun. Under their own Strategic Arms Limitation Treaty, both she and Alyosha had agreed to put away their weapons, for now. 'Tell me the way to this tampon factory.

I've got precisely an hour to retrieve the man you kidnapped.' She was lying, but people always worked better to a deadline. In any case, she really should get back to Sasha in time for his next tartrazine-infected meal.

'I'll show you,' said Georgi from the back. 'You need to get onto the Garden Ring and towards Ostankino and I'll direct you from there.'

'Look, are you sure you know how to drive one of these things?' asked Peter. He was sitting up front with her and she could read genuine concern in his face.

One of Katya's recent forays into barter capitalism had been buying an ancient ambulance to transport prison-made furniture (she'd hatched the deal on her only visit to her jailed sister-in-law) bought with jars of pickled cucumbers, for which she gave the dying state-run factory that produced them a pittance. She then sold the furniture to a Swedish company who had recently set up in Moscow. The experiment had netted her a thousand which she kept safe in a pickled cucumber jar. She trusted banks about as much as she trusted everybody else. Russian savings could deflate overnight quicker than a drunk's erection.

She looked at Peter. 'Prepare to meet thy maker,' she said as she put the ambulance into first and wheel-spun out of the institute's car park.

'Excellent,' said Alyosha.

The ambulance sounded as if the last time it had been used was in the 1993 coup. How fitting that it should be on its way back to the TV tower at Ostankino where most of the bloodshed had been.

As she pulled out into the flow of traffic, Katya thought back to the scene in the embalming parlour.

Raevitch: 'Where's the body?'

Bridges: 'Why do you want to see it so much?'

Raevitch: 'That's none of your business. The mourners' charter says—'

Bridges: 'The mourners' charter states viewing the body, prior to embalming, is at the discretion of the funeral director.'

Raevitch: 'I think you've stolen it.'

Bridges: 'For Christ's sake, why would I want to steal a body?'

Raevitch: 'You know perfectly well why.'

Bridges: 'What, you think I'm some sort of necrophiliac—'

Raevitch: 'Don't be ridiculous.'

At this point Katya had intervened and Alyosha had passed round a hip flask. 'This is getting us nowhere,' she said. 'You've tried to get hold of your partner who takes care of the embalming and he's not in. For want of an alternative, I suggest we at least find my missing client.'

They'd all looked as if they wanted to disagree but could think of no good reason to. And no one wanted a return to the gun tussle. Katya usually succeeded in getting people to do things her way.

In the drizzle the streets had a look of early-morning desertion to them, even though it was past lunchtime. The ambulance made a satisfying swoosh as it sailed down Tverokaya Ulitsa. They'd just turned onto Petrovka when Katya spotted Sonya, looking as radiant as ever but slightly more pensive.

Horns blared as Katya swerved across two lanes of traffic to pick her up. 'For God's sake,' she muttered.

'can't they see this is an ambulance?'

IV

There was a neatness about bodies, an ordered precision which made them easy to comprehend unlike the living. Bodies were like oysters. Their true beauty was on the inside, though not in all of them. From the first incision you knew what to expect; they rarely disappointed. The body could tell you everything *physically* about a man. The fatty globules in the liver informed you that he drank too much. The porous quality of the lungs with their tar-black deposits pronounced him a smoker. But it could tell you nothing of the nature of the man. Professor Modin trusted bodies, people less so.

'The body is the most wondrous machine on the planet. What the mind makes a body do is between him and his God. But when I have finished work on a body, I leave it in a state of perfection. As a mother would want to remember her son. It is an act of transubstantiation. That is the skill of the embalmer.' This was a conversation he often had with his wife, though more one-sided than most conversations because Marina, though she understood evil, had never understood her husband's obsession with embalming.

Marina rarely pointed out what his job had cost them, still cost them. Nor did he ever recall how it had saved them. The professor distrusted people because he had spent nearly two years in the camps. Though they were both arrested in the early hours of that same July morning,

Marina hadn't followed him to the gulag, but her loss – by the boot of an NKVD officer – had been greater.

They knew they hadn't suffered more than anyone else. They were, after all, still alive. The baby Marina had been carrying had been lost, but so had millions more. She'd had to learn to concentrate not on the specifics, but to philosophise. In retrospect they'd been lucky to have lost just one. Only, even now, on most days it didn't seem like that.

She (Marina had been carrying a girl) would have been a grown woman by now. In fact a middle-aged woman in her forties. A mother herself. A childless woman imagining other childless woman.

They never spoke of their loss, or of his time at Solovki, an island in the eyeball-freezing north which was dark round the clock for months and shrouded by mosquitoes for the rest of the year. He'd spent four months in the Lubyanka and then two in Butyrskaya before being cattle-herded onto the train. They'd read recently that the archipelago had opened up for tourism so that Russians could revisit the scene of the barbarism. They didn't plan to go.

Maybe her husband was right, maybe he could restore the goodness to people – even those guards, her own countrymen. In the end it had been the embalming that had saved her husband, an intellectual and a Jew, from the purges.

It had been simple. No one but he knew the formula the recipe for the fluid which kept Lenin's body preserved Without the knowledge, the founding father of the nation would rot like a lump of meat. After eighteen months he was brought back to Moscow. Lenin had saved him.

Marina had been still a young woman when the doctor told her she'd never bear children – apart from the baby she'd given birth to after ten hours' labour on a cell floor in front of twenty others. She'd wrapped her daughter in a headscarf and held on to her body for three minutes before the guards had taken her away.

That was why the professor took solace from the body. Not the mind. He knew about bodies. Knew that the outside had so little bearing on the inside. Not just beauty but evil was skin deep. None knew it better than he did.

V

Peter elected to stay in the ambulance. 'You don't need me, and someone might steal the van. I think Sonya should wait as well.' It was as definitive a statement as he felt capable of making. He saw Alyosha nudge Georgi in the ribs with his elbow. Peter continued, 'It's muddy and she's only wearing thin shoes. And apart from that—'

'All right, all right. We can all see *why* you want to stay in the van,' said Alyosha who was wearing a stethoscope and pair of rubber gloves which Peter hoped he'd found in the glove compartment. He lowered his voice. 'No doubt, mate, I'd call that a five star, no questions asked MARX.'

'Alyosha, this is no time for your idiotic word games,' said Peter, racking his brain. MARX, he recalled, stood for Modest Although Really X-rated. 'And take that bloody thing off.'

'Will you two shut up and tell me where you left my

friend?' Katya said as she reversed the ambulance into a gravel parking space.

This district on the outskirts of Moscow had all the charm of a post-nuclear wasteland. It was made up of a sea of lockup garages, small factories and sheds and was deserted apart from the occasional pair of feet sticking out from under the chassis of a Lada. An old woman in a full-length grey nylon coat tied at the waist with string was carrying a basket of kittens. Either she enjoyed taking cats on day trips or she was on her way to sell or kill them.

'I don't think all four of us need to go.' Katya had unlocked the front seat.

Alyosha sniffed loudly and yanked the sliding back door across. A freezing current of cold air streamed in. 'Why not? You never know, he might be dangerous.' There was thinly disguised optimism in his voice.

'The man is a visiting English lecturer. I hardly think so.' She sighed. 'All right then.'

The four clambered out.

The conversation inside the van had caused the windows to steam up. It was like conducting negotiations in a rainforest, thought Peter. He smiled as he leaned across Sonya to wipe away the condensation with the sleeve of his Burberry. It was waterproof and the water slid off it. Sonya smiled at him. He used the blue and purple tassels from his De Montfort scarf.

'So how do you know Katya?'

'A friend,' she said quietly just as an engine revved to the right of them.

'Sorry?'

'She's just a friend.'

'You work with her?'

She was wearing a thin brown mac and a long loose grey jumper over blue lace-up shoes. She had a Kate Moss fragility to her with the same ingenuousness, though in this case, Peter imagined, the naivety was for real. He wanted to get a better look at her but short of climbing into the back was unable to.

'No, she's . . . I don't know, a friend.'

'Right.'

They fell silent. Peter watched the other four disappear into a lockup. Alyosha, ridiculously, was still wearing his stethoscope.

'Why do you sound so funny?' Sonya addressed the question to the gap between the passenger and driver's seat. Peter thought he could see the mist of her breath.

'My accent, it's English. You see,' Peter wanted to explain about De Montfort, 'I went—'

'You dress funny, too.'

Peter looked down at his trousers. Maybe jumbo cords did have more of an eighties look to them. 'Everyone in England dresses like this.'

'Oh.'

He couldn't bear the disappointment in her voice. 'Well, I can change. I can wear jeans if you'd prefer, or chinos?'

'I don't mind. I suppose you want to marry me, then?' She looked straight at Peter.

'Er, no, I mean yes, but isn't it a bit sudden?' Alyosha had told him that Russian girls weren't shy, but this was ridiculous. 'You don't even know my name.'

'So what's your name?'

'Peter.'

She wrinkled her nose. 'That was my father's name.'

'Oh.' Peter smiled. Women, he knew from Em's library, liked men who reminded them of their fathers. It had made him think on more than one occasion how lucky it was that only Hard Currency's male chromosomes had reproduced.

'He died in a car crash.' She looked down.

'Oh right, well I'm—' Peter caught sight of the gang returning from the lockup. Bridges, Katya, Georgi and Alyosha – in order from left to right. The mood looked grave. Three of the four brows were creased. Alyosha was intently taking his own pulse. Peter wished he and Sonya could have spent more time alone.

Both front doors sprang open at the same time. Katya looked far from happy.

'Not bloody well there. He's gone. Sawed his way out,' she said to no one in particular.

On his other side Peter felt Alyosha nudge him. 'S' mate,' he lowered his voice, 'how did you get on?'

Peter eyed him nervously. He was close enough to see the flecks in his eyes and smell the faint odour of alcohol on his breath. He spoke down towards his chest. 'I think we're engaged.'

Alyosha, impressed, nodded and with a smile placed the stethoscope over Peter's heart.

VI

Terry felt tears of frustration welling up. It was a tiny

when – had he been able to – he would have pulled his hair out. How could *anyone* not carry any money with them? What was the point of him being the mother of all Steve McQueens if, when you made it to Switzerland (in his case the other side of the lockup), you were stony broke. How could it be that the jacket he'd mistakenly swiped from the gym was not only *not* a Cecil Gee original but contained no roubles, no dollars, marks (Finnish or German), no French francs, Spanish pesetas or even any Kenyan bloody shillings. And certainly no sterling. Had the owner of that jacket never been a Boy Scout? He'd bet even the Queen carried 10p in case she had to make a phone call. The jacket, he felt like screaming, held less money than the Russian central bloody reserve.

He sank down on a pile of boxes away from the road and tried to cheer himself up by thinking back to the skill and ingenuity of the escape. He needed to get it straight in his mind for the press conference, if nothing else. He imagined the lights and the hordes in front of his podium. He cleared his throat and started to speak. A hush fell in the auditorium.

'Digging, I realised early on in my imprisonment, would get me nowhere. I was against the clock, never knowing when my captors might return. Clearly there had to be a better way. I searched the cell for something else. Don't forget, ladies and gentlemen (should he add of the press? It worked for Clinton) I hadn't eaten for more than three days. It is at times like these that I fall back on the spirituality of the Gender Awareness Forum. Yes, ladies and gentlemen, I chanted and in a matter of minutes my eyes alighted on a saw. Yes, I saw a saw. (Note to self:

maybe too evangelical.) I took the saw and I sawed through the garage door and I saw the light. Yes, ladies and gentlemen, I saw the light. And I went towards that light. And I was free.'

In the film version there might be room for a black choir, but for the immediate press conference it seemed to hit the right pitch, midway between President Clinton and Billy Graham. On reflection Terry decided that the KGB couldn't have used the lockup as a prison very often because, in reality, there had been many means of escape. He'd used a wooden mallet from a rusty workbench to make a hole with a large sharpened screw. Then he'd haphazardly made a few more, like breaking into a can of condensed milk when you were camping, and used the saw to join them up. After what he guessed was a couple of hours, he'd made a hole big enough to climb through

The corrugated iron had slashed his clothes, tearing a large rip down one leg of his trousers and pulling a great hole in his jumper. His hands, from the attempt to tunnel his way out, were filthy and having periodically wiped his brow he imagined his face was too. His mouth tasted of something metallic, though when he cupped his hands over it and exhaled, his breath didn't smell too bad. He rubbed his teeth with his finger but stopped abruptly when he remembered how long it was since he'd last washed his hands. Also, he feared it might leave a brownish deposit around his lips, making it look as if he'd been eating something entirely unpleasant.

Before the possibility of breaking free had presented itself, he'd urinated behind the workbench in the corner. From the smell of the place, he didn't think he'd been th first. That had been it as far as his morning toilet had gone. He'd read somewhere that soldiers in the field did their number twos on a sheet of cling film and took them wherever they went. Ever since, he'd not been able to view the chocolate brownies Grace used to wrap in polythene to take to the WI bring-and-buy sale in the same light. He'd considered doing similar this morning but as the only container to hand was a discarded empty bottle of vodka, he'd decided against it. If he's slipped he'd have been the butt (literally) of every casualty joke going.

He sniggered. Good one, Terry, he said to himself. How like a British soldier to keep his sense of humour behind enemy lines. But onwards and upwards, old son. Onwards and upwards.

He stood up. He did not, he knew, look his sartorial best. In fact the phrase down and out sprang to mind, but this was no time for elegance. He reappraised the situation. He was somewhere in Moscow, Russia, with no money and unsure of how far he was from, and in which direction lay, base camp (aka Katya's). Nervously he started pinging the PrUS pen in his trouser pocket. He looked around. There was no sign of anyone. The lockup was sandwiched between two more identical ones and stood apart from larger sheds in the foreground. There was a still larger industrial building a hundred yards away. The soil was clayish and yellow and liberally peppered with dog mess.

In a strange way this was the most terrifying part of his ordeal. Before this he'd been reacting to events, albeit heroically maintaining his silence under interrogation and escaping captivity. Now he had to be the decision maker.

He looked over his shoulder.

The whole place had the eeriest feel to it, and it was so quiet. In a terrifying blast of panic he thought he might not be in Moscow but had been drugged and moved to God knew where. Maybe Siberia. That was where they shipped convicts in Russia. Had there been a period in his abduction that he couldn't remember? He frowned. He didn't think so, but they could have done anything – given him one of those date-rape drugs which he'd once tried to buy at the chemist on the high street. Christ, the more he thought about it, the less convinced he was that he was in Moscow. The *feel* of the place, the smell, entirely different. He shuddered to say it above the dog turds and empty oil drums, but it was *cleaner*.

His Navaho tracker instincts were obviously badly shaken because he didn't hear the man approach.

'*Sto vi zdes delayete?*' He was wearing a boiler suit and a fur hat with untied flaps over ears which stuck out like a cartoon character's. It was the only endearing part of his persona which looked as if it belonged to the days of Ivan the Terrible. He had a thick dark moustache and bushy hair. Worse than that, he had a wrench in his hand.

'I beg your pardon?' His own voice sounded, even to himself, shaky.

'*Chevo?*'

Chevron? He must be some sort of oil vendor. 'No, no thank you. No oil for me.' Terry shook his head and criss-crossed his hands in front of him to denote the negative.

'*Chevo?*'

'No, no oil ski for me ski.' He kept smiling. 'Thank you

ski.' The man reminded him of someone from *Deliverance, the Cossack Version*. He himself would, of course, have played Burt Reynolds.

A gust of wind heralded the start of a shower. The sky was solid grey, the colour of socks, though the moustached man seemed oblivious of the weather. Terry thought he might have been drinking. He continued a diatribe in Russian. Give them their due, though, they were keen to sell their oil. An admirable sign of capitalism, brought on, no doubt, by the falling world crude prices.

'Listen, Boris,' Terry felt a wave of exhaustion mingled with a sharp migraine of misery, 'I have no interest *whatsoever* in buying any oil, petrol, diesel or WD 40 from you.' He moved forward. 'In fact,' he took another step towards him, 'it is more likely you can help me. Is this,' he slowed his speech and pointed to a Snickers ice-cream wrapper on the ground, 'Moscow?' He smiled. 'Here ski,' and pointed, 'Moscow ski?'

Abruptly the man turned to leave. He seemed bigger viewed from the back. Ox-like shoulders filled out the army green boiler suit. Afterwards, Terry justified the attack as having been provoked over some time. And in many respects – if you took into account the troll with the lead-lined handbag and the demented shopkeeper – he had. But at the time it was just the sheer *rudeness* of the man that made him swing the plastic bag he was carrying and crash it down on the oil vendor's head. Of course, had he remembered it contained the empty vodka bottle (gleaned in case he changed his mind about a bowel movement), he might not have done it. He meant merely to assert himself.

It was certainly the bottle that caused the oil man to go down. He staggered slightly as his knees caved under him, reminding Terry how detonated high-rise blocks fell. For a second he thought the bottle had killed him. The sense of how hard the blow had been lived on in his arm. He flexed his fingers and shook his arm from the shoulder to try and loosen it. After a few moments, the man gurgled, and twenty seconds later, while Terry waited frozen to the spot, he started to snore.

It was too good an opportunity to miss, thought Terry. He looked round briefly and then bent towards the prone oil man. The material felt grimy as he slipped his hand into the pocket of the boiler suit and rummaged for loose change. His nails filled with sand. There was nothing. Nada, nyet, nothing. No wallet, no coins, nothing. He looked at the man's insensible face in obscenely intimate detail. The ruddy bottom lip from which saliva was dribbling, the shaving cut, the open pores around his nose. Adrenaline still racing, Terry felt like hitting him again. Instead he let out a 'Grrrrrrrrrrr' and almost spat. He lumbered off towards the road, swinging his plastic bag from side to side. He didn't even notice the rain.

VII

The senator clenched his buttocks as he pushed himself further into the bucket seat. He picked up his drink. That was another advantage of Moscow over, say, London or Paris, they appreciated the importance of a straw. He was a man who couldn't bear his lips to come in contact with anything as unsavoury as a recycled glass. As he sucked on the vodka and tonic, he looked towards the stage. What a find, a strip joint open round the clock. Well worth paying the taxi driver $50 for, though it was probably the sonofabitch's brother who ran the place. Probably his sister in a G-string on the stage right now. The conniving dog. Not worth getting in a stew about, though. Life was, after all, swings and roundabouts. Like now, for example, the club was freezing cold – good for erect nipples, bad for goose flesh.

The act finished, with a redhead pulling a feather boa between her legs like a saw, to a Europop song. He couldn't see her feet from where he was sitting. He tried to imagine them, slim and smooth with perfect red nails. It was all routine stuff. In fact, pretty amateurish compared to what he was used to in the US but, as in market reforms, it was good to see Russians making an effort. Apart from their bodies he'd never been *that* impressed by Russian strippers. It was the whole *service* thing. When a woman took her clothes off, she had to look like she was enjoying it. She should act like she was there just to please you. Not here. Oh no. Some of these babes undressed like they were getting ready for bed in a power cut.

He glanced round the club and signalled for another drink. All the men here were foreigners – two Japanese and what looked like a couple of Finns three-quarters of their way down a bottle of Absolut.

He looked at his watch. There was no point in him hurrying over to her apartment. He'd tried to call her from Houston to tell her what time he would be landing – she usually arranged a car from the Sheremetyvo airport to her place – but there'd been no reply. He thought about leaving another message. In the club the music hadn't returned, and there was this *intermission* feeling to the show. He squeezed a gold nugget on his pinky, considering whether it was worth tracking down a pay phone, and decided against it. Better just to enjoy the view.

He could hardly remember how he had hit upon the whole former USSR thing in the first place. From memory it'd been recommended by a friend who said Russia now outstripped, literally, the Far East for easy pussy. That was when he'd come up with an *official*, vote-winning reason for going there. The trade delegations came later. If he could get the American taxpayer to sponsor his trips, so much the better. He'd even invested in some spurious company which exported ex-military night-vision goggles – very big after *Silence of the Lambs* – bought in the States via the classifieds of combat magazines. He even made a point, every trip, of visiting Ilya, his shadowy Russian partner in the joint venture, whom he'd met in a co-ed sauna on his very first fact-finding mission five years ago. Truth was, the biggest fact that he'd found in the course of half a decade was that Russian women suited him.

Not so long ago, when you mentioned a Soviet chick to any American male his immediate thought was shot putter at worst, tractor driver at best – either way with enough body hair to carpet a condo. But uh-uh. No way. How to explain it? He'd once heard that the Soviet government used to put some growth hormone in the bread that made the women tall and thin. But, unless they had some sort of segregation in their bakeries, that couldn't have been it, because the men were mostly short and ugly. Then he figured it was the lack of food. It didn't take a $100-an-hour nutritionist tell you that people who queue for hours to get a loaf of bread are gonna be thin, while people who dial in pizza are gonna be fat.

Whatever the reason, the women were triple A gorgeous. And as for body hair, they didn't have any. Even their bushes were tweaked to a line no fatter than a cigar.

Sure, in nightclubs women looked the same the world over, but *here* . . . Sometimes he would ride the Metro, not because he couldn't afford a cab but just to look at them. None of the sloppy Joe style of dressing that had afflicted young women in the United States. No, from the age of fourteen upwards, almost without exception, they dressed like *hookers*.

He drained the last of his drink and raised his hand for a refill. The base line from a tech tune was crackling through the speakers. Two girls in cowboy boots, waistcoats and a short tasselled skirt under which you could see their panties came on stage. Hell, he chuckled, they couldn't have been more than sixteen.

VIII

'To be honest with you I don't give, how do you say, a flying fuck about your father – no disrespect to the dead – but my client is lost and I have a five-year-old son to get home to.'

Luckily for Bridges, English had become the mother tongue of negotiations. He noticed, with affection, that when she was mad Katya's nostrils flared and her cheeks became slightly blotchy. On Georgi's insistence, they had adjourned to a Russian *stolovya*, a workers' collective cookhouse, most of which had reincarnated into Italian furniture shops or *obmen valuti*, currency exchanges. He was glad that at least some of the old traditions remained. Such as E-coli on demand.

No one wanted to fill the void after Katya's rant. Bridges studied the progress of a cockroach scaling a dirt-brown plastered wall. There were no seats in a *stolovya*, and the five of them stood round a pole which ran from floor to ceiling through a chest-high circular table.

Katya bristled in a purposeful way that suggested she was leaving. It was an exercise in futility; Bridges knew she feared that Peter and Alyosha were now as much a part of her as a tapeworm. He smiled in her direction. By way of response she turned to him and hissed, 'Look, tell them where the body is, then we can go.'

He put down the aluminium spoon standing in his glass of fruit compote, which had a dried apricot festering in the bottom. 'I would if I knew what had happened to it. It must have been stolen.'

'Who would want to steal the corpse of a Russian mobster?' she snapped.

Bridges swallowed a smile. He and Katya had already shared their first lie, now they were arguing. They were only a couple of affairs short of a full-blown marriage. He moved closer to her ear. He was so close he could see the blonde down on her lobe and the slight drag of her silver earring. She smelt of peaches. Wisps of hair curled on her neck and there was a faint sideburn on her cheek. Close up she was taller than he'd thought and gave the impression of solidity. Not physically but somehow palpably nonetheless.

'I don't know,' he said. 'All I'm saying is, it was in the morgue yesterday and now it's gone.' The rotation was strictly fridge, lab, and out. It was possible the reference system had fouled up, but he had checked the other dozen or so drawers. Unsurprisingly they had been empty. The professor was right, it was the slow season when, prior to the winter freeze, bodies were thick in the water but thin in the embalming parlour. Losing a corpse, he had to admit, was pretty bad.

The young woman, Sonya, had started to fidget with the slice of stale bread and black-edged salmon in front of her. Only Georgi was eating with gusto. Katya, who had passed over the fruit compote in favour of a bottle of Czech beer, poured a second glass.

Peter looked at her. 'Well, I suppose there's no reason why you can't go home—'

'Thanks,' she interrupted sarcastically.

'After all, it's only him that we really need.' He nodded towards Bridges.

'Oh, fantastic,' said Bridges. 'Why me?'

'We need you because you are the only surviving link between us and my recently departed father. That's why.'

'Look, if your father's corpse has disappeared, that's nothing to do with me. Maybe he, I dunno, sort of spontaneously combusted.'

Peter spluttered on a swig of black tea.

Katya began fastening her coat. At this rate, thought Bridges, she could disappear from him forever. Truth be told, she didn't look overly sad at the prospect.

'I promised this lady I'd help her find her friend and that's what I intend to do.'

Katya looked at him. 'No, really, I'm sure—'

'Nonsense. We can start now if you're ready.'

Despite the language barrier and the fact he was midway through a Danish pastry the size of Copenhagen, Alyosha had a keen grasp on proceedings. As Bridges turned to take Katya's arm, without looking up Alyosha drew his pistol from his inside pocket and laid it threateningly on the table.

'*Stop*,' he growled. Even if the word hadn't been the same in both languages Bridges would have got the gist. He was being told to stay.

A cook in a white overall stained grey around the midriff continued to move between them collecting plates.

IX

It was after six before Katya made it back to her apartment. Even Mrs Voronsheva had given up with the Russian classics and was allowing the boys to play Doom while she read Gogol in the corner.

The red button of the answer phone was beeping faster than the pacemaker of a man with a coronary. Katya didn't dare play back the tape, knowing it would be Clive after Terry again. The apartment smelt of young boys who hadn't been allowed out all day. She opened a window and then looked in her purse for a twenty dollar note for Mrs Voronsheva who, for a woman raised to abhor foreign currency, now understood more about exchange rates than a futures dealer. Katya almost managed a smile as she pulled out the bill, her last, from the wallet.

'I cooked borscht and kasha for the boys. But they refused to eat it,' said Mrs Voronsheva, squeezing chunky fingers into home knitted gloves.

'I'm afraid Sasha only eats orange food,' replied Katya absently, most of her thoughts devoted to her lack of cash.

Mrs Voronsheva tutted and shook her head. She took the money and left.

'Will pizza do you?' Katya called to the boys.

'What flavour?' shouted back Sasha.

'Tuna,' said Katya, her head in the fridge.

There was a prolonged silence from the sitting room.

'Look, Sasha,' Katya was getting cross, 'if you put a pizza into a blender, it would come out orange because tomatoes are red and tuna is,' she studied the picture on the packet, 'beige.'

'OK, then.'

'Great,' Katya muttered to herself and checked the sell-by date on the carton. The shops were full of suspect food which European companies sold to Russia. That or the shipping time was so long they went off en route. Few knew to check a best-by date.

She slid the pizza into the oven and sat down. As she pushed her hand through her hair she weighed up the debits and credits of the day. Lost, one moronic Englishman. Found, one attractive Russian woman whose passivity, luckily, had caused her not to probe in the events of the past twenty-four hours.

It hadn't been all bad.

X

'Look, guys, I think it's time you levelled with me. Exactly why do you want to see your father's body so much?' The dacha which Bridges had been taken to made his KGB-issued country home look like a lean-to. Even the artwork looked as if it had come straight out of the Hermitage. He thought at least one of the pictures he'd seen was a Chagall. The mood was on the convivial side of muted.

There'd been some frantic Russian debate over dinner, an odd meal even by local standards, which Bridges hadn't understood but at least the gun had disappeared. Alyosha had tried to assert himself but Peter had managed to restrain him. Georgi, after eating more than the rest of them put together, had retired. Now, seated on a white leather settee in front of a fire, and with a couple of brandies inside him, Bridges felt confident enough to confront Peter and Alyosha.

'I'd rather not say,' said Peter who had stripped down to an open-necked silk shirt and tailored trousers. 'It's personal.'

'Fair enough, but you gotta realise that until I can track down the professor there's really not a hell of a lot I can do.'

Peter sighed. 'By which time it may be too late.' He stared moodily into his brandy glass.

'Why? You're not worried he's gonna, you know, *decompose*.'

Peter shuddered. 'Good heavens no. It's nothing like that. It's, well, I . . . well, I suppose I might as well tell you. There's really no harm—'

In the corner, Alyosha, sensing danger, grunted.

Peter just glanced at him. 'You see, my father, Mr, er, Bridges, was quite a colourful man. You may know how his demise actually, er, you know, took place.' He was wriggling in his seat. Bridges loved it. Even the English accent didn't grate as much as usual. 'When we read the will we learned that the number of the combination to his personal safe, where most, if not all, his wealth lies, had been . . . Well, there's no easy way to say this. Tattooed to his, er, member.'

'His member,' repeated Bridges gravely. 'You mean his *weeny*.'

'Precisely,' said Peter. 'We could have waited until the funeral and then had a look, as it were, had it not been for the week's other unfortunate incident.'

'You mean there's more?' This was better than a Bruce Willis video dubbed into English any day of the week.

'I'm afraid so. You see, Father brought me back from England in the hope that I would take over his business affairs. I am not, by nature, a businessman. Literature's more my thing.'

'Literature,' repeated Bridges. A log shifted in the grate. Alyosha picked up the poker purposefully.

'Well, to cut a long story short, my first attempts in that field were not, shall we say, overly successful.' He looked directly at Bridges: 'Though one might argue that introducing English spring water to Russia would not have been without merit.'

Bridges smiled sympathetically.

'Anyway,' Peter continued quickly, 'we think as a result of my efforts at, shall we say, free trade, my half-brother has been kidnapped.'

'Holy shit.'

'Precisely. Though Alyosha assures me that in Moscow business circles, kidnapping is an accepted negotiating tool. He says there really is no need for alarm. Unless, of course, we don't pay.'

'Of course,' Bridges nodded.

'Which is why we urgently need the money from the safe, which is why we need—'

'To see your father,' finished Bridges.

'Exactly,' said Peter.

The atmosphere bristled with unanswered questions and half-explained statements. Bridges paused to take it all in. Alyosha, slumped in an armchair in the corner, sensing the import, stopped picking his teeth. Peter sat in motionless defeat. Then, 'Oh my God.' The words came from Peter in reasoned, even tones. 'I can't believe it.' He leapt to his feet, spilling brandy on the sofa. 'What a bloody idiot I've been.' Bridges and Alyosha exchanged glances. Peter went on excitedly, 'The photocopies! The genitals!' He was laughing. 'Gentlemen, follow me. Salvation is at hand.'

XI

The market, illuminated by the single arc of a street light, was deserted. Terry had been walking for hours in this industrial landscape. He was exhausted. Too exhausted even to make an entry in *Terry's Log*. His hands were numb and his shoulders ached from the weight of a discarded and now sodden coat he'd found on a dump. A couple of the market trestle tables were piled high with cardboard boxes. Terry made his way over to them. His feet hurt and his stomach ached with hunger. He read the labels which were illustrated with pictures of improbable happiness. Oranges from Israel. He sorted through the crates like a man possessed. He was hungry and thirsty. He couldn't believe anywhere on earth could be this inhospitable.

In the third box he found two mouldering oranges which he put to his mouth and sucked. A moving light to his left made him turn his head. He saw a yellow bus, empty but for the driver. He tried to run towards it but the weight of his coat and his exhaustion made him stumble. When he reached the bus he fell onto his elbows and tried to drag himself up the metal steps. He looked up at the driver and pleaded, 'Me ski. Please ski. Home ski.'

The driver sucked on his teeth in irritation at another late-night drunk and flicked a switch which shut the doors like a concertina, squeezing Terry out onto the pavement.

A cloud scudded across the sky to reveal a full moon over the city. Terry put his head back and howled.

XII

Sasha asked, 'Are you scared?'

'Nah,' said Misha, trying to sound brave. It was several hours past lights out, though neither boy, sandwiched together under a Teletubbies duvet, could sleep.

'Trust me,' said Sasha. 'You know I won't let you down.'

In the dark they heard a short blast on the doorbell. Sasha sat bolt upright.

'Who's that?' he said.

'Don't ask me,' said Misha.

'Maybe it's my dad.'

They heard Katya unbolt the inner and outer doors.

It wasn't Sasha's dad. The voice was loud and foreign. It boomed down the corridor into their room, disturbing everything. It said, 'Surprise, surprise, Katya. Wakey, wakey. The senator is back.'

CHAPTER TWELVE

I

Neither the curtains, which billowed slightly in the night air, nor the blinds were drawn. When Peter flicked on the overhead strip light, which hummed like a mosquito, the moonlight outside bounced off the windows into infinity.

He led Alyosha and Bridges into the study with the hesitant stealth of a burglar. In an ideal world, he reasoned, he wouldn't have to do this, but in an ideal world he would not have been the son of a sociopath. The room smelt of disinfectant and the faint chemical odour given off by new office machinery. Because of the unnatural strain his father had put on hi-tech durables, he had had to update his computers and fax machines regularly.

Peter tried to look on the bright side. If they succeeded in their midnight foray, then all they would have to do was open the safe, pay the kidnappers and bury his father. Itemised like that it didn't seem so insurmountable. Then perhaps he could return to writing the modern Russian classic.

He puffed out his cheeks in wary anticipation as he

flipped the lid of a steel-grey box file. Bridges and Alyosha loitered by the door, neither sure what this moonlit madness signified. The first thing to hit Peter was an impression of Tanya's breasts. In the grey relief of a mammogram, her nipples were like benchmarks on an Ordnance Survey map at the summer of a mountainous swell. He shuddered and put it to the bottom of the pile. Next came her buttocks. It might have been a reflection of her pear-shaped Russian figure, but he couldn't help noticing his father had changed the paper size to A3.

'What are you doing?' asked Alyosha carefully from inside the oak door jamb, as if he didn't want to interrupt.

'The combination to the safe,' Peter explained. 'My father and Tanya used to photocopy their,' he paused, 'you know, bits.' Saying it out loud gave the whole thing a bit of credence, he thought.

'So?' asked Alyosha, raising his blond eyebrows as if Xeroxing genitals was as normal a leisure pursuit as tennis.

'So,' replied Peter, not looking up from the box, 'we should be able to see the tattoo and make out the combination for the safe.' He continued flicking through the photocopies as he spoke. Suddenly he looked up at Alyosha and said, 'Here we are.'

The penis was back on A4 paper. Peter held it up towards the fluorescent light. One thing could be said for it, it was erect. Bridges looked baffled. Peter took the sheet and sat behind Hard Currency's desk, placing the photocopy in front of him with the precision of an exam student. The desk had collected a thin layer of dust which he disturbed as he shoved a pile of papers towards an overflowing in-tray. Other than letters which looked as if they were from the kidnappers – which were mostly hand-delivered – he hadn't touched his father's correspondence since he'd died. He re-registered the chore on his mental 'to do' list.

Peter explained again, in English, for the sake of Bridges, what he was going to do. Bridges didn't seem that impressed. He was more intent on familiarising himself with the specs of his father's laptop. 'Does that come with a pentium processor as standard?' he asked, pointing towards a grey Toshiba.

It wasn't the first time Peter had noticed the avarice with which Americans stored up technical knowledge. When you saw two or more of them together – there had been several at De Montfort – they didn't so much *converse* as download information from each other.

'I really couldn't tell you,' said Peter irritably. For one of the greatest ideas of the past week, his ingenuity was receiving scant praise. He turned to Alyosha. 'I don't suppose you've got a magnifying glass on you?' With Alyosha it was always worth a shot.

Alyosha checked his pockets before saying, 'No, but I'll get one.' He left the room walking on tiptoe with his body slightly forward, which was his normal gait.

Peter meanwhile plucked a pen from a black and white beaker with a red heart which said 'I love Moscow'. He couldn't help thinking that, as a line, it must have enjoyed a very limited production run. Then he swept the Anglepoise lamp down to within an inch of the paper.

Success lay, he discovered after the first minute, in not thinking of the image as his father's genitals, but rather a sort of spot-the-ball competition which he'd seen a couple of times in an English paper. The black-and-white granular quality of the paper was similar.

The first number he read (the figures were tattooed in a column, like a totem) he thought was a one, but what with the poor reproduction and veined skin it could well have been a seven. There appeared to be seven numbers in all. He wondered if he could somehow blow the image up. He sat back and sighed, one hand knocking the lamp upwards. If only his father had invested in a colour photocopier. He sighed again. If only Tanya could remember more about her husband's genitals (in a rare moment of lucidity, she'd claim that a blindfold fashioned from post-it stickers had restricted her view). If only, he thought, his father hadn't been such a *freak*.

'How's it going?' asked Bridges.

'Not great,' replied Peter. 'I think it begins one, three, seven, but I can't be sure. That's as far as I've got.'

Bridges still had his brandy glass in his hand. He swilled it round before taking an extended gulp. 'Mind if I try?' He put his hand out for the photocopy.

Peter sensed he should be embarrassed, but after the events of the past week he was all coyed out. 'Be my guest. I don't suppose, if you saw the body, you remember anything?'

'I'm afraid not. Professor Modin's the one who does the embalming part. I'm more, you know, PR.'

'Right,' said Peter. 'And I suppose the professor's still not—'

'At home or at the lab,' finished Bridges. 'Being the weekend he's probably at his dacha. As I said, I guess he'll be back on Monday, if you can wait.'

The question was answered for him from the other side of the open door. 'I don't think so,' said Alyosha. 'In his left hand he held a child's magnifying glass, in the other a brown envelope. 'This must have been delivered by the kidnappers sometime this evening.'

'What does it say?' asked Peter, nervously tapping the desk with his index finger.

'Everything's fine, your brother's well, only they want the money sooner rather than later.'

'How soon?' asked Peter.

'Tomorrow at noon.'

Peter looked at his watch. At the same time the clock in the dining room struck twice. 'That gives us exactly ten hours,' he said.

II

The drizzle woke Terry before dawn. Apart from the cold, it wasn't an unpleasant sensation. There was something fresh about it, almost cleansing. He hunched the coat over his head. He knew that eighty per cent of all body heat was lost through the head – and that, he guessed, was through a well turfed head. He was as stiff as a poker down the whole of his left side. He'd tried to sleep on his back in case he rolled off the trestle table but in the night he must have turned himself to try to relieve the soreness. His mattress and duvet were fashioned out of cardboard fruit boxes for warmth. The alternative would have been to risk the ground and he'd spotted several rats chasing in and out of plastic bags as he'd been making up his billet.

He'd meant to write an entry in *Terry's Log* but found his hands were too frozen by the time he'd levered himself into bed.

He went back to sleep and when he woke again it was to the sound of voices nearby. Terry raised his head a couple of inches and tried to look round. A spasm of stiffness caused him to collapse again. He must have dozed off once more because he came round – he had no idea how much later – to find himself being shaken roughly. From his horizontal vantage point Terry was only aware of the man's gold teeth, not just fillings but an entire front row of them. He was youngish, in his forties, with dark glossy hair and dark skin. He was shaking Terry by the shoulder and trying to push him at the same time. Terry went rigid to stop himself being shoved off his bed. Somehow it struck him as a Russian version of the princess and the pea. Through his peripheral vision he was dimly aware that more people had started to gather round. Then two more men began to lift a corner of the table to make him slide off. The air around his assailants had the acrid smell of alcohol – though Terry had to admit that, in the whiff department, he was far from potpourri. He swung his legs off the table and onto the ground which was muddy and soft underfoot. His hip ached and when he looked at his hands, which were scratched and caked in dirt, he didn't recognise them. He was sore all over and tried to do some muscle-relaxing exercises but the weight of his coat made it impossible. His eyes, he sensed, were puffy, the result of too little sleep and the lingering effects of last week's handbag attack.

What he wouldn't do for a Badedas bath and a ninety-eight per cent fat-free bagel, though given his hunger he would have gladly tucked into an FEB including fried bread. The first man was shouting something incomprehensible at him, gold teeth flashing like a character from a Bond film. Next to the swarthy man, a woman of the same age and with the same teeth – so much for these people being poor, Terry said to himself – was laughing. She was wearing a brightly coloured headscarf and sitting on her haunches over an improvised table cutting a salami into slices and hacking at a loaf of bread.

Elsewhere around the market, stalls were being set up. Old women sat behind neatly stacked piles of tomatoes and oranges. A couple pulled bunches of green and purple grapes from huge canvas bags and hung the fruit on hooks. He was starving. He tried to ignore Gold Tooth who was still shouting in front of him. On another day he might have harangued him in return, but he wasn't at his best this morning. Lost, cold, dirty and hungry were words that sprang to mind. The fear that he might never find his way home gnawed at him worse than his hunger. The rain was more persistent now. He noticed a couple of men and some women drinking huge glasses of what he guessed was vodka. After they downed it they shuddered and bit on a piece of black bread. Most of the stallholders were dark-haired men and women whom Terry now took to be Gypsies, though they clearly lacked the legendary Romany hospitality. On the periphery Russians were laying out their goods, most of which made Basingstoke's Three-for-a-Pound store look like Selfridges. One was selling a plug and two pairs of socks, another a couple of chipped plates. They all seemed oblivious of the weather.

Terry decided to make a circuit of the market, less out

of interest in Russian horticulture than because he didn't have a clear idea what else to do. He didn't know which way to walk and he had no money for a cab. Even if he dared risk the incomprehensible Russian Metro, he couldn't pay for a ticket. He had no money to call anyone, and in any case he didn't have Katya's number.

Then, just past a table of dull aubergines, it came to him quite suddenly, the refuge of all Englishmen abroad, the salvation of the weary, where he would be welcomed like a lost son. The British Embassy.

Two outstanding problems, though, Terry, my son, he said to himself. Where was it and how would he get there? Finding it ought to be easy. His circuit now finished, he was back opposite the man who had crudely evicted him from his bed half an hour ago. It was amazing, Terry thought with pride, how soon a trained man could familiarise himself with foreign terrain.

He smoothed down his hair and adjusted his coat lapels. Even if the plan didn't work, he might get an orange out of it. In the distance he heard the mechanical clank of a trolley bus making its first journey of the day.

Terry coughed. 'Excuse me ski. Where is Britishski Embasski?' It had been so long since he had spoken that his voice sounded strange, even to him. He felt unconnected to it.

Gold Tooth looked up from the headscarved woman who was now sitting on his knee. They both studied him curiously. It was still early and, other than the traders, there were few people at the market. Consequently, it was Terry who provided the bulk of the breakfast-time entertainment.

The couple clearly didn't know what he was talking about – there was a chance, after all, that they didn't speak Russian. He would have to be more visual. Come in with a few of his legendary charades, of which Una Stubbs would have been proud. He coughed again, inhaled and started to sing. 'Land of hope and glory, mother of the free, where is the embassy? You have got to tell me.' He was hoarse but he was pleased with the rhyme and scan of the tune. He repeated the verse, adding a salute.

No reaction, although the woman sitting on the man's knee had started to laugh, shaking her long dark mane and flashing her teeth like a horse.

Terry continued, 'Michael Owen, Elton John, Margaret Thatcher, Spice Girls. *Où est-il?*'

Nothing.

'William Shakespeare, Lionel Blair ski.' What was the matter with these people? Britain had ruled half the known world at one point and they were staring at him as if he came from Guatemala. 'Oh, for goodness sake.' He suddenly felt very defeated. Everything just seemed too much trouble. He'd had it with Russians. Who cared if the whole country sank into chaos or civil war? All he wanted was things to be normal again: a trip round the Savacentre, a pineapple juice with the lads after work, a shared double entendre with Joan from accounts.

He retreated to his abandoned pile of cardboard boxes in the corner and sat down. His trouser bottoms were covered in grey mud and by the look of it he was already on his way to contracting trench foot. Or Lassa fever. Or both. He thought he heard a rat scrabble out from under the boxes but he couldn't be bothered to move. Resting his full weight on them, he found the cardboard moulded itself to the contours of his body. He dozed off. When he woke he became aware of a steady trickle of warm water on his leg. It wasn't unpleasant. Even when he saw the dog, a pepper-coloured sort of mongrel, he could hardly be bothered to shoo it away.

He suddenly knew what he had to do. His fingers were chapped and cold, which made undoing the buttons doubly difficult. Then he started peeling off his coat and slowly undoing his shirt.

III

It was getting on for five, the black night sky lifting to bruised purple, when they finally cracked it. It was the scanner that saved them in the end, a consumer durable which had served more as one of his father's *outré* sex aids than for any recognised office function. Bridges was the first to spot its potential just before dawn when they had all but given up on illumination either by magnifying glass or the naked eye.

According to Bridges, if the image was scanned onto a screen it could be enlarged and, not only that, they could *zoom* in on any part of the organ they wanted. Peter squirmed. The idea of enlarging his father's penis smacked of indecency, if not incest.

'Wicked idea,' said Alyosha when it was explained to him. Whereas Bridges and Peter had been flagging since two, Alyosha looked as fresh as a Young Pioneer at summer camp.

It must have been the whipping potential of the plastic flex that had appealed to his father, thought Peter, because once you examined the Medusa-like spray of them behind his word processor, you saw that very few were actually connected to anything.

'Do you know what you're doing?' he asked Bridges as he held the lead to the scanner gently between thumb and forefinger.

'Sure. We just have to . . .' he looked hesitantly at the back of the computer.

'Attach it to the scanner port on the right,' said Alyosha, taking the lead from him.

'Exactly,' said Bridges. 'Now all we have to do is—'

Alyosha switched on the computer which sprang to life with a metallic jingle. Then he started flicking the mouse across the screen, clicking it like a Geiger counter in a nuclear plant.

'Where did you learn all this stuff?' Peter asked him sceptically.

'De Montfort University is not the only seat of learning in the world,' he replied with offended superiority.

'So you learnt it at college?' said Peter, half shocked, half impressed.

'Nah, we had a load of knocked-off Turkish computers. I had to show the punters how they worked before they bought them.'

'Great. Why didn't you say anything before?'

'You never asked,' said Alyosha.

In less than five minutes they were confronted with what they wanted to see. The numbers weren't completely visible but, from their configuration and what you could see, they were possible to read. A flurry of excitement went round the room. Peter and Alyosha embraced and Bridges said, 'Great, now I guess I can go.' They ignored him.

Peter spoke while Alyosha wrote: 'One, eight, seven, nine, two five, three.'

'Eighteen seventy-nine to fifty-three. A patriot to the end,' said Alyosha with hushed reverence. 'Stalin's date of birth and death.'

'Fascinating,' said Peter. 'Now can we get on?' They both knew where the safe was kept, shrouded by a topless calendar forever stuck on June 1992 showing Olga astride an armoured personnel carrier, her striped army pullover hoisted up to chin height.

'Does that mean I'm free to go, then?' repeated Bridges wearily.

All eyes were on Olga as her bare breasts were swept up in an arc to reveal the safe beneath.

'Fingers crossed,' said Peter.

'Here we go,' said Alyosha.

IV

Sasha couldn't resist a bit of improvised begging on the Metro into town. It was hardly worth trying in the empty outlying stations near home, but as they approached Kutosovski Prospekt he started to prepare himself. Prior to Kutosovski the train clanked its way through the high-rises above ground. When it was raining or, like today, there was a slight drizzle of snow, light flurries leaked in through the badly fitting windows. Misha and Sasha opened their mouths and turned their faces up, laughing at the cold touch of the flakes on their tongues.

The carriage was deserted but for a girl and an old couple carrying baskets of food back from their dacha. They reminded Sasha of his grandparents in the Ukraine. Simple peasant folk, he thought, so ignorant of market forces. Why plant potatoes when everyone else did? Why stick with your boring old Giffen goods when you could go for the exotic – a mange tout or asparagus?

The woman was big and, in black-rimmed glasses the thickness of a goldfish bowl, looked like a barn owl. The man was wiry with a flat nose and down-turned mouth which reminded Sasha that they'd left Leonid at home. Today's trip was no place for small pets and women.

'Come on Mish. Stand up.' He nudged his friend.

'Oh, must we?' Misha hung back.

'Certainly, it's always good to keep your hand in.'

Misha tutted but allowed himself to be hauled to his feet by the shoulders.

Sasha started in his singsong voice, 'Dear ladies and gentlemen, my brother and I are victims of the Chernobyl nuclear accident. Though we may look well enough, in fact we both suffer from a series of internal disorders including—'

'What do you mean Chernobyl? You can't be more than seven, the pair of you. Chernobyl was in nineteen eighty-seven.' It was the pug-faced man, and he sounded mighty indignant.

The train swerved round a corner and Sasha nearly lost his balance. As it was he crashed into the knees of a young blonde woman who pushed him away angrily.

'I meant we are the *hidden* victims of Chernobyl,' he explained patiently.

'And what exactly is a *hidden* victim of Chernobyl?' asked the old man who, prior to this outburst, Sasha thought, had an under-the-thumb look. Though that could just have been because of his size in comparison to his wife's. Then he reminded himself that he, more than most, should remember that size had very little to do with power.

He continued indignant and unabashed. He was speaking as if by rote and hardly pausing for breath. 'It means my father was one of the liquidators at the plant, and the radiation in his thyroid gland was passed on to me, which means that my – and my brother's,' he nodded at Misha, 'internal organs are not all they should be.'

'Completely shot away,' murmured Misha by way of encouragement, and coughed.

The old man looked suitably chastised and the woman reached for her purse and pressed a five rouble note into his hand.

'For our operations,' said Sasha, nodding. 'We thank you.'

'Not at all,' she replied with a tear in her eye.

The boys leapt off at Kievski station – Sasha never liked to overplay an audience – and made their way to the Circle Line past the old men selling newspapers on tables where the new glossy *Vogue* rubbed shoulders with *Pravda*. Every station had its own smell, Sasha thought. He could've recognised them all with his eyes shut. Kievski reminded him of vanilla, which reminded him how much he would like an ice cream. But there was work to be done.

He liked the mosaics of rural life on the walls at Kievski. His mother had told him that when she'd been his age, life had been completely different. She said under what was called Communism, people thought of the state as their mum and dad. He didn't know much about governments, but he couldn't imagine the men he saw on the TV as his parents, no matter how much he missed his dad. Now he just liked to look at the colours of the mosaics. They reminded him of his story books. His grandparents in Byelorus used to tell him how much better it was in the olden days, but he thought things were pretty good these days. Admittedly, they would improve tenfold with a mobile phone, but that was just a question of time. Old people always complained.

They took a Circle Line train to Barakadnia station, too busy to do any freelance begging. There was a time when he might have indulged in some minor pickpocketing but not now that he was older. Not at his age. Their destination was 1905 Ulitsa.

V

Katya put the senator to sleep in Terry's room. If she'd had a washing machine, she might have washed the sheets – she calculated three men had slept in the same bedclothes – but, while she still hand-washed, the sheets would just have to do. She'd tidied most of Terry's belongings into a suitcase and pushed them under the

361

bed, apart from that damned piece of moulded metal which wouldn't fit. In a paroxysm of rage she'd twisted it out of shape and shoved it down the communal rubbish chute in the hall.

In one of the scenarios currently running through her head, Terry Small would never return to see it. Despite the obvious advantages, it wasn't a prospect she cherished. Clive hadn't called last night, though it was just a question of time before he did. Not only that but Terry's flight home was in a few days.

She looked at her watch. Sasha and Misha had been gone an hour. She sighed. She should get dressed. The senator would be round as soon as he woke up, or, more exactly, sobered up. She'd known a visit to Moscow was on the cards, she just hadn't imagined it would be so soon. She poured herself another cup of tea from the pot, bone china from Minsk which she'd bought on her last visit to her parents. She'd sent Sasha out without breakfast this morning which she hated to do, but she simply hadn't had time to shop. She'd given him a couple of roubles and told him to get himself and Misha some *piroshki*, which would no doubt have ended up as half a Snickers bar. She really must get dressed for the senator – but then again, her age put her at least twenty years outside his acceptable parameters of sexual attractiveness.

It reminded her that she should go through her Rolodex to pick out some suitable girls, try him out with a few before introducing him to Sonya. If everything went according to plan, she was in line for her $20,000 bonus. In which case she needn't worry whether Terry Small had been run over by a trolley bus or joined the Red Army.

But she had a growing feeling of unease. She shuddered. Some might have recognised it as conscience. She sat back and was sipping her tea, trying to dispel the sensation, when the phone rang. Katya overrode her usual instinct of letting the machine pick it up. Today, she felt, might be the day to really start taking charge. Things in the last few days had ever so slightly started to slip.

'Hello, Katya?' The unmistakable soft lilt of Sonya. She sounded as if she was trying not to be overheard.

'Sonya, hello. How are you?' Katya began doodling on an open pad.

'Fine. I'm very well.'

Katya could hardly hear her. Apart from Sonya's hushed voice, the line was bad.

'Listen, the foreigner,' then something muffled. The only word Katya grasped was 'foreigner'. 'I want to meet him.'

Katya smiled over the knot in her stomach. 'Of course, and I know he wants to meet you too.'

'He does?' She sounded surprised. 'It's just that . . .' She paused. 'It's just that I've been thinking it over and I have decided that, I have decided that I really do want to marry him.'

Katya's jaw dropped. 'Well, this is great Sonya. It's a little unexpected. I mean, you haven't even—'

'I know, I know, it's just a feeling I have.'

Katya's stomach twisted as she thought of the man next door. 'And you're sure you really want to marry him?'

'Absolutely.'

'OK. Actually, Sonya, he'll be here this morning, why don't you come over?'

'Oh no, I couldn't.'

'Of course you could. I insist.' She gave her the address, they said goodbye and Katya hung up. 'Jesus Christ,' she said out loud. Sonya's fortunes must have really taken a tumble for her to be in such a hurry to marry him. She hadn't even met the senator. Katya looked down at the doodle. It was in the shape of a dollar sign.

VI

'You're very happy this morning.' Nikita looked up from the jigsaw at his sister. 'Don't tell me it's because it's your day off. That usually makes you fed up.'

Sonya stopped humming. 'What do you mean?'

'You start getting anxious and moping about, as if you don't want to be here.' He picked up a piece and pretended to study it.

'That's not true.'

'I wouldn't blame you. You're young, you should be getting out with your friends, not staying here looking after me.' Sonya could see how much it was hurting him to say it and how much he was hoping she would deny it. And yet they both knew it was true.

She thought her news would make him happy, and in any case she had to tell someone. She'd barely been able to stop thinking of the tall man in the strange trousers with the funny accent since Katya had introduced them.

'Listen, darling. I've met someone, he's foreign and I think we're going to get married.' It tumbled out.

The tray with the jigsaw, a view of Odessa, slipped or

Nikita's lap. 'What? Where? I mean how? What will happen to me?' He forgot the *who*, though she knew it didn't mean he didn't care.

'You, darling, are going to be fine.' She kissed his head. 'I promise. Trust me, everything is going to be all right. But now I have to go out.'

VII

Just after she put the phone down, the door buzzer went. Katya tutted loudly. If she had wanted all these unheralded interruptions she would have stayed in the village. In the city it was only manners to call before you turned up. More than that, it was only sense. Katya lived an hour out of the centre. It surely couldn't be the senator. Jet lag and hangover should at least have put him out of action till lunchtime. 'Who on earth . . .?' She hushed Leonid, who as a guard dog could be relied on to bark at one out of every five guests.

'Good morning,' came the greeting as she opened the door.

'Mr Bridges. I . . . What the . . .? I mean, you did well to find me again.' The American looked tired and more dishevelled than previously.

'Yeah, well. The jacket I picked up in the gym had your name and number on it. I called this morning and your son – Sasha? – gave me directions.' He was standing in the doorway. Katya's hand immediately went to gather her dressing gown at the throat. She never knew why it was such an instinctive reaction, bearing in mind it hardly covered her backside.

'Come in. I'll just get dressed.'

'Not on my account,' said Bridges, smiling. He went on, as if he needed to explain, 'I came because I promised to help you find the English professor, Dr Small, and I,' he paused, 'I guess I'm a man of my word. I feel real bad that I might have caused you any inconvenience.'

One thing about Americans, they had, or at least pretended to have, the pleasantest manners, she thought as she led him into her flat. Despite the hurried explanation, the way he was looking at her legs made Katya think she knew the real reason why he'd spent an hour on the Metro.

She smiled to herself. At least he was taking the initiative. Or was he? Was this part of western courtship? Two Russians of the opposite sex in an empty apartment would have been in bed within seconds even if they weren't that keen on each other, just to take advantage of the privacy. With him, Katya wasn't sure. She watched *Santa Barbara*, she knew Americans lived on ranches and could have sex any time. She was confused. She was well acquainted with the courtship rituals of her American clients, which had about as much finesse as a nature documentary on rutting deers, but what were the real rules of western affairs?

'Why don't you wait in the kitchen?' She ushered him through the glass door and pulled out a stool for him. 'There's tea in the pot, though no milk.' She reached up to get some sugar.

Katya had an entire kitchen cabinet devoted to boxes of sugar cubes which she'd bought cheap from an Azerbaijani former accountant at the local market. As she pulled the door open, two boxes tumbled out, spilling their contents over the bench and onto the floor. Bridges rushed to help her. There was a tussle of bumped shoulders but he backed away. Typical, thought Katya. She threw some of the cubes into the cardboard box and stalked into the bathroom.

When she returned twenty minutes later in jeans and a sweatshirt, putting her hair into a ponytail, he had just finished with the brush and dustpan.

'I found them under the sink,' he said almost apologetically.

'Great. Thanks a lot,' replied Katya, sitting beside him. 'So where do we start?'

'Excuse me?' He sounded shocked.

'Where do we start to look for Mr Small? Don't tell you'd forgotten why you were here, Mr Bridges?'

'No, of course not. I thought maybe we could ring round some of the hospitals. In case—'

'Pah! This is not *ER*. In Russia once someone gets caught in our system he can be lost for months and no one will find him. What you fail to understand, Mr Bridges, is that in my country you can be imprisoned for not carrying personal documents. You can be locked up for being drunk. It is easy to, how do you say, to fall through the hole.' She had reddened slightly at the neck as she spoke.

'OK then, let's start with what we know. Let's imagine you were him.'

Katya twitched internally.

'You have escaped from imprisonment. Surely you would return here? Does Mr Small speak any Russian?'

'Not a word.'

367

'But he knows where you live. He would make his way back here, right?'

Katya was starting to get bored with this line of inquiry and resentful of the interrogation. 'Mr Bridges, if I were a mind-reader I would join the circus. As it is, I really don't feel qualified to speak of someone's imagined where-abouts.'

Bridges looked chastised.

Katya felt a stab of pity. 'I do appreciate that you're trying to help and I am grateful, but in this country you quickly learn that the best approach is to wait and see. And that, I'm afraid, is what we shall have to do with Small.' She got up and went to the window. She toyed with the idea of inquiring what had happened after she'd left Bridges with the three Russians, but experience had taught her not to ask about anything that didn't exactly correspond to her immediate needs.

The morning was overcast, the way it would stay for the next six or seven months. Moscow didn't have seasons. You were plunged in a fortnight from summer to snow, and then at the beginning of May the snow would stop and the trees would explode into greenery. It was so breathtaking that it was the only few days in the year when she felt close to religious. In today's gloom, lights shone from most of the windows in every tower block. Chronic unemployment meant people stayed at home, diverted only by the television and vodka. Domestic violence was as closely linked to the unemployment rate as inflation was. She often thought that if the state had granted them more than a two-roomed apartment, she wouldn't have posted her husband to Siberia or dispatched her sister-in-law to jail.

She looked at Bridges, whose brow was furrowed in thought. It was a relief to know that he was pretending to look for Small because he fancied her. Lust was so much easier to understand than altruism.

'Look, Mr Bridges—' She was interrupted by a double toot at the door, jaunty and yet with an undercurrent of menace, like Morse code. 'Could you excuse me, please?'

'Sure.' He was absently stirring his tea as she left the room. She kicked Sasha's football into the sitting room as she passed it and tidied away a couple of photographs of her girls which were lying on the telephone table. Bridges hadn't noticed them, though she knew her next guest would home in on them like a nuclear warhead. She breathed deeply and forced a smile as she twisted the plastic doorknob.

'Mornin',' said the senator as he pushed past Katya uninvited. He smelt of linseed oil and cigars. 'Jesus Christ, I swear the beds you give me get more uncomfortable every visit. It might be time for me to review my accommodation. But you know how I need my privacy.' He turned to Katya and winked.

'Come in,' said Katya redundantly. He was dressed in cowboy boots, fading denim jeans, a leather belt with a star-shaped buckle, a checked shirt and a fringed suede jacket. And a stetson. It was an amazing costume, she thought, considering he'd only crossed the two-metre prairie from next door. He didn't attempt to remove his hat or his coat. The incongruity of his presence struck Katya. If the world had gone according to plan, he would have lived his entire life thinking Moscow was a type of marsh-eating cattle. But the world hadn't gone according to plan and he was here in her hall.

It used to be against the law to fraternise with Americans, and now she had two of them in her apartment. Something told her she should keep them apart. Even with her acting ability it would be difficult to pass the senator off as a visiting lecturer. In return the senator would take Bridges for another client and she knew from experience that all clients over the age of fifty-five reacted badly to the younger ones. Especially not bad-looking ones.

'Do go into the sitting room,' she said, glad she had already converted her bed back into a sofa.

He walked as if his balls were the only part of his body affected by gravity.

As the senator sank into the sofa, Katya recoiled slightly, thinking how a couple of hours earlier her head had been lying where his backside was now plumply resting.

'How are you this morning?' She sat primly on the edge of a wooden-backed chair. She seemed to remember that the senator responded best to prim.

'Just fine, ma'am. And yourself?' His hair was white and oily. It was balding on top and long at the back. Maybe it was the light from the window – the curtains weren't fully open – but his hair seemed to have a green sheen to it. His skin was red and porous. It was impossible to imagine the man in front of her to be any age other than the one he was. In Bridges, for example, she could see the young man; in the senator anything younger than fifty was impossible.

She knew from what he'd told her that he had two

grown-up sons, one an insurance broker, the other a bum. At first she thought he'd meant a criminal. It later transpired he was a sculptor, married to a Hispanic with two children. The senator had been married three times; after twenty years with his first wife he had moved on progressively to younger women, weeded out by feet size and willingness to sign a pre-nup. 'I've tried going out with older women,' he'd told her on his first visit three years ago, 'but I'd find myself looking at them and saying, "Barry, what are you doing out with Grandma?"'

Since then his upper age limit had been twenty. Katya had twice introduced him (she was sure she wouldn't have done it had Sasha been a daughter) to girls who claimed not to be underage but she guessed were. Late last year in a 4 a.m. phone call, the senator had declared he wanted another wife. The travel was taking its toll and he found trips to Moscow increasingly uncomfortable.

Katya thought a conversational preamble would be good. 'Did you have a pleasant evening yesterday?'

'I sure as hell did. Found the greatest club and spent most of it watching the pride of Russian womanhood.' His thighs looked close to covering the divan and his stomach lopped over his belt like a Sumo wrestler's.

For a moment Katya thought he meant a sports club. He'd been to *Dynamo*? Then it clicked. 'Oh, you mean a strip club.'

'Sure as hell do. And let me tell you, they put me in the mood. I'm raring to go.' His arms, which were draped over the back of the divan, slapped his thighs. His legs were akimbo. He was a huge man and seemed to colonise

371

the room. 'So, Katya, what have you got for me this trip?' He smiled at her, more leer than pleasure. His voice was rasping, almost asthmatic.

Katya suddenly wondered what it might take for a woman to have sex with him. Before today, she'd assumed the women she matched with foreigners were as stupid as the men. It was perfect supply and demand. Young women wanted security and wealth, men wanted beautiful, docile wives. The fact that neither party ever got what they wanted didn't concern her. She just facilitated the unions. Morals didn't come into it.

Then she thought of Sonya. Sonya didn't fit the mould. She shouldn't have to sleep with the man sitting in front of her. She should at least have a choice. They might have Swedish fish fingers in the shops and American lingerie, but Russians really didn't have a *choice*. That why she wanted to get herself and Sasha out.

'I said, who have you got for me this time?'

Katya looked at his face, his eyes empty of anything but lustful anticipation. 'I'll just have—' She saw the colour drain from the senator's face. He was staring past her to the doorway where Bridges had appeared.

The senator spoke to Katya but he didn't stop staring at Bridges. 'My God, what in the name of sweet fanny Jesus is *he* doing here?'

VIII

The statue outside the Metro was one of Peter's favourites. He'd always been a sucker for Soviet realism. Huge bronze casts of men, women and children walking towards the new dawn of communism. How different from the men and women of today stumbling around the statue's base. Had it ever been like that, two hundred millions people united in one ideal? If it had, then the two generations of Party followers hadn't managed to pass on anything but materialism in their genes. In the weak midday sun, he almost felt a chapter coming on.

The bronze woman at the front of the statue was bravely clutching a huge flag chest high. Her hair was cast flowing behind her. Her arms were strong. Her legs were apart, walking towards the future. Her expression was one of joyful determination. She reminded Peter of Sonya. Sonya was more fragile but the almond-shaped eyes and high Slavonic cheekbones were the same. He thought back to yesterday's encounter. Could she really have suggested they should get married? Would she really be the devoted Sonya to his – he paused – Raskolnikov?

Father Georgi and Alyosha were arguing as the three of them left the hexagonal station, its skylight dappled with bird droppings. The scent as they were deposited at the top of the escalator was floral, the exit surrounded by glum-faced middle-aged women selling elegant long-stemmed roses, seemingly immune to their stock. Alyosha held the Slazenger holdall clasped to his chest. He'd refused to part with his Tommy Hilfiger bag.

'*You* leave the money,' he said to Georgi sternly. 'I mean, who's going to shoot a man of God?'

'Need I point out the fate of Gregory Rasputin?' On Alyosha's explicit instructions he was wearing his full religious kit.

'That was different,' said Alyosha. Peter wondered if the name Rasputin really had any resonance, other than as a Boney M song, for Alyosha. 'Exactly what do you think you're getting paid for, *confession*? Employer-employee relations depend on one person doing what the other says, savvy?'

'But I'm not employed by—'

'Look,' Peter intervened, will you two shut up? This is difficult enough without you arguing. Father, you will *please* leave the holdall in the allotted spot.'

Georgi was silent, which Alyosha took as capitulation. He gave a grin of triumph.

After they'd made it inside the safe, a few hours earlier, getting the money had been a cinch. In fact the $250,000 they took was a drop in the ocean of greenbacks stuffed into the safe. Thousands of thousands of them, as well as details of the offshore accounts. There'd been no clue to the whereabouts of the safety deposit box or its key, but Peter understood he would never, unless he wanted to, have to work again.

They crossed Krasna Presninskaya, past the Soviet statue. There was a McDonald's to their immediate left and a couple of metres further down a Union flag outside the English John Bull pub. Peter looked at his watch. Ten to twelve. They dodged a tram as it came towards them and then a trolley bus on their left. The park where they were to make the drop was a long, thin, wooded avenue where, even in the cold weather, couples mingled with drunks. In the centre was a clearing containing a statue of Lenin.

The exchange was to be simple. Three seats formed an arc round the far side of the statue, behind Lenin's head, nd according to the letter one of them was to leave the oldall on the left-hand side of the end bench. After the oldall had been in place for two minutes, Peter's brother vould appear in the clearing. The note hadn't bothered to ell them not to inform the police. It was taken as read hat the only operation the militia were capable of was the ollection of bribes.

The statue as covered in graffiti which Peter couldn't nderstand. Lenin's head dripped with bird droppings, naking him look as if someone had cracked an egg on his ead.

The three of them hung back among the glittering silver irches. Peter's hands were clammy with sweat and he had hard knot of dread in his stomach. Alyosha, on the other and, looked as if he was on his way to a game of football. oth he and Georgi were smoking. A semi-circle of their iscarded butts lay on the reddish earth in front of them, ven though there was a moulded communal ashtray a netre to their left.

One thing about Moscow was that you were always ithin easy reading distance of a clock and, unlike in ritain, Peter thought, they always told the right time. ime wasn't for the people's benefit, people were for the enefit of time. Shaping history. So the kidnappers had no xcuse to be late.

'What's the time now?' asked Alyosha.

'Two minutes to,' said Peter.

'Well, I suggest we get the priest out there, then.'

'Must I?' countered Father Georgi.

'Look, are you part of this firm or not?' snapped lyosha.

Peter sized up the people on the benches: an earnest young woman in glasses reading, two lank-haired teenagers kissing, and an old woman in a grey vinyl coat and bobble hat watching over her grandchild playing on a blue and white tricycle.

'Did you remember to bring your Bible?' Alyosha asked Georgi.

'Yes.'

'Right, go to the end of the third seat, with the holdall, sit down and read a couple of psalms. Then get up, leaving the bag. Got that?'

'What if they shoot me?'

'No one's going to shoot you,' said Alyosha with less than a hundred per cent conviction. 'Now get out there.'

Georgi took the holdall and walked unsteadily out of the trees towards the statue. Alyosha and Peter watched him with the rapt attention of parents watching a toddler's first steps. Georgi looked around then brushed some leaves off the seat and sat down. The old woman smiled at him and crossed herself. Georgi waved in her direction and opened his Bible.

He had been reading for no more than thirty seconds when he snapped the book shut and stumbled to his feet.

'What a prat,' mumbled Alyosha, shaking his head.

As Georgi hurried towards them, the old woman in the bobble hat stood up and called after him.

'Father, you've forgotten your bag. Father.' The kissers didn't look up, but the reading woman stared at her.

After that things happened very quickly. To the right of them they heard a young boy's voice crying, 'Help, help!' Peter immediately identified it, before the wind carried it away, as his brother. He and Alyosha instinctively moved towards it, while to the left someone grabbed the holdall from the old woman and ran hell for leather. But when the three of them turned to look, they saw nothing but a raggle-taggle gang of boys having a kick-about on the path.

IX

Calvin Kleinski original.' Terry held the shirt by its collar at arm's length. It wasn't as clean as it might be but then again neither were the wares his neighbours were selling. To his left a middle-aged woman in an army jacket was selling a used set of saucepans and another woman, older, around fifty – in a *fur coat* – was selling a pile of muddy carrots. In a fur coat, selling vegetables? He looked at her again. Maybe she was a down-on-her-luck Russian pop star, no doubt with a heroin habit. Or a ballerina, though he didn't have, and seemed unlikely ever to have had, a figure which could have been described as balletic.

But hadn't the troll at the nightclub with the lead-lined bag been wearing a fur? So many of them did. And the red assailant had had gold teeth. The were all probably rolling in it, just pretending to be poor to get more IMF loans. Russians, eh? The world equivalent of the council house state subsidy scrounger. They were probably all on drugs.

He turned to the woman in the coat. 'Drugski. In the armski.' He mimed shooting up. 'And who pays for it all? Mugginsski hereski.'

The woman edged away from him. All he was trying to do was to get enough money for a Metro ride or a cab fare home. Surely his shirt was worth that much. He now felt dizzy with hunger. He fixed his attention on the pile of carrots laid out on a sheet of newspaper beside him.

'Carrotski, give me. Nowski.' He started the mantra low but determined. If he concentrated hard enough, the woman, oblivious of the power of chanting, should just pick up a carrot and give it to him.

Terry wasn't sure if he'd somehow got his cosmic wires crossed because what happened next was unprecedented in chanting history. The stallholders and street hawkers started to disappear, as when a flock of birds is startled by an imperceptible noise. They moved en masse, seemingly not knowing if they were reacting to a supposed threat or the threat itself. The fur-coated woman next to Terry grabbed her pile of carrots and stuffed them in a carrier bag. The other one pulled at the saucepans. It was all so quick, Terry had no idea what had hit the hawkers. In one seamless manoeuvre the marketplace was transformed into a crowd scene.

Which is why when three militiamen, dressed in a colour Terry associated with the duck-egg blue of the Airfix models of his youth, and with semi-automatics slung over their shoulders as casually as handbags, appeared two minutes later, he was the only one still standing there. The larger of the three, who was dark with a moustache and wearing boots the size of buckets, approached him first.

'Morning, gentlemen,' said Terry, as an electric current

of fear shot up his spinal column. 'Can I interest any of you in an original Calvin Klein shirt?'

Within two minutes he was in handcuffs and being frog-marched towards a waiting car. It was all a long way from the market in *EastEnders*, Terry thought as he was pushed onto the back seat.

X

Bridges' heart finally stopped pumping like a Caspian oilwell a few metres away from Katya's apartment block. He ran past the startled babushkas gossiping in the doorway to the back of the building and collapsed against the cold plaster wall. How the *hell* had Senator Barry Foreman tracked him down to Katya's? Bridges had known it was him even before he introduced himself. 'I am Senator Barry Foreman and you, you sonofabitch traitor, are under arrest,' he'd half spat, half drawled as he hoisted himself from the sofa like a walrus in a dragnet.

Bridges had been out of the flat in less time than it took the senator to make it across the room. He closed both doors behind him, hoping they would stall his adversary until the lift had dragged itself towards him. Something had told him he was being followed, even after the Raevitch fiasco. But how was Katya tied up in it? She worked at the English department of MGU. Didn't she? Maybe it was just because he was feeling exceptionally vulnerable but as he turned in his sweat-sodden shirt to look behind him, he could have sworn he saw Blue Eyes entering the Metro.

CHAPTER THIRTEEN

I

His face was the same colour as the gingham check of his shirt. He fumed, 'Have you any *idea* who that man *is*?' The senator was hyperventilating and salivating in a way that reminded Katya of a bull about to enter the ring.

'I believe his name is Mr Bridges. And that he's, um, an international banker. A banker-cum-sort of, well, embalmer,' replied Katya less than persuasively. The truth was, she didn't really know that much about him.

'*What* in the name of Jesus H. Christ are you talking about?' demanded the senator as if she was speaking Swahili. He was on his feet, pacing and shouting. 'What he *is* a threat to every law-abiding American man, woman and child in the country.'

Katya felt herself instinctively warm to Bridges. 'How so?' she asked innocently.

'That, that *man* is a goddamned *spy*!' He spat the word out with a gobbet of saliva.

'You mean he—'

'I mean he should be shipped back to the States, tried

before a grand jury and then taken out and shot for being the ass-picking traitor he is.' Katya winced. She'd never held with capital punishment. 'And I'm the man to do it. Why do you think I get to visit this hellhole country of yours so often?'

'Because it's the only country with so few human rights where you can screw white underage girls to your heart's content?' She was getting angry now.

Her tone was lost on him. 'No, because I have pledged to the people of my country that I will seek out the betrayer Bridges and bring him home. Had I been a younger man I might have chased his butt, but a man of my age . . .' He sank down heavily on the sofa. 'Still, I guess it means I've got a handle on him now. D'you know where the cocksucker hangs out?'

Katya ignored the question.

'You know I can make it worth your while,' he added in a voice he must have thought was beseeching.

She struggled to control the anger rising in her chest. She really must try to end the day with at least one client on her books.

She left the senator and went next door to the kitchen to make a cup of tea. She turned on the radio to try to calm her nerves and neutralise the events of the last half hour. If she doused herself in the normal, the abnormal might disappear.

It wasn't that easy. The news bulletin reported a short piece on how a pensioner had been caught in Vladivostok with the half-eaten remains of her dead husband. Katya turned the radio off and was pouring boiling water from the kettle into the pot when the door buzzed again. He slippers made a flip-flop sound on the parquet as she sashayed indignantly past the senator to answer it.

'Now, Katya, you tell me if that's pussy or a spy. Either way, I'll take it,' he said, gulping like a wart hog. She saw in passing that he was helping himself to a bottle of cognac she kept in case of emergencies.

She felt a hole in her stomach, not just from hunger. It was strange. An hour ago she had been happy enough to introduce Sonya to the senator. Now, as she opened the door to her and saw her young face full of childish expectation, she wasn't so sure.

'Sonya, you made it. Come in.'

Sonya was carrying a box of German cherry liqueurs which she handed silently to Katya. 'It's to say thanks,' she said hesitantly, with her head bowed.

'For what?' asked Katya cautiously, unwilling to hear the reply.

'Oh, you know, everything.' Sonya smiled as she passed Katya her thin coat. Much too thin for the time of year, and the red beret, Katya guessed, had been added as a touch of sophistication.

They lingered in the corridor. Sonya fussed over Leonid who had joined them.

When Katya spoke, her voice was hushed, even though she knew the senator didn't understand Russian. 'Look, Sonya, he's in there,' she nodded towards the sitting room. Sonya's eyes lit up. 'Only don't feel, you know, don't feel you have to do anything you don't want to.' Katya smiled maternally. She checked herself. What was happening to her, for God's sake? There was $20,000 at stake. Then she calmed herself. After all, she could always find another wife for the senator, one more suited to wreaking revenge on his credit card.

Sonya, in a green skirt and matching waistcoat with a white blouse open at the neck, shuffled shyly through the double doors into the sitting room.

The noises which emerged, Katya thought later, were best described as farmyard. The senator snorted in rapid succession and Sonya gave a sort of frightened low which was terror mingled with surprise.

Katya hurried into the sitting room. 'What's the matter?' she asked in panicky Russian.

'Ugh! Who is *he*?' said Sonya, her face white with shock. She was physically withdrawing behind the door.

'Well, hello, young lady. My, my, Katya, you've certainly surpassed yourself with this piece of pussy,' said the senator, trying to lever himself off the sofa.

The noise of the springs and Sonya's rapid shallow breathing were superseded by the ring of the phone in the hall. Sonya ran to pick it up and thrust it into Katya's hand.

'Don't leave me in there with him,' she hissed as she clung to her like a pleading toddler.

Katya spoke into the receiver. 'Hello?'

'Hello, is that Katya Popova?' The accent was British and clipped. Katya guessed his age at around fifty, recently divorced and after a brunette between twenty-five and thirty. She had an instinct for such things. 'I'm sorry to bother you but I got your number from Clive Pickford at Reds In—'

'Where are you?' interrupted Katya. 'Are you in Moscow?' The ring hadn't been the rapid trill of an international call.

384

'Yes, I am,' replied the man, sounding surprised.

'Shit,' said Katya. 'I had no idea he was sending any more this month.'

'You don't – I—'

'Listen. You can come over and see the catalogue but I won't be able to put you up for a couple of days.' Katya tried to loosen Sonya's stranglehold.

'I *have* a place to stay in Moscow—'

'Don't say with that bloody Valentina, From Russia with Love,' said Katya. Clive had been right, they were losing their market share.

'No, really, Mrs Popova. My name is Arnold Dixon. I'm from the British Embassy. One of your clients, a Mr Terry Small, has been arrested and is being held by the militia.'

'Oh shit,' said Katya.

'They're not pressing charges but you'll have to go and pick him up.' She didn't ask what he'd been arrested for. Dixon gave the address of the police station. 'Oh, and Mrs Popova?'

'Mmm?' Katya was still writing.

'We take a pretty dim view of the sort of outfit you and Mr Pickford are running.'

That stopped Katya. She looked at Sonya, who was choking back muffled sobs. In the sitting room she could hear the senator whistling *Voulez-vous couchez avec moi?*

'Mr Dixon,' she was trying for indignant, 'all I do is bring true love matches together,' but it came out sleazy.

It took three cups of sweet tea before Sonya was anything like back to normal.

'Who *is* that man in there?' she asked Katya when her voice returned.

'For goodness sake, Sonya, it's only a man. I thought you wanted to marry a foreigner?'

'I do, but not that one. He's so old. And so fat. And—'

'Well, which one did you have in mind, then? I'm afraid Leonardo DiCaprio may be spoken for,' said Katya wearily. Maybe she'd been wrong. Maybe Sonya was dumb enough for one of her clients.

'The tall one I met in the ambulance.'

Katya cast her mind back. Surely not Bridges. She felt an unusual twang that to her surprise she associated with jealousy. 'You don't mean the dark one in the green jacket?'

'No, silly, the tall one with the long hair swept back, like this.' She mimed someone sweeping hair off their face with the palm of their hand.

'What? You mean the Raevitch boy? But he was, he *is* Russian.'

'Oh,' said Sonya, sipping her tea with her head on one side. 'Well, I told you at the start, I could never see myself marrying a foreigner.'

Katya sighed and stood up from the kitchen table. 'Come on.'

'Where?'

'I've got to pick someone up from the centre of town. So unless you want to be left alone with Lavrenti Beria in there—'

'Who?' asked Sonya, wide-eyed.

'A member of Russia's illustrious past. Though he used to kill his young conquests afterwards,' said Katya from the coat rack. 'Are you coming or not?'

She checked on the senator before she closed the double door into the sitting room so he couldn't see Sonya sneak past. He'd undone his belt buckle and had settled down with the 1997 catalogue. It would at least buy them a couple of hours.

II

It was no good keeping up with the Russian mute façade, Terry thought as he eyed his latest set of captors. They weren't plain-clothed, so he doubted they were KGB. The driver, who had a face like a bandit in a spaghetti Western, growled at him in the mirror.

'You Engleez?'

'Si, I mean da. I mean yes.' After his recent ordeal, a drive in a Russian Panda car – albeit the inevitable suspensionless Lada – came as quite a treat. For the first time in thirty-six hours he was warm and dryish, though the spectre of John McCarthy still raised its ugly head. Who would be his Jill Morrell? Certainly not Jean from accounts, that much he knew.

The car was driving down a deserted two-lane road. There was a canal or small river to their left. The road was dotted with kiosks selling car parts. A few yards on, Terry saw a primitive garage with a sign in English saying 'Benzene'. Before the shock wave of pain, he was determined to note everything – if only for his appearance on Russian *Crimewatch*.

Jill Dandoski (short skirt): Were you that babushka? Or

the vodka-swigging pensioner? Either way we need to speak to you.

Nick Rosski (grave): This was a particularly nasty crime. But, please, don't have nightmares, Russian police brutality only affects ninety-nine out of every hundred arrests.

The militiaman continued. 'Street trading is against article four seven six of the Russian constitution. Now you give me dollars.' The driver spoke with not inconsiderable menace, thought Terry.

'No can do, mate. I am absolutely skint, boracic flint. Penniless. Nothing. Nada.' He gave his best trying-to-co-operate-with-long-arm-of-the-law-but-can't smile.

'You no understand.'

'No, you – aaaagh.' The duck-egg blue militiaman on the back seat next to Terry ground his rifle butt into his groin.

Terry's eyes started to water. He spoke through the pain. 'No, please, I haven't. No, stop—'

'Illegal street trading comes with a ten-year sentence. You want Russian jail?'

Terry groaned as they pulled up outside a building that looked like a municipal WC.

'Get out,' said the driver. 'We are at the police station.'

III

Even Katya felt her pity gland secrete something when she saw him. The cell smelt of damp woollen clothes, alcohol and urine. Two of its walls consisted entirely of bars and it was slotted into the corner of a windowless room. I

388

seemed colder inside than out. She'd gone down a short flight of stairs to get there. That, and the vegetal smell of dirt, made Katya think they must be underground. She guessed there were half a dozen men in the cage, though the general gloom and a natural aversion to looking closer made it difficult to be sure. If Terry was in there, which the gruff young sergeant on the front desk had assured her he was, it was impossible to tell which one was him. She'd already given her last $20 as a bribe to the desk sergeant to get Terry out, and she was not in the best of tempers.

Two bodies were curled foetally on the concrete floor. Only the occasional wriggle and scratch indicated they were anything more than a pile of discarded blankets. Another two, their faces disfigured by bruises and cuts, sat hunched over with their backs against the bare bricked wall.

'Hello, Terry?' Katya addressed the cell in general. A couple of the men looked up. One even gave a wolf whistle. She looked more closely at a shape against the far wall to which the festering cell had lent perfect camouflage.

'Terry, is that you?' Katya tried to remember the jaunty man who had nervously shaken her hand at the airport a week ago. He was unrecognisable, Katya imagined, even to his own mother. It wasn't just the dirt that covered him like a second skin, or the torn clothes, or the huge misshapen overcoat which seemed to be pinning him to the ground as he tried to stand. It was the haunted look in his eyes, the gaunt cheekbones surrounding the hollow, purple eyes. At first he didn't seem able to speak, then he stumbled over to the bars. What he said was unintelligible to Katya but sounded like 'Homeski. Take me homeski.'

They left Holding Prison Number 195 to join Sonya, waiting outside in the taxi.

IV

By the time they'd cajoled the incoherent Terry into the lift at her apartment block, both Katya and Sonya were sweating. Because of his smell, Katya had allowed Sonya to take more of a hands-off role and done the majority of the manhandling herself. Even the cab driver had demanded extra fare.

'Where do you think he got these awful clothes from?' asked Katya, her hand over her nose as she pushed the button for the sixteenth floor.

'From a tramp by the look of it. Poo, what a stink.' Sonya positioned herself diametrically opposite Terry, not just because of the smell but because of the unnatural smile he was giving her. 'How do you know this man? Is he some sort of vagrant?'

Katya was facing the lift doors, with her back to Sonya. She thought vagrant-cum-would-be husband best described him.

'It's a long story,' she said. Sonya had already seen enough of the dregs of western manhood for one day.

'But what will you do with him? You're not going to look after—'

The lift jolted to a halt and the doors opened.

'Oh!' Sonya gave a quick intake of breath.

In the hallway a man in a green waxy jacket was stooped

over, trying to read the apartment numbers. His shoulder-length hair and beige trousers didn't signify much to Katya but clearly the same could not be said of her young companion.

He swung round and only then did Katya recognise him as the Raevitch boy. He reddened and nervously tried to hide a bouquet of flowers he was carrying.

'Sonya,' he said.

'Peter.'

'Christ,' said Katya, girding her irritation. 'Look, you may think I run a commune for the lovelorn but could someone give me a hand? She was not in an enviable position. Terry had one arm over her shoulders and she was trying to support him round his waist.

'Yes, yes, of course.' Peter moved forward. 'Sonya, why don't you go on ahead?'

'Yes, Sonya, why don't you? This is, after all, a job for men and old crones,' said Katya more crossly than she would have liked.

'I wouldn't dream of it,' said Sonya. 'Here, let me help.'

Katya found her keys and they half pushed, half lifted Terry into the flat.

Logistics were now a definite problem. While she could put Terry in the bath for the moment, not even her inventiveness with regard to accommodation reshuffles could allow him to stay there until his flight home in two days. Sasha had to have his evening bath, after all.

Temporarily she pushed him into the bathroom and turned the taps on. 'Can you manage, Mr Small?' she asked, not sure what she would do if he said no.

More nonsense. 'Radoxski, please,' it sounded like. She put an old carrier bag by the door and told him to pass out his clothes when he was undressed.

The doors to the sitting room were still tightly closed. Sonya and Peter seemed to have taken up a spooning position in the hall.

'But how did you know I'd be here?' Sonya was asking.

'I didn't,' he beamed back. 'I thought I'd start tracking you down via Katya.'

Katya was hanging up her coat when the double doors burst open. The first thing that sprang to her mind was Bill Clinton. The 1997 catalogue must have had some profound effect on the senator; his trousers were round his ankles and pointing up shyly from under his shirt tails was an erection.

He lunged towards Sonya, grabbing her slim wrist in his bear-like paw. As well as the cognac he'd evidently also discovered the remains of a bottle of vodka which now lay empty, Katya saw, by her bookcase. The senator groaned as he dragged Sonya into the room, moving backwards and simultaneously pushing her head down with his free hand as they went.

Sonya's screams came out more as yelps. It was then that the senator noticed Peter who had moved forward and was trying to put himself between Sonya and his naked lower half. The senator took his hand from Sonya's head and swung at him. The force of the punch sent Peter reeling back towards the glass door.

'Now, you lovely bit of pussy, come to daddy. You know you—'

The click of a safety catch got his attention. Katya levelled the gun at him. 'OK, I've really had enough of this.'

At first, even the acknowledgement that a firearm was pointing at his head didn't seem to transform the dull look of lust in the senator's eyes. He continued as if he was in a trance, his voice low and determined. 'You know daddy'll make it worth your while. Just put those lovely lips of—'

'Let her go,' said Katya, raising her voice. She walked towards the senator to make her presence felt and put the gun half a metre from his head. Sonya was on the floor, sobbing. The senator suddenly sank back on the sofa, his shirt covering his lap like a napkin.

Katya's voice was calm and determined. 'Now this is what I want you to do. Stand up,' she jerked the gun over his discarded trousers, 'get dressed and leave.' She turned to Sonya. 'Are you OK?'

Sonya nodded. In the corner Peter Raevitch seemed to be coming round.

Katya went back to the senator. 'You can go next door and collect your things or you can leave immediately. Either way, I never want to see your face again.'

'But what about our deal?'

'The deal is off, Mr Foreman. And let me tell you, if you ever try to hurt me or my business interests, I will personally see to it that the great American public really does understand what your real Russian business interests are. Now get out.'

The room was silent. Even Sonya checked her sobs as they watched him hoist his Star of Texas belt waist high. After he left, the only sound that could be heard was coming from the bathroom. It was a man's voice singing 'Land of Hope and Glory'.

V

Katya kicked her slippers off and tucked her legs underneath her. She shuddered as another gulp of Moldovan cognac hit her stomach. She replaced the glass on the armrest. Not much of the bottle was left after she'd restored Sonya this afternoon. Still, the girl was young, she'd get over it.

Katya had tidied the apartment before Sasha returned at six and outwardly there was nothing to indicate what had gone on. Inwardly, of course, there was the loss of $20,000, but she imagined they'd get by. Only the smell of the senator, even after she'd opened the windows to let in the freezing twilight air, lingered.

At just after ten the phone went.

'Hello.'

'Katya, this is Bridges. Listen, is he still there?'

'Who?'

'The senator.'

'No, he's gone.'

There was a silence which neither seemed inclined to fill.

'Katya, you don't work at the university, do you?' He sounded weary.

'No.'

Then, anxiously, 'But you don't work for him, do you?'

'Who?'

'The senator.'

'Not in the way you think. Anyway—'

'He's trying to get me tried in the States, which would mean twenty years in a state penitentiary.'

'So you *are* a spy?' She knew it would sound judgmental to him. If he'd known her better he would have realised she was smiling.

'Yeah, well. Was, I was a spy. Small spy.'

'I thought the English phrase was small fry.'

There was a pause.

'Why was he in your apartment?'

'It's not like you think.' She stalled. 'It's a long story.'

"Look, can I see you again?'

'Maybe. We'll see. Yes, and . . .'

'What?'

'I don't think you'll get any more trouble from the senator.'

'What do you mean? He's still in Moscow, isn't he? He won't give up until—'

'Mr Bridges, please, trust me.' She replaced the receiver and smiled.

On her way to check on Sasha she tripped on his football abandoned in the corridor. Why couldn't he keep the damn thing under his bed?

His room smelt of soap and sleep. She inhaled and then crouched by him and lifted the corner of his eiderdown to replace the ball. Among the socks, old toy cars and Power Rangers under and around his bed, she saw a bag she didn't recognise.

'Mum?'

'Yes, darling.' She smoothed the hair on his forehead.

'We won't ever have to leave Russia, will we?'

'I doubt it, darling.' She kissed him. 'Now go to sleep.' As she said good night she couldn't help noticing the bag said Slazenger.

'What's in the bag, Sasha?' she asked wearily.

He smiled. 'It's a present so you needn't ever have to worry again.' His teeth shone in the moonlight. A moment later he upended the bag and dollars came tumbling out like a tidal wave of green.

V

He sent Marina down to the Dodi and Diana memorial on the ground floor and told her he would join her to an hour for tea in the Georgian restaurant.

It was nearly forty years since they'd both been to London, on a day trip from Oxford where he was attending an international conference. That had been when life was good. Since then his only contact with Britain, until a few days ago, had been with a colleague at the institute who had visited the country as part of a delegation. The colleague had made a video recording of the Food Hall. Not Buckingham Palace or Big Ben, but Harrods Food Hall.

Professor Modin had known all along there was something special about the Raevitch body, only he wasn't sure what. That was why he'd taken it to his special place, his secret room at the back of the institute, before he started work on it.

The key had been lodged halfway down his oesophagus. In fact, it had probably been the cause of death. What it was doing there, he simply couldn't imagine, though he'd once read that people indulging in the sort of activity Gleb Raevitch had enjoyed sometimes used a device to keep the air passage open.

The body was an oyster and this one had offered up a pearl. A small key-shaped pearl with an 'H' on it.

It had been Marina who had understood the importance of the key. On the day trip to Harrods four decades before, she'd bought a teapot with the same logo on it.

The safety deposit boxes were down a flight of steps near entrance three. The smell of the store was intoxicating. Everything was so clean and new. The professor's feet sank into the red carpet as he descended the staircase. At the bottom a barred door opened automatically in front of him and a man's voice from nowhere bade him come forward.

To the right of him, behind a small hatch, a security man with a round face and glasses asked him his name.

The professor cleared his throat and pushed out his hollowing chest. 'Mr Gleb Raevitch and I want to review the contents of my deposit box.'

Four storeys up Marina ordered tea, Russian style, with no milk. She loved the delicate china and the linen napkins. She smiled and felt a great relief. They were about to be happy again.

CHAPTER FOURTEEN

I

There was little doubt in Katya's mind that Orthodox churches were a shocking waste of urban resources. It had been one of the few points on which she agreed with Stalin – much better to blow them up and turn them into something useful like car parks or swimming pools. She looked around the gloomy interior lit by spindly mutton-fat candles and a shaft of cold light from the open door.

She glanced at Bridges beside her. In grey suit and black tie, he was contemplating the scene with feigned gravity. As a date, the funeral rivalled a trip she'd had around the Lubyanka in 1977 with a sixteen-year-old Latvian Young Pioneer called Andrei who had tried to lure her into the toilets in Red Square in the interests of furthering international socialism. The difference this time was that she had an agenda of her own to promote.

She had already declined the opportunity to file past the body of the recently departed, and recently found, Gleb Raevitch lying in an open casket like a waxwork effigy. In fact from where she stood, close to the back of the church, as far away from the malevolent gaze of the icons on the far wall as possible, all she could see was the tip of a human nose above a valance of purple silk.

Father Georgi was quietly reciting an incantation which she couldn't hear. At first she'd assumed the spiral of smoke was coming from the incense burner to his right. Only on closer inspection did she see the ashtray containing a cigarette from which he was taking occasional puffs as he leaned over the body. Around him scurried wizened women in black, crossing and re-crossing themselves with fervour. The church was full. Katya caught the mourners in profile as they passed by the coffin in the two-dimensional relief of a mug shot.

Amid the crowd she caught a glimpse of Peter, deep in conversation with a man in a dark leather coat. Sonya stood on his left clutching his hand.

Katya turned to Bridges. 'How come the body turned up again?' She was wearing a black wool dress. His eyes were fixed on her lips as she spoke. Unusually for Katya, she was wearing lipstick.

'One of the technicians found it laid out in the lab a few days ago. According to the make-up girl, it was one of the finest embalmings she'd ever seen.'

'But the professor's still not turned up?'

'No. But you know about the letter.' Bridges had told her two days ago of the envelope addressed in English that he'd found on the mat of his dacha. Part of the perfectly scripted note told him that Professor Modin and his wife had gone into retirement abroad. It was up to Bridges to decide the fate of Bodies Beautiful.

The string quarter in the corner jolted into life. It began

playing selections from American musicals.

Katya frowned. 'What the . . .'

'I couldn't find the orchestra the professor usually used. This one comes from the foyer of the Metropole.' Bridges looked apologetic. 'No one seems to mind.' He glanced at the mourners. 'And I have asked them to restrict themselves to *Porgy and Bess*. How's Sasha?'

Katya sucked in her cheeks with a stab of irritation. Bridges' ability to deflect a conversation was matched only by her own.

'He's fine. Listen, about the business.' She paused to think of her son who, with Misha, was using their recently acquired booty to invest in a sunflower-processing factory in Rostov on Don. He'd informed her this morning that they expected their first share issue in two years. 'Tell me again,' Katya wished she hadn't left her coat in Bridges' car, 'how much to you stand to make from this funeral?'

'Thirty grand.'

'US?' she asked contemplatively.

'Of course.'

'It seems a shame to let Bodies Beautiful go.'

'There's not much choice. I'm no embalming expert and there are overheads.'

'It's just that I find I have some money to invest at the moment and— *ouch*.' She felt an electric current of pain in her ankle.

'Sorry, coming through. Access please. Access.'

Katya turned to see Alyosha, wearing a black tracksuit with three stripes down the side, pushing a wheelchair uncertainly towards the front.

'Katya, hello,' he said expansively, turning to look at

her. He must have recognised her from her legs or the string of expletives, she thought. He appeared oblivious of the fact that their last meeting had been under conditions of armed hostility. 'How are you? Have you met—'

'Nikita. Yes, of course. How are you, Nikita?'

Before he could answer, Alyosha butted in, 'He's on top of the world, aren't you, Nikita? In fact, I've just asked him to join the firm.'

Nikita tried to say something but Alyosha had commandeered her ear. He spoke as if Nikita was out of earshot. 'I mean, in our line of work, the boy will be invaluable. I ask you, who would ever shoot a cripple? First a priest, and now a disabled war veteran. It's classic. Must go.' He winked at Katya and accompanied by Bridges, carried on towards the front of the church.

'That chap you told me was following you, if it's Mafia we'll sort it,' Alyosha said casually.

Bridges looked momentarily non-plussed. 'No, no, actually Ol' Blue Eyes turned out to be just my usual tail – KGB but re-vamped. I had no idea those guys were so smart these days.'

Alyosha nodded and continued down the aisle.

Two minutes later Katya took her place alongside Bridges. He was, she noted with approval, almost Russian in his ability to blot out the absurd. He was humming quietly to *Summertime*.

She thought of her kitchen table, for the last three days littered with books from the Moscow Institute of Biochemistry. 'I can do it,' she said.

'Do what?' Bridges seemed unmoved.

'Embalm them.' She recited from memory. 'Fix the

tissues with formalin, a powerful antiseptic which inhibits autolysis. Next, place wads of cotton wool steeped in one per cent solution of formaldehyde over face, hands and body. Clean the body cavities with acetic acid. How much more do you want to know?'

'Katya, what are you talking about?'

'I'll do it. I've recently acquired some spare cash which I need to invest. I'll buy into the business and then I can do the actual, you know, medical bits.' She paused. 'What do you think?'

'I think you're mad.'

'Yes, but do you think it'll work?'

Bridges smiled, took her hand and squeezed it. He said, 'We'll see.' And watched the quartet prepare for their next number.

Chapter Fifteen

I

Clive opened the letter with caution. The address, in green ink, was written by hand. Moving his lips slightly as he read, his eyes skidded across the page.

> Terry Small
> 7 Damson Court
> Basingstoke

Clive Pickford
Reds In Your Bed
PO Box 412
Norwich

Dear Mr Pickford,
  I write to inform you that I have instructed my solicitors to seek compensation for the recent experiences I encountered on one of your holidays, namely the To Russia For Love package, all incl. £1,295.

In your brochure (page 13, chapter 2, 'How To Win the Cold Phwoar'), the package guarantees at least one sexual experience or your money back. Not only did I *not* have a sexual experience during my stay, I was attacked and abducted while under the care of your so-called 'representative', Katya Popova. In fact during the only physical contact I had with a woman, her hair came off in my hand. Which, as you might imagine, was a deeply scarring experience.

The conditions of my stay were indescribable and, save for my foresight in packing several dozen Nutri-Grain bars, I might well have starved to death.

Consequently I expect the full price of the package, at least, to be reimbursed. I am prepared to take this matter to the highest court in the land. Far from being 'gentle, loving and demure' (page 3, *Nothing Square About Our Reds*) Russian women are as bad as the rest of them.

Yours sincerely,
Terry Small
cc Anne Robinson, *Watchdog*, BBC1

Clive carefully folded the letter before filing it under dissatisfied customers, subsection nutters. The file, he noted with some discomfort, was bulging. Still, this was no time for the faint-hearted. South America was biting at his heels and Katya had recently, inexplicably, told him where he could stick his international love.

He picked up his pen and surveyed the latest batch of photographs. He uncapped the Biro and thought. Could he really get away with 'Get your fill in Brazil'?

A Coffin for Two

Quintin Jardine

After cracking their first case together as a private investigation team, Oz Blackstone and Primavera Philips find themselves simultaneously in love and in the money. And where better to lie back and contemplate life than the picturesque village of St Marti, on the rugged Costa Brava.

But is their new home quite so idyllic as it looks? Some very dark secrets begin to emerge as the inhabitants draw them into the intrigue which bubbles away beneath the surface, until suddenly, faced with a mysterious skeleton and an unauthenticated Dali masterpiece, Prim and Oz stumble across one of the century's most amazing stories . . .

'Entertaining . . . keeps you intrigued'
Carlisle News & Star

0 7472 5575 X

HEADLINE

Written in Blood

Caroline Graham

It is clear to the more realistic members of the Midsomer Worthy's Writers' Circle that asking best-selling author Max Jennings to talk to them is a little ambitious. Less clear are the reasons for secretary Gerald Hadleigh's fierce objections to seeing the man – a face from his past – again. But, astonishingly, Jennings accepts the invitation and before the night is out, Gerald is dead.

Summoned to investigate, Chief Inspector Barnaby finds that Gerald's solitary life was as much of a mystery to his well-heeled neighbours as his violent death. The key is surely their illustrious guest speaker – but where is he now?

Now part of the major television drama series, *Midsomer Murders*, starring John Nettles as Chief Inspector Barnaby.

'Plenty of horror spiked by humour, all twirling in a staggering *danse macabre*' *The Sunday Times*

'Very funny, with a brilliant cast of eccentrics' *Yorkshire Post*

'Enlivened by a very sardonic wit and turn of phrase, the narrative drive never falters . . . a most impressive performance' *Birmingham Post*

0 7472 4664 5

HEADLINE

If you enjoyed this book here is a selection of other bestselling titles from Headline